David Garrick Portrait by Robert Edge Pine.
Victoria and Albert Museum

THE PLAYS OF DAVID GARRICK

A COMPLETE COLLECTION OF THE SOCIAL SATIRES, FRENCH ADAPTATIONS, PANTOMIMES, CHRISTMAS AND MUSICAL PLAYS, PRELUDES, INTERLUDES, AND BURLESQUES, to which are added the Alterations and Adaptations of the Plays of Shakespeare and Other Dramatists from the Sixteenth to the Eighteenth Centuries

VOLUME 2

Garrick's Own Plays, 1767-1775

EDITED WITH COMMENTARY AND NOTES BY
HARRY WILLIAM PEDICORD AND
FREDRICK LOUIS BERGMANN

SOUTHERN ILLINOIS UNIVERSITY PRESS
CARBONDALE AND EDWARDSVILLE

PRINTED IN THE UNITED STATES OF AMERICA
DESIGNED BY GEORGE LENOX

LIBRARY OF CONGRESS CATALOGUING IN PUBLICATION DATA

Garrick, David, 1717–1779.
The plays of David Garrick.

Bibliography: p.
Includes indexes.
CONTENTS: v. 1. Garrick's own plays, 1740–1766.–
v. 2. Garrick's own plays, 1767–1775.
I. Pedicord, Harry William. II. Bergmann,
Fredrick Louis, 1916– III. Title.
PR3465 1980 822'.6 79–28443
ISBN 0–8093–0863–0 (v. 2)

Contents

Illustrations

Acknowledgments

THE EDITORS and the publishers gratefully acknowledge the permissions granted by the following libraries, museums, and publishers: The Folger Shakespeare Library, Washington, D.C., the Lilly Library of Indiana University, the University of Pennsylvania Libraries, and the University of Illinois Library at Urbana-Champaign, for permission to reproduce the title pages of first editions of Garrick's plays; the Folger and the Harvard Theatre Collection, and the Theatre Collection of the Victoria and Albert Museum, London, for permission to reproduce the illustrations in these volumes; The Huntington Library, San Marino, California, for permission to edit the Prologue to and the text of *The Jubilee*, the text of *The Institution of the Garter* and *The Meeting of the Company* (and the introductory letter to the play), for permission to quote from The Huntington's copy of *Lethe*, and for permission to reprint The Huntington's copy of the Prologue to *The Tempest: An Opera*; the Boston Public Library, Boston, Massachusetts, for permission to edit *Harlequin's Invasion*; Mr. J. Edward Eberle and the Edward-Dean Museum of Decorative Arts, Cherry Valley, California, for permission to photograph and reproduce a portrait supposed to be one of David Garrick; Doubleday for permission to quote from the Preface to Maurice Evans's *G.I. Production of Hamlet by William Shakespeare*, copyright 1946 by Maurice Evans and reprinted by permission of Doubleday and Company, Inc.; the Modern Language Association of America for permission to quote from "Garrick's Long Lost Alteration of *Hamlet*" by George Winchester Stone, Jr. (*PMLA*, 49 [1934], 890–921), copyright 1934 by the Modern Language Association of America and reprinted by permission of the Association.

Acknowledgments

The Garrick Canon

[Dates indicate the season each play or adaptation was first presented.]

GARRICK'S OWN PLAYS

1. Lethe; or, Esop in the Shades. A Dramatic Satire (1740)
2. The Lying Valet (1741)
3. Miss in Her Teens; or, The Medley of Lovers (1747)
4. Lilliput. A Dramatic Entertainment (1756)
5. The Male-Coquette; or, Seventeen Hundred Fifty-Seven (1757)
6. The Guardian. A Comedy (1759)
7. Harlequin's Invasion; or, A Christmas Gambol (1759)
8. The Enchanter; or, Love and Magic. A Musical Drama (1760)
9. The Farmer's Return from London. An Interlude (1762)
10. The Clandestine Marriage. A Comedy (1766)
11. Neck or Nothing. A Farce (1766)
12. Cymon. A Dramatic Romance (1767)
13. Linco's Travels. An Interlude (1767)
14. A Peep Behind the Curtain; or, The New Rehearsal (1767)
15. The Jubilee (1769)
16. The Institution of the Garter; or, Arthur's Roundtable Restored (1771)
17. The Irish Widow (1772)
18. A Christmas Tale. A New Dramatic Entertainment (1773)
19. The Meeting of the Company; or, Bayes's Art of Acting (1774)
20. Bon Ton; or, High Life Above Stairs (1775)
21. May-Day; or, The Little Gipsy. A Musical Farce (1775)
22. The Theatrical Candidates. A Musical Prelude (1775)

GARRICK'S ADAPTATIONS OF SHAKESPEARE

23. Macbeth (1744)
24. Romeo and Juliet (1748)
25. The Fairies. An Opera (1755)

26. Catharine and Petruchio (1756)
27. Florizel and Perdita. A Dramatic Pastoral (1756)
28. The Tempest. An Opera (1756)
29. King Lear (1756)
30. Antony and Cleopatra (1759)
31. Cymbeline (1761)
32. A Midsummer Night's Dream (1763)
33. Hamlet (1772)
34. The Tempest (1773)

GARRICK'S ALTERATIONS OF OTHERS

35. The Alchymist (1747)
36. The Provok'd Wife (1747)
37. The Rehearsal (1749)
38. The Roman Father (1750)
39. Alfred. A Masque (1751)
40. Every Man in His Humour (1751)
41. Zara (1754)
42. Thc Chances (1754)
43. Rule a Wife and Have a Wife. A Comedy (1756)
44. Isabella; or, The Fatal Marriage (1757)
45. The Gamesters. A Comedy (1757)
46. Mahomet (1765)
47. The Country Girl (1766)
48. King Arthur; or, The British Worthy (1770)
49. Albumazar. A Comedy (1773)

Chronology

Year	Events	Garrick
1685		David Garric arrives in London from Bordeaux.
1687		Peter Garrick, son of David Garric, born in France, arrives in England.
1707		Peter Garrick married to Arabella Clough of Litchfield.
1717		David Garrick born in the Angel Inn, Hereford, 19 February.
1718	France and England declare war against Spain.	
1720	Failure of South Sea Company and Law's Mississippi Company in Paris.	
1722	Jacobite Plot.	
1724	The Drapier's Letters and Wood's Halfpence.	
1725	Treaty of Hanover.	Brother George Garrick born 22 August.

1727	Accession of George II.	David attends Litchfield Grammar School.
1728		David sent to Lisbon, Portugal, to enter Uncle's wine business. After a brief stay returns to England.
1729	Resolutions against the reporting of Parliamentary debates.	David re-enters Litchfield Grammar School.
1730	Walpole and Townshend quarrel, Townshend resigns.	
1731	Full Walpole administration.	
1735	Porteous Riots in Edinburgh.	David enrolled under Samuel Johnson at Edial Hall.
1736		Father returns from Army and David drops out of Edial. Johnson's academy a failure.
1737	Censorship established with the passing of the theatrical Licensing Act.	Garrick and Samuel Johnson set out for London on 2 March. Garrick enrolled as student at Lincoln's Inn on 9 March.
1738	Jenkin's Ear.	
1739	England declares war against Spain.	
1740		Garrick's first play, *Lethe; or, Esop in the Shades*, produced at Drury Lane, 1 April.
1741		Charles Macklin's revolutionary performance as Shylock, Drury Lane, 14 February. Garrick plays summer engagement at Ipswich under name

		of Lydall–Capt. Duretête in Farquhar's *The Inconstant*, 21 July. Garrick's debut as Richard III at Goodman's Fields, 19 October. Appears in seven other roles during the season. *The Lying Valet* produced at Goodman's Fields, 30 November. Garrick retires from wine trade in London.
1742	Resignation of Walpole.	Garrick plays three performances at Drury Lane: Bayes, 26 May; Lear, 28 May; Richard III, 31 May. Plays summer season at Smock Alley Theatre, Dublin. Returns to London as a member of the Drury Lane company, opening with Chamont in Otway's *The Orphan* and playing twelve other roles before end of season.
1743	Defeat of French at Dettingen.	Actors' strike against manager Fleetwood at Drury Lane. Garrick plays second season at Smock Alley, Dublin.
1745		Plays Dublin, 9 December to 3 May, 1746.
1746		Mlle. Violetti arrives from Continent in February to dance at Haymarket Theatre. Garrick and James Quin compete in performance of Rowe's *The Fair Penitent* at Covent Garden, 14 November.

1747		*Miss in Her Teens* produced at Covent Garden, 17 January. James Lacy and David Garrick become joint-patentees of Drury Lane, 9 April. New managers alter and refurbish Drury Lane Theatre.
1748	Peace of Aix-la-Chapelle.	
1749		Garrick and Violetti married, 22 June, and reside at 27 Southampton Street, Covent Garden. The "Battle of the Romeos."
1751	Death of Frederick, Prince of Wales.	Garricks set out for trip to the Continent, 19 May.
1753	Founding of the British Museum.	
1754	Death of Pelham, who is succeeded by Newcastle as Prime Minister.	Garrick leases villa at Hampton.
1755	Publication of Johnson's *Dictionary*.	The Chinese Festival Riots at Drury Lane, 8–18 November. Garrick buys Hampton villa.
1756	Seven Years' War begins.	
1760	Accession of George III.	
1762	War against Spain.	Drury Lane Theatre altered and enlarged. Half-Price Riots at Drury Lane and Covent Garden.
1763	John Wilkes and *The North Briton.*	Garricks tour the Continent 1763–65.
1764		Garrick stricken with typhoid fever in Munich.

1765	The Stamp Act.	Publication of *The Sick Monkey* precedes Garrick's return from abroad. Returns to stage by command as Benedict in *Much Ado About Nothing*, 14 November.
1766	Repeal of the Stamp Act.	
1768		*The Dramatic Works of David Garrick* published in three volumes.
1769	The letters of "Junius."	Garrick becomes Steward of Shakespeare Jubilee at Stratford-upon-Avon, 6–9 September. Stages *The Jubilee* at Drury Lane on 14 October.
1772		Garrick buys house in Adam Brothers' Adelphi Terrace; moves in on 28 February. Isaac Bickerstaffe flees to France in disgrace, and Garrick is attacked by William Kenrick's publication of *Love in the Suds*. Garrick goes to court and Kenrick publishes apology on 26 November.
1773	The Boston Tea-Party.	
1774	Death of Oliver Goldsmith.	*The Dramatic Works of David Garrick* published in two volumes by R. Bald, T. Blaw and J. Kurt.
1775	War of American Independence.	Drury Lane altered and decorated by the Adam Brothers.

1776		Garrick's sale of Drury Lane patent announced in the press on 7 March—to Richard Brinsley Sheridan, Thomas Linley and Dr. James Ford. Garrick's farewell performances upon retirement, 1 April to 10 June. Final performance as Don Felix in Mrs. Centlivre's *The Wonder*, 10 June.
1777	Burgoyne surrenders at Saratoga	Garrick reads *Lethe* before the Royal Family at Windsor Castle in February.
1778	Alliance of France and Spain with the United States.	
1779		Garrick dies at Adelphi Terrace home on 20 January. Burial in Poets' Corner, Westminster Abbey, on 1 February. Roubillac statue of Shakespeare and large collection of old plays willed to the British Museum. George Garrick dies on 3 February.

Cymon
A Dramatic Romance
1767

CYMON.

A

DRAMATIC ROMANCE.

As it is Performed at the

THEATRE-ROYAL, in DRURY-LANE.

The MUSIC by Mr. ARNE.

——— SOLI CANTARE PERITI
ARCADES. *Virg.*

L O N D O N:
Printed for T. BECKET and P. A. DE HONDT, in
the Strand. MDCCLXVII.

[Price One Shilling and Six Pence.]

Facsimile title page of the First Edition.
Lilly Library, Indiana University.

Prologue

For New Year's Day.
Spoken by Mr. King

I come, obedient at my brethren's call,
From top to bottom, to salute you all;
Warmly to wish, before our piece you view,
A happy year—to you—you—you—and you!
(Box^{s}*—Pit—1 Gall*^{y}*—2 Gall*^{y}*).*
From you the players enjoy and feel it here,
The merry Christmas and the happy Year.
There is a good old saying—pray attend it:
As you begin the year you'll surely end it.
Should any one this night incline to evil,
He'll play for twelve long months the very devil!
Should any married dame exert her tongue,
She'll sing the zodiac round the same sweet song.
And should the husband join his music too,
Why then 'tis cat and dog the whole year thro'.
Ye sons of law and physic, for your ease
Be sure this day you never take your fees.
Can't you refuse? Then the disease grows strong;
You'll have two itching palms—Lord knows how long!
Writers of news by this strange fate are bound;
They fib today, and fib the whole year round.
You wits assembled here, both great and small,
Set not this night afloat—your critic gall;
If you should snarl and not incline to laughter,
What sweet companions for a twelvemonth after!

Prologue] Prologue lacking in *O1*, *O2*.

4.1. Box^{s}—Pit—1 Gall^{y}—2 Gall^{y}] *O3*, *O4*, *O5*; Boxes *D*; Box—Pit—1 Gall—2 Gall. *O6*.

You must be muzzled for this night at least;
Our author has a right this day to feast.
He has not touched one bit as yet. Remember,
'Tis a long fast—from now to next December.
'Tis holiday! You are our patrons now
(*to the Upper Gallery*):
If you but grin, the critics won't bow wow.
As for the plot, wit, humor, language—I
Beg you such trifles kindly to pass by;
The most essential part, which something means,
As dresses, dances, sinkings, flyings, scenes –
They'll make you stare—nay, there is such a thing
Will make you stare still more—for I must sing!
And should your taste and ears be over nice,
Alas! you'll spoil my singing in a trice.
If you should growl, my notes will alter soon;
I can't be in—if you are out of tune!
Permit my fears your favor to bespeak,
My part's a strong one, and poor I but weak
[*alluding to his late accident*].
If you but smile, I'm firm; if frown, I stumble –
Scarce well of one, spare me a second tumble!

Dramatis Personae

Merlin	Mr. *Bensley*.
Cymon	Mr. *Vernon*.
Dorus	Mr. *Parsons*.
Linco	Mr. *King*.
Damon	Mr. *Fawcett*.
Dorilas	Mr. *Fox*.
Hymen	Mr. *Giorgi*.
Cupid	Miss *Rogers*.

Demons of Revenge, Mr. Champness, &c. &c.
Knights, Shepherds, &c. &c. &c. &c.

Urganda	Mrs. *Baddeley*.
Sylvia	Mrs. *Arne*.
Fatima	Mrs. *Abington*.
First Shepherdess	Miss *Reynolds*.
Second Shepherdess	Miss *Plym*.
Dorcas	Mrs. *Bradshaw*.

SCENE, Arcadia.

Cymon

ACT I.

SCENE [I], Urganda's *Palace.*
Enter Merlin *and* Urganda.

URGANDA. But hear me, Merlin, I beseech you, hear me.

MERLIN. Hear you! I have heard you, for years have heard your vows, your protestations. Have you not allured my affections by every female art? And when I thought that my unalterable passion was to be rewarded for its constancy, what have you done? Why, like mere mortal woman, in the true spirit of frailty, [you] have given up me and my hopes. For what? a boy, an idiot.

URGANDA. Ev'n this I can bear from Merlin.

MERLIN. You have injured me and must bear more.

URGANDA. I'll repair that injury.

MERLIN. Then send back your favorite, Cymon, to his disconsolate friends.

URGANDA. How can you imagine that such a poor, ignorant object as Cymon is can have any charms for me?

MERLIN. Ignorance, no more than profligacy, is excluded from female favor. The success of rakes and fools is a sufficient warning to us, could we be wise enough to take it.

URGANDA. You mistake me, Merlin. Pity for Cymon's state of mind, and friendship for his father, have induced me to endeavor at his cure.

MERLIN. False, prevaricating Urganda! Love was your inducement. Have you not stolen the prince from his royal father and detained him here by your power, while a hundred knights are in search after him? Does not everything about you prove the consequence of your want of honor and faith to me? Were you not placed on this happy spot of Arcadia to be the guardian of its peace and innocence? And have not the Arcadians lived for ages the envy of less happy, because less virtuous, people?

URGANDA. Let me beseech you, Merlin, spare my shame.

MERLIN. And are they not at last, by your example, sunk from their state of happiness and tranquility to that of care, vice, and folly? Their once happy lives are now embittered with envy, passion, vanity, selfishness, and inconstancy. And who are they to curse for this change? Urganda, the lost Urganda.

AIR. [Omitted in the representation.]

If pure are the springs of the fountain,
As purely the river will flow,
If noxious the stream from the mountain,
It poisons the valley below.
So of vice or of virtue possessed,
The throne makes the nation,
Through every gradation,
Or wretched, or blessed.

URGANDA. Let us talk calmly of this matter.

MERLIN. I'll converse with you no more, because I will be no more deceived. I cannot hate you, though I shun you. Yet in my misery I have this consolation, that the pangs of my jealousy are at least equalled by the torments of your fruitless passion.

Still wish and sigh, and wish again,
Love *is dethroned,* Revenge *shall reign*!
Still shall my power your arts confound.
And Cymon's *cure shall be* Urganda's *wound.*

Exit Merlin.

URGANDA. *And* Cymon's *cure shall be* Urganda's *wound*! What mystery is couched in these words? What can he mean?

Enter Fatima, *looking after* Merlin.

FATIMA. I'll tell you, Madam, when he is out of hearing. He means mischief, and terrible mischief too. No less, I believe, than ravishing you and cutting my tongue out. I wish we were out of his clutches.

URGANDA. Don't fear, Fatima.

FATIMA. I can't help it. He has great power and is mischievously angry.

URGANDA. Here is your protection (*showing her wand*). My power is

33–33.1. Urganda, the lost] *O*1, *O*2, *O*3, *O*4, *O*5, *D*; Urganda, the false, the lost *O*6. AIR] *O*6; omitted in the representation *O*1, *O*2, *O*3, *O*4, *O*5, *D*.

at least equal to his. (*Muses.*) *And* Cymon's *cure shall be* Urganda's *wound*!

FATIMA. Don't trouble your head with these odd ends of verses which were spoke in a passion, or, perhaps for the rhyme's sake. Think a little to clear us from this old mischief-making conjurer. What will you do, madam?

URGANDA. What can I do, Fatima?

FATIMA. You might very easily settle matters with him, if you could as easily settle 'em with yourself.

URGANDA. Tell me how.

FATIMA. Marry Merlin and send away the young fellow. (Urganda *shakes her head.*) I thought so. We are all alike, and that folly of ours of preferring two-and-twenty to two-and-forty runs through the whole sex of us. But, before matters grow worse, give me leave to reason a little with you, madam.

URGANDA (*sighing*). I am in love, Fatima.

FATIMA. And poor reason may stay at home—me exactly! Ay, ay, we are all alike, but with this difference, madam. Your passion is surely a strange one. You have stolen away this young man, who, bating his youth and figure, has not one single circumstance to create affection about him. He is half an idiot, madam, which is no great compliment to your wisdom, your beauty, or your power.

URGANDA. I despise them all, for they can neither relieve my passion or create one where I would have them.

AIR.

What is knowledge, and beauty, and power,
Or what is my magical art?
Can I for a day, for an hour,
Have beauty to make the youth kind,
Have power o'er his mind,
Or knowledge to warm his cold heart?
Oh, no! A weak boy all my magic disarms,
And I sigh all the day with my power and my charms.

FATIMA. Sigh all the day! More shame for you, madam. Cymon is incapable of being touched with anything. Nothing gives him pleasure but twirling his cap and hunting butterflies. He'll make a sad lover indeed, madam.

URGANDA. I can wait with patience for the recovery of his understanding. It begins to dawn already.

FATIMA. Where, pray?

URGANDA. In his eyes.

80. idiot] *O*1, *O*2, *O*3, *O*4, *D*; ideot *O*5, *O*6.

FATIMA. Eyes! Ha, ha, ha! Love has none, madam; the heart only sees on these occasions. Cymon was born a fool, and his eyes will never look as you would have them. Take my word for it.

URGANDA. Don't make me despair, Fatima.

FATIMA. Don't lose your time then. 'Tis the business of beauty to make fools, and not cure 'em. Even I, poor I, could have made twenty fools of wise men in half the time that you have been endeavoring to make your fool sensible. Oh, 'tis a sad way of spending one's time.

URGANDA. Hold your tongue, Fatima. My passion is too serious to be jested with.

FATIMA. Far gone indeed, madam. And yonder goes the precious object of it.

URGANDA. He seems melancholy. What's the matter with him?

FATIMA. He's a fool, or he might make himself very merry among us. I'll leave you to make the most of him.

URGANDA. Stay, Fatima, and help me to divert him.

FATIMA. A sad time, when a lady must call in help to divert her gallant. But I'm at your service.

AIR.

URGANDA.
Hither, all my spirits, bend,
With your magic powers attend,
  Chase the mists that cloud his mind.
Music, melt the frozen boy,
Raise his soul to love and joy.
  Dulness makes the heart unkind.

Enter Cymon *melancholy.*

CYMON. What do you sing for? (*Sighing.*) Heigho!

FATIMA. What's the matter, young gentleman?

CYMON. Heigho!

URGANDA. Are you not well, Cymon?

CYMON. Yes, I am very well.

URGANDA. Why do you sigh then?

CYMON. Eh! (*Looks foolishly.*)

FATIMA. Do you see it in his eyes now, madam?

URGANDA. Prithee, be quiet.—What is it you want? Tell me, Cymon. Tell me your wishes and you shall have 'em.

CYMON. Shall I?

URGANDA. Yes, indeed, Cymon.

FATIMA. Now for it!

CYMON. I wish—heigho!

---

111. No stage direction *O1, O2, D*; *looking out* added *O3, O4, O5, O6.*

URGANDA (*aside to* Fatima). These sighs must mean something.

FATIMA. I wish you joy, then. Find it out, madam.

URGANDA. What do you sigh for?

CYMON. I want—(*Sighs.*)

URGANDA (*eagerly*). What, what, my sweet creature?

CYMON. To go away.

FATIMA. Oh, la! The meaning's out.

URGANDA. What, would you leave me then?

CYMON. Yes.

URGANDA. Why would you leave me?

CYMON. I don't know.

URGANDA. Where would you go?

CYMON. Anywhere.

URGANDA. Had you rather go anywhere than stay with me?

CYMON. I had rather go anywhere than stay with anybody.

URGANDA. But you can't love me if you would leave me, Cymon.

CYMON. Love you! What's that?

URGANDA. Do you feel nothing here in your heart, Cymon?

CYMON. Yes, I do.

URGANDA. What is it?

CYMON. I don't know. (*Sighs.*)

URGANDA. That's a sigh, Cymon. Am I the cause of it?

CYMON. Yes, indeed you are.

URGANDA. Then I am blest!

FATIMA. Poor lady!

URGANDA. But how do I cause it?

CYMON. You won't let me go away.

FATIMA (*aside*). Poor lady!

URGANDA. Will you love me if I let you go?

CYMON. Anything, if you'll let me go. Pray let me go.

URGANDA. You can't love me and go too.

CYMON. Let me try.

FATIMA. I'm out of all patience. What the deuce would you have, young gentleman? Had you one grain of understanding, or a spark of sensibility in you, you would know and feel yourself to be the happiest of mortals.

CYMON. I had rather go, for all that.

FATIMA (*aside to* Urganda). The picture of the whole sex. Oh, madam, fondness will never do. A little coquetry is the thing. I bait my hook with nothing else, and I always catch fish.

URGANDA. What! Had you rather go away than live here in splendor, be caressed by me, and have all your commands obeyed?

CYMON. All my commands obeyed?

URGANDA. Yes, my dear Cymon. Give me your affections and I will give you my power. You shall be lord of me and mine.

CYMON. Oh, Lord!

FATIMA. Oh, the fool!

URGANDA. I will show him my power and captivate his heart through his senses.

FATIMA. You'll throw away your powder and shot.

Urganda *waves her wand, and the stage changes to a magnificent garden.* Cupid *and the* Loves *descend.*

AIR.

CUPID.
Oh, why will you call me again,
'Tis in vain, 'tis in vain.
The powers of a god
Cannot quicken this clod,
Alas! It is labor in vain.
Oh Venus! my mother, some new object give her!
This blunts all my arrows and empties my quiver.

A Dance by Cupid *and followers.*
During the entertainments of singing and dancing Cymon *at first stares about him, then grows inattentive, and at last falls asleep.*

URGANDA. Look, Fatima. Nothing can affect his insensibility—and yet, what a beautiful simplicity!

FATIMA. Turn him out among the sheep, madam, and think of him no more. 'Tis all labor in vain, as the song says, I assure you.

URGANDA. Cymon, Cymon! What, are you dead to these entertainments?

CYMON (*starts*). Dead! I hope not.

URGANDA. How can you be so unmoved?

CYMON. They tired me so, that I wished 'em a good night and went to sleep. But where are they?

URGANDA. They are gone, Cymon.

CYMON (*getting up*). Then let me go too.

FATIMA. The old story!

URGANDA. Whither would you go? Tell me, and I'll go with you, my sweet youth.

CYMON. No, I'll go by myself.

URGANDA. And so you shall. But where?

CYMON. Into the fields.

183. Oh, Lord] *O*1, *O*2, *D*; O la *O*3, *O*4, *O*5, *O*6.
197. Turn him out . . .] p. 13 misnumbered 31 and pages misgathered *O*5.

URGANDA. But is not this garden pleasanter than the fields, my palace than cottages, and my company more agreeable to you than the shepherds?

CYMON. Why how can I tell till I try? You won't let me choose.

AIR.

You gave me last week a young linnet,
Shut up in a fine golden cage;
Yet how sad the poor thing was within it,
Oh how did it flutter and rage!
Then he moped and he pined
That his wings were confined,
Till I opened the door of his den.
Then so merry was he,
And because he was free,
He came to his cage back again.

And so should I too, if you would let me go.

URGANDA. And you would return to me again?

CYMON. Yes, I would. I have nowhere else to go.

FATIMA. Let him have his humor. When he is not confined and is seemingly disregarded, you may have him and mould him as you please. 'Tis a receipt for the whole sex.

URGANDA. I'll follow your advice. Well, Cymon, you shall go wherever you please, and for as long as you please.

CYMON. Oh, la! And I'll bring you a bird's nest and some cowslips. And shall I let my linnet out too?

FATIMA. Oh, ay, pretty creatures. Pray, let 'em go together.

URGANDA. And take this, Cymon. Wear it for my sake and don't forget me. (*Gives* Cymon *a nosegay.*) (*Aside.*) Though it won't give passion, it will increase it if he should think kindly of me, and absence may befriend me. [*To* Cymon.] Go, Cymon. Take your companion and be happier than I can make you.

CYMON. Then I'm out of my cage and shall mope no longer.

URGANDA. His transports distract me. I must retire to conceal my uneasiness. (*Retires.*)

FATIMA. And I'll open the gate to the prisoners.

Exit.

CYMON. And I'll fetch my bird, and we'll fly away together.

---

242. No acting cue in *O*1, *O*2, *D*; *overjoyed* added *O*3, *O*4, *O*5, *O*6.

AIR.

Oh liberty, liberty! Dear happy liberty!
Nothing's like thee!
So merry are we,
My linnet and I
From prison we're free.
Away we will fly,
To liberty, liberty,
Dear happy liberty!
Nothing's like thee!

End of the First Act.

ACT II.

SCENE [I], *A Rural Prospect.*

Enter two Shepherdesses.

FIRST SHEPHERDESS. What, to be left and forsaken! And see the false fellow make the same vows to another almost before my face. I can't bear it, and I won't.

SECOND SHEPHERDESS. Why, look ye, Sister, I am as little inclined to bear these things as yourself. And if my swain had been faithless too, I should have been vexed at it, to be sure. But how can you help yourself?

FIRST SHEPHERDESS. I have not thought of that. I only feel I can't bear it. And as to the *won't*—I must trust in a little mischief of my own to bring it about. Oh that I had the power of our enchantress yonder! I would play the devil with them all.

SECOND SHEPHERDESS. And yet folks say she has no power in love-matters. You know, notwithstanding her charms and her spirits, she is in love with a fool and has not wit enough to make him return it.

FIRST SHEPHERDESS. No matter for that. If I could not make folks love me, I would make them miserable. And that's the next pleasure to it.

SECOND SHEPHERDESS. And yet, to do justice to her who makes all this disturbance among you, she does not in the least encourage the shepherds. And she can't help their falling in love with her.

FIRST SHEPHERDESS. Maybe so. Nor can I help hating and detesting her because they do fall in love with her. Sylvia's good qualities cannot

15.1. cue word for next page is erroneously given as SECOND in *O1*, *O2*, *O3*; correctly FIRST *O4*, *O5*, *D*, *O6*.

excuse her to me. My quarrel to her is that all the young fellows follow her, not because she does not follow the young fellows.

SECOND SHEPHERDESS (*affectedly*). Well, but really now, Sister, 'tis a little hard that a girl who has beauty to get lovers, or merit enough to keep 'em, should be hated for her good qualities.

FIRST SHEPHERDESS. Marry come up, my insulting sister! Because you think your shepherd constant, you have no feeling for the false-heartedness of mine. But don't be too vain with your success. My Dorilas is made of the same stuff as your Damon. And I can't for the life of me see that you have any particular security for your fool more than I had for mine.

SECOND SHEPHERDESS. Why are you so angry, my dear sister? I am not Sylvia. And, to oblige you, I will abuse her wherever I go and whenever you please. I think she is a most provoking creature, and I wish she was out of the country with all my soul.

FIRST SHEPHERDESS. And so she ought to be. She has no business here with her good qualities. Nobody knows who she is or whence she came. She was left here with old Dorcas, but how, or by whom, or for what, except to make mischief among us, I know not. There is some mystery about her, and I'll find it out.

SECOND SHEPHERDESS. But will your quarreling with her bring back your sweetheart?

FIRST SHEPHERDESS. No matter for that. When the heart is overloaded, any vent is a relief to it. And that of the tongue is always the readiest and most natural. So if you won't help me to find her, you may stay where you will.

Linco, *singing without.*
Care flies from the lad that is merry.

SECOND SHEPHERDESS. Here comes the merry Linco, who never knew care or felt sorrow. If you can beat his laughing at your griefs or singing away his own, you may get some information from him.

Enter Linco, *singing.*

LINCO. What, my girls of ten thousand! I was this moment defying love and all his mischief, and you are sent in the nick by him to try my courage. But I'm above temptation, or below it. I duck down, and all his arrows fly over me.

AIR.

Care flies from the lad that is merry,
Who's heart is as sound,
And cheeks are as round,
As round and as red as a cherry.

FIRST SHEPHERDESS. What, are you always thus?

LINCO. Ay, or Heaven help me! What, would you have me do as you do, walking with your arms across—thus? Heighhoing by the brookside among the willows? Oh, fye for shame, lasses! Young and handsome, and sighing after one fellow apiece, when you should have a hundred in a drove following you like—like—you shall have the simile another time.

SECOND SHEPHERDESS. No. Prithee, Linco, give it us now.

LINCO. You shall have it. Or, what's better, I'll tell you what you are *not* like. You are not like our shepherdess Sylvia. She's so cold and so coy that she flies from her lovers but is never without a score of them. You are always running after the fellows, and yet are always alone—a very great difference, let me tell you. Frost and fire, that's all.

SECOND SHEPHERDESS. Don't imagine that I am in the pining condition my poor sister is. I am as happy as she is miserable.

LINCO. Good lack, I'm sorry for it.

SECOND SHEPHERDESS. What, sorry that I am happy?

LINCO. Oh, no! Prodigious glad.

FIRST SHEPHERDESS. That I am miserable?

LINCO. No, no! Prodigious sorry for that—and prodigious glad of the other.

FIRST SHEPHERDESS. Be my friend, Linco, and I'll confess my folly to you.

LINCO. Don't trouble yourself. 'Tis plain enough to be seen. But I'll give you a receipt for it without fee or reward. There's friendship for you.

FIRST SHEPHERDESS. Prithee, be serious a little.

LINCO. No, Heaven forbid! If I am serious 'tis all over with me. I should soon change my roses for your lilies.

SECOND SHEPHERDESS. Don't be impudent, Linco, but give us your receipt.

AIR.

LINCO.

I laugh and sing,
I am blithsome and free,
The rogue's little sting,
It can never reach me:
For with fal, la, la, la!
And ha, ha, ha, ha!
It can never reach me.

---

92. I laugh and sing] *O1*, *O2*, *D*; I laugh, and I sing *O3*, *O4*, *O5*, *O6*.

II.

My skin is so tough,
Or so blinking is he,
He can't pierce my buff,
Or he misses poor me.
  For with fal, la, la, la!
  And ha, ha, ha, ha!
  He misses poor me.

III.

Oh, never be dull,
By the sad willow tree;
Of mirth be brim full,
And run over like me.
  For with fal, la, la, la!
  And ha, ha, ha, ha!
  Run over like me.

FIRST SHEPHERDESS. It won't do!

LINCO. Then you are far gone indeed.

FIRST SHEPHERDESS. And as I can't cure my love, I'll revenge it.

LINCO. But how, how, shepherdess?

FIRST SHEPHERDESS. I'll tear Sylvia's eyes out.

LINCO. That's your only way, for you'll give your nails a feast and prevent mischief for the future. Oh, tear her eyes out, by all means.

SECOND SHEPHERDESS. How can you laugh, Linco, at my sister in her condition?

LINCO. I must laugh at something. Shall I be merry with you?

SECOND SHEPHERDESS. The happy shepherd can bear to be laughed at.

LINCO. Then Sylvia might take your shepherd without a sigh, though your sister would tear her eyes out.

SECOND SHEPHERDESS. *My* shepherd? What does the fool mean?

FIRST SHEPHERDESS (*eagerly*). *Her* shepherd! Pray tell us, Linco.

LINCO. 'Tis no secret, I suppose. I only met Damon and Sylvia together.

SECOND SHEPHERDESS. What, *my* Damon?

LINCO. Your Damon that was and that would be Sylvia's Damon, if she would accept him.

SECOND SHEPHERDESS. Her Damon! I'll make her to know—a wicked slut! a vile fellow! Come, Sister, I'm ready to go with you. We'll give her her own. If our old governor continues to cast a sheep's eye at me, I'll have her turned out of Arcadia, I warrant you.

FIRST SHEPHERDESS. This is some comfort, however. Ha, ha, ha!

---

123. The happy shepherd] *O1*, *O2*, *O3*, *O4*, *O5*, *D*; Shepherd, the happy *O6*.
131. accept him] *O1*, *O2*, *D*; accept of him *O3*, *O4*, *O5*, *O6*.

SECOND SHEPHERDESS. Very well, Sister. You may laugh if you please, but perhaps it is too soon. Linco may be mistaken. It may be your Dorilas that was with her.

LINCO. And your Damon too—and Strephon, and Colin, and Alexis, and Egon, and Corydon, and every fool of the parish but Linco. And he,

With fal, la, la!
And ha, ha, ha!

FIRST SHEPHERDESS. I can't bear to see him so merry when I am so miserable.

Exit.

SECOND SHEPHERDESS. There is some satisfaction in seeing one's sister as miserable as one's self.

Exit.

LINCO. Ha, ha, ha! Oh, how the pretty sweet-tempered creatures are ruffled.

AIR.

This love puts 'em all in commotion,
For preach what you will,
They cannot be still,
No more than the wind or the ocean.

Exit.

---

142. And he,] *O*1, *O*2, *O*3, *O*4, *O*5, *D*; And he sticks to *O*6.
143. With fal, la, la!] *O*1, *O*2, *O*3; Sticks to fal, lal, la, la! *O*4; Sticks to fal, la, la! *O*5; With Fal, la, la, la! *D*; With Fal, lal, la, la! *O*6.
144. And ha, ha, ha!] *O*1, *O*2, *O*3, *O*4, *O*5; And ha, ha, ha, ha! *D*, *O*6.
146.1. (*Exit*)] *O*1, *O*2, *O*3, *O*4, *O*5, *D*; (*going*) *O*6.
148.1. (*Exit*)] *O*1, *O*2, *O*3, *O*4, *O*5, *D*; (*going*) O6.
149–50. are ruffled. AIR.] *O*1, *O*2, *O*3, *O*4, *O*5, *D*; are ruffled.
One word more, lasses, if you please. I see you are both brimful of wrath, and will certainly scratch one another if you don't find Sylvia. Now hear but another song, and if it does not cool you, I'll show you where the enemy lies, and you shall draw your tongues upon her immediately. AIR. *O*6.
151. This love puts 'em . . .] *O*6 substitutes the following Air:

If you make it your plan,
To have but one man,
By one you are surely betrayed.
Should he prove untrue,
Oh! what can you do?
Alas, you must die an old maid.
And you too must die an old maid.

SCENE [II] *changes to a rural prospect.*
Sylvia *discovered lying upon a bank.*
Enter Merlin.

MERLIN. My art succeeds, which hither has conveyed,
To catch the eye of Cymon, this sweet maid.
Her charms shall clear the mists which cloud his mind.
And make him warm, and sensible, and kind.
Her yet cold heart with passion's sighs shall move,
Melt, as he melts, and give him love for Love.
This magic touch shall to these flowers impart,

(*Touches a nosegay in her hand.*)

A power, when beauty gains, to fix the heart;
A power the false enchantress shall confound,
And Cymon's *cure shall be* Urganda's *wound.*

Exit.

Enter Cymon *with his bird.*

II.

Would you ne'er take a sup,
But out of one cup,
And it proves brittle ware, you are curst.
If down it should tip,
Or thru' your hands slip,
Oh how would you then quench your thirst?
Oh how, &c.

III.

If your palate to hit
You choose but one bit,
And that dainty tit-bit should not keep,
Then restless you lie,
Pout, whimper and cry,
And go without supper to sleep.
And go, &c.

IV.

As your shepherds have chose
Two strings to their bows,
Shall one for each female suffice?
Take two, three, or four,
Like me take a score,
And then you'll be merry and wise. *Exeunt severally.*

9.1. (*Touches a nosegay in her hand.*)] O1, O2, D; (*Touches a basket of flowers with his wand.*) O3, O4, O5, O6.

CYMON. Away, prisoner, and make yourself merry. (*Bird flies.*) Ay, ay, I knew how it would be with you. Much good may it do you, Bob. What a sweet place this is—hills and greens and rocks and trees and water and sun and birds! Dear me, 'tis just as if I had never seen it before. Bob, Bob, much good may it do you, Bob.

Whistles about till he sees Sylvia, *then stops and sinks his whistling by degrees, with a look and attitude of astonishment.*

Oh, la, what's here! 'Tis something dropped from the heavens sure, and yet 'tis like a woman too. Bless me, is it alive? (*Sighs.*) It can't be dead, for its cheek is as red as a rose, and it moves about the heart of it. I am afraid of it and yet can't leave it. I begin to feel something strange here. (*Lays his hand on his heart and sighs.*) I don't know what's the matter with me. I wish it would wake, that I might see its eyes. If it should look gentle and smile upon me, I should be glad to play with it. Ay, ay, there's something now in my breast that they told me of. It feels oddly to me, and yet I don't dislike it.

AIR.

All amaze!
Wonder, praise,
Here forever could I gaze!
Creep still near it, (*Advancing.*)
Yet I fear it, (*Retiring.*)
I can neither stay nor go.
Can't forsake it, (*Advancing.*)
Dare not wake it, (*Retiring.*)
Shall I touch it? No, no, no! (*Retires.*)

II.

[*This stanza omitted in the acting.*]

Cymon, sure thou art possessed,
Something's got into thy breast,
Strangely feeling,
Gently stealing,
And my heart is panting so,
I'm sad and merry, sick and well,
What it is I cannot tell
Makes me thus. Heigho! Heigho!

I am glad I came abroad. I have not been so pleased ever since I can remember. But perhaps it may be angry with me. I can't help it if

17.2. *attitude of astonishment.*] O1, O2, D; *attitude of foolish astonishment* O3, O4, O5, O6.

35. (*Retires.*)] O1, O2, D; (*Advances and retires.*) O3, O4, O5, O6.

it is. I had rather see her angry with me than Urganda smile upon me. Stay, stay! (Sylvia *stirs.*) La, what a pretty foot it has! (Cymon *retires.*)

Sylvia, *raising herself from the bank.*

AIR.

SYLVIA.
Yet awhile, sweet Sleep, deceive me,
Fold me in thy downy arms,
Let not care awake to grieve me,
Lull it with thy potent charms.

I, a turtle, doomed to stray,
Quitting young the parent's nest,
Find each bird a bird of prey,
Sorrow knows not where to rest.

Sylvia *wakes by degrees, supported by her right hand, while he gazes strongly on her, and retires gently, pulling off his cap.*

SYLVIA (*speaking gently and surprised*). Who's that?

CYMON (*bowing and hesitating*). 'Tis I.

SYLVIA. What's your name?

CYMON. Cymon.

SYLVIA. What do you want, young man?

CYMON. Nothing, young woman.

SYLVIA. What are you doing there?

CYMON. Looking at you there.

SYLVIA (*aside*). What a pretty creature it is.

CYMON (*aside*). What eyes it has!

SYLVIA. You don't intend me any harm?

CYMON. Not I, indeed. I wish you don't do me some. Are you a fairy, pray?

SYLVIA. No, I am a poor harmless shepherdess.

CYMON. I don't know that. You have bewitched me, I believe.

SYLVIA. Indeed I have not. And if it was in my power to harm you, I'm sure it is not in my inclination.

CYMON. I'm sure I would trust you to do anything with me.

SYLVIA. Would you? (*Sighs.*)

CYMON. Yes, indeed I would. (*Sighs.*)

SYLVIA. Why do you look so at me?

CYMON. Why do you look so at me?

55.1. Sylvia *wakes by degrees, supported by her right hand, while* . . .] *O1, O2, D*; Sylvia *sees* Cymon *with emotion, while* . . . *O3, O4, O5, O6.*

Joseph Vernon as Cymon.
Harvard Theatre Collection

SYLVIA. I can't help it.

CYMON. Nor I neither. I wish you'd speak to me and look at me as Urganda does.

SYLVIA. What, the enchantress? Do you belong to her?

CYMON. I had rather belong to you. I would not desire to go abroad if I did.

SYLVIA. Does Urganda love you?

CYMON. So she says.

SYLVIA. I'm sorry for it.

CYMON. Why are you sorry, pray?

SYLVIA. I shall never see you again. I wish I had not seen you now.

CYMON. If you did but wish as I do, all the enchantresses in the world could not hinder us from seeing one another.

SYLVIA. Do you love Urganda?

CYMON. Do you love the shepherds?

SYLVIA. I did not know what love was this morning.

CYMON. Nor I, 'till this afternoon. Who taught you, pray?

SYLVIA. Who taught you?

CYMON (*bashful*). You.

SYLVIA (*blushing*). You.

CYMON. You could teach me anything, if I was to live with you. I should not be called Simple Cymon anymore.

SYLVIA. Nor I, hard-hearted Sylvia.

CYMON (*transported*). Sylvia—what a sweet name! I could speak it forever.

SYLVIA. I can never forget that of Cymon, though Cymon may forget me.

CYMON. Never, never, my sweet Sylvia. (*Falls on his knees and kisses her hand.*)

SYLVIA. We shall be seen and separated forever. Pray let me go. We are undone if we are seen. I must go. I am all over in a flutter.

CYMON. When shall I see you again? In half an hour?

SYLVIA. Half an hour! That will be too soon. No, no, it must be three quarters of an hour.

CYMON. And where, my sweet Sylvia?

SYLVIA. Anywhere, my sweet Cymon.

CYMON. In the grove by the river there.

SYLVIA. And you shall take this to remember it. (*Gives him a nosegay.*) I wish it were a kingdom. I would give it you, and a queen along with it.

---

78. help it.] *O1*, *O2*, *D*; help it. (*Sighs.*) *O3*, *O4*, *O5*, *O6*.

79. I neither.] *O1*, *O2*, *D*; I neither. (*Sighs.*) *O3*, *O4*, *O5*, *O6*.

103–4. forget me.] *O1*, *O2*, *D*; forget me. (*Sighs.*) *O3*, *O4*, *O5*, *O6*.

114. *a nosegay*] *O1*, *O2*, *D*; *the nosegay enchanted by* Merlin *O3*, *O4*, *O5*, *O6*.

CYMON. How my heart is transported! And here is one for you too, which is of no value to me unless you will receive it. Take it, my sweet Sylvia. (Cymon *gives her* Urganda's *nosegay*.)

DUET.

SYLVIA. Take this nosegay, gentle youth,
CYMON. And you, sweet maid, take mine.
SYLVIA. Unlike these flowers be thy fair truth.
CYMON. Unlike these flowers be thine.
These changing soon
Will soon decay,
Be sweet till noon,
Then pass away.
Fair for a time their transient charms appear;
But truth unchanged shall bloom forever here.

(*Each pressing their hearts.*)

Exeunt.

End of the Second Act.

ACT III.

SCENE [I], *before* Urganda's *Palace.*

Enter Urganda *and* Fatima.

URGANDA. Is he not returned yet, Fatima?

FATIMA. He has no feelings but those of hunger. When that pinches him, he'll return to be fed like other animals.

URGANDA. Indeed, Fatima, his insensibility astonishes and distracts me. I have exhausted all my arts to overcome it. I have run all dangers to make an impression upon him. And, instead of finding my passion in the least abated by his ingratitude, I am only a greater slave to my weakness and most incapable of relief.

FATIMA. Why then I may as well hold my tongue. But before I would waste all the prime of my womanhood in playing such a losing game, I would—but I see you don't mind me, madam, and therefore I'll say no more. I know the consequence and must submit.

URGANDA. What can I do in my situation?

FATIMA. What you ought to do. And you belie your beauty and understanding by not doing it.

URGANDA. Explain yourself.

---

15. by not doing it.] *O1*, *O2*, *O3*, *O4*, *O5*, *D*; by not doing it. 'Tis a fashionable scheme. *O6*.

FATIMA. To secure my tongue and your honor (for Merlin will have you by hook or by crook), marry him directly. It will prevent mischief at least. So much for prudence. During your honeymoon I will hide the young gentleman, and if he has any tinder in him kindle him up for you. If your husband should be tired of you, as ten to one he will, I'll step in his way. He may be glad of the change. And in return, I'll restore young Simplicity to you. That's what I call a fashionable scheme.

URGANDA. I can't bear trifling at this time. You'll make me angry with you. But see where Cymon approaches. He seems transported. Look, look, Fatima! He is kissing and embracing my nosegay. It has had the desired effect and I am happy. We'll be invisible, that I may observe his transports.

Urganda *waves her wand and retires with* Fatima.
Enter Cymon, *hugging a nosegay.*

CYMON. Oh my dear, sweet, charming nosegay! To see thee, to smell thee, and to taste thee (*Kisses it.*) will make Urganda and her garden delightful to me. (*Kisses it.*)

FATIMA. What does he say?

URGANDA. Hush, hush! All transport, and about me. What a change is this?

CYMON. With this I can want for nothing. I possess everything with this. My mind and heart are expanded. I feel—I know not what. Every thought that delights and every passion that transports gather like so many bees about this treasure of sweetness. Oh, the dear, dear nosegay and the dear, dear giver of it!

URGANDA. The dear, dear giver. Mind that, Fatima. What heavenly eloquence! Here's a change of heart and mind. Heigho!

FATIMA. I'm all amazement, in a dream. But is that your nosegay?

URGANDA. Mine? How can you doubt it?

FATIMA. Nay, I'm near-sighted.

CYMON. She has not a beauty that is not brought to mind by these flowers. This the color of her hair, this of her skin, this of her cheeks, this of her eyes, this of her lips, sweet, sweet—and those rosebuds. Oh, I shall go out of my wits with pleasure!

FATIMA. 'Tis pity to lose 'em the moment you have found 'em.

URGANDA. Oh, Fatima, I never was proud of my power or vain of my beauty till this transporting moment.

CYMON. Where shall I put it? Where shall I conceal it from everybody? I'll keep it in my bosom next my heart all the day. And at night I will put it upon my pillow and talk to it, and sigh to it, and swear to it, and sleep by it, and kiss it forever and ever.

AIR.

What exquisite pleasure!
This sweet treasure
From me they shall never
Sever.
In thee, in thee,
My charmer I see.
I'll sigh and caress thee,
I'll kiss thee and press thee,
Thus, thus to my bosom forever and ever.

Urganda *and* Fatima *come forward.*
Cymon *puts the nosegay in his bosom and looks confused and astonished.*

URGANDA (*smiling*). Pray, what is that you would kiss and press to your bosom forever and ever?

CYMON. Nothing but the end of an old song the shepherds taught me, (*Pretends to sing.*) "I'll sigh and caress thee, I'll kiss thee and press thee," &c.

FATIMA (*aside to* Urganda). Upon my word, a very hopeful youth indeed, and much improved in his singing. What think you now?

URGANDA. Nothing but his bashfulness struggling with his passion. [*To* Cymon] What was that you was talking to?

CYMON. Myself, to be sure. I had nothing else to talk to.

URGANDA. Yes, but you have, Cymon. Don't be ashamed of what you ought to be proud of. There is something in your bosom next your heart.

CYMON. Yes, so there is.

URGANDA (*smiling*). What is it, Cymon?

FATIMA (*aside*). Now his modesty is giving way. We shall have him at last.

CYMON. Nothing but a nosegay.

URGANDA. That which I gave you? Let me see it.

CYMON. What! Give a thing and take it away again?

URGANDA. I would not take it away for the world.

CYMON. Nor would I give it you for a hundred worlds.

FATIMA (*aside to* Urganda). See it by all means, Madam. I have my reasons.

URGANDA. I must see it, Cymon, and therefore no delay. You cannot

---

65.2–3. *puts the nosegay in his bosom and looks confused and astonished.*] O1, O2, D; *starts at seeing* Urganda *and puts the nosegay in his bosom with great confusion.* O3, O4, O5, O6.

have the love you seemed to have but now and refuse me.

CYMON. Oh, but I can, and for that reason.

URGANDA. Don't provoke me. I will see it or shut you up forever.

CYMON. What a stir is here about nothing. Now are you satisfied?

He holds the nosegay at a distance. Urganda *and* Fatima *look at one another with confusion.*

FATIMA. I was right.

URGANDA. And I am miserable.

CYMON. Have you seen it enough?

URGANDA. That is not mine, Cymon.

CYMON. No, 'tis mine.

URGANDA. Who gave it you?

CYMON. A person.

URGANDA. What person? Male or female?

CYMON. La! How can I tell?

FATIMA (*aside*). Finely improved indeed. A genius!

URGANDA (*aside*). I must dissemble. [*To* Cymon.] Lookee, Cymon, I did but sport with you. The nosegay was your own, and you had a right to give it away or throw it away.

CYMON. Indeed, but I did not. I only gave it for this, which, as it is so much finer and sweeter, I thought would not vex you.

URGANDA (*aside*). Heigho!

FATIMA. Vex her? Oh, not in the least. But you should not have given away her present to a vulgar creature.

CYMON. How dare you talk to me so? I would have you to know she is neither ugly nor vulgar.

FATIMA. Oh, she! Your humble servant, young Simplicity. La, how can you tell whether it is male or female? (Cymon *is confused.*)

URGANDA. Don't mind her impertinence, Cymon. I give you leave to follow your own inclinations. I brought you hither for your pleasure. Indulge yourself in everything you like, and be as happy as following your desires can make you.

CYMON. Then I am happy indeed. Thank you, Lady; you have made me quite another creature. I'm out of my wits with joy. I may follow my inclinations. Thank you, thank you, and thank you again!

I'll sigh and caress thee,
I'll kiss thee and press thee,
Thus, thus, to my bosom, forever and ever.

Exit Cymon *singing.*

93.2. with confusion.] *O1*, *O2*, *D*; *with surprise O3*, *O4*, *O5*, *O6*.

116. (Cymon *is confused.*)] *O1*, *O2*, *D*; (*Mimicks* Cymon, *who seems confused.*) *O3*, *O4*, *O5*, *O6*.

FATIMA. You are a philosopher indeed.

URGANDA. A female one. Fatima, I have hid the most racking jealousy under this false appearance in order to deceive him. I shall by this means discover the cause of his joy and my misery; and when that is known, you shall see whether I am most of a woman or a philosopher.

FATIMA. I'll lay ten to one of the woman in matters of this nature.

URGANDA. Let him have liberty to go wherever he pleases. I will have him watched. That office be yours, my faithful Fatima. About it instantly. Don't lose sight of him—no reply, not a word more.

FATIMA. That's very hard, but I'm gone.

Exit.

URGANDA. When I have discovered the object of his present transports, I will make her more wretched than any of her sex—except myself.

AIR.

Hence every hope and every fear!
Awake, awake, my power and pride,
Let Jealousy, stern Jealousy appear!
With Vengeance at her side!

II.

Who scorns my charms, my power shall prove.
Revenge succeeds to slighted love!
Revenge! But oh, my sighing heart
With rebel Love takes part;
Now pants again with all her fears,
And drowns her rage in tears.

Exit.

SCENE [II], Dorcas's *cottage.*

Sylvia *at the door with* Cymon's *nosegay in her hand.*

AIR.

SYLVIA. These flowers, like our hearts, are united in one,
And are bound up so fast that they can't be undone;
So well are they blended, so beauteous to sight,
There springs from their union a tenfold delight;
No poison nor weed here our passion to warn,
But sweet without briar, the rose without thorn.

The more I look upon this nosegay, the more I feel Cymon in my heart and mind. Ever since I have seen him, heard his vows, and received this nosegay from him, I am in continual agitation and cannot rest a moment. I wander without knowing where; I speak without knowing to whom; and I look without knowing at what. Heigho! How my poor heart flutters in my breast. Now I dread to lose him, and now again I think him mine forever.

AIR.

Oh why should we sorrow, who never knew sin?
Let smiles of content show our rapture within.
'Tis love has so raised me, I now tread in air.
He's sure sent from heaven to lighten my care.

II.

Each shepherdess views me with scorn and disdain;
Each shepherd pursues me, but all is in vain.
No more will I sorrow, no longer despair,
He's sure sent from heaven to lighten my care.

Enter Linco.

LINCO. If you were as wicked, Shepherdess, as you are innocent, that voice of yours would corrupt justice herself, unless she was deaf as well as blind.

SYLVIA. I hope you did not overhear me, Linco.

LINCO. Oh, but I did though. And, notwithstanding I come as the deputy of a deputy governor to bring you before my principal for some complaints made against you by a certain shepherdess, I will stand your friend though I lose my place for it. There are not many such friends, Shepherdess.

SYLVIA. What have I done to the shepherdesses that they persecute me so?

LINCO. You are much too handsome, which is a crime the best of 'em can't forgive you.

SYLVIA. I'll trust myself with you and face my enemies.

As they are going, Dorcas *calls from the cottage.*

DORCAS. Where are you going, Child? Who is that with you, Sylvia?

LINCO. Now shall we be stopped by this good old woman, who will know all and can scarce hear anything.

DORCAS. I'll see who you have with you.

Enter Dorcas *from the house.*

21.1. *Enter* Linco.] O1, O2, D; Linco *is seen listening to her singing.* O3, O4, O5, O6.

39. with you. *Enter* Dorcas *from the house.*] O1, O2, D; DORCAS (*coming forward*). I'll see who you have with you. O3, O4, O5, O6.

LINCO (*speaks loud in her ear*). 'Tis I, Dame, your kinsman Linco.

DORCAS. Oh, is it you, honest Linco? (*Takes his hand.*) Well, what's to do now?

LINCO. The governor desires to speak with Sylvia. A friendly enquiry, that's all.

DORCAS. For what, for what? Tell me that. I have nothing to do with his desires, nor she neither. He is grown very inquisitive of late about the shepherdesses. Fine doings, indeed! No such doings when I was young. If he wants to examine anybody, why don't he examine me? I'll give him an answer, let him be as inquisitive as he pleases.

LINCO (*speaks loud at her ear*). But I am your kinsman, Dame, and you dare trust me sure.

DORCAS. Thou art the best of 'em, that I'll say for thee. But the best of you are bad when a young woman is in the case. I have gone through great difficulties myself, I can assure you, in better times than these. Why must not I go too?

LINCO (*still speaking loud*). We shall return to you again before you can get there.

SYLVIA. You may trust us, Mother. My own innocence and Linco's goodness will be guard enough for me.

DORCAS. Eh, what?

LINCO (*speaking loud*). She says you may trust me with her innocence.

DORCAS. Well, well, I will then. Thou art a sweet creature, and I love thee better than even I did my own child. (*Kisses* Sylvia.) When thou art fetched away by him that brought thee, 'twill be a woeful day for me. Well, well, go thy ways with Linco. I dare trust thee anywhere. I'll prepare thy dinner at thy return. And bring my honest kinsman along with you.

LINCO. We will be with you before you can make the pot boil.

DORCAS. Before what?

LINCO. We will be with you before you can make the pot boil.

Speaks very loud, and goes off with Sylvia.

DORCAS. Heaven shield thee for the sweetest, best creature that ever blessed old age. What a comfort she is to me. All I have to wish for in this world is to know who thou art, who brought thee to me, and then to see thee as happy as thou hast made poor Dorcas. What can

---

41. is it you] *O1*, *O2*, *O3*, *O4*, *O5*, *D*; it is you *O6*.
43. LINCO. The governor . . .] *O1*, *O2*, *D*; LINCO (*speaks aloud.*) The governor . . . *O3*, *O4*, *O5*, *O6*.
51. (*speaks loud at her ear*)] *O1*, *O2*, *D*; (*speaks loud*) *O3*, *O4*, *O5*, *O6*.
62. (*speaking loud*)] *O1*, *O2*, *D*; (*speaking louder*) *O3*, *O4*, *O5*, *O6*.

the governor want with her? I wish I had gone too. I'd have talked to him, and to the purpose. We had no such doings when I was a young woman. They never made such a fuss with me.

AIR.

When I were young, though now am old,
The men were kind and true;
But now they're grown so false and bold,
What can a woman do?
Now what can a woman do?
For men are truly,
So unruly,
I tremble at seventy-two!

II.

When I were fair, though now so-so,
No hearts were given to rove.
Our pulses beat nor fast nor slow,
But all was faith and love.
Now what can a woman do?
For men are truly,
So unruly,
I tremble at seventy-two!

Exit.

SCENE [III], *the Magistrate's House.*
Enter Dorus *and* Second Shepherdess.

DORUS. This way, this way, damsel. Now we are alone, I can hear your grievances and will redress them, that I will. You have my good liking, damsel, and favor follows of course.

SECOND SHEPHERDESS. I want words, your Honor and Worship, to thank you fitly.

DORUS. Smile upon me, damsel. Smile and command me. Your hand is whiter than ever, I protest. You must indulge me with a chaste salute. (*Kisses her hand.*)

SECOND SHEPHERDESS. La, your Honor! (*Curtsies.*)

DORUS. You have charmed me, damsel, and I can deny you nothing. Another chaste salute. 'Tis a perfect cordial. (*Kisses her hand.*) Well, what shall I do with this Sylvia, this stranger, this baggage, that has affronted thee? I'll send her where she shall never vex thee again, an impudent wicked–(*Kisses her hand.*) I'll send her packing this very day.

SECOND SHEPHERDESS (*leering*). I vow your Worship is too good to me.

DORUS. Nothing's too good for thee. I'll send her off directly. Don't fret and tease thyself about her. Go she shall, and speedily too. I have sent my deputy Linco for that Dorcas who has harbored this Sylvia without my knowledge, and the country shall be rid of her tomorrow morning. Smile upon me, damsel. Smile upon me.

SECOND SHEPHERDESS. I would I were half as handsome as Sylvia; I might smile to good purpose.

DORUS. I'll Sylvia her! An impudent vagrant. She can neither smile or whine to any purpose while I am to govern. She shall go tomorrow, damsel. This hand, this lily hand, has signed her fate. (*Kisses it.*)

Enter Linco.

LINCO. No bribery and corruption, I beg of your Honor.

DORUS. You are too bold, Linco. Where did you learn this impertinence to your superiors?

LINCO. From an old song, and please your Honor, where I get all my wisdom. Heaven help me!

AIR.

If she whispers the judge, be he ever so wise,
  Though great and important his trust is,
His hand is unsteady, a pair of black eyes
  Will kick up the balance of justice.

II.

If his passions are strong, his judgment grows weak,
  For love through his veins will be creeping;
And his worship, when near to a round dimpled cheek,
  Though he ought to be blind, will be peeping.

DORUS. Pooh, pooh, 'tis a very foolish song, and you're a fool for singing it.

SECOND SHEPHERDESS. Linco's no friend of mine. Sylvia can sing and has enchanted him.

LINCO. My ears have been feasted, that's most certain. But my heart, damsel, is as uncracked as your virtue or his honor's wisdom. There is not too much presumption in that, I hope.

DORUS. Linco, do your duty and know your distance–What is to come to the fellow? He is so altered I don't know him again.

LINCO. Your Honor's eyesight is not so good as it was. I am always the same, and heaven forbid that mirth should be a sin. I am always laughing and singing. Let who will change; I will not. I laugh at

16. (*leering*)] *O1*, *O2*, *D*; (*leering at him*) *O3*, *O4*, *O5*, *O6*.

the times, but I can't mend 'em. They are woefully altered for the worse. But here's my comfort. (*Showing his tabor and pipe.*)

DORUS. I'll hear no more of this ribaldry. I hate poetry and I don't like music. Where is this vagrant, this Sylvia?

LINCO. In the justice chamber, waiting for your Honor's commands.

DORUS. Why did you not tell me so?

LINCO. I thought your Honor better engaged, and that it was too much for you to try two female causes at one time.

DORUS. You thought! I won't have you think but obey. Times are changed indeed. Deputies must not think for their superiors.

LINCO. Must not they! What will become of our poor country? (*Going.*)

DORUS. No more impertinence, but bring the culprit hither.

LINCO. In the twinkling of your Honor's eye.

Exit.

SECOND SHEPHERDESS. I leave my griefs in your Worship's hands.

DORUS. You leave 'em in my heart, damsel, where they soon shall be changed into pleasures. Wait for me in the justice chamber. Smile, damsel, smile upon me and edge the sword of justice.

Enter Linco *and* Sylvia.

SECOND SHEPHERDESS. Here she comes. See how like an innocent she looks. But I'll be gone. I trust in your Worship. I hate the sight of her; I could tear her nasty eyes out.

Exit.

DORUS (*gazing at* Sylvia). Hem, hem! I am told, young woman—hem, hem!—that—(*Aside, and turning from her.*) She does not look so mischievous as I expected.

---

68. of justice. *Enter* Linco . . .] *O1*, *O2*, *O3*, *O4*, *O5*, *D*; of justice.

AIR.

Smile, damsel, smile,
I'll frown upon your foe,
I'll pack her off, the vagrant vile,
This moment she shall go.
Smile, damsel, smile.
Sweet hazlenut,
The wicked slut
Shall trudge for many a mile,
And all that I shall ask for this
Is now and then a harmless kiss.
Smile, damsel, smile.

Enter Linco . . . *O6*.

71. her nasty eyes] *O1*, *O2*, *O3*, *O4*, *O5*, *D*; her eyes *O6*.

LINCO. Bear up, sweet shepherdess. Your beauty and innocence will put injustice out of countenance.

SYLVIA. The shame of being suspected confounds me, and I can't speak.

DORUS. Where is the old woman, Dorcas, they told me of? Did not I order you to braing her before me?

LINCO. The good old woman is so deaf, and your reverence a little thick of hearing, I thought the business would be sooner and better done by the young woman.

DORUS. What, at your thinking again? Young shepherdess, I hear—I hear —Hem! (*Aside.*) Her modesty pleases me.—What is the reason, I say—Hem!—that—that I hear—(*Aside, and turning from her.*) She has very fine features.

LINCO. Speak, speak, Sylvia, and the business is done.

DORUS. Is not your name Sylvia?

LINCO. Yes, your Honor, her name is Sylvia.

DORUS. I don't ask you.—What is your name? Look up and tell me, Shepherdess.

SYLVIA (*sighs and curtsies*). Sylvia.

DORUS (*aside*). What a sweet look with her eyes she has!—What can be the reason, Sylvia—that—Hem! (*Aside.*) I protest she disarms my anger.

LINCO. Now is your time. Speak to his Reverence.

DORUS. Don't whisper the prisoner.

SYLVIA. Prisoner? Am I a prisoner then?

DORUS. No, not absolutely a prisoner; but you are charged, damsel. Hem, hem! Charged, damsel. (*Aside.*) I don't know what to say to her.

SYLVIA. With what, your Honor?

LINCO. If he begins to damsel us, we have him sure.

SYLVIA. What is my crime?

LINCO. A little too handsome, that's all.

DORUS. Hold your peace.—Why don't you look up in my face if you are innocent? (Sylvia *looks at* Dorus *with great modesty.*) I can't stand it. She has turned my anger, my justice, and my whole scheme topsy-turvy. Reach me a chair, Linco.

LINCO. One sweet song, Sylvia, before his Reverence gives sentence. (*Reaches a chair for* Dorus.)

DORUS. No singing. Her looks have done too much already.

LINCO. Only to soften your rigor.

Sylvia *sings.*

AIR.

SYLVIA. From duty if the shepherd stray,
And leave his flocks to feed,

The wolf will seize the harmless prey,
And innocence will bleed.

II.

In me a harmless lamb behold,
Oppressed with ev'ry fear.
Oh guard, good shepherd, guard your fold,
For wicked wolves are near. (*Kneels.*)

DORUS. I'll guard thee and fold thee too, my lambkin, and they shan't hurt thee. This is a melting ditty indeed! Rise, rise, my Sylvia. (*Embraces her.*)

Enter Second Shepherdess.
Dorus *and she start at seeing each other.*

SECOND SHEPHERDESS. Is your Reverence taking leave of her before you drive her out of the country?

DORUS. How now! What presumption is this, to break in upon us so and interrupt the course of justice?

SECOND SHEPHERDESS. May I be permitted to speak three words with your Worship?

DORUS. Well, well, I will speak to you. I'll come to you in the justice chamber presently.

SECOND SHEPHERDESS (*aside*). I knew the wheedling slut would spoil all. But I'll be up with her yet.

Exit.

DORUS. I'm glad she's gone. Linco, you must send her away. I won't see her now.

LINCO. And shall I take Sylvia to prison?

DORUS. No, no, no. To prison? Mercy forbid! What a sin should I have committed to please that envious, jealous-pated shepherdess! Linco, comfort the damsel.—Dry your eyes, Sylvia. I will call upon you myself, and examine Dorcas myself, and protect you myself, and do everything myself. [*Aside.*] I profess she has bewitched me. I am all agitation.—I'll call upon you tomorrow, perhaps tonight—perhaps in half an hour. Take care of her, Linco. [*Aside.*] She has bewitched me, and I shall lose my wits if I look on her any longer. Oh, the sweet, lovely, delightful creature!

LINCO. Don't whimper now, my sweet Sylvia. Justice has taken up the sword and scales again, and your rivals shall cry their eyes out. The day's our own.

AIR.

Sing high derry derry,
The day is our own,

Be wise and be merry,
Let sorrow alone.
Alter your tone
To high derry derry,
Be wise and be merry,
The day is our own.

Exeunt.

End of the Third Act.

ACT IV.

SCENE [I], *an old castle.*

Enter Urganda *greatly agitated.*

URGANDA. Lost, lost Urganda! Nothing can control
The beating tempest of my restless soul.
While I prepare in this dark witching hour
My potent spells and call forth all my power,
Arise ye demons of revenge, arise!
Begin your rites unseen by mortal eyes.
Hurl plagues and mischiefs through the poisoned air,
And give me vengeance to appease despair!

CHORUS (*underground*). We come, we come, we come.

She waves her wand and the castle vanishes.
The first Demon of Revenge *arises.*

AIR.

While mortals charm their cares in sleep,
And demons howl below,
Urganda calls us from the deep.
Arise ye sons of woe!
Ever busy, ever willing,
All those horrid tasks fulfilling,
Which draw from mortal breasts the groan,
And make their torments like our own.

CHORUS (*underground*). We come, we come, we come!

Demons arise and perform their rites.
Then Exeunt, with Urganda *at their head.*

9.2. *arises.*] *O1, O2, O3, O4, O5, D*; *arises, with his followers. O6.*
18.1. Demons arise . . .] *O1, O2, O3, O4, O5, D*; *Other demons arise . . . O6.*

SCENE [II], *the Country.*

Enter Linco, *drawing in* Damon *and* Dorilas.

LINCO. Nay, nay, but let me talk to you a little. By the lark, you are early stirrers. Has not that gadfly jealousy stung you up to this same mischief you are upon?

DAMON. We are commanded by our governor, who has orders from Urganda, to bring Cymon and Sylvia before her.

LINCO. And you are fond of this employment, are you? Fye, for shame! I know more than you think I know. You were each of you (good souls!) betrothed to two shepherdesses, but Sylvia comes in the nick and away go vows, promises, and protestations, she loving Cymon and despising you and you. You (hating one another) join cordially to distress them for loving one another. Fye, for shame, shepherds!

DAMON. What will the governor say to this? This is fine treatment of your betters.

LINCO. If my betters are no better than they should be, 'tis their fault, not mine. Urganda, Dorus, and you, not being able to reach the grapes, won't let anybody else taste them. Fye, for shame, shepherds!

DAMON. We have no time to lose. We must raise the shepherds and hunt after these young sinners. And you, Mr. Deputy, for all your airs, must make one in the chase.

LINCO. Before I would follow unlawful game to please a hot-livered enchantress, an old itching governor, and two such jealous-pated noodles as yourselves, I would thrust my pipe through my tabor, chuck it into the river, and myself after it.

DAMON. Here comes the governor. Now we shall hear what you will say to him.

LINCO. Just what I have said to you. An honest laughing fellow like myself don't mind a governor, though I should raise his spleen and lose my place into the bargain. There are not many deputies in Arcadia of the same mind.

DORILAS. Come, come, let us mind our business and not his impertinence.

DAMON. If the governor would do as I wish him, you would have your deserts, Mr. Deputy Linco.

LINCO. And if Cymon could do as I wish him, you would have your deserts, my gentle shepherds.

Enter Dorus *and* Arcadians.

DORUS. Where have you been, Linco? I sent for you an hour ago.

LINCO. I was in bed, your Honor; and as I don't walk in my sleep, I could not well be with you before I was dressed.

DORUS. No joking, no joking! We are ordered by the Enchantress to search for Cymon and Sylvia and bring them before her.

LINCO. I hate to spoil sport, so I'll go home again. (*Going.*)

DORUS. Stay, Linco. (*He returns.*) I command you to do your duty and go with me in pursuit of these young criminals.

LINCO. Criminals! Heaven bless them, I say! I'll go home again. (*Going.*)

DORUS. Was there ever such insolence? Come back, Linco. How dare you disobey what I order and Urganda commands? Give me an answer.

LINCO. Conscience! Conscience, Governor, an old fashioned excuse, but a true one. I cannot find in my heart to disturb two sweet young creatures, whom, as heaven has put together, I will not attempt to divide. 'Twould be a crying sin. I'll go home again. (*Going.*)

DORUS. You are a scandal to your place, and you shall hold it no longer. I'll take it from you instantly.

LINCO. You cannot take from me a quiet conscience and a merry heart. You are heartily welcome to all the rest, Governor.

DORUS. I dismiss you from this moment; you shall be no deputy of mine. You shall suffer for your arrogance. I shall tell the Enchantress that you are leagued with this Sylvia and will not do your duty.

LINCO. A word with your Honor. Could you have been leagued with this Sylvia too, you would not have done your duty, Mr. Governor.

DORUS. Hem! Come along, shepherds, and don't mind his impudence.

Exeunt Dorus *and* Shepherds.

LINCO. I wish your Reverence a good morning, and I thank you for all favors. Any fool now that was less merry than myself would be out of spirits for being out of place. But as matters are now turned topsy-turvy, I won't walk upon my head for the best office in Arcadia. And so, my virtuous old governor, get what deputy you please. I shall stick to my tabor and pipe, and sing away the loss of one place till I can whistle myself into another.

AIR.

When peace here was reigning,
And love without waining,
Or care or complaining,
Base passions disdaining,
This was my way,
With my pipe and tabor,
I laughed down the day,
Nor envied the joys of a neighbor.

II.

Now sad transformation
Runs through the whole nation;
Peace, love, recreation,
All changed to vexation.
This, this is my way,
With my pipe and my tabor,
I laugh down the day,
And pity the cares of my neighbor.

III. [Omitted in the representation]

While all are designing,
Their friends undermining,
To mischief inclining,
This, this is my way,
With my pipe and my tabor,
I laugh down the day,
And pity the cares of my neighbor.

Exit.

SCENE [III], *another part of the country.*
Enter Fatima.

[FATIMA.] Truly a very pretty mischievous errand I am sent upon. I am to follow this foolish young fellow all about to find out his haunts. Not so foolish neither, for he is so much improved of late we shrewedly suspect that he must have some female to sharpen his intellects. For love, among many other strange things, can make fools of wits and wits of fools. I saw our young partridge run before me and take cover hereabouts. I must make no noise, for fear of alarming him; besides, I hate to disturb the poor things in pairing time. (*Looks through the bushes.*)

Enter Merlin.

MERLIN. I shall spoil your peeping, thou evil counselor of a faithless mistress. [*Aside*] I must torment her a little for her good. Such females must feel much to be made just and reasonable creatures.

FATIMA (*peeping through the bushes*). There they are. Our fool has made no bad choice. Upon my word, a very pretty couple! and will make my poor lady's heart ache.

9.1. *Enter* Merlin.] O1, O2, O3, O4, O5, *D*; *Enter* Merlin, *behind her O6.*

MERLIN [*aside*]. I shall twinge yours a little before we part.

FATIMA. Well said, Cymon! Upon your knees to her! Now for my pocket-book, that I may exactly describe this rival of ours. She is much too handsome to live long; she will be either burnt alive, thrown to wild beasts, or shut up in the black tower. The greatest mercy she can have will be to let her take her choice. (*Takes out a pocket-book.*)

MERLIN [*aside*]. Maybe so, but we will prevent the prophecy if we can.

FATIMA (*writing in her book*). She is of a good height, about my size; a fine shape, delicate features, charming hair, heavenly eyes, not unlike my own, with such a sweet smile. She must be burnt alive. Yes, yes, she must be burnt alive.

Merlin *taps her upon the shoulder with his wand.*

Who's there? Bless me, nobody. I protest, it startled me. I must finish my picture. (*Writes on.*)

Merlin *waves his wand over her head.*

Now let me see what I have written. Bless me, what's here? All the letters are as red as blood! My eyes fail me. Sure I am bewitched. (*Reads and trembles.*) Urganda *has a shameful passion for* Cymon, Cymon *a most virtuous one for* Sylvia. *As for* Fatima, *wild beasts, the black tower, and burning alive are too good for her.* (*Drops the book.*) I have not power to stir a step. I knew what would come of affronting that devil Merlin.

Merlin *is visible.*

MERLIN. True, Fatima, and I am here at your service.

FATIMA. Oh, most magnanimous Merlin, don't set your wit to a poor foolish weak woman.

MERLIN. Why, then, will a foolish weak woman set her wit to me? But we will be better friends for the future. Mark me, Fatima. (*Holds up his wand.*)

FATIMA. No conjuration, I beseech your Worship, and you shall do anything with me.

MERLIN. I want nothing of you but to hold your tongue.

FATIMA. Will nothing else content your fury?

MERLIN. Silence, babbler.

FATIMA. I am your own forever, most merciful Merlin. I am your own forever. Oh, my poor tongue. I thought I never should have wagged thee again. What a dreadful thing it would be to be dumb.

MERLIN. You see it is not in the power of Urganda to protect you, or to injure Cymon and Sylvia. I will be their protector against all her arts, though she has leagued herself with the demons of revenge. We have no power but what results from our virtue.

FATIMA. I had rather lose anything than my speech.

MERLIN. As you profess yourself my friend (for with all my art I cannot see into a woman's mind), I will show my gratitude and my power by giving your tongue an additional accomplishment.

FATIMA. What, shall I talk more than ever?

MERLIN (*smiling*). That would be no accomplishment, Fatima. No, I mean that you should talk less. When you return to Urganda, she will be very inquisitive, and you very ready to tell her all you know.

FATIMA. And may I without offence to your Worship?

MERLIN. Silence, and mark me well. Observe me truly and punctually. Every answer you give to Urganda's questions must be confined to two words, *Yes* and *No*. I have done you a great favor and you don't perceive it.

FATIMA (*aside*). Not very clearly, indeed.

MERLIN. Beware of encroaching a single monosyllable upon my injunction. The moment another word escapes you, you are dumb.

FATIMA. Heaven preserve me! What will become of me!

MERLIN. Remember what I say. As you obey or neglect me, you will be punished or rewarded.

Merlin *strikes the scene, which opens and discovers his dragons and chariot, which carry him away.*

Farewell. (*Bowing to her.*) Remember me, Fatima.

FATIMA. I shall never forget you, I am sure. What a polite devil it is, and what a woeful plight am I in. This confining my tongue to two words is worse than being quite dumb. I had rather be stinted in anything than in my speech. Heigho! There never sure was a tax upon the tongue before.

---

72. or rewarded.] *O1*, *O2*, *O3*, *O4*, *O5*, *D*; or rewarded.

AIR.

Be sure you regard what I say;
My commands to a tittle obey.
Beware, beware,
I ride in the air,
And will watch you by night and by day.
Tho' I raise both the sea and the wind,
The tempest in fetters can bind,
Yet my magic, more powerful and strong,
Can stop the full tide of a woman's tongue. *O6*.

AIR.

Tax my tongue! it is a shame.
Merlin, sure, is much to blame,
Not to let it sweetly flow.
Yet the favors of the great,
And the silly maiden's fate,
Often follow Yes or No.
Lack-a-day!
Poor Fatima!
Stinted so,
To Yes or No.

II.

Should I want to talk and chat,
Tell Urganda this or that,
How shall I about it go?
Let her ask me what she will,
I must keep my clapper still,
Striking only Yes or No.
Lack-a-day!
Poor Fatima!
Stinted so,
To Yes or No.

Exit.

SCENE [IV], *Enter* Cymon *and* Sylvia (*arm in arm*).

CYMON. You must not sigh, my Sylvia. Love like ours can have no bitter mingled with its sweets. It has given me eyes, ears, and understanding; and till they forsake me, I must be Sylvia's.

SYLVIA. And while I retain mine, I can know no happiness but with Cymon. And yet Urganda –

CYMON. Why will you sully again the purity of our joys with the thoughts of that unhappy, because guilty, woman? Has not Merlin discovered all that was unknown to us? Has he not promised us his protection and told us that we are the care of superior beings, and that more blessings, if possible, are in store for us? What can Sylvia want, when Cymon is completely blessed?

SYLVIA. Nothing but my Cymon. When that is secured to me, I have not a wish for more.

CYMON. Thy wishes are fulfilled then, and mine in thee!

SYLVIA. Take my hand, and with it a heart which, till you had touched, never knew nor could even imagine what was love. But my passion now is as sincere as it is tender, and it would be ungrateful to disguise my affections, as they are my greatest pride and happiness.

CYMON (*kisses her hand*). Transporting maid!

AIR.

SYLVIA. This cold, flinty heart, it is you who have warmed,
You wakened my passions, my senses have charmed;
In vain against merit and Cymon I strove;
What's life without passion, sweet passion of love?

II.

The frost nips the bud, and the rose cannot blow,
From youth that is frost-nipped no raptures can flow,
Elysium to him but a desert will prove;
What's life without passion, sweet passion of love?

III.

The spring should be warm, the young season be gay,
Her birds and her flowrets make blithsome sweet May,
Love blesses the cottage, and sings through the grove;
What's life without passion, sweet passion of love?

CYMON. Thus then I seize my treasure, will protect it with my life, and will never resign it but to heaven, who gave it me. (*Embraces her.*)

Enter Damon *and* Dorilas *on one side, and* Dorus *and his followers on the other, who start at seeing* Cymon *and* Sylvia.

DAMON. Here they are.

SYLVIA (*starting*). Ha! Bless me!

DORUS. Fine doings indeed!

Cymon *and* Sylvia *stand amazed and ashamed.*

DORILAS. Your humble servant, modest Madam Sylvia.

DAMON. You are much improved by your new tutor.

DORUS. But I'll send her and her tutor where they shall learn better. I am confounded at their assurance. Why don't you speak, culprits?

CYMON. We may be ashamed without guilt, to be watched and surprised by those who ought to be more ashamed at what they have done.

SYLVIA. Be calm, my Cymon. They mean us mischief.

CYMON. But they can do us none. Fear them not, my shepherdess.

DORUS. Did you ever hear or see such an impudent couple? But I'll secure you from these intemperate doings.

DAMON. Shall we seize them, your Worship, and drag 'em to Urganda?

DORUS. Let me speak first with that damsel.

As he approaches, Cymon *puts her behind him.*

CYMON. That damsel is not to be spoken with.

DORUS. Here's impudence in perfection. Do you know who I am, stripling?

CYMON. I know you to be one who ought to observe the laws and protect innocence. But having passions that disgrace both your age and place, you neither do one nor the other.

DORUS. I am astonished. What, are you the foolish young fellow I have heard so much of?

CYMON. As sure as you are the wicked old fellow I have heard so much of.

DORUS. Seize them both this instant!

CYMON. That is sooner said than done, Governor.

As they approach on both sides to seize them, he snatches a staff from one of the shepherds and beats them back.

DORUS. Fall on him, but don't kill him, for I must make an example of him.

CYMON. In this cause I am myself an army. See how the wretches stare and cannot stir.

AIR.

Come on, come on,
A thousand to one,
I dare you to come on.
Though unpracticed and young,
Love has made me stout and strong;
Has given me a charm,
Will not suffer me to fall;
Has steeled my heart, and nerved my arm,
To guard my precious all. (*Looking at Sylvia.*)
Come on, come on, *&c.*

Exit.

SYLVIA. Oh Merlin, now befriend him!
From their rage defend him!

While Cymon *drives off the party of shepherds on one side, enter* Dorus *and his party, who surround* Sylvia.

DORUS. Away with her, away with her.

SYLVIA. Protect me, Merlin! Cymon, Cymon! Where art thou, Cymon?

DORUS. Your fool Cymon is too fond of fighting to mind his mistress. Away with her to Urganda, Away with her. [*Exit with* Sylvia.]

Enter shepherds, running across,
disordered and beaten by Cymon.

DAMON (*looking back*). 'Tis the devil of a fellow! How he has laid about him!

Exit.

DORILAS. There is no way but this to avoid him.

Exit.

Enter Cymon, *in confusion and out of breath.*

[CYMON]. I have conquered, my Sylvia! Where art thou, my life, my love, my valor, my all? What, gone, torn from me? Then I am conquered indeed.

He runs off and returns several times during the symphony of the following song.

AIR.

Torn from me, torn from me, which way did they
take her?
To death they shall bear me,
To pieces shall tear me,
Before I'll forsake her.
Though fast bound in a spell,
By Urganda and hell,
I'll burst through their charms,
Seize my fair in my arms;
Then my valor shall prove
No magic like virtue, like Virtue and Love!

End of the Fourth Act.

ACT V.

SCENE [I], *a grotto.*

Enter Urganda *and* Fatima.

URGANDA. Yes! No! Forbear this mockery. What can it mean? I will not bear this trifling with my passion. Fatima, my heart's upon the

1. URGANDA.] *O1, O2, O3, O4, O5, D*; URGANDA (*angry*). *O6.*

rack and must not be sported with. Let me know the worst and quickly. To conceal it from me is not kindness but the height of cruelty. Why don't you speak? (Fatima *shakes her head.*) Won't you speak?

FATIMA. Yes.

URGANDA. Go on then.

FATIMA. No.

URGANDA. Will you say nothing but "No"?

FATIMA. Yes.

URGANDA. Distracting, treacherous Fatima. Have you seen my rival?

FATIMA. Yes.

URGANDA. Thanks, dear Fatima. Well, now go on.

FATIMA. No.

URGANDA. This is not to be borne. Was Cymon with her?

FATIMA. Yes.

URGANDA. Are they in love with each other?

FATIMA (*sighing*). Yes.

URGANDA. Where did you see my rival? (Fatima *shakes her head.*) False, unkind, obstinate Fatima! Won't you tell me?

FATIMA. No.

URGANDA. You are bribed to betray me?

FATIMA. No.

URGANDA. What, still "Yes" and "No"?

FATIMA. Yes.

URGANDA. And not a single word more?

FATIMA. No.

URGANDA. Are you afraid of anybody?

FATIMA. Yes.

URGANDA. Are you not afraid of me too?

FATIMA. No.

URGANDA. Insolence! Is my rival handsome? Tell me that.

FATIMA. Yes.

URGANDA. Very handsome?

FATIMA. Yes, yes.

URGANDA. How handsome? Handsomer than I or you?

FATIMA (*hesitating*). Yes–No –

URGANDA. How can you see me thus miserable and not relieve me? Have you no pity for me?

FATIMA (*sighing*). Yes!

URGANDA. Convince me of it and tell me all.

FATIMA (*sighing*). No.

URGANDA. I shall go distracted. Leave me.

FATIMA. Yes.

URGANDA. And dare not come into my presence.

FATIMA. No.

Curtsies and Exit.

URGANDA (*alone*). She has a spell upon her, or she could not do thus. Merlin's power has prevailed; he has enchanted her, and my love and my revenge are equally disappointed. This is the completion of my misery.

Enter Dorus.

DORUS. May I presume to intrude upon my sovereign's contemplations?

URGANDA. Dare not to approach my misery, or thou shalt partake of it.

DORUS (*going*). I am gone. And Sylvia shall go too.

URGANDA. Sylvia, said you? Where is she, where is she? Speak, speak, and give me life or death.

DORUS. She is without and attends your mighty will.

URGANDA. Then I am queen again! Forgive me, Dorus, I was lost in thought, sunk in despair. I knew not what I said. But now I am raised again. Sylvia is safe!

DORUS. Yes, and I am safe too, which is no small comfort to me, considering where I have been.

URGANDA. And Cymon? Has he escaped?

DORUS. Yes, he has escaped from us; and, what is better, we have escaped from him.

URGANDA. Where is he?

DORUS. Breaking the bones of every shepherd he meets.

URGANDA. Well, no matter. I am in possession of the present object of my passion, and I will indulge it to the height of luxury. Let 'em prepare my victim instantly for death.

DORUS. For death! Is not that going too far?

URGANDA. Nothing is too far. She makes me suffer ten thousand deaths, and nothing but hers can appease me. (Dorus *going*.) Stay, Dorus, I have a richer revenge. She shall be shut up in the Black Tower till her beauties are destroyed, and then I will present her to this ungrateful Cymon. Let her be brought before me, and I will feast my eyes and ease my heart with this devoted Sylvia. No reply, but obey.

DORUS. It is done. (*Aside*.) This is going too far.

Exit, shrugging up his shoulders.

URGANDA.
Though still of raging winds the sport,
My shipwrecked heart shall gain the port;
Revenge, the pilot, steers her way,
No more of tenderness and love,

The eagle in her grip has seized the dove,
And thinks of nothing but her prey.

Enter Sylvia, Dorus, *and Guards.*

URGANDA. Are you the wretch, the unhappy maid, who has dared to be the rival of Urganda?

SYLVIA. I am no wretch, but the happy maid who am possessed of the affections of Cymon, and with them have nothing to hope or fear.

URGANDA. Thou vain, rash creature! I will make thee fear my power and hope for my mercy. (*Waves her wand, and the scene changes to the black rocks.*)

SYLVIA (*smiling*). I am still unmoved.

URGANDA. Thou art on the very brink of perdition, and in a moment will be closed in a tower, where thou shalt never see Cymon or any human being more.

SYLVIA. While I have Cymon in my heart, I bear a charm about me to scorn your power or, what is more, your cruelty.

Urganda *waves her wand and the Black Tower appears.*

URGANDA. Open the gates and enclose her insolence forever.

SYLVIA (*smiling at* Urganda). I am ready.

AIR.

Though various deaths surround me,
No terrors can confound me;
Protected from above,
I glory in my love!
Against thy cruel might,
And in this dreadful hour,
I have a sure defence,
'Tis innocence,
That heavenly right
To smile on guilty power.

URGANDA. Let me no more be tormented with her; I cannot bear to hear or see her. Close her in the tower forever! (*They put* Sylvia *in the tower.*) Now let Merlin release you if he can.

It thunders. The tower and rocks give way to a magnificent amphitheatre, and Merlin *appears in the place where the tower sunk. All shriek and run off except* Urganda, *who is struck with terror.*

111. he can.] *O1*, *O2*, *D*; he can (*exultingly*). *O3*, *O4*, *O5*, *O6*.

MERLIN. Still shall my power your arts confound;
And Cymon's cure shall be Urganda's wound.

Urganda *waves her wand.*

MERLIN. Ha, ha, ha! Your power is gone.

URGANDA. I am all terror and shame. In vain I wave this wand. I feel my power is gone, yet I still retain my passions. My misery is complete!

MERLIN. It is indeed! No power, no happiness were superior to thine till you sunk them in your folly. You now find, but too late, that there is no magic like virtue. (*Sound of warlike instruments.*)

URGANDA. What mean those sounds of joy? My heart forbodes that they proclaim my fall and dishonor.

MERLIN. The orders of chivalry are assembled, sent by Cymon's father to celebrate and protect the marriage of Cymon with Sylvia.

URGANDA. Death to my hopes! Then I am lost indeed.

MERLIN. From the moment you wronged me and yourself I became their protector. I counteracted all your schemes. I continued Cymon in his state of ignorance till he was cured by Sylvia, whom I conveyed here for that purpose. That shepherdess is a princess equal to Cymon. They have obtained by their virtues the throne of Arcadia, which you have lost by—But I have done. I see your repentance, and my anger melts into pity.

URGANDA. Pity me not. I am undeserving of it. I have been cruel and faithless and ought to be wretched. Thus I destroy the small remains of my sovereignty. (*Breaks her wand.*) May power, basely exerted, be ever thus broken and dispersed. (*Throws away her wand.*)

Forgive my errors and forget my name,
Oh, drive me hence with penitence and shame;
From Merlin, Cimon, Sylvia, let me fly,
Beholding them, my shame can never die.

Exit Urganda.

123–24. The orders of chivalry . . . with Sylvia.] *O1*, *O2*, *D*; The knights of the different orders of chivalry, who were sent by Cymon's father in quest of his son, were drawn hither by my power from their several stations to one spot, and at the same instant. The general astonishment at their meeting was soon changed into general joy when they were told by what means and upon what occasion they were so unexpectedly assembled; and they are now preparing to celebrate and protect the marriage of Cymon and Sylvia. *O3*, *O4*, *O5*, *O6*.

139. Cimon] *O1*, *O2*, *O3*; Cymon *O4*, *O5*, *D*, *O6*.

MERLIN. Falsehood is punished, virtue rewarded, and Arcadia is restored to peace, pleasure, and innocence!

MARCH.

Enter the procession of knights of the different orders of Chivalry, *with* Enchanters, *&c., who range themselves round the amphitheatre, followed by* Cymon, Sylvia, *and* Merlin, *who are brought in triumph drawn by* Loves, *preceded by* Cupid *and* Hymen *walking arm and arm. Then enter the* Arcadian *shepherds, with* Dorus *and* Linco *at their head,* Damon *and* Dorilas *with their shepherdesses, &c. They sing the following* chorus.

CHORUS. [Omitted in the representation.]
Each heart and each voice
In Arcadia rejoice;
Let gratitude raise
To great Merlin our praise.
Long, long may we share
The blessings of this pair!
Long, long may they live
To share the bliss they give!

After the chorus and procession, Linco *comes forward.*

LINCO. My good neighbors and friends (for now I am not ashamed to call you so), your deputy Linco has but a short charge to give you. As we have turned over a new, fair leaf, let us never look back to our past blots and errors.

DORUS. No more we will, Linco. No retrospection.

141–42. is restored to peace, pleasure, and innocence.] *O*1, *D*; is happy! *O*2, *O*3, *O*4, *O*5, *O*6.

142.8. *shepherdesses, &c. They sing the following chorus.*] *O*1, *D*; shepherdesses, &c. Merlin, Cymon, *and* Sylvia *descend from the car.* Merlin *joins their hands, and then speaks the following lines.*

MERLIN. Now join your hands, whose hearts were joined before;
This union shall Arcadia's peace restore.
When virtues such as these adorn a throne,
The people make their sovereign's bliss their own.
Their joys, their virtues shall each subject share,
And all the land reflect the royal pair.

*O*2, *O*3, *O*4, *O*5, *O*6.

150.1. Linco *comes forward.*] *O*1, *D*; Cymon, Sylvia, *and* Merlin *retire to the knights, while* Linco *call* [*sic*] *the shepherds about him. O*2, *O*3; . . . calls . . . *O*4, *O*5, *O*6.

LINCO. I meant to oblige your Worship in the proposition. I shall ever be a good subject (*bowing to* Cymon *and* Sylvia), and your friend and obedient deputy. Let us have a hundred marriages directly, and no more inconstancy, jealousy, or coquetry from this day. The best purifier of the blood is mirth, with a few grains of wisdom. We will take it every day, neighbors, as the best preservative against bad humors. "Be merry and wise," according to the old proverb, and I defy the devil ever to get among you again. And that we may be sure to get rid of him, let us drive him quite away with a little singing and dancing, for he hates mortally mirth and good fellowship.

AIR.

DAMON. Each shepherd again shall be content and kind,
And every strayed heart shall each shepherdess find.
DELIA. If faithful our shepherds, we always are true.
Our truth and our falsehood we borrow from you.
CHORUS. Happy Arcadians still shall be;
Ever be happy while virtuous and free.
FATIMA. Let those who the sword and the balance must hold,
To int'rest be blind, and to beauty be cold.
When justice has eyes her integrity fails,
Her sword becomes blunted, and down drop her scales.
CHORUS. Happy Arcadians still shall be;
Ever be happy while virtuous and free.
LINCO. The bliss of your heart no rude care shall molest,
While innocent mirth is your bosom's sweet guest.
Of that happy pair let us worthy be seen,
Love, honor, and copy your king and your queen.
CHORUS. Happy Arcadians still shall be;
Ever be happy while virtuous and free.
SYLVIA. Let love, peace, and joy still be seen hand in hand,
To dance on this turf and again bless the land.
CYMON. Love and Hymen of blessings have opened their store,
For Cymon with Sylvia can wish nothing more.
BOTH. Love and Hymen of blessings have opened their store,

165–66. good fellowship.] *O*1, *D*; good fellowship. *A dance of* Arcadian Shepherds *and* Shepherdesses. *O*2, *O*3, *O*4, *O*5, *O*6.

171–72. Happy Arcadians still shall be;
Ever be happy while virtuous and free. *O*1, *O*2, *O*3, *O*4, *O*5, *D*;
While we're virtuous, while we're free,
Ever happy shall we be! *O*6

177–78. *O*6 repeats lines 171–72.

183–84. *O*6 repeats lines 171–72.

HE. For Cymon with Sylvia }
SHE. For Sylvia with Cymon } can wish nothing more.
CHORUS. Happy Arcadians still shall be;
Ever happy while virtuous and free.

A Dance of Arcadian Shepherds and Shepherdesses.

Finis.

192–93. *O6* repeats lines 171–72.
193. virtuous and free. *A dance of Arcadian shepherds and shepherdesses.*] *O1*, *D*; virtuous and free. *O2*, *O3*, *O4*, *O5*, *O6*.

Epilogue

Written by GEORGE KEATE, Esq.
Spoken by Mrs. Abington

Enter, peeping in at the stage door.

Is the stage clear? Bless me, I've such a dread!
It seems enchanted ground where'er I tread!

Coming forward.

What noise was that? Hush! 'Twas a false alarm –
I'm sure there's no one here will do me harm.
Amongst you can't be found a single knight
Who would not do an injured damsel right.
Well–Heaven be praised! I'm out of magic reach
And have once more regained the power of speech.
Aye, and I'll use it, for it must appear
That my poor tongue is greatly in arrear.
There's not a female here but shared my woe,
Tied down to *yes*, or still more hateful *no*.
No is expressive–but I must confess,
If rightly questioned I'd use only *yes*.
    In Merlin's walk this broken wand I found,

Showing a broken wand.

Which to two words my speaking organs bound.
Suppose upon the town I try his spell –
Ladies, don't stir! You use your tongues too well!
How tranquil every place, when, by my skill,
Folly is mute, and even Slander still!
Old Gossips speechless, Bloods would breed no riot,
And all the tongues at Jonathan's lie quiet!
Each grave procession must new bush the wig;

EPILOGUE.] Epilogue lacking in *O*1, *O*2.

Nothing to say, 'twere needful they look big!
The reverend doctor might the change endure,
He would sit still and have his sine cure!
Nor could great folks much hardship undergo;
They do their bus'ness with an *aye* or *no*!
But, come, I only joked—dismiss your fear;
Tho' I've the power, I will not use it here.
I'll only keep my magic as a guard
To awe each critic who attacks our bard.
I see some malcontents their fingers biting,
Snarling, "The Ancients never knew such writing.
"The drama's lost! The managers exhaust us
"With op'ras, monkies, Mab, and Dr. Faustus."
Dread sirs, a word! The public taste is fickle;
All palates in their turn we strive to tickle.
Our cat'rers vary; and you'll own at least
It is variety that makes the feast.
If this fair circle smile and the gods thunder,
I with this wand will keep the critics under.

Linco's Travels

An Interlude

1767

LVII.

LINCO's TRAVELS*.

Linco, - - - Mr. KING.
Dorcas, - - - Mrs. BRADSHAW.

Enter Arcadian *Men and Women*; *and among them* Dorcas, *gathering about* Linco.

CHORUS of ARCADIANS.

WELCOME Linco, welcome home.
Linco. Happy am I, that am come;
Tho' I've been in countries rare,
Seen ſuch ſights would make you ſtare!
Arcadian. Tell us, tell us!
Linco. Give me air to blow my bellows.
Arcadian. Tell us, tell us!
Linco. A moment ſpare.
Arcad. Make your neighbours ſome amends.
Linco. Never more I'll wander,
Simple, ſilly gander,
From my flock and cackling friends. (*Shakes hands, and kiſſes the women.*)
Chorus. Welcome, Linco, welcome home.

* An Interlude, acted at Drury-lane, for Mr. King's Benefit, April 1767.

Facsimile first page of *Linco's Travels* in *The Poetical Works of David Garrick*, 1785. Folger Shakespeare Library.

Dramatis Personae

Linco	Mr. *King*.
Dorcas	Mrs. *Bradshaw*.

Linco's Travels, *An Interlude*

Enter Arcadian *Men and Women*; *and among them* Dorcas, *gathering about* Linco.

CHORUS OF ARCADIANS. Welcome Linco, welcome home.

LINCO. Happy am I that am come;
Tho' I've been in countries rare,
Seen such sights would make you stare!

ARCADIANS. Tell us, tell us.
LINCO. Give me air to blow my bellows.
ARCADIANS. Tell us, tell us.
LINCO. A moment spare.
ARCADIANS. Make your neighbors some amends.

LINCO. Never more I'll wander,
Simple, silly gander,
From my flock and cackling friends.

(*Shakes hands, and kisses the women.*)

CHORUS. Welcome, Linco, welcome home.

LINCO. Don't crowd so, neighbors. You confound me.
Stand back and make a circle round me.
I'll move my elbows in the center –
And on my travels thus I enter.
O yes! Keep silence old and young.
Do you find ears while I find tongue.

DORCAS. I am so deaf I must come near thee. (*Approaches.*)

LINCO. And pray be dumb, or you'll not hear me.
Seized with a strange desire of gadding,

Which sets your Englishmen a madding,
I rather chose like them to roam,
To play the fool than stay at home.
But though like them abroad I roved,
I'm not returned so much improved. (*Ironically.*)

DORCAS. Those English folks are very strange.

LINCO. In politics much giv'n to change,
They are in temper like the weather –
Fair, storm, foul, sunshine all together.
Strange contradictions: gay and sad,
Moped, merry, moody, wise, and mad,
A strange hodge-podge of good and bad.

DORCAS. 'Tis said they are so fierce and bold
No woman's safe.

LINCO. Unless she's old.

DORCAS. I hate such wantonness and riot.

LINCO. You'd live among 'em very quiet. (*Loud.*)

ARCADIAN. But are they so prodigious stout?

LINCO. Best go and try 'em, if you doubt.
Be honest, and they'll kindly treat you;
Be pert and saucy, and they'll beat you.
If you dissect an English skull,
Of politics 'tis so brimful,
Of papers, pamphlets, prose and verse,
The furniture can't well be worse.
So furious are they to be free,
Nothing so common as to see
Britons dead-drunk for liberty.
This draws the sword of Englishmen,
Of English women draws the pen.
I ne'er shall see such folks again.
Their very children on the lap
Are fed with liberty and pap.
But hold –
True travellers have various ways
To ease their bones. They quit their chaise,
To mount a horse and pace along.
So I, to ease my half-tired tongue,
Leave doggrel trot to pace it in a song.

AIR.

I saw sprightly France,
 That nation so gay,
Where they sing and they dance
 All their sorrows away.
  For with fal, lal, la,
  And ha, ha, ha!
They drive sorrow away.

II.

The German so brave,
 Not a smile must come near.
When they laugh they are grave;
 'Tis thus with mynheer.
  They fal, lal, la,
  And ha, ha, ha!
Nicht laughter, mynheer.

III.

The Italians so sly
 Have one simple plan.
On your purse they keep eye,
 And their hand, if they can.
  If you fal, lal, lal,
  Then they fal, lal, lal,
So Signor, Signora, if they can.

IV.

But England's strange folk
 Are my greatest delight.
They'll scold and they'll joke,
 Shake hands, and they'll fight.
  One moment fal, lal, lal,
  The next fal, lal, lal,
Curse, kiss you, and fight.

I will now leave my horse and my chaise for a time,
And will foot it for change in prose tagged with rhyme.

ARCADIAN. Of England tell more, what their sport and their trade is.

DORCAS. And tell us, good Linco, some news of their ladies.

LINCO. Their women are fair, but fantastical grown,
To Dame Nature owe much, would they let her alone.
They challenge the world for good hearts and sweet faces,
But use all their *tongues* as they do in *all places*.

Portrait of Thomas King.
Folger Shakespeare Library

For their sports they have plays, where all ranks and degrees
Take places to sweat, to be squeezed, and to squeeze.
'Tis strange but 'tis true what I saw with my eye:
They give money to laugh, and what's stranger—*to cry*.
They build 'em fine places to meet in and talk,
To walk round and round, and then round and round walk.
When tired, to drink tea and to eat buttered bread,
Then again round and round, and go home almost dead.
Of all human things there a traffic is made —
Religion, law, physic—nay, beauty's a trade.

ARCADIAN. Beauty! (*Starts.*)

LINCO. Yes, beauty, I say. At midnight you'll meet
Kind damsels who offer their charms in the street —
"*Ah, so you! Where go you? Sir, pray stay a while.*"
Then so softly they talk and so sweetly they smile
That they tempt you to buy by alluring approaches.
Such females are hired as they hire hackney coaches.

DORCAS. Fye, for shame! For their kingdom they should not have me.

LINCO. In that, my good dame, you and they will agree.
For ev'ry disorder they'll publish a cure,
Whose virtue much puffing and swearing insure.
Should he kill the poor patient, the doctor must gain,
And still have good trade—for the dead won't complain.
Though they talk of their rights, which they'll fight for and die,
Yet to know what's their right to the law they apply.
For two bits of gold a black gown reads your case,
Hums and haws, and thus speaks with a wise puckered face:
"*That coat on your back you have bought and may use it.*"
'Tis proved the next day 'tis not mine, and I *lose it*.
Among these green bags, if you are not alert,
With your coat you may lose both your waistcoat and shirt.
And happy I am that I've brought home my skin.

DORCAS. To forsake all your friends was a shame and a sin. Leave roving, and make your own country your wife.

LINCO. From this moment I wed her and take her for life,
Shall quit all the world and think her the most comely;
For home is still home, though never so homely.

SONG.

I'll never go abroad again,
Nor ever will I roam;

For he has but a flimsy brain,
Who wanders far from home.
See nine in ten
Of Englishmen
Who run the nations o'er;
Though pert and gay,
Yet, pray, are they
Much wiser than before?

CHORUS. See nine in ten, *&c*,*&c*.

II.

Contented here, I'll pass my life,
For roving's but a curse.
I'll take my country for a wife,
For better and for worse.
See nine in ten
Of Englishmen
Who run the nations o'er;
Though pert and gay,
Yet, pray, are they
Much wiser than before?

CHORUS. See nine in ten, *&c*., *&c*.

III.

While I can see such sights as these,
And such a harvest bring;
And while I can my betters please,
For ever will I sing –
That nine in ten
Of Englishmen
Who choose abroad to roam,
Among mankind
Will ever find
The worth they leave at home.

CHORUS. See nine in ten, *&c*., *&c*.

A Peep Behind the Curtain; or, The New Rehearsal
1767

A

PEEP BEHIND THE CURTAIN;

O R,

THE NEW REHEARSAL:

AS IT IS NOW PERFORMED AT THE

THEATRE ROYAL

N

DRURY-LANE

THE SECOND EDITION.

LONDON
Printed for T. BECKET and P. A. DE HONDT,
near Surry-Street, in the Strand.
MDCCLXVII.

[Price One Shilling.]

Facsimile title page of the Second Edition.
Folger Shakespeare Library.

Prologue

Bold is the man, and *compos mentis*, scarce –
Who, in these nicer times, dares write a Farce;
A vulgar long-forgotten taste renew;
All now are Comedies, five acts, or two.
Authors have ever in a canting strain,
Begged mercy for the bantling of their brain;
That you, kind nurse, would fondle 't on your lap,
And rear it with applause, that best of pap –
Thus babes have in their cradles 'scaped a blow,
Tho' lame and rickety from top to toe;
Our bard, with prologue-outworks has not fenced him,
For all that I shall say, will make against him.
Imprimis, this his piece–a Farce we call it –
Ergo, 'tis low–and ten to one you maul it!
Would you, because 'tis low, no quarter give?
Black-guards, as well as Gentlemen, should live.
'Tis downright English too–nothing from France;
Except some beasts, which treat you with a dance.
With a Burletta too we shall present you –
And, not Italian–that will discontent you.
Nay, what is worse–you'll see it, and must know it –
I, Thomas King, of King-street, am the poet:
The murder's out–the murderer detected;
May in one night, be tried, condemned, dissected.
'Tis said, for Scandal's tongue will never cease;
That mischief's meant against our little piece:
Let me look round, I'll tell you how the case is –
There's not one frown a single brow disgraces;
I never saw a sweeter set of faces!
Suppose Old Nick, before you righteous folk,

Produce a farce, brimful of mirth and joke;
Tho' he, at other times, would fire your blood;
You'd clap his piece, and swear, 'twas devilish good!
Malice prepense! 'tis false!—it cannot be –
Light is my heart, from apprehensions free –
If you would save Old Nick, you'll never damn poor me.

Dramatis Personae

Men

Sir Toby Fuz	[Mr. *Love*]
Glib, the Author	[Mr. *King*]
Wilson	[Mr. *J. Palmer*]
Mervin	[Mr. *Aickin*]
Sir Macaroni Virtu	[Mr. *Dodd*]
Patent, the Manager	[Mr. *Packer*]
Hopkins, Prompter	[Mr. *Bannister*]
Saunders, Carpenter	[Mr. *Moody*]
Johnston, Housekeeper	[Mr. *Johnston*]

Women

Lady Fuz	[Mrs. *Clive*]
Miss Fuz	[Miss *Pope*]
First Sweeper	[Mrs. *Bradshaw*]
Second Sweeper	[Mrs. *Love*]

Dramatis Personae to ORPHEUS

Orpheus	[Mr. *Vernon*]
Old Shepherd	[Mr. *Dodd*]
Chorus of Shepherds	[Messrs. *Parsons*, *Hartry*, *Bannister*, *Faucet*, *Kear*]
Rhodope	[Mrs. *Arne*]

A Peep Behind the Curtain; or, The New Rehearsal

ACT I. SCENE I.

Covent Garden
Enter Wilson *and* Mervin, *booted.*

WILSON. My dear Jack! Ten thousand thanks for your punctuality. Ready equipped, I see, to serve your friend.

MERVIN. But how can I serve you, my young Don Quixote? Am I to be your Sancho while your Knight Errantship is running away with this Dulcinea del Toboso?

WILSON. I have given orders that my post chaise shall wait in the broad way by Exeter-Change, and the moment the lady steps from her chair to the chaise, the postilions will crack their whips and drive away like lightning.

MERVIN. You are a romantic fellow! How can you possibly imagine that your hot-headed scheme to run away with this young lady can ever be executed?

WILSON. From the justice of my cause, Jack.

MERVIN. Justice! Make that out and my conscience will be easy.

WILSON. Did not her father's uncle, who was a good lawyer and cheated my father of three-fourths of his fortune, leave her near thirty thousand pounds? Now, this is my reasoning. Sir Toby's uncle ran away with some thousands from my father. I shall run away with Sir Toby's daughter. This will bring the said thousands back to me again, with which I'll pay off old scores, strike a balance in my favor, and get a good wife into the bargain. There's justice for you!

MERVIN. Ay, justice with a vengeance. But why must Sir Toby be punished for the sins of his uncle?

WILSON. I'll ease your conscience there too. My mother, at my father's death, took me a boy to Sir Toby and my Lady, to solicit their kindness for me. He gave me half a crown to buy gingerbread, and her Ladyship, who was combing a fat lap dog, muttered, "There was no end of maintaining poor relations."

MERVIN. I have not a qualm left. But did you really pass for a strolling player last summer to have a pretence of being near her father's house?

WILSON. Yes, I did, and as Polonius says, "was accounted a good actor."

MERVIN. What could put that unaccountable frolic in your head?

WILSON. To gain the favor of Sir Toby's family as a strolling player, which I could not as a poor relation. They are fond of acting to madness, and my plan succeeded. I was so altered they did not know me. They liked me much, came to a benefit which I pretended to have, invited me to their house, and Miss met me privately, after I had played Ranger and Lothario.

MERVIN. Ay, ay, when a young lady's head is crammed with combustible scraps of plays, she is always ready-primed and will *go off* (if you will allow me a pun) the very first opportunity.

WILSON. I discovered myself to the young lady, and her generosity was so great that she resolved to marry me to make me amends. There are refined feelings for you.

MERVIN. Ay, double refined! She is more romantic than you, Will. But did you not run a great risk of losing her, when she knew you was only a gentleman and not a player?

WILSON. Read that letter and tell me if my castles are built in the air? (*Gives a letter.*)

MERVIN (*reads*). "I shall be with my Papa and Mama to see a rehearsal at Drury-Lane Playhouse on Tuesday morning. If my present inclinations hold, and my heart does not fail me, I may convince honest Ranger what confidence I have in his honor." Postscript. "If I don't see you then, I don't know when I shall see you, for we return into the country next week."

WILSON. Well, what think you?

MERVIN. O she'll run away with you most certainly.

WILSON. I must not lost time then. (*Looking at his watch.*) I must go and take my stand, that the *Deer* may not escape me.

MERVIN. And I'll go and take mine, to help you to carry off the venison. This is very like poaching, Will. But how will you get admittance into Drury-Lane Theatre?

WILSON. I was very near being disappointed there. For unluckily the acting manager, who scarce reached to my third button, cocked up his head in my face and said I was much to tall for a hero. However, I got the liberty of the scenes by desiring to rehearse Hamlet next week. But I hope to cross the Tweed with the fair Ophelia before that time and finish my stage adventures by appearing the first time in the character of a good husband.

MERVIN. Success attend you.

WILSON. This is the day,
Makes me or mars, for ever and for aye! If I succeed I shall be restored to my father's estate, drink claret, and live like a gentleman with the wife of my heart, and, egad, for aught I know, stand for the County.

MERVIN. If not, you must be confined to your little one hundred and twenty pounds a year farm, make your own cheese, marry the curate's daughter, have a dozen children, and brew the best October in the parish.

WILSON. Whichever way fortune will dispose of me, I shall be always happy to see my friends, and never shall forget my obligations to thee, my dear Jack. (*Shakes him by the hand.*)

MERVIN. Well, well, let us away. We have too much business to mind compliments.

(*Exeunt severally.*)

SCENE II, *The Playhouse.*

Two women *sweeping the stage.*

FIRST WOMAN. Come, Betty, dust away, dust away, girl, the managers will be here presently. There's no lying in bed for them now. We are up early and late, all hurry and bustle from morning to night. I wonder what the deuce they have got in their heads?

SECOND WOMAN. Why to get money, Mrs. Besom, to be sure. The folks say about us, that the other house will make them stir their stumps and they'll make us stir ours. If they are in motion we must not stand still, Mrs. Besom.

FIRST WOMAN. Ay, ay, girl, they have met their match, and we shall all suffer for it. For my part I can't go through the work if they are always in this plaguy hurry. I have not drank a comfortable dish of tea since the house opened.

SECOND WOMAN. One had better die than be scolded and hurried about as we are by the housekeeper. He takes us all for a parcel of Negers, I believe. Pray give us a pinch of your snuff, Mrs. Besom.

(*They lean upon their brooms and take snuff.*)

---

73. mars] *O*1, *O*2, *O*3, *D*1, *D*2, *O*5; marrs *O*2, *O*4.

FIRST WOMAN. Between you and I, Betty, and our two brooms, the housekeeper is grown a little purse-proud. He thinks himself a great actor, forsooth, since he played the Scotch fellow and the fat cook in Queen Mab.

SECOND WOMAN. The Quality spoils him too. Why, woman, he talks to them for all the world as if he was a Lord.

FIRST WOMAN. I shall certainly "resign," as the great folks call it in the newspaper, if they won't promise to give me the first dresser's place that falls and make our little Tommy a page. What, woman, though we are well paid for our work, we ought to make sure of something when our brooms are taken from us. 'Tis the fashion, Betty.

SECOND WOMAN. Right, right, Mrs. Besom. Service is no inheritance, and to be always doing dirty work and to have no prospect to rest and clean ourselves, is the curse only of us poor folks.

FIRST WOMAN. You and I will drink a dish of tea together in comfort this afternoon and talk over these and other matters. But mum! here's the prompter. (*They sing and sweep again.*)

Enter Hopkins, *the prompter.*

PROMPTER. Come, come, away with your brooms and clear the stage. The managers will be here directly.

(*The sweepers hurry off.*)

Where are the carpenters? Carpenters!

A CARPENTER (*above*). What do you want, Mr. Hopkins?

PROMPTER. What do I want? Come down and set the scene for the new burletta of Orpheus.

CARPENTER. We an't ready for it. The beasts are now in hand. They an't finished.

PROMPTER. Not finished the beasts? Here's fine work! The managers and author will be here directly, and nothing ready. Fie, fie, fie! (*Calls out.*) Saunders! Saunders!

Enter Saunders.

SAUNDERS. Here, here! Zooks, what a bawling you make. Do keep your breath for your prompting, Master Hopkins, and not send it after me at this rate. I'm not deaf.

PROMPTER. But your men are—and asleep too, I believe. I can't get a soul of 'em near me. (*Looking at his watch.*) 'Tis ten o'clock, and not a scene prepared for the rehearsal. 'Tis I shall be blamed and not you.

SAUNDERS. Blamed for what? 'Tis but a rehearsal, and of one act only.

17. grown] *O*1, *O*2, *O*3, *D*2, *O*4, *O*5; growing *D*1.

Garrick with Shakespearean Characters, Commemorating the Jubilee at Stratford-upon-Avon, 1769. By Isaac Taylor.
Victoria and Albert Museum

Would you have us to finish our work before the poet has done his? Don't you know that carpenters are always the last in a house? And yet you want us to get out of it before the author has covered in.

PROMPTER. You may be as witty as you please, but the managers will do as they please. And they have promised the author to rehearse the first act of his burletta of Orpheus this morning as he pleases, with all the proper scenes, dresses, machinery, and music. So what signifies all our prating?

SAUNDERS. Very little, as you say. But damn all these new vagaries that put us all upon our heads topsy versy. My men have sat up all night, and I have finished everything but the dancing cows.

PROMPTER. Bless my heart, man, the author depends most upon his cows.

SAUNDERS. His cows! How came they to be his? They are *my* cows. These poets are pretty fellows, faith. They say I'll have a flying devil or a dancing bear or any such conundrum. Why, 'tis easily said. But who is to make 'em fly and dance? Ha, Mr. Prompter? Why poor Pill Garlick. The audience applauds, the author is conceited, but the carpenter is never thought of.

PROMPTER. These are bold truths, Mr. Saunders.

SAUNDERS. Why then out with 'em, I say. Great men spin the brains of the little ones and take the credit of 'em. Do you know how I was served in our dramatic romance of *Cymon*?

PROMPTER. You did your business well there, particularly in the last scene.

SAUNDERS. And what was the consequence? One fine gentleman in the boxes said my master brought it from Italy. "No, damn it," says another taking snuff, "I saw the very same thing at Paris," when you all know here behind the scenes that the whole design came from this head and the execution from these hands. But nothing can be done by an Englishman nowadays, and so your servant, Mr. Hopkins. (*Going.*)

PROMPTER. Hark'ee, Saunders. The managers have ordered me to discharge the man at the lightning. He was so drunk the last time he flashed that he has singed all the clouds on that side the stage. (*Pointing to the clouds.*)

SAUNDERS. Yes, yes, I see it. And hark'ee, he has burnt a hole in the new cascade and set fire to the shower of rain. But mum!

PROMPTER. The deuce! He must be discharged directly.

(*Exit* Saunders.)

53. always last] *O*1, *O*2, *O*3, *D*2, *O*4, *O*5; always the last *D*1.
69. Pill Garlick] *O*1, *O*2, *O*3, *D*1, *D*2, *O*5; Pill Garlic *O*4.

PATENT (*without*). Where's the prompter?

PROMPTER. Here I am, Sir.

Enter Patent.

PATENT. Make haste with your scenes, Saunders. So clear the stage, Mr. Hopkins, and let us go to business. Is the extraordinary author of this very extraordinary performance come yet?

PROMPTER. Not yet, Sir, but we shall soon be ready for him. 'Tis a very extraordinary thing, indeed, to rehearse only one act of a performance, and with dress and decorations as if it were really before an audience.

PATENT. It is a novelty indeed and a little expensive too, but we could not withstand the solicitations that were made to us. We shan't often repeat the same experiment.

PROMPTER. I hope not, Sir. 'Tis a very troublesome one and the performers murmur greatly at it.

PATENT. When do the performers not murmur, Mr. Hopkins? Has any morning passed in your time without some grievance or another?

PROMPTER. I have half a dozen now in my pocket for you. (*Feeling in his pockets for papers.*)

PATENT. O pray let's have 'em, my old breakfast. (*Prompter gives 'em.*) And the old story, actress quarrelling about parts. There's not one of 'em but thinks herself young enough for any part, and not a young one but thinks herself capable of any part. But their betters quarrel about what they are not fit for. So our ladies have at least great precedents for their folly.

PROMPTER. The young fellow from Edinburgh won't accept of the second Lord. He desires to have the first.

PATENT. I don't doubt it. Well, well, if the author can make him speak English, I have no objection.

PROMPTER. Mr. Rantly is indisposed and can't play tomorrow.

PATENT. Well, well, let his lungs rest a little. They want it, I'm sure. What a campaign shall we make of it. All our subalterns will be general officers and our generals will only fight when they please.

GLIB (*without*). O he's upon the stage, is he? I'll go to him.

PATENT. Here comes the author. Do you prepare the people for the rehearsal. Desire them to be as careful as if they were to perform before an audience.

---

90. Patent (*without*).] *O*1, *O*2, *O*3, *D*2, *O*5; Manager (*without*).] *D*1, *O*4.
95. shall soon] *O*1, *O*2, *O*3, *D*2, *O*5; shall be soon *D*1, *O*4.
97. dress] *O*1, *O*2, *O*3, *D*2, *O*5; dresses *D*1, *O*4.
108. actress] *O*1, *O*2, *O*3, *D*2, *O*5; actresses *D*1, *O*4.

PROMPTER. I will, Sir. Pray let us know when we must begin.

(*Exit* Prompter.)

Enter Glib, *the author.*

GLIB. Dear Mr. Patent, am not I too late? Do make me happy at once. I have been upon the rack this half hour. But the ladies, Mr. Patent, the ladies –

PATENT. But where are the ladies, Sir?

GLIB. They'll be here in the drinking of a cup of tea. I left 'em all at breakfast. Lady Fuz can't stir from home without some refreshment. Sir Macaroni Virtu was not come when I left them. He generally sits up all night, and if he gets up before two o'clock he only walks in his sleep all the rest of the day. He is perhaps the most accomplished connoisseur in the three kingdoms, yet he is never properly awake till other people go to bed. However, if he should come, our little performance, I believe, will rouse him. Ha, ha, ha! You understand me? A pinch of cephalic only.

PATENT. I have the honor of knowing him a little. Will Sir Macaroni be here?

GLIB. Why, he promised; but he's too polite to be punctual. You understand me? Ha, ha, ha! However, I am pretty sure we shall see him. I have a secret for you, not a soul must know it. He has composed two of the songs in my burletta. An admirable musician, but particular. He has no great opinion of me, nor indeed of anybody else, a very tolerable one of himself. And so I believe he'll come. You understand me? Ha, ha, ha!

PATENT. I do, Sir. But pray, Mr. Glib, why did not you complete your burletta? 'Tis very new with us to rehearse but one act only.

GLIB. By a sample, Mr. Patent, you may know the piece. If you approve you shall never want novelty. I am a very spider at spinning my own brains, ha, ha, ha! Always at it, spin, spin, spin. You understand me?

PATENT. Extremely well. In your second act, I suppose, you intend to bring Orpheus into hell.

GLIB. O yes. I make him play the devil there. I send him for some better purpose than to fetch his wife, ha, ha, ha! Don't mistake me. While he is upon earth I make him a very good sort of man. He keeps a mistress, indeed, but his wife's dead, you know. And were she alive not much harm in that, for I make him a man of fashion. Fashion,

125.2. Glib] *O1*, *O2*, *O3*, *D2*, *O5*; Author *D1*, *O4*.
130. Glib] *O1*, *O2*, *O3*, *D1*, *D2*, *O5*; Author *O4*.

you know, is all in all. You understand me? Upon a qualm of conscience he quits his mistress and sets out for hell with a resolution to fetch his wife.

PATENT. Is that, too, like a man of fashion, Mr. Glib?

GLIB. No, that's the *moral* part of him. He's a mixed character. But as he approaches and gets into the infernal regions, his principles melt away by degrees, as it were by the heat of the climate. And finding that his wife Eurydice is kept by Pluto, he immediately makes up to Proserpine and is kept by her. Then they all four agree matters amicably, change partners, as one may say, make a general *partie quarrée*, and finish the whole with a song and a chorus. And a stinger it is. The subject of the song is the old proverb, "Exchange is no robbery," and the chorus runs thus:

> We care not or know,
> In matters of love,
> What is doing *above*,
> But his, this is the fashion *below*.

I believe that's true satire, Mr. Patent, strong and poignant. You understand me?

PATENT. O very well. 'Tis cayenne pepper indeed. A little will go a great way.

GLIB. I make Orpheus see in my hell all sorts of people of all degrees and occupations. Ay, and of both sexes. That's not very unnatural, I believe. There shall be very good company too, I assure you. "High life below stairs," as I call it, ha, ha, ha! You take me. A double edge, no boys' play. Rip and tear; the times require it. Fortè, fortissimè.

PATENT. Won't it be too fortè? Take care, Mr. Glib, not to make it so much above proof that the boxes can't taste it. Take care of empty boxes.

GLIB. Empty boxes! I'll engage that my Cerberus alone shall fill the boxes for a month.

PATENT. Cerberus?

GLIB. Be quiet a little. You know, I suppose, that Cerberus is a dog and has three heads?

PATENT. I have heard as much.

GLIB. Then you shall see some sport. He shall be a comical dog, too, I warrant you. Ha, ha, ha!

PATENT. What, is Cerberus a character in your performance?

GLIB. Capital, capital! I have thrown all my fancy and invention into

---

180. cayenne] *O1, O2, O3, D2, O5*; chian *D1, O4*.
186. boys'] *O1, O2, O3, D1, D2, O5*; boys *O4*.

his mouth, or rather mouths. There are three of 'em, you know.

PATENT. Most certainly, if there are three heads.

GLIB. Poh, that's nothing to what I have *in petto* for you. Observe me now. When Orpheus comes to the gates of hell, Cerberus stops him. But how, how? Now for it—guess –

PATENT. Upon my soul, I can't guess.

GLIB. I make his three heads sing a trio.

PATENT. A trio?

GLIB. A trio! I knew I should hit you. A trio, treble, tenor and bass, and what shall they sing? Nothing in the world but "Bow, wow, wow!" Orpheus begins,

O bark not, Cerberus, nor grin –
A stranger sure to pass within,
Your goodness will allow?
Bow, wow, wow –

Treble, tenor and bass. Then Orpheus shall tickle his lyre and treble, tenor and bass shall fall asleep by degrees, and one after another, fainter and fainter. "Bow, wow, wow" fast. You understand me?

PATENT. Very ingenious and very new. I hope the critics will understand it.

GLIB. I will make everybody understand it, or my name is not Derry-Down Glib. When I write, the whole town shall understand me. You understand me?

PATENT. Not very clearly, Sir. But it is no matter. Here's your company.

Enter Sir Toby, Lady Fuz, Sir Macaroni Virtu, *and* Miss Fuz.

GLIB. Ladies and gentlemen, you do me honor. Mr. Patent—Sir Toby and Miss Fuz. And this is Sir Macaroni Virtu. (*All bow and curtsy.*) Sir Toby, one of the managers. (*Introducing* Patent.)

SIR TOBY. I am one of the manager's most humble and obedient.

GLIB. I take it as a most particular compliment, Sir Macaroni, that you would attend my trifle at so early an hour.

SIR MACARONI (*yawns*). Why, faith, Glib, without a compliment, I had much rather be in bed than here or anywhere else.

LADY FUZ. I have a prodigious curiosity to see your playhouse by daylight, Mr. Manager. Have not you, Sir Macaroni?

SIR MACARONI (*half asleep*). O no, my Lady. I never have any curiosity to see it at all.

PATENT. I will prepare some tea and chocolate in the Green Room for the ladies, while the prompter prepares matters for the rehearsal.

---

226. this is Sir Macaroni] *O*1, *O*2, *O*3, *D*1, *D*2, *O*5; this Sir Macaroni *O*4.
228. manager's] *O*1, *O*2, *O*3, *D*1, *D*2, *O*5; managers *O*4.

LADY FUZ. I never breakfast but once a day, Mr. Manager. Sir Toby indeed never refuses anything at any time. He's at it from morning till night.

SIR TOBY. I love to be social, my dear. Besides, trifling with tea, chocolate, macaroons, biscuits, and such things is never reckoned eating, you know.

GLIB. You are indefatigably obliging, Mr. Patent.

(*Exit* Patent.)

MISS FUZ. Bless me, Papa, what a strange place this is! I am sure I should not have known it again. (*Aside and looking about.*) I wonder where he is? I wish I could get a peep at him. And yet I am frighted out of my wits.

SIR TOBY. Now the manager is gone, one may venture to say that the playhouse is no morning beauty. Paint and candlelight are as great friends to the theatres as to the ladies. They hide many wrinkles, don't they, Mr. Glib? Ha, ha, ha!

GLIB. You have hit it, Sir Toby, and this is the old house too. Ha, ha, ha!

Sir Toby *shows his daughter the scenes.*

LADY FUZ (*looking about with a glass*). My dear Sir Toby, you, you may be as sarcastical as you please. But I protest a playhouse is a prodigious odd sort of a thing, now there's nobody in it. Is it not, Sir Macaroni?

SIR MACARONI. O yes, and a prodigious odd sort of thing when 'tis full too. I abominate a playhouse. My ingenious countrymen have no taste now for the high seasoned comedies, and I am sure that I have none for the pap and loplolly of our present writers.

GLIB. Bravo, Sir Macaroni! I would not give a pin for a play, no more than a partridge, that has not the fumet.

SIR MACARONI. Not amiss, faith! Ha, ha, ha!

LADY FUZ. Don't let us lose time, Mr. Glib. If they are not ready for the rehearsal, suppose the manager entertains us with thunder and lightning. And let us see his traps, and his whims and harlequin pantomimes.

SIR TOBY. And a shower of rain or an eclipse. And I must beg one peep at the Patagonians.

MISS FUZ. Pray, Mr. Glib, let us have some thunder and lightning.

GLIB. Your commands shall be obeyed, Miss. I'll whip up to the clouds and be your Jupiter Tonans in a crack.

(*Exit* Glib.)

---

257. there's nobody] *O*1, *O*2, *O*3, *D*1, *D*2, *O*5; there is nobody *O*4.

SIR MACARONI. A playhouse in England is to me as dull as a church and fit only to sleep in.

LADY FUZ. Sir Toby thinks so too. I'll tell you what happened the last time we were there.

MISS FUZ. Ay, do, my dear lady, tell what happened to Papa. 'Twas very droll.

SIR TOBY. Fie, fie, Fanny. My Lady, you should not tell tales out of school. 'Twas an accident.

LADY FUZ. A very common one with you, my dear. We dined late. Sir Toby could not take his nap. And we came early to the house. In ten minutes he fell fast asleep against the box door, his wig half off, his mouth wide open, and snoring like a rhinoceros.

SIR MACARONI. Well, but the catastrophe, Lady Fuz?

LADY FUZ. The pit and galleries fell a-laughing and clapping. I jogged and pulled him till my arms ached. And if the boxkeeper had not luckily opened the door, and Sir Toby fell headlong into the passage, I should have died with shame.

SIR TOBY. You'll not die with tenderness, I believe, for I got a lump upon my head as big as an egg and have not been free from the headache ever since.

MISS FUZ. I shall never forget what a flump my papa came down with. Ha, ha, ha!

SIR MACARONI. The tenderness runs in the family, Sir Toby?

LADY FUZ. Pray don't you adore Shakespeare, Sir Mac?

SIR MACARONI (*yawning*). Shakespeare!

LADY FUZ. Sir Toby and I are absolute worshippers of him. We very often act some of his best tragedy scenes to divert ourselves.

SIR MACARONI. And it must be very diverting, I dare swear.

SIR TOBY. What, more family secrets! For shame, Lady Fuz.

LADY FUZ. You need not be ashamed of your talents, my dear. I will venture to say you are the best Romeo that ever appeared.

SIR TOBY. Pooh, pooh!

SIR MACARONI. I have not the least doubt of Sir Toby's genius. But don't your Ladyship think he rather carries too much flesh for the lover? Does your Ladyship incline to tragedy too?

LADY FUZ. I have my feelings, Sir. And if Sir Toby will favor you with two or three speeches, I will stand up for Juliet.

SIR TOBY. I vow, Lady Fuz, you distress me beyond measure. I never have any voice till the evening.

MISS FUZ. Never mind being a little husky, Papa. Do tear your wig, throw yourself upon the ground and poison yourself.

SIR MACARONI. This is a glorious scene, faith. (*Aside.*) Sir Toby looks as if he were susceptible of the tender passions.

LADY FUZ. Too much so, indeed. He is too amiable not to be a little faithless. He has been a great libertine. Have not you, Sir Toby? Have you not wronged me? Come, give me a pinch of your snuff. (*Takes snuff out of his box.*)

SIR TOBY. Forget and forgive, my dear. If my constitution erred, my affections never did. I have told you so a thousand times.

SIR MACARONI (*aside*). A wonderful couple, upon my soul!

Enter Glib.

GLIB. Ladies, you can't possibly have any thunder and lightning this morning. One of the planks of the thunder-trunk started the other night, and had not Jupiter stepped aside to drink a pot of porter he had been knocked o' the head with his own thunderbolt.

LADY FUZ. Well, let us go into the Green Room then, and see the actors and actresses. Is Clive there? I should be glad of all things to see that woman off the stage.

GLIB. She never attends here but when she is wanted.

LADY FUZ. Bless me! If I was an actress I should never be a moment out of the playhouse.

SIR MACARONI. And if I had my will, I would never be a moment in it.

LADY FUZ. I wish I could have seen Clive! I think her a droll creature. Nobody has half so good an opinion of her as I have.

(*Exit* Lady Fuz.)

MISS FUZ (*going*). For my part I had rather have had a little thunder and lightning than all the tea and chocolate in the world. (*Aside.*) I wonder I don't see him.

(*Exit* Miss Fuz.)

SIR MACARONI. What a set of people am I with! What a place I am in, and what an entertainment am I to go through! But I can't go through it. So I'll e'en get into my chair again and escape from these Hottentots. I wish with all my soul that Sir Toby, my Lady, and Miss, the author and his piece, the managers, their playhouse and their performers, were all at the bottom of the Thames, and that I were fast asleep in my bed again.

(*Exit.*)

Enter Wilson.

WILSON (*peeping*). I durst not discover myself, though I saw her dear eyes looking about for me. If I could see her for a moment now, as the stage is clear and nobody to overlook us, who knows but I might kindle up her spirit this moment to run away with me. Hah! What noise is that?—There she is! Miss Fanny! Miss Fanny—here I am! By heavens, she comes!

Enter Miss Fuz.

MISS FUZ. O dear, how I flutter! I can't stay long. My Papa and Mama were going to rehearse *Romeo and Juliet*, or I could not have stole out now.

WILSON. Let you and I act those parts in earnest, Miss, and fly to Lawrence's cell. Love has given us the opportunity, and we shall forfeit his protection if we don't make the best use of it.

MISS FUZ. Indeed I can't go away with you now. I will find a better opportunity soon, perhaps tomorrow. Let me return to the Green Room. If we are seen together we shall be separated forever.

WILSON. To prevent that let me lead you a private way through the house to a post chaise. We shall be out of reach before Sir Toby and my Lady have gone half through *Romeo and Juliet.*

MISS FUZ. Don't insist upon it now. I could not for the world. My fear has taken away all my inclinations.

WILSON. I must run away with you now, Miss Fuz. Indeed I must.

MISS FUZ. Have you really a post chaise ready?

WILSON. I have indeed! A post chaise and four.

MISS FUZ. A post chaise and four! Bless me!

WILSON. Four of the best bays in London, and my postilions are in blue jackets with silver shoulderknots.

MISS FUZ. With silver shoulderknots! Nay, then there is no resisting. And yet . . . ?

WILSON. Nay, quickly, quickly determine, my dear Miss Fuz.

MISS FUZ. I will determine then. I will sit by my Papa at the rehearsal. And when he is asleep, which he will be in ten minutes, and my Mama will be deaf, dumb, and blind to everything but Mr. Glib's wit—I'll steal out of the box from them, and you shall run away with me as fast as you can wherever your four bays and silver shoulderknots please to take me.

WILSON. Upon my knees I thank you and thus take an earnest of my happiness. (*Kisses her hand.*) Zounds! Here's your Mama, Miss. Don't be alarmed. "Lady! by yonder blessed moon I vow!"

MISS FUZ. "Oh! swear not by the moon, th'inconstant moon!"

LADY FUZ (*approaching*). Let us have no sun and moon and stars now. What are you about, my dear? Who is this young gentleman you are so free with?

MISS FUZ. This is the young gentleman actor, Mama, whose benefit we were at last summer. And while you were busy acting in the Green Room, I stole out to try how my voice would sound upon the stage. And finding him here, I begged him to teach me a little how to play Juliet.

356–57. Lawrence's cell] *O1*, *O2*, *O3*, *D2*, *O5*; Laurence's cell *D1*, *O4*.

LADY FUZ. O very well, my dear. We are obliged to the young gentleman, to be sure. Your Papa will teach you, child, and play Romeo with you. (*Aside.*) You should not be too free with these actors.— I am much obliged to you, Sir, for the pains you have taken with my daughter. We are very sensible of your politeness, and you may bring us some tickets when your benefit time comes.

WILSON. I am greatly honored by your Ladyship and will go through all the scenes of *Romeo and Juliet* with Miss whenever she pleases.

LADY FUZ. O no, young man. Her Papa is a very fine actor and a great critic, and he will have nobody teach her these things but himself. Thank the gentleman, child. (*She curtsies.*) Why did not you stay to hear your Papa and me? Go, go, my dear, and I'll follow you.

(*Exit* Miss [Fuz].)

Upon my word, a likely young man. Your servant, Sir. And very likely to turn a young woman's head. Were it not for setting my daughter a bad example, I should like to go over some scenes of Juliet with him myself.

(*Exit, looking at him.*)

End of the First Act.

ACT II.

The Stage.

Enter Glib, Sir Toby, Lady *and* Miss Fuz, Patent, *&c.*

GLIB. What, we have lost Sir Macaroni! No great matter, for he was half asleep all the time he was here, very little better than a *caput mortuum.* Now, ladies and gentlemen of the jury, take your places. Hiss and clap, condemn or applaud me as your taste directs you, and Apollo and the Nine send me a good deliverance.

LADY FUZ. We'll go into the front boxes. What is the matter with you, Fanny? You had rather be at your inconstant moon than hear Mr. Glib's wit.

MISS FUZ (*sighs*). I never was happier in all my life, Mama. (*Aside.*) What will become of me?

SIR TOBY. I shall be very critical, Mr. Author.

LADY FUZ. Pray are we to have a prologue, Mr. Glib? We positively must have a prologue.

GLIB. Most certainly. *Entre nous*, I have desired the manager to write

0.3. Glib] *O1, O2, O3, D1, D2, O5*; Author *O4*.

me one, which has so flattered him that I shall be able to do anything with him. (*Aside to Lady Fuz.*) I know 'em all from the Patentees down to the waiting fellows in green coats.

SIR TOBY. You are very happy in your acquaintance, Sir.

LADY FUZ. I wish some of the stage folks would show me round to the boxes. Who's there?

Enter Johnston.

JOHNSTON. I'll conduct your Ladyship round, if you please.

LADY FUZ. Thank you, Mr. Johnston. Remember my box the first night. And don't forget Clive's benefit.

JOHNSTON. I won't, my Lady.

LADY FUZ. Come, now for it, Glib. I shall have both my ears open, and I hope Sir Toby will do as much by his eyes. Come, Fanny, my dear, this way.

(*Exit* Lady Fuz, *etc.*)

MISS FUZ. I'll go my own way for the first time. Now my spirits are up again. I have slipped my leading strings, and if dear Mr. Wilson's bays and postilions keep pace with my fancy, my Papa and Mama must run a little faster than they do to overtake me.

(*Exit* Miss Fuz.)

Enter Prompter.

GLIB. I hope, Mr. Hopkins, that nobody has got secretly into the house. I would have none but friends at the first rehearsal. (*Looking round the house.*)

PROMPTER. You see the house is quite clear, Sir.

GLIB. I would not have the town have the least idea of my performance beforehand. I would open a masked battery of entertainment upon the public.

PROMPTER. You'll surprise 'em, I believe, Sir.

GLIB. Pray be so good as to ring down the curtain that we may rehearse in form. So, so, so, well well. (*Curtain drops.*) And now I'll say a word or two to the gentlemen in the orchestra. (*To the orchestra.*) Gentlemen, I shall take it as a particular favor if you would be careful of your *pianos* and *fortès*. They are the light and shade, and without 'em music is all noise and singing nothing but bawling.

MUSICIAN (*from the orchestra*). I don't quite understand this movement. Is it allegro, Sir?

GLIB. Allegro, spiritoso! Flash, flash, fire! My friends, you gentlemen

36. masked] *O1*, *O2*, *O3*, *D1*, *D2*, *O5*; mask *O4*.
40. well, well] *O1*, *O2*, *O3*, *D2*, *O5*; very well *D1*, *O4*.

hautboys, take particular care of your little solos. You bassoons support 'em *con gusto*, not too powerfully. Mind a delicacy of feeling in your second movement. Make yourselves ready, gentlemen. Shoulder your fiddles, cock your bows, and the moment I vanish fire away, crash. I leave my fame in your hands. My Lady, Sir Toby, are you got round? O very well; I see you. (*Speaking to the audience and making a sign of clapping.*) Don't forget a cordial now and then for the poor author.

During the Burletta, Glib, *the author, goes out and comes in several times upon the stage and speaks occasionally to the performers, as his fancy prompts him, in order to enliven the action and give a proper comic spirit to the performance.*

OVERTURE

To the

BURLETTA OF ORPHEUS

The curtain rises to soft music after the Overture and discovers Orpheus *asleep upon a couch with his lyre near him. After the Symphony—Recitative accompanied.*

ORPHEUS (*dreaming*). I come—I go—I must—I will. (*Half awake.*)
Bless me!—Where am I?—Here I'm still. (*Quite awake.*)
Though dead, she haunts me still, my wife.
In death my torment as in life,
By day, by night, whene'er she catches
Poor me asleep, she thumps and scratches.
No more she cries with harlot's revel,
But fetch me, Orpheus, from the devil.

AIR.

I.

Though she scolded all day, and all night did the same,
Though she was too rampant, and I was too tame;
Though shriller her notes than the ear-piercing fife,
I must and I will go to hell for my wife.

II.

As the sailor can't rest if the winds are too still,
As the miller sleeps best by the clack of his mill,
So I was most happy in tumult and strife.
I must and I will go to hell for my wife.

(*Going out.*)

Enter Rhodope.

RECIT[ATIVE].

RHODOPE. Your wife, you driv'ler! Is it so?
But I'll play hell before you go.

RECIT[ATIVE].

ORPHEUS (*aside*). With fear and shame my cheeks are scarlet.
I've praised my wife before my harlot.

RECIT[ATIVE].

RHODOPE. Go, fetch your wife, thou simple man.
What, keep us both? Is that your plan?
And darest thou, Orpheus, think of two,
When one's too much by one for you?

RECIT[ATIVE].

ORPHEUS. My mind is fixed. In vain this strife.
To hell I go to fetch my wife.

(*Going*, Rhodope *holds him.*)

AIR.

RHODOPE (*in tears*). Is this your affection,
Your vows and protection,
To bring back your wife to your house?
When she knows what I am,
As a wolf the poor lamb,
As a cat she will mumble the mouse.

AIR AND RECIT[ATIVE].

ORPHEUS. Pray cease your pathetic,
And I'll be prophetic,
Two ladies at once in my house;
Two cats they will be,
And mumble poor me.
The poor married man is the mouse.

RECIT[ATIVE].

RHODOPE. Yet hear me, Orpheus, can you be
So vulgar as to part with me
And fetch your wife? Am I forsaken?
O give me back what you have taken!
In vain I rave, my fate deplore,
A ruined maid is maid no more.
Your love alone is reparation.
Give me but *that*, and *this* for reputation. (*Snaps her fingers.*)

100. reparation] *O1*, *O2*, *O3*, *D1*, *D2*, *O5*; reputation *O4*.

AIR.

I.

When Orpheus you
Were kind and true,
Of joy I had my fill.
Now Orpheus roves
And faithless proves.
Alas, the bitter pill!

II.

As from the bogs
The wounded frogs
Called out, I call to thee.
O naughty boy,
To you 'tis joy.
Alas, 'tis death to me.

RECIT[ATIVE].

ORPHEUS. In vain are all your sobs and sighs,
In vain the rhet'ric of your eyes.
To wind and rain my heart is rock.
The more you cry, the more I'm block.

RECIT[ATIVE].

RHODOPE. Since my best weapon, crying, fails,
I'll try my tongue and then my nails.

AIR.

Mount if you will and reach the sky,
Quick as lightning would I fly,
And there would give you battle.
Like the thunder I would rattle.
Seek if you will the shades below,
Thither, thither will I go,
Your faithless heart appall!
My rage no bounds shall know.
Revenge my bosom stings,
And jealousy has wings
To rise above 'em all.

Orpheus snatches up the lyre.

RECIT[ATIVE].

ORPHEUS. This is my weapon. Don't advance!
I'll make you sleep or make you dance.

115. rhet'ric] *O1*, *O2*, *O3*, *D2*, *O5*; rhet'rick *D1*, *O4*.

AIR.

One med'cine cures the gout,
Another cures a cold.
This can drive your passions out,
Nay, even cure a scold.
Have you gout or vapours,
I in sleep
Your senses steep
Or make your legs cut capers.

DUETTO (*accompanied with the lyre*).

RHODOPE. I cannot have my swing.
ORPHEUS. Ting, ting, ting.
RHODOPE. My tongue has lost its twang,
ORPHEUS. Tang, tang, tang.
RHODOPE. My eyes begin to twinkle,
ORPHEUS. Tinkle, tinkle, tinkle.
RHODOPE. My hands dingle dangle,
ORPHEUS. Tangle, tangle, tangle.
RHODOPE. My spirits sink,
ORPHEUS. Tink, tink, tink.
RHODOPE. Alas, my tongue,
ORPHEUS. Ting, tang, tong.
RHODOPE. Now 'tis all o'er.
I can no more
But-go-to-sleep—and—sno-o-re. (*Sinks by degrees upon a couch and falls asleep.*)

RECIT[ATIVE].

ORPHEUS. 'Tis done, I'm free.
And now for thee,
Eurydice!
Behold what's seldom seen in life,
I leave my mistress for my wife.

Who's there? (*Calls a servant, who peeps in.*)
Come in. Nay, never peep.
The danger's o'er—she's fast asleep.
Do not too soon her fury rouse.
I go to hell to fetch my spouse.

AIR (*repeated*).

Though she scolded all day, and all night did the same,
Though she was too rampant and I was too tame;

152. Ting] *O1*, *O2*, *O3*, *D1*, *D2*, *O5*; Tang *O4*.

Though shriller her notes than the ear-piercing fife,
I must and I will go to hell for my wife.

(*Exit singing.*)

Scene changes to a mountainous country, with cows, sheep, goats, etc.

After a short Symphony,
Enter Orpheus, *playing upon his lyre.*

AIR.

Thou dear companion of my life,
My friend, my mistress and my wife,
Much dearer than all three;
Should they be faithless and deceive me,
Thy Grand Specific can relieve me.
All med'cines are in thee,
Thou veritable *Beaume de Vie*!

RECIT[ATIVE].

Now wake my lyre to sprightlier strains,
Inspire with joy both beasts and swains.
Give us no soporific potion,
But notes shall set the fields in motion.

AIR.

Breathe no ditty,
Soft and pretty,
Charming female tongues to sleep.
Goats shall flaunt it,
Cows *courante* it,
Shepherds frisk it with their sheep!

Enter Old Shepherd *with others.*

RECIT[ATIVE].

[OLD SHEPHERD]. Stop, stop your noise, you fiddling fool.
We want not here a dancing school.

RECIT[ATIVE].

ORPHEUS. Shepherd, be cool, forbear this vap'ring,
Or this (*his lyre.*) shall set you all a-cap'ring.

185. *courante*] O1, O2, O3, D2, O5; currant D1, O4.

RECIT[ATIVE].

[OLD SHEPHERD.] Touch it again and I shall straight
Beat time with this (*his crook.*) upon your pate.

RECIT[ATIVE].

ORPHEUS. I dare you all, your threats, your blows,
Come one and all we now are foes.

RECIT[ATIVE].

OLD SHEPHERD. Zounds! what's the matter with my toes? (*Begins to dance.*)

AIR.

From top to toe,
Above, below,
The tingling runs about me.
I feel it here,
I feel it there,
Within me and without me.

AIR.

ORPHEUS.
From top to toe,
Above, below,
The charm shall run about you.
Now tingle here,
Now tingle there,
Within you and without you.

AIR.

OLD SHEPHERD.
O cut those strings,
Those tickling things
Of that same cursed scraper.

Chorus of Shepherds.

We're dancing too,
And we like you
Can only cut a caper.

AIR.

ORPHEUS.
They cut the strings,
Those foolish things,
They cannot hurt the scraper!
They're dancing too,
And they like you
Can only cut a caper.

Chorus of Shepherds.

We're dancing too,
And we like you
Can only cut a caper.

AIR.

OLD SHEPHERD.
As I'm alive,
I'm sixty-five,
And that's no age for dancing.
I'm past the game,
O fie, for shame.
Old men should not be prancing.
O cut the strings,
Those tickling things
Of that same cursed scraper.

Chorus of Shepherds.

We're dancing too,
And we like you,
Can only cut a caper.

AIR.

ORPHEUS.
They cut the strings,
Those foolish things,
They cannot hurt the scraper.
They're dancing too,
And they like you
Can only cut a caper.

CHORUS.
We're dancing too,
And we like you
Can only cut a caper.

Orpheus *leads out the shepherds in a grand chorus of singing and dancing, and the beasts following them.*

GLIB. Here's a scene, Lady Fuz. If this won't do, what the devil will? (*Dancing.*) tal, lal, lal, lal. (*To the orchestra.*) Thank you, gentlemen, admirably well done indeed. I'll kiss you all round over as much punch as the double bass will hold.

Enter Patent.

There, Mr. Manager, is an end of an act. Every beast upon his hind legs! I did intend that houses and trees (according to the old story) should have joined in the dance, but it would have crowded the stage too much.

PATENT. Full enough as it is, Mr. Glib.

LADY FUZ (*without*). Let me come! Let me come, I say!

GLIB. D'ye hear, d'ye hear? Her Ladyship's in raptures I find. I knew I should touch her.

Enter Lady Fuz.

LADY FUZ. These are fine doings, fine doings, Mr. Glib.

GLIB. And a fine effect they will have, my Lady, particularly the dancing off of the beasts.

LADY FUZ. Yes, yes, they have danced off, but they shall dance back again. Take my word for it. (*Walks about.*)

GLIB. My dear Lady, and so they shall. Don't be uneasy. They shall dance back again directly. Here, Prompter. I intended to have the scene over again. I could see it forever.

LADY FUZ. Was this your plot, Mr. Glib? Or your contrivance, Mr. Manager?

PATENT. Madam!

GLIB. No, upon my soul, 'tis all my own contrivance, not a thought stole from Ancients or Modern, all my own plot.

LADY FUZ. Call my servants. I'll have a post-chaise directly. I see your guilt by your vain endeavors to hide it. This is the most bare-faced impudence!

GLIB. Impudence? May I die if I know an indecent expression in the whole piece.

PATENT. Your passion, Madam, runs away with you. I don't understand you.

LADY FUZ. No, Sir, 'tis one of your stage-players has run away with my daughter. And I'll be revenged on you all. I'll shut up your house.

PATENT. This must be inquired into.

(*Exit* Patent.)

GLIB. What, did Miss Fuz run away without seeing *Orpheus*?

LADY FUZ. Don't say a word more, thou blockhead.

GLIB. I am dumb, but no blockhead.

Enter Sir Toby *in confusion.*

SIR TOBY. What is all this? What is it all about?

LADY FUZ. Why, it is all your fault, Sir Toby. Had not you been asleep, she could never have been stolen from your side.

SIR TOBY. How do you know she is stolen? Inquire first, my Lady, and be in a passion afterwards.

LADY FUZ. I know she's gone. I saw her with a young fellow. He was upon his knees, swearing by the moon. Let us have a post-chaise, Sir Toby, directly and follow 'em.

SIR TOBY. Let us dine first, my dear, and I'll go wherever you please.

LADY FUZ. Dine? Dine! Did you ever hear the like? You have no more feeling, Sir Toby, than your periwig. I shall go distracted. The greatest curse of a poor woman is to have a flighty daughter and a sleepy husband.

(*Exit* Lady Fuz.)

SIR TOBY. And the greatest curse of a poor man, to have everybody flighty in his family but himself.

(*Exit.*)

Enter Patent.

PATENT. 'Tis true, Mr. Glib. The young lady is gone off, but with nobody that belongs to us. 'Tis a dreadful affair.

GLIB. So it is, faith, to spoil my rehearsal. I think it was very ungenteel of her to choose this morning for her pranks. Though she might make free with her father and mother, she should have more manners than to treat me so. I'll tell her as much when I see her. The second act shall be ready for you next week. I depend upon you for a prologue. Your genius –

PATENT. You are too polite, Mr. Glib. Have you an epilogue?

GLIB. I have a kind of address here, by the way of epilogue, to the Town. I suppose it to be spoken by myself as the author. Who have you can represent me? No easy task, let me tell you. He must be a little smart, *dégagé*, and not want assurance.

PATENT. Smart, *dégagé*, and not want assurance. King is the very man.

GLIB. Thank you, thank you, dear Mr. Patent. The very man! is he in the house? I would read it to him.

PATENT. O no! Since the audience received him in Linco, he is practicing music whenever he is not wanted here.

GLIB. I have heard as much, and that he continually sets his family's teeth on edge with scraping upon the fiddle. Conceit, conceit, Mr. Patent, is the ruin of 'em all. I could wish when he speaks this address that he would be more easy in his carriage, and not have that damned jerk in his bow that he generally treats us with.

PATENT. I'll hint as much to him.

GLIB. This is my conception of the matter. Bow your body gently. Turn your head semicircularly on one side and the other. And smiling thus agreeably begin:

All fable is figure. I your bard will maintain it,
And lest you don't know it, 'tis fit I explain it.
The lyre of our Orpheus means your approbation,
Which frees the poor poet from care and vexation.

324. figure] O1, O2, O3, D1, D2, O5; fiction O4.

Should want make his mistress too keen to dispute,
Your smiles fill his pockets, and madam is mute.
Should his wife, that's himself, for they two are but one,
Be in hell, that's in debt and the money all gone.
Your favor brings comfort, at once cures the evil,
For 'scaping Bum Bailiffs is 'scaping the devil.
Nay, Cerberus Critics their fury will drop,
For such barking monsters your smiles are a sop.
But how to explain what you most will require,
That cows, sheep, and calves should dance after the lyre,
Without your kind favor, how scanty each meal.
But with it comes dancing Beef, Mutton, and Veal.
For sing it, or say it, this truth we all see,
Your applause will be ever the true *Beaume de Vie*.

The End.

The Jubilee
1769

SONGS, CHORUSSES, &c.

WHICH ARE INTRODUCED IN THE

NEW ENTERTAINMENT

OF THE

J U B I L E E.

AT THE

THEATRE ROYAL.

IN

DRURY-LANE.

LONDON:
PRINTED FOR T. BECKET, AND P. A. DE HONDT,
IN THE STRAND.
MDCCLXIX.
[PRICE SIX-PENCE.]

Facsimile title page of the First Edition.
Folger Shakespeare Library.

Prologue

From London, your Honors, to Stratford I'm come.
I'm a waiter, your Honors,—you know bustling Tom,
Who, proud of your orders and bowing before ye,
Till supper is ready will tell ye a story. —
Twixt Hounslow and Colbrooke—two houses of fame,
Well known on that road—the two Magpies by name.
The one of long standing, the other a new one
That boasts he's the old one, and this he's the true one.
Tho' we the old Magpie, as well as the younger,
May puff that our liquors are clearer and stronger,
Of puffing and bragging you make but a jest,
You taste of us both and will stick to the best.
A race we have had for your pastime and laughter —
Young Mag started first, with old Mag hopping after.
'Tis said the old house hath possess'd a receipt
To make a choice mixture of sour, strong and sweet —
A Jubilee Punch—which, right skilfully made,
Insur'd the old Magpie a good running trade.
But think you we mean to monopolize?—No, no!
We're like Brother Ashley—*pro publico bono*!
Each Magpie, your Honors, will peck at his brother,
And their nature's we've always to crib from each other.
Young landlords and old ones are taught by their calling
To laugh at engrossing and practice forestalling.
Our landlords are game cocks—and fair play but grant 'em,
I'll warrant you pastime from each little bantam.
To return to the Punch—I hope from my soul
That now the old Magpie may sell you a bowl.
We've all sorts and sizes—a quick trade to drive.
We've one shilling, two shillings—three shillings—five!

From this town of Stratford you'll have each ingredient,
Besides a kind welcome from Your Obedient.
I'll now squeeze my fruit, put the sugar and rum in,
And be back in a moment–(*bell rings*). I'm coming, Sir, coming!

Exit running.

Dramatis Personae

Prologue	Mr. *King*.

The PAGEANT, *as it was intended for Stratford-upon-Avon.*

Ralph	Mr. *King*.
Irishman	Mr. *Moody*.
Ballad Singer	Mr. *Vernon*.
Ostler	Mr. *Parsons*.
Country Girls	Mrs. *Baddeley*.
	Miss *Radley*.
Margery Jervis	Mrs. *Love*.
Female Ballad Singer	Mr. *Dibdin*.

Other parts by: *Ackman*, *Hurst*, *Waldron*, *Castle*, *Wheeler*, *W. Palmer*, *Wright*, *Keen*, *Hartry*, *Messink*, *Clough*, *Booth*, *J. Burton*, *Mas. Cape*, *Mrs. Bradshaw*, *Mrs. Lowe*.

Vocal parts by: *Vernon*, *Dibdin*, *Bannister*, *Champnes*, *Fawcett*, *Kear*, etc., *Miss Radley* and *Mrs. Baddeley*.

The dances by: *Dagueville*, *Mrs. King*, *Sga. Vidini*, *Miss Rogers*, etc.

Characters in the Pageant:

Benedict	Mr. *Garrick*.
Beatrice	Miss *Pope*.
Touchstone	Mr. *King*.
Richard III	Mr. *Holland*.
Romeo	Mr. *Brereton*.
Hamlet	Mr. *Cautherly*.
Falstaff	Mr. *Love*.

Lear	Mr. *Reddish.*
Antony	Mr. *Aikin.*
Portia	Mrs. *W. Barry.*
Apollo	Mr. *Vernon.*
Tragic Muse	Mrs. *Barry.*
Comic Muse	Mrs. *Abington.*

Also: *Hurst, Wheeler, Castle, Waldron, Wright, Keen, Clough, Hartry, Messink, Booth, J. Burton, Master Cape, Mrs. Bradshaw, Mrs. Love.*

Dancing and singing. New dresses, scenes.

Music by Dibdin.

The Jubilee

SCENE [I], [FIRST PART] *An old woman's house.*
An old woman asleep in a wicker chair, a bottle by her.

SECOND OLD WOMAN (*without*). Goody Benson! Goody Benson! What, an't you up, woman? 'Tis near five o'clock.

FIRST OLD WOMAN (*waking*). Bless me! Who's there? I'm frightened out of my wits. Who calls?

SECOND OLD WOMAN. 'Tis I, 'tis I, neighbor, Margery Jarvis. Let me speak with you.

FIRST OLD WOMAN. Ay, ay, and thank you too, Margery. (*Puts the bottle under the chair and goes to the door.*)

Enter Second Old Woman.

SECOND OLD WOMAN. What, are you up, Dame?

FIRST OLD WOMAN. Up, Woman? Why I hanno' been abed, not I, nor canno' rest since this racket begun. I durst not lay me down, but was taking a little nap in my chair when you knocked at the door. I verily think, neighbor, this Jubillo will be death o' me.

SECOND OLD WOMAN. I canno' rest neither, not I. I wish 'twas all over and these Londoners were well out of town. One is not safe in one's bed. I canno' guess what they'd be at.

FIRST OLD WOMAN. I darn't trust 'em neither. I have not pulled off my clothes this week, but doze, doze in my chair. I wish they have not more in their yeads than we are aware of.

SECOND OLD WOMAN. Our Ralph swears there's mischief in hond. And the poor soul has ne'er been his own mon since the Jubillo was talked of. He verily believes that the Pope is at bottom on't all.

RALPH (*peeps in*). Introth, and so I do, Neighbor.

BOTH OLD WOMEN. Mercy on us! Who's there?

Enter Ralph.

SECOND OLD WOMAN. Why would you startle us so, Ralph, in these frightful times? I'm glad you are come though. You are up, I see, as well as us.

RALPH. Is this a time to lie abed, when the town may be flown away with, for aught we know? I should not like to wake and find myself a hundred miles off. And so I don't sleep at all, nor will I, till the devil has done his worst.

FIRST OLD WOMAN. Prithee, don't talk so, Ralph. You set my back a aching and I tremble every joint of me.

RALPH. And not without reason, Neighbor. I'll be hanged up alive (and may be, for aught I know), but there is some plot afoot with this Jubillo.

BOTH OLD WOMEN. Bless us!

RALPH. Why, there are a hundred tailors in town. And all from London. 'Tis certainly a plot of the Jews and Papishes.

FIRST OLD WOMAN. Terrible indeed!

RALPH. Why Dame, the tailors and barbers alone would breed a famine. Then they have brought cannon guns down with them, and a mortal deal of gunpowder. What's gunpowder for? To blow us all up in a fillip. Another Powder Plot, Heav'n preserve us! Little Dolly Dobson will take her Bible oath that she saw fifty devils at work in Farmer Thornton's barn and cowhouse. She has been partly out of her mind ever since.

SECOND OLD WOMAN. They are at the same work in the College here. Such a cargo of all sorts of conjuration!

RALPH. O yes, they keep all their hobgoblins there. And if they're let loose about the town, not all our parson's preaching will drive them out again.

FIRST OLD WOMAN. Prithee, Ralph, does know why they build such a large, great round house in the Meadow for?

RALPH. Why to drive all us poor folks in, to be sure, like cattle into a pound. Then lock us in, while they may be firing the town and running away with and ravish—ay, that's what they will—ravish man, woman and child! How can one sleep with such thoughts in one's head?

SECOND OLD WOMAN. Ravishing, O law! And yet were there no mischief afoot, there's a power of money to be got. I might have let my little room for a good sum. And I would. But "Auld you," said I, "gold may be bought too dear." And yet I'de have ventured for t'other guinea.

RALPH. More shame for you. Do you think they would make such a

56–57. ravish man, woman and child!] "ravishing our Wives & Children," crossed out.

rout about our Shakespur the poet, if they had not other things in their pates? I knew something was abrewing when they would not let his image alone in the church, but had the show people paint it in such fine colors to look like a Popish saint. Ay, ay! That was the beginning of it all.

FIRST OLD WOMAN. Have you seen, Ralph, the mon that is the ring leader of the Jubillo, who is to fly about the town by conjuration?

SECOND OLD WOMAN. Ay, the mon that came from London, the Steward, as they call 'en. Have you seen he, Ralph?

RALPH. Yes, I ha' seen him. Not much to be seen, though, I did not care to come too near him. He's not so big as I, but a great deal plumper. He's auld enough to be wiser, too. But he knows what he's about, I warrant 'en. He has brought the pipers and, 'Ecod, he'll make us pay for 'em. Let him alone for that. He's a long yead of his own. (*Cannon fires without.*)

ALL (*starting and trembling*). Lud have mercy upon us! (*Cannon fires again.*)

RALPH. Now they are at it. (*Cannon fires again.*) We shall all be blown up. Lud have mercy upon us! (*Cannon fires again.*) I'll go and take a peep at a distance and bring you word if I see any mischief. (*Cannon fires again.*)

FIRST OLD WOMAN. Ralph, don't leave us alone. We'll take a peep too.

SECOND OLD WOMAN. Have they begun ravishing, Ralph?

RALPH. O Lud have mercy upon us! Nay, nay, don't you be frightened. What the devil should you be frightened for? (*Cannon fires again.*) O Lud! have mercy upon us!

Exit trembling and much frightened.

SCENE II, *The street, with a postchaise on one side.*
Enter musicians and singers in dominoes to give a serenade, ladies looking out at a window.

AIR.

Let beauty with the sun arise,
To Shakespeare tribute pay,
With heavenly smiles and sparkling eyes
Give grace and lustre to the day.

2.

Each smile she gives protects his name:
What face shall dare to frown?
Not envy's self can blast the fame,
Which beauty deigns to crown.

IRISHMAN (*peeping out of the chaise window*). What a plague do you mean there below, with your noise, and your music, and your colored surplusses, disturbing gentlemen in their beds before they are got to sleep?

MUSICIAN. Oh, Sir, this is part of the Jubilee, Sir.

IRISHMAN. Yes, and I dare say you think it very entertaining. I could not get to the Jubilee 'till twelve o'clock last night, and I walked about the streets for two hours to get a bed and a bit of supper. But the devil a toothful of neither one nor t'other could I get, and so I was forced to take lodgings in the first floor of this postchaise at a half crown a head. And here they have crammed a bedfellow with me into the bargain. Not being able to lie down upright in my bed, I could not get a wink of sleep 'till you were pleased to wake me with your damned scraping and caterwauling. I never had such a night in all my days. And is this what you call a Jubilee? It's truly worthwhile to travel from Dublin to be sure of such a recreation. But what is your Jubilee, Honey? 'Tis full time to know.

MUSICIAN. If your honor pleases to come out, I'll sing you a song about the Jubilee.

IRISHMAN. With all my heart, fait, for I am ready drest though I'm in bed you see. And if you'll do me the honor to open my chamber door, you'll greatly oblige me. (*Musician opens the door and he comes out.*) Mr. Musicioner, I'm your humble servant. But stay, let me shut the chamber door upon my bedfellow that he may not catch cold. Upon my conscience I was forced to make a nightcap of my wig, that the hair may keep me warm. And now, pray inform me, what is this same Jubilee that I am come so far to see and know nothing of the matter.

MUSICIAN.
This is, Sir, a Jubilee
Crowded without company.
Riot without jollity,
That's a Jubilee.

26–27. I'll sing you . . . Jubilee] "we'll give you an Account—what a Jubilee is," crossed out.

32. the chamber door] "my chamber door." "My" crossed out.

37. Song, "This is, Sir, a Jubilee" substituted for Musician's speech in manuscript ("imitating Foote"): "I'll tell you, Sir; a Jubilee is to invite the people of England to go a hundred miles post without horses—to a Borough without Representatives—govern'd by a Mayor and Aldermen who are no Magistrates. There, in a Crowd without Company, you'll find Music without Melody, Odes without Poetry, Dinners without Victuals, and Lodgings without beds." Garrick's note opposite this speech reads: "This is what Foote said of Ye Jubilee in his Devil upon Two Sticks."

Thus 'tis night and day, Sir,
I hope that you will stay, Sir,
To see our Jubilee.

2.

On the road such crosses, Sir,
Cursing jolts and tossing, Sir,
Posting without horses, Sir,
Thus 'tis *etc.*

3.

Odes, Sir, without poetry
Music without melody
Singing without harmony.
Thus 'tis *etc.*

4.

Holes to thrust your head in, Sir,
Lodgings without bedding, Sir,
Beds as if they'd lead in, Sir
Thus 'tis *etc.*

5.

Blankets without sheeting, Sir,
Dinners without eating, Sir,
Not without much cheating, Sir,
Thus 'tis *etc.*

IRISHMAN. 'Tis a comical kind of a song to be sure, and you did not stale it from what they say of little Kilkenny. There we have –

Fire without smoke
Wit without joke
Air without fog
Land without bog
Men without heads
Lodging without beds.

O no! that's your Jubilee Rig, *Ecce signum* (*pointing to the post-chaise.*) We have

Water without mud,
Beds without bug,
Pudding without eggs
Rabbits without legs.

---

60. 'Tis a comical kind of a song] substituted for "He was a Comical Devil that told you that—To be sure he did not Stale [steal, crossed out] from what they say, etc."

MUSICIAN. Rabbits without legs?

IRISHMAN. Yes, rabbits without legs—welsh ones. Besides, rabbits' fore-legs are two of 'em wings, Honey. Then I was upon you now. But what are we to have next? For I went to the great big Inn, where all the plays are writ upon the doors, and so I thought to see a play and popped my head into *Much Ado About Nothing*. And there was nothing at all but the Steward with his mulberry box upon his breast, speaking his fine Ode to music.

TWO BALLAD SINGERS (*behind*). This is entitled and called "O Rare Warwickshire!"

MUSICIAN. O Sir, here's something will rouse you if you are not awake. Here they come!

Enter Ballad Singers, *etc.*

MAN BALLAD SINGER (*Vernon*). Ye Warwickshire lads and ye lasses.
See what at our Jubilee passes,
Come revel away, rejoice and be glad,
For the lad of all lads was a Warwickshire lad,
Warwickshire lad,
All be glad!
For the lad of all lads was a Warwickshire lad.

WOMAN (*Dibdin*). Be proud of the charms of your country,
Where nature has lavished her bounty,
Where much she has giv'n, and some to be spared,
For the Bard of all bards was a Warwickshire bard,
Warwickshire bard,
Never paired
For the Bard of all bards was a Warwickshire bard.

MAN. Old Ben, Thomas Otway, John Dryden,
And half a score more, we take pride in,
Of famous Will Congreve we boast too the skill,
But the Will of all Wills was a Warwickshire Will;
Warwickshire Will,
Matchless still!
For the Will of all Wills was a Warwickshire Will.

WOMAN. As ven'son is very inviting,
To steal it our bard took delight in,
To make his friends merry he never was lag,
And the wag of all wags was a Warwickshire wag,
Warwickshire wag,
Ever brag,
For the wag of all wags was a Warwickshire wag.

[MAN.] There never was seen such a creature,
Of all she was worth he robbed nature;

He took all her smiles, and he took all her grief,
And the thief of all thieves was a Warwickshire thief,
Warwickshire thief
He's the chief,
For the thief of all thieves was a Warwickshire thief.
He took *etc.*

Exeunt singing.

IRISHMAN. The devil burn me, but I believe you are all Tieves.
Jubilee thief,
'Tis my belief,
The thief of all thieves is a Jubilee thief.

Exit singing.

SCENE III, *The White Lion Inn Yard.*

A crowd of people, some with portmanteaux, etc., going across the stage. (Bar bell rings.)

SERVANT (*at a window*). Here, waiter. Why don't you bring the hot rolls to the Julius Caesar?

FIRST WAITER. Coming, sir. Hot rolls to the Julius Caesar. (*Bar bell rings.*)

Enter three ladies.

What do you want, Ladies?

FIRST LADY (*whispers to the Waiter*). Pray is Captain Patrick O'Shoulder here?

WAITER. He is, Ladies. Here, Will, show these ladies into Harry the Eighth. (*Bar bell rings.*)

Exeunt Ladies.

FRIBBLE (*at a window*). Waiter! Will ye or will ye not bring the refreshment I ordered an hour ago?

FIRST WAITER. Coming, Sir. Coming, Sir.

FRIBBLE. You're always acoming and never stir a step. The Lady and I are almost perished. Waiter, let me have half a dozen more jellies.

Exit.

FIRST WAITER. I shall, Sir. Do, Tom, carry half a dozen jellies to that fribbling gentleman and the tall lady in *Love's Labor Lost.* (*Bar bell rings.*)

Enter Gentleman *in slippers.*

FIRST GENTLEMAN. Ostler! Bootcatcher! Where are those fellows? I can get nobody near me. Damn the Jubilee, I can neither eat or drink or sleep here, nor get my boots to go somewhere else. Why, Bootcatcher, you, Sirrah! Where are my boots?

Enter Bootcatcher.

[BOOTCATCHER.] I wish I could tell you, sir. But you mun do as the rest on 'em. The boots are all thrown together in a heap yonder, and first come, first sarv'd.

FIRST GENTLEMAN. Zounds! Mine's a new pair, made a purpose for the Jubilee and never worn before. I would not lose them for all the Jubilees and Shakespears –

Runs off.

BOOTCATCHER. You need not run so fast, Measter, for all the new boots ha' been gone this half hour. (*Bar bell rings.*)

Exit Bootcatcher.

Enter Second Gentleman.

SECOND GENTLEMAN. I shall be too late for the pageant. Where's my breakfast, Waiter?

Enter Second Waiter *with breakfast.*

SECOND WAITER. Here, Sir.

SECOND GENTLEMAN. Bring it this way then.

Exit Second Gentleman.

Enter Third Gentleman, *meeting the breakfast.*

THIRD GENTLEMAN. This is my breakfast. Where are you carrying it?

SECOND WAITER. To the other gentleman.

THIRD GENTLEMAN. One is as good as another. There's for you (*gives him money*). He's a book customer. Ready money is always served first.

Exit with breakfast.
(*Bar bell rings.*)

SECOND WAITER (*crying*). Coming up, Sir.

Exit.

Enter Fourth and Fifth Gentlemen *running with some ribs of beef.*

FOURTH AND FIFTH GENTLEMEN. I have got something at last. Come along, this is better than starving.

Exeunt with the beef.

Enter Fat Cook *running after him* [*them*].

[COOK.] Here you with the three ribs of beef! Don't touch 'em! They are for my Lord's servants, and they must be served first. See, see, hunger has no manners. They are at it already. What shall I do? Here, Boy! Roger!

Enter Roger.

[ROGER.] What mun ye ha, measter. Look I'm ready to do anything for you, so I am.

COOK. Hold your tongue then.

ROGER. I'll do anything for you, measter. Indeed I will.

COOK. Hold your tongue then, you dog, and hear what I have to say. (*Strikes him.*) Run to the butcher's as fast as you can. Bid him send me all he has, fat and lean, fresh or not fresh. And bid him kill away, or I must run away.

Exeunt Cook *and* Boy *severally.*
(*Bar bell rings.*)

IRISHMAN. Faith and troth, I never complain of want of sleep whilst I am drinking. But to have no sleep and no drink is a little too much upon the Jubilee rig.

WAITER (*at the window*). Here, where are you all, John, Tom, Harry?

IRISHMAN. Hollo! Fait, here is a fine hurry and boddering and confusion. There's no pleasure at all like a Jubilee. The delight is to be wanting everything and get nothing, to see everybody busy and not know what they're about.

WAITER (*at the window*). John, Tom, Harry!

IRISHMAN. Hey dey, what's the matter now?

Enter Waiter.

WAITER. Where's my master? Call him, John. There's the devil to do. The gentlemen and ladies are quarrelling again in the *Catherine and Petruchio*.

Exit Waiter.

FIRST GENTLEMAN. O, let 'em alone. They know what they are about. It is some of the married gentry from the playhouse. It is family business and must be settled by themselves. The only way to make peace is to let them fight it out.

Enter Fellow *with a box of wooden ware, etc.*

[FELLOW.] Toothpick cases, needle cases, punch ladles, tobacco stoppers, inkstands, nutmeg graters, and all sorts of boxes made out of the famous Mulberry Tree.

FIRST GENTLEMAN. Here you, Mulberry Tree. Let me have some of the true dandy to carry back to my wife and relations in Ireland. (*Looks at the ware.*)

Enter Second Man *with ware.*

[SECOND MAN.] Don't buy of that fellow, your honor, he never had an inch of the Mulberry Tree in his life. His goods are made out of old chairs and stools and colored to cheat gentlefolks with. It was I, your honor, bought all the true Mulberry Tree. Here's my affidavit of it.

FIRST MAN. Yes, you villain, but you sold it all two years ago, and you have purchased since more mulberry trees than would serve to hang your whole generation upon. He has got a little money, your honor, and so nobody must turn a penny or cheat gentlefolks but himself. I wonder you an't ashamed, Robin. Do, your honor, take this punch ladle.

IRISHMAN. I'll tell you what, you mulberry scoundrels you. If you don't clear the yard of yourselves this minute and let me see you out of my sight, you thieves of the world, my oak plant shall be about your trinkets and make the mulberry juice run down your rogue-pates. Get away, you spalpeens you. (*Beats 'em off.*)

[*Exit.*]

Re-enter Irishman *immediately.*

A parcel of rascals want to impose upon a gentleman that has travelled in all the foreign parts both at home and abroad. They may talk as they will of their mulberry bushes, but commend me to a bit of old shellalee.

Enter a Man *beating a drum, and* Another *leading a large bird with a crowd following.*

[MAN.] The Notified Porcupine Man, and all sorts of outlandish birds and other strange beasts to be seen without loss of time on the great Meadow near the Ampi-Theatre at so small a price as one shilling apiece. Alive, alive, alive, ho!

Exit, beating the drum etc.

IRISHMAN. This foolish fellow won't make his fortune at the Jubilee. To ax a Tirteen to see strange animals in a house, when one may see 'em for nothing going along the streets, alive, alive, ho!

93.1. a large bird] "a Maucow etc.," crossed out.
95. strange beasts] "animals," crossed out.

Enter Trumpeter *blowing the trumpet, and* Mr. *and* Mrs. Samson *and a crowd of people. They give away bills, etc.*

TRUMPETER. Ladies and Gentlemen. The famous Samson is just going to begin, just going to mount four horses at once with his feet upon two saddles. Also the most wonderful surprising feats of horsemanship by the most *notorious* Mrs. Sampson.

Exeunt blowing the trumpet.

IRISHMAN. I warrant her she rides astride, Honey, with a pommel, as they do in Ireland. This is a new way of riding upon one's feet—Though fait and trot, many a good gentleman rides upon his feet from Ireland, and Scotland too.

Enter Waiter.

Harkee, young fellow, here's tree tirteens for you. Let me have a bowl of hot punch and a little something to ate in any snug little corner, and here's another tirteen for yourself.

WAITER. Follow me, Sir, and I'll take care of you—I'll take care of you, upon my honor, Sir.

Exit.

IRISHMAN. Upon my soul, there is nothing to be done at the Jubilee, nor nowhere else, fait, without a little bribery and corruption. Upon my conscience I am very cold with going to bed in a postchaise, so I'll warm myself with a little hot punch, and steal a nap for nothing into the bargain, to refresh me for their pageant and fringes and the rest of their Jubilee.

Exit Irishman.

Enter Bannister *and* Vernon *and a number of men, boys, etc.,* Mr. Vernon *with the Mulberry Cup in his hand and fuddled.*

VERNON. Hollo, boys! Don't let us selfishly and niggardly confine our joys to ourselves, but let every Jubilee soul partake of our mirth and our liquor, at least kiss the cup and be happy.

BANNISTER. With all my heart, my boy. We have fuddled ourselves in the house, and now we'll sober ourselves in the open air. Let us take t'other taste of the dear mulberry juice.

I

BANNISTER SINGS. Behold this fair goblet, 'twas carved from the tree
Which, O my sweet Shakespear, was planted by thee.
As a relic I kiss it and bow at the shrine,
What comes from thy hand must be ever divine!

All shall yield to the Mulberry Tree,
Bend to thee,
Blest Mulberry,
Matchless was he
Who planted thee,
And thou like him immortal be!

VERNON. The fame of the patron gives fame to the tree,
From him and his merits this takes its degree.
Let Phoebus and Bacchus their glories resign,
Our tree shall surpass both the Laurel and Vine.
All shall yield to the Mulberry Tree, *etc.*

2

Ye trees of the forest, so rampant and high,
Who spread round their branches, whose heads sweep the sky,
Ye curious exotics, whom taste has brought here,
To root out the natives at prices so dear.
All shall yield to the Mulberry Tree, *etc.*

3

The oak is held royal, is Britain's great boast
Preserved once our king and will always our coast,
But of fir we make ships, we have thousands that fight;
But where is there one like our Shakespeare can write.
All shall yield to the Mulberry Tree, *etc.*

4

Let Venus delight in her gay myrtle bowers,
Pomona in fruit trees and Flora in flowers;
The Garden of Shakespeare all fancies will suit,
With the sweetest of flowers and fairest of fruit.
All shall yield to the Mulberry Tree, *etc.*

5

With learning and knowledge the well-lettered birch
Supplies Law and Physic and grace for the Church.
But Law and the Gospel in Shakespeare we find,
And he gives the best physic for body and mind.
All shall yield to the Mulberry Tree, *etc.*

---

136. Garrick's note opposite this line: "Sh[d] this Stanza be repeated twice? Better as Stanza 6."

6

The fame of the patron gives fame to the tree,
From him and his merits this takes its degree.
Let Phoebus and Bacchus their glories resign,
Our tree shall surpass both the Laurel and Vine.
All shall yield to the Mulberry Tree, *etc.*

7

KEAR. The genius of Shakespear outshines the bright day,
More rapture than wine to the heart can convey.
So the tree which he planted, by making his own,
Has Laurel, and Bays and the Vine all in one.
All shall yield to the Mulberry Tree, *etc.*

8

VERNON. Then each take a relic of this hallowed tree,
From folly and fashion a charm let it be.
Fill, fill to the planter, the Cup to the brim,
To honor your country do honor to him.
All shall yield to the Mulberry Tree,
Bend to thee,
Blest Mulberry,
Matchless was he
Who planted thee,
And thou like him immortal be!

Drums, fifes, and bells ring.

They all exit in a hurry, going to see the Pageant.

HERE FOLLOWS THE PAGEANT

With bells ringing, fifes playing, drums beating, and cannon firing.

Order of the Pageant in the Jubilee.

All enter from the top of the stage. They dance down the stage to music.

9 Men dancers with tambourines
3 Graces
9 Women Dancers–Muses

0.3. Order of the Pageant in the Jubilee.] Opposite this line is Garrick's note: "N.B. in the Procession Every Scene in y[e] different Plays represents some capital part of it in Action."

2 Men dressed in Old English, with mottos of the Theatre *upon rich standards with proper decorations.*
2 Fifes
and
2 Drums.

As You Like It

Shepherd with a banner
Touchstone
Audrey
Rosalind in boy's clothes with a crook
Orlando
Duke Senior, with a spear.
4 Foresters with spears, two and two.
Jaques with a spear, melancholy.

Tempest

Sailor with a banner
Ariel with a wand, raising a tempest.
A ship in distress sailing down the stage –
Prospero with a wand
Miranda
Caliban with a wooden bottle and
2 Sailors all drunk

Merchant of Venice

Lancelot with a banner –
2 Men with the caskets in a rick
Bassanio
Portia
Shylock with a knife, and bond and scales.

Much Ado [*About Nothing*] *etc*

Town Clerk with banner
Benedick and Beatrice in masquerade.

Two Gentlemen of Verona

Man with the banner
The Two Gentlemen of Verona
Launce with his dog Crab

Garrick Delivering His Ode on the Drury Lane Stage. Engraving by Lodge.
Harvard Theatre Collection

Twelfth Night

Clown, a banner
Sir Andrew Aguecheek } fuddled.
Sir Toby Belch }
Malvolio with a letter and
his stockings cross-gartered.

Midsummer Night's Dream

Bottom with ass's head and banner
16 Fairies with banners
Chariot drawn by Butterflies
King and Queen of the Fairies in the chariot.

Merry Wives of Windsor

Nym with a banner.
Justice Shallow }
Sir Hugh }
Host }
Dr. Caius }
Mrs. Quickly }
Rugby }
Slender
Bardolph with a cup.
Mrs. Ford }
Falstaff } on horseback
Mrs. Page }
Page with sword and shield
Pistol
Mouldy
Bullcalf
Wart
Feeble
Shadow
Venus and Cupid
The Comic Muse in a chariot drawn by 5 Satyrs
attended by 6 Loves with large antique masks.

36.1. Opposite *Midsummer Night's Dream* is Garrick's note: "Suppose Bottom & 2 of F^{s} asleep in ye Chariot—& K. of F. drops her eyes with ye Flower, turns out Bottom & takes his Place. Bottom & she awakes, etc."

50–52. Opposite the trio on horseback is Garrick's note: "What is ye Whim of having These particularly on Horseback? Cath^{e} & Petruchio, with ye same dismal Horse & all P's miserable Geer, as describ'd by Grumio w^{d} have had a fine Effect. I w^{d} introduce C & P in this Manner & four Fellows sh^{d} bring in Sr John in ye Buck Basket ye Wives on either Side covering him with foul Cloaths, & he endeavouring to get out."

All the Chorus (6 Boys and 20 Men dressed in a uniform like Arcadian Shepherds), two and two, singing.

Chorus for the Pageant, by Bickerstaff.

Hence, ye profane! And only they,
Our Pageant grace our pomp survey,
Whom love of sacred genius brings.
Let pride, let flattery decree
Honors to deck the memory
Of warriors, senators, and kings.
No less in glory and desert
The Poet here receives his part,
A tribute from the feeling heart.

3 Graces
Apollo with his lyre.
The statue of Shakespear supported by the Passions and surrounded by the Seven Muses with their trophies.
The kettle drum drawn in a car
6 Trumpets

King Richard Third

Old English Gentleman with a banner
6 Old English Soldiers with spears, two and two
King Richard with a ring
Tyrrell
Queen leading Prince Edward and the Duke of York.
Richmond with a truncheon.

Cymbeline

Old English Gentleman with a banner
Bellarious with a spear
Arviragus and Guyderius with spears leading Imogen
Posthumus, a sword and shield.

Hamlet

Gentleman with a banner
Ghost with a truncheon
Hamlet }
Queen } in the Closet Scene follows the Ghost in horror
Ophelia mad, with straw, *etc.*
2 Gravediggers, a pickax and spade.

---

63. All the Chorus] opposite is Garrick's note: "6 Boys—& 20 Men dress'd in a Uniform like Arcadian Shepherds."

Othello

Soldier, a banner
2 Senators.
Duke }
Brabantio in a nightgown }
Othello }
Desdemona }
Iago
Roderigo

Romeo and Juliet

A Gentleman with a banner.
Peter with a fan }
Nurse with a crutch stick }
Romeo }
Friar }
Juliet }
Apothecary

King Henry Fifth

Old English Gentleman with a banner
2 Old English Soldiers
2 Ditto
King Henry Fifth
Fluellen with a leek }
Pistol } Fluellan makes Pistol eat the leek.

King Lear

Old English Gentleman, a banner
Edgar in the mad dress with a staff
King Lear }
Kent } Thunder and Lightning
Cordelia }

King Henry Eighth

Old English Gentleman with a banner
2 Old English Gentlemen
2 Beef Eaters
Wolsey }
King Henry }
Bishop Cranmer }
Queen Catherine }
4 Beef Eaters

Macbeth

Gentleman with a banner
Macbeth }
Lady Macbeth }
Caldron drawn by 4 Demons, the caldron burning, Hecate and 3 Witches following the caldron.

Julius Caesar

A Roman Gentleman with a banner.
6 Romans with lictors.
Julius Caesar
Roman Gentleman with the Eagle.
Soothsayer.
6 Romans with trophies
Brutus }
Cassius }

Antony and Cleopatra

Soldier with a banner in a Persian dress
4 Persian Guards with spears
4 Blacks
2 Black Boys with fans of peacock feathers fanning
= Antony }
and }
Cleopatra }
2 Blacks with umbrellas
2 Black Boys to hold up Cleopatra's train
4 Eunuchs
Minerva
Demon of Revenge with a burning torch
The Tragic Muse drawn in a chariot by
6 Furies, and attended by
Fame
Grief
Pity
Despair
Madness
3 Furies following the chariot.
Mars
6 Soldiers with swords and shields
9 Soldiers with spears.

The bells ring 'em off and the scene changes to a street in Stratford

End of the first part.

SECOND PART

SCENE [I], *a street in Stratford.*
Enter Sukey *and* Nancy.

SUKEY. There was a sight for you! There was a Pagan! If I had not a Shakespur ribbon to pin upon my heart, I could not have shown my face. The dear creature is nearest my heart. I dote upon Shakespur.

NANCY. Law, Cousin Sue, how you talk to a body. I swear I know no more about the Jubillo and Shakespur, as you call him, that I do about the Pope of Rome.

SUKEY. Nancy, you have not been out of this poor hole of a town, or you would not have such low, vulgar fancies in your head. Had you lived at Birmingham or Coventry, or any other polite cities, as I have done, you would have known better than to talk so of Shakespur and the Jewbill.

NANCY. Why who is this Shakespur, that they make such a rout about 'en. He was not a lord?

SUKEY. Lord help you, Cousin. He is worth fifty lords. Why he could write. He could write finely your plays and your tragedies and make your heart leap or sink in your bosom as he pleased. 'Twas a wonder of a man! I'm sure I cried for a whole night together after hearing his Romy and July at Birmingham, by the London gentlemen and ladies player people. I never let Mr. Robin keep me company till I had been moved by that fine piece. Why he cuts Romeo into little stars as fine as fipence. O, the sweet Creature, the dear Willy Shakespur.

The pride of all nature was sweet Willy O,
The first of all swains,
He gladdened the plains,
None ever was like to the sweet Willy O.

2.

He sung it so rarely did sweet Willy O,
He melted each maid,
So skilful he played,
No shepherd e'er piped like the sweet Willy O.

3.

He would be a soldier, the sweet Willy O,
When armed in the field
With sword and with shield,
The laurel was worn by the sweet Willy O.

8. low vulgar fancies] "foolish," crossed out.

4.

He charmed 'em when living the sweet Willy O,
And when Willy died,
'Twas nature that sighed,
To part with her all in her sweet Willy O.

NANCY. I know nothing of what you talk about, not I. But I can't think all this crowding, trumpeting, drumming, eating, drinking, ringing, cannon firing, and all this mummery would be for a poor poet that lived I don't know how many hundred years ago. I canno' believe what you tell me.

All this for a poet—o no,
Who lived Lord knows how long ago.
How can you jeer one,
How can you fleer one,
A poet, a poet—o no,
'Tis not so,
Who lived Lord knows how long ago.

2.

It must be some great man,
A prince or a state-man,
It can't be a poet—o no.
Your poet is poor,
And nobody sure
Regards a poor poet, I trow.
The rich ones we prize,
Send 'em up to the skies,
But not a poor poet—o no,
Who lived Lord knows how long ago.

SUKEY. If you are so vulgar, Cousin Nancy, I vow you shan't go along with me to the Ample-Theatre. Don't you remember the verses Parson Shrimp wrote upon him?

If he saw ye he knew ye,
Would look through and through ye,
Through skin and your flesh and your clothes,
Had you vanity, pride,
Fifty follies beside,
He would see 'em as plain as your nose.

NANCY. Though sins I have none,
I am glad he is gone,
No maid would live near such a mon.

Duet by Sukey *and* Nancy.

Let us sing it and dance it,
Rejoice it and prance it,
That no man has now such an art.
What would come of us all,
Both the great ones and small,
Should he now live to peep in each heart.
Though sins I have none,
I am glad he is gone,
No maid could live near such a mon.

Exeunt singing and dancing.

[*Enter* Irishman.]

IRISHMAN (*drunk*). Hollo! You sweet Jubilee wenches, come here you dear craturs. Stand still and see who you are running away from, you little precious devils. Here's old Ireland for you, you dear craturs. I'll follow you, you dear little Jewels, I will.

Exit.

SCENE [II], *a Landship.*
Re-enter Irishman.

[IRISHMAN.] Where are you, you dear precious craturs. I'll find you out after your Pageant fringes are gone by.

Enter Roger *and crosses the stage.*

IRISHMAN. Here you boy with the strait colored head of hair.

BOY. What would you have, Master? Make haste for I'm in a wounded hurry.

IRISHMAN. When will the Pageant fringes be after coming by here?

ROGER. La, Sir, the Pagans are all gone by already. And now they are all crowding like mad folks into the great, round house on the Meadow. And I'm going there too. Your servant. I mun go. I munno lose the fine sight. Your servant. The Pagans are all gone by.

Exit running.

IRISHMAN. O this is fine usage, faith! After coming all the way from Ireland to see the Shakespear fringes and Pageant, and them thieves of the world, them waiters, to let a gentleman sleep all the while it was going past, because they knew very well I could not see it if I was not awake. (*Rain behind.*) Och hone! It does not rain, to be sure. 'Tis a fine affair to bring gentlemen out in such weather. This would not be suffered in Dublin without calling this fellow of a Steward to an account. I shall give a fine account of my travels. I came here three hundred miles to lie in a postchaise without sleep, and to sleep when I should be awake, to get nothing to ate, and pay double for that. And now I must return back in the rain, as great a fool as those who hate to stay in their own country and return from their travels as much improved as I myself shall when I go back to Kilkenny. However, I'll try and get into some corner of the round house too. And if I can't get in–Ara! I'll go home and be nowhere.

Exit.

[SCENE III] LAST SCENE

is a magnificent transparent one in which the capital characters of Shakespeare are exhibited at full length, with Shakespeare's statue in the middle crowned by Tragedy and Comedy, fairies and cupids surrounding him, and all the banners waving at the upper end. Then enter the Dancers, and then the Tragic and Comic Troops, and range themselves in the scene.

Chorus from the first entrance singing.

This is the day, a holiday! a holiday!
Drive spleen and rancor far away,
This is the day, a holiday! a holiday!
Drive care and sorrow far away.
Here nature nursed her Darling Boy
From whom all cares and sorrow fly
    Whose harp the muses strung;
From heart to heart let joy rebound,
Now, now, we tread enchanted ground
    Here Shakespeare walked and sung.

A Dance of the Graces, Muses, etc.
After the Dance they all come forward and sing the following Roundelay.

MRS. BADDELEY *as Venus.* Sisters of the tuneful strain,
Attend your parents' jocund train.
'Tis fancy calls you, follow me
    To celebrate the Jubilee.

0.1–0.6. "A Fine Transparent Scene The Statue of Shakespeare discov'd with Tragedy & Comedy etc.," crossed out.

MR. VERNON 2 *as Apollo.* On Avon's banks, where Shakespeare's bust
Points out and guards his sleeping dust,
The sons of scenic mirth decree
To celebrate this Jubilee.
MISS RADLEY 3 *as a Muse.* Come, daughters, come, and bring with you
The aerial sprites and fairy crew,
And the sister Graces three,
To celebrate our Jubilee.
MR. VERNON 4. Hang around the sculptured tomb
The broidered vest, the nodding plume,
And the mask of Comic Glee,
To celebrate our Jubilee.
MR. BANNISTER 5 *as Comus.* From Birnam Wood and Bosworth's Field,
Bring the standard, bring the shield,
With drums and martial symphony,
To celebrate our Jubilee.
MRS. BADDELEY 6. In mournful numbers now relate
Poor Desdemona's hapless fate,
With frantic deeds of jealousy,
To celebrate our Jubilee.
MISS RADLEY 7. Nor be Windsor's Wives forgot,
With their harmless merry plot,
The whit'ning mead and haunted tree,
To celebrate our Jubilee.
MR. BANNISTER 8. Now in jocund strains recite
The revels of the braggard Knight,
Fat Knight! and Ancient Pistol he!
To celebrate our Jubilee.
MR. VERNON 9. But see in crowds, the gay, the fair,
To the splendid scene repair,
A scene as fine, as fine can be,
To celebrate our Jubilee.

Every character, tragic and comic, join[s] *in the Chorus and go*[es] *back, during which the guns fire, bells ring, etc. etc. and the audience applaud*[s].
Bravo Jubilee!
Shakespeare forever!

The End.

29. Garrick's note opposite: "Branches—The Battle was at Dunsinane."

The Institution of the Garter; or, Arthur's Roundtable Restored

1771

THE

SONGS, CHORUSES,

AND

SERIOUS DIALOGUE

OF THE

MASQUE

CALLED

The Inftitution of the GARTER,

OR,

ARTHUR'S ROUND TABLE reftored.

LONDON:
Printed for T. BECKET, and P. A. DE HONDT, in the STRAND.

MDCCLXXI.

Facsimile title page of the First Edition.
Folger Shakespeare Library.

Advertisement

The eager and almost universal curiosity, which the late Installation of the Knights of the Order of the Garter excited in the public, seemed in a manner to command our attention and justify our endeavors to exhibit a representation of it in the following Masque. The difficulty was to give an adequate idea, in a small compass, of the various circumstances of this great solemnity, consisting of the Installation, Procession, and Feast.

The late Mr. Gilbert West published some years ago a dramatic poem called *The Institution of the Order of the Garter*, which has been much admired. It was, however, impossible to bring it on the stage as it was originally written because, though rich in machinery, it was little more than a poem in dialogue without action. Some select parts of it, however, with a few necessary alterations and the addition of some comic scenes, were thought a proper vehicle for the different ceremonies of this great festival. The scene is laid in the reign of Edward the Third, who was the founder of the Order, after having restored that of the Knights of the Round Table, which we have supposed, with some writers, to be continued at the Institution of the Garter.

No expense has been spared, nor, we hope, any object of attention overlooked, which might conduce to make the following Masque as short, as various, and as faithful to the original Institution as possible.

The songs, choruses, and serious dialogue are published, that they may be better understood from the stage. The comic parts, which are intended merely for the preparation of the principal scenes, are not printed, as they would lose much of their effect by being separated from the action of the performer.

Mr. West, in order to give a greater variety and to introduce some particular characters into his poem, has taken (as he acknowledges in a note) the advantage of a licence usually allowed to poets of departing a little from chronology and postponing the Institution of the Order for a few years.

Under the sanction of this authority, we have ventured to make use of the same poetical licence by throwing the Institution of the Order as many years backward as Mr. West has brought it forward. We have made the Black Prince nine years younger than he was when he was knighted; and we flatter ourselves that this anachronism will be excused for the sake of the application.

Some other liberties of less consequence are necessarily taken for the sake of rendering the whole more theatrical. We have had too long an experience of the public indulgence not to know that they will be readily overlooked, should the rest of the performance have the good fortune to be approved.

Dramatis Personae

Spirits	Miss *Hayward.* Mrs. *Morland.* Miss *Rogers.* Mrs. *Simson.*
Genius of England	Mr. *Reddish.*
Chief Druid	Mr. *Inchbald.*
King Edward	Mr. *Aickin.*
Sir Dingle, *court fool*	Mr. *King.*
Edward, the Black Prince	Miss *Hopkins.*
Nat Needle	Mr. *Parsons.*
Roger	Mr. *Weston.*
Squallini	Mrs. *Wrighten.*
Queen Philippa	Mrs. *Johnston.*

The Institution of the Garter; or, Arthur's Roundtable Restored

[PART THE FIRST]

After the Overture,
The curtain rises and discovers,
in SCENE the FIRST,
Three Spirits.

FIRST SPIRIT. Hither, all ye heav'nly powers,
From your empyreal bowers;
From the fields forever gay,
From the star-paved Milky Way,
From the Moon's relucent horn,
From the star that wakes the morn;
From the bow, whose mingling dyes
Sweetly cheer the frowning skies;
From the silver cloud that sails,
Shadowy o'er the darkened vales;
From the elysiums of the sky,
Spirits immortal, hither fly!

CHORUS OF SPIRITS. Fly, and through the limpid air
Guard in pomp the sliding car,
Which to his terrestrial throne
Wafts Britannia's genius down.

SECOND SPIRIT. Hither all ye heav'nly powers,
From your empyreal bowers:
Chiefly ye whose brows divine
Crowned with starry circlets shine,
Who in various labors tried,
Once Britannia's strength and pride,
Now in everlasting rest
Share the glories of the blessed.

Peers and nobles of the sky,
Spirts immortal, hither fly.

CHORUS OF BARDS AND SPIRITS answer[s].
We fly, and charm the limpid air,
While the softly-sliding car
To his sea-encircled throne
Wafts Britannia's genius down.

THIRD SPIRIT. Hither, too, ye tuneful throng,
Masters of enchanting song,
Sacred bards! whose rapt'rous strains
Sooth the toiling hero's pains,
Sooth the patriot's gen'rous cares;
Sweetly through their ravished ears,
Whisp'ring to th' immortal mind,
Heav'nly visions, hopes refined;
Hopes of endless peace and fame,
Safe from envy's blasting flame,
Pure, sincere in those abodes,
Where to throngs of list'ning gods,
Hymning bards to virtue's praise
Tune their never-dying lays.
Sweet encomiasts of the sky,
Spirits immortal, hither fly!

The scene opens and discovers the Genius of England descending, attended by Spirits and Bards, who sing the following Chorus.

We wake our harps to Britain's weal,
Our bosoms glow with heav'nly love,
The bliss that spotless patriots feel,
Is kindred to the bliss above.

GENIUS *speaks.* Disdain not, ye blest denisons of air,
To breathe this grosser atmosphere a while,
Your service I shall need; meantime resort
To yon imperial palace, and in air
Shed your choice influence on the noble train,
There on the solemn day assembled round
The throne of British Edward; I a while
Must here await th' approach of other spirits,
Sage Druids, Britain's old philosophers,
Who, still enamored of their ancient haunts,
Unseen of mortal eyes, they hover round
Their ruined altars and these sacred oaks.
But hence, aerial Spirits; lo, they come!

The Spirits go off—the Genius and Bards come forward to meet the Druids in scene the third.

CHIEF DRUID. Inform us, happy Spirit, protecting power
Of this our ancient country, wherefore now
From our sequestered valleys, pensive groves
And dark recesses, thou hast summoned us
To wait thy orders 'mongst these sacred oaks.
GENIUS. A great event, sage Druids, that no less
Imports than this your ancient country's fame
From contemplation and your silent shades
Calls you to meet me in this dark recess.
CHIEF DRUID. Our country's weal, ev'n from the bliss of heav'n,
Can charm down patriot souls to visit earth,
And in her cause exert their holiest ardors.
GENIUS. Know, in yon castle, whose proud battlements
Sit like a regal crown upon the brow
Of that high-climbing lawn, doth Edward hold
His solemn session, and this hour receives
The pleas of all th' aspiring candidates,
Who, summoned by the herald's public voice
To Windsor, as to Fame's bright temple, haste
From every shore; the noble, wise, and brave,
Knights, senators and statesmen, lords and kings;
Ambitious each to gain the splendid prize
By Edward promised to transcendent worth.
For who of mortals is too great and high
In the career of virtue to contend?
Of these, selecting the most glorious names,
Doth England's monarch purpose to compose
A princely brotherhood, himself the chief
And worthy sovereign of th' illustrious band;
A band of heroes, listed in the cause
Of honor, virtue, and celestial truth,
Under the name and holy patronage
Of Cappadocian George, Britannia's saint.
CHIEF DRUID. A plan of glory, which beyond the reach
Of his own conqu'ring arms may propagate
The sovereignty of Britain and erect
Her monarchs into judges of mankind!
How, Spirit, can we aid this glorious work?
GENIUS. Straight to the chapel, sages, bend your way,
And there, unseen, support me in the task

To guide our Edward's choice, clear from the mists
It haply hath contracted from a long
Unebbing current of prosperity,
His intellectual eye. From this day's choice
Of his first colleagues shall succeeding times
Of Edward judge, and on his fame pronounce.
For dignities and titles, when misplaced
Upon the vicious, the corrupt, and vile,
Like princely virgins to low peasants matched,
Descend from their nobility and, soiled
By base alliance, not their pride alone
And native splendor lose, but shame retort
Ev'n on the sacred throne from whence they sprung.
So may the lustre of this order bright,
This eldest child of chivalry be stained,
If, at her first espousals, her great fire,
Caught by the specious outsides that deceive
And captivate the world, admit the suit
Of vain pretenders void of real worth;
Light, empty bubbles by the wanton gale
Of fortune swelled, and only formed to dance
And glitter in the sunshine of a court.

CHIEF DRUID. We will attend thee, Spirit; from thy hallowed lips
Breathe forth the sacred oracles of truth.

GENIUS. And you, immortal bards, charm with your lays,
The sacred songs of virtue, the pure air,
That evil sprites, if any such lurk here,
May quit the hallowed and enchanted ground,
Nor counteract our sacred operations.

Exit Genius *and* Druids.

Bards remain and sing the following semi-Chorus.

CHORUS OF BARDS. Gentle spirit, we obey,
Thus we charm the silent air;
Fiends and demons shall not stay,
Raptures of the blest to share.

SONG.

I.

FIRST BARD. Ye southern gales, that ever fly
In frolic April's vernal train,
Who, as you skim along the sky,

Dip your light pinions in the main;
Then shake them fraught with genial show'rs,
O'er blooming Flora's primrose bow'rs.

II.

Now cease awhile your wanton sport,
Now drive each threat'ning cloud away;
Then to the flow'ry vale resort,
And hither all its sweets convey;
And ever, as you dance along,
With softest murmurs aid our song.

Repeat the Chorus. *Gentle spirit, etc.*

SCENE IV. *The Chapel of St. George.*
The knights seated in their stalls.
King Edward *comes forward and meets the Prince of* Wales.

KING EDWARD. Edward, approach, beloved and noble son,
In whom my heart more joys and glories, more
Than in the highest pride of sovereign pow'r:
Last I admit thee, Edward Prince of Wales;
Thus to complete the number of our order.
In evidence whereof—receive this robe
Of heavenly hue, ennobled by the shield
And ensign of our faith. About thy knee
Be bound that mystic Garter, to denote
The bond of honor that together ties
The brethren of St. George in friendly league,
United to maintain the cause of truth
And justice only. May propitious heav'n
Grant that thou may'st henceforth wear it to his praise,
The exaltation of this noble Order
And thy own glory. With like reverence,
My son, receive and wear this golden chain,
Graced with the image of Britannia's saint,
Heav'n's valiant soldier, Cappadocian George;
In imitation of whose glorious deeds,
May'st thou triumphant in each state of life,
Or prosperous or adverse, still subdue
Thy spiritual and carnal enemies;
That not on earth alone thou may'st obtain
The guerdon of thy valor, endless praise,
But with the virtuous and the brave above,

In solemn triumph, wear celestial palms
To crown thy final noblest victory.

Embraces the Prince.

PRINCE EDWARD. Accept, my sovereign liege, my grateful thanks,
That thou hast thus vouchsafed to place thy son
So near thyself upon the roll of fame:
And may thy benediction, gracious lord,
May thy paternal vows be heard in heav'n!
That he whom thou hast listed in the cause
Of truth and virtue never may forget
His vowed engagements, nor defraud the hopes,
By soiling with dishonorable deeds
The lustre of that order which thy name
Should teach him to respect and to adorn.

CHORUS.

Let his name,
With honor and fame,
Down the tide of ages roll:
Glory shall fire him,
Virtue inspire him,
'Till, blessed and blessing,
Power possessing,
From earth to heav'n he lifts his soul!

First Part ends.

PART THE SECOND.

SCENE [I], *A gate of Windsor Castle.*

This scene passes among the Comic Characters, and the following Song *is introduced.*

[SCENE [IV], *The outside of the Castle Gate.*]

[*Enter different characters of Men & Women looking about to get into the Castle.*]

[1st WOMAN.] [Why this gate is shut too–The devil's in the folks–there's no entrance, sure enough–'tis a sin and a shame to serve us so.–We come I don't know how many miles to see the Estallation –have our pockets picked by the innkeepers, and can't get a peep neither into the bargain.–What does it signify to have fine sights, when folks can't get in to see 'em.]

[*Enter* Roger.]

[ROGER.] [Why, I can see nothing, not I, but crowds of folks who are as great fools as myself.—Unless I had eyes to see thro' stone walls, I have walked near thirty miles to suck a bull, and I am as great a caulf for my pains.]

[1st COUNTRY MAN.] [Roger will ha' his joke, if he has nothing else.]

[ROGER.] [Indeed wull I. I'se neer be mollencholy while I have something to loffat. Could I have seen what I came to see, the lords dressed out in their mummery, I'd ha' loft at them; but since they are so hard to come at, why I'll make the best on't, and loff at the poor fools who can't see the great ones. Ha! ha! ha!]

[2nd COUNTRY MAN.] [Wounds, Roger! you'll speak treason.]

[ROGER.] [Let 'em take me before the King for't. Then I might see the show, though I should be hanged after. Ha! ha! ha!]

[ONE OF THE CROWD.] [See, see, neighbors, here comes Sir Dingle, the King's Fool, as fine as a lord. He'll certainly be let into the gate, and then we may follow him.]

[ROGER.] [Ay, ay, let the Fool alone. He has more interest within than wiser or better folks, I warrant him.]

[*Enter* Sir Dingle, *the King's Fool, and* Signior Catterwawlins with a paper in his hand, followed by different characters.]

[2nd WOMAN.] [Nay, pray now, dear Cousin Dingle—]

[FOOL.] [Nay, pray now, good folks, don't *dear* me and Cousin Dingle me so. I am too busy and too great to know anybody, especially creditors and poor relations.]

[2nd WOMAN.] [Nay, but Sir Dingle—]

[FOOL.] [Nay but Madam Dangle—I am in a hurry I tell you. I am poet laureat for the day, and this beardless fellow here, Signior Catterwawlins, is my gentleman usher. And with my want of wit and his want of manhood, we are to throw into ecstacies half a score dutchesses, thirteen to the dozen of countesses, and uncountable numbers of inferior quality. Here is the choice fruit of my fancy. Such a song! But I must be gone; there can be no sport without me. Come along, Signior Catterwawlins. (*Going.*)]

[CATTERWAWLINS.] [I'm with you, Sir Dingle.]

[2nd WOMAN.] [But you gave me a promise yesterday.]

[FOOL.] [Why keep it then, for I won't. I live in the land of promises, and I'll give you a hundred more. We give nothing else here. Besides, I am a wit and have a very short memory, and yesterday is an age. Do you think I am so vulgar, or so little of a courtier, to remember what I promised yesterday? Fie, for shame. Come along, Signior.]

[CATTERWAWLINS.] [I'm with you, Sir Dingle.]

Portrait of Parsons by Condé.
Harvard Theatre Collection

[Tailor *comes forward out of breath.*]

[TAILOR.] [O, your Honor, Sir Dingle, I am glad I have found you. Here we all are. (*Showing his family.*)]

[FOOL.] [What, my old friend Nat Needle! What brought you here? You an't come a dunning sure?]

[TAILOR.] [Dunning! Lord help, not I. Your Honor's welcome a month or six weeks longer.—I hope your Honor likes your new suit. I was in high luck—never better—no dunning, your Honor, but a little curiosity to peep at matters brought my wife and I and young Natty to Windsor. Why don't you bow, Nat? Will your Honor help me to a peep? One good turn deserves another, you know.]

[FOOL.] [So it does, you know,—if one could get another. But you have done with me, friend Nat, and I with you. I owe you money, 'tis true, but you will trust me no more. And therefore I must oblige those that will. *One good turn deserves another, you know.* (*Mimics him.*)]

[SEVERAL TOGETHER, *crowding him.*] [Nay but, Sir Dingle! for heaven's sake—]

[FOOL.] [Well, well, for Heaven's good Christians don't smother me so. If you don't give me air, I shall die; and if I die I can neither serve you or myself. Elbow room, I beseech you, good friends!—So, so,—now tell me *your* wants and I'll tell you *mine*; then we'll hustle 'em together, and mend the breed if we can.—Pray young man with your mouth open, what would you please to have; you are gaping after something, I'm sure.]

[ROGER.] [I wanted a sight of the King's Fool; and one need not shut one's mouth, you know, for a mouthful of moonshine. Are you a lord, pray?]

[FOOL.] [I live at the next door. I am a fool, at your service.]

[ROGER.] [I took you for a lord. Can you get me a place, Fool?]

[FOOL.] [I'll give you a promise, fool. And you can get nothing else here. But what place do you want?]

[ROGER.] [Yours, when you have done with it; for to talk much, say little, do nothing, and be paid for it would fit me nicely.]

[FOOL.] [What an unconscionable fellow are you, to wish to be a great man without serving your time to it. Talk much! Say little, do nothing, and be paid for it! Do you know, Booby, that you have crammed into a nutshell the very quintessence of a court life? Law, Physick, and Divinity keep their coaches by the same receipt. Though you are a booby, Roger, you was born a wit.]

[ROGER.] [Though you was born a fool, I believe you're something else. For my part, I was born poor, bred to work hard, and get little. Had I been a fool at Court, I might have been as fine and as fat as other folks. There's a douse in the chops for you, (*half-aside*) ha! ha! ha!]

[1st COUNTRY MAN.] [Well said, Roger. Ha! ha! ha!]

[FOOL.] [Very well said, Roger. But take a fool's advice: don't grin at your own jokes; for it shows little wit and a very bad set of teeth. *There's a douse in your chops, Roger.*]

[ROGER.] [You have dashed my teeth down my throat, but I won't be choked for all that.]

[FOOL.] [But, Signior of the Neuter Gender, let our good friends have something to stay their longing. Swell your notes to the highest raptures of conceit, and my vanity shall beat time to it. What luxury for your ears, if you have not lost 'em, to hear voice and my poetry. Fasten 'em by the ears, and I'll sneak off.]

SONG.

I.

[CATTERWAWLINS *sings.*] O the glorious Installation!
Happy nation!
You shall see the King and Queen,
Such a scene!
Valor he, sir,
Virtue she, sir,
Which our hearts will ever win;
Sweet her face is,
With such graces,
Show what goodness dwells within.

II.

O the glorious Installation!
Happy nation!
You shall see the noble Knights!
Charming sights!
Feathers wagging,
Velvet dragging,
Trailing, sailing on the ground;
Loud in talking,
Proud in walking,
Nodding, ogling, smirking round –
O the glorious *etc.*

[(*Noise of cannon, etc.*)]

[FOOL.] [Hark! hark! they have done in the chapel, and now they are going in grand procession to feast in the hall. I must be gone.]

[ROGER.] [Nay, do now good, Mr. Fool; take us in, pray now, take us in.]

[FOOL.] [Well, well. You shall be taken in. But do as I bid you—say not a word more nor stir one step 'till I come back; for, if you do, you spoil all. I'll whip round a secret way that I know of. So put yourselves in order. Let the ladies look as simpering and the men as wise as they can. Settle your ruffs and faces, brush up your fardingales and wipe the sweat off your brows. And then—you shall be taken in, I assure you.]

[ROGER.] [Shall we indeed now?]

[FOOL.] [That you shall, I promise you. In the meantime, there's my song to divert you. (*Gives it to* Roger.) Read it, you who can; sing it, you who may. And I'll be back again before that fellow has tied up his hose, that booby has washed his face, or Roger got half through a stanza. Come along, Signior Catterwawlins.]

[CATTERWAWLINS.] [I'm with you, Sir Dingle.]

[*Exeunt.*]

[ROGER.] [Ecod, and so you may. Zooks, what pothooks are here! But this, I have been told, is your quality scrawl. 'Tis too much like tradesfolk to write what can easily be read. If I could but conjure it out, I'll be hanged if I would not try to sing it. The De'el himself cannot make out the top; let's take a touch at the bottom. (*He reads:*)

O the glorious Exhalation
    Happy nature
You shall see the noble knights,
    Charming frights!
    Feathers waggling,
    Velvet draggling,
Taleing, staleing on the ground;
    Loud in talking,
    Proud in walking,
Noddling, goggling, smirking round.

But where's our friend the Fool? (*Then tries to sing it.*)]

[*The* Fool *thrusts his head through a hole near the gate.*]

[FOOL.] [Friends, neighbors, brethren, countrymen and countrywomen! I have pleaded your cause upon my knees to our gracious King. *Imprimis*—as a skillful orator for my own sake. *Secundo*—as a very loving fool for yours. His Majesty frowned terribly at first, but, as I have stroked a roaring lion before now, I patted him gently 'till I got my fingers in his shaggy mane, and then I scratched and melted his most princely heart till the tears trickled down his cheeks with a most pathetic laughter, and at last he most generously resolved –]

[ROGER.] [That we shall be taken in.]

[FOOL.] [Yes, yes, you shall be taken in—but not into the castle, for it is so thronged that my good friend and generous creditor there, Nathaniel Needle the Tailor, could not possibly be squeezed in edgeways. Therefore, if you will come round to a certain wicket under a certain window, you will be admitted at a certain time, for a certain business—for his Majesty has given his royal word, and I am his security, that after he and his Knights Companions have regaled their royal, princely, and noble appetites, that you shall enter at a certain signal as freebooters, and then –

With stomachs keen and eager for your prey,
Through baked, and boiled, and roast shall hewway,
Attack fish, flesh and fowl, both great and small,
Joints, haunches, turkies, turbots, bones and all!
In vain for quarter custards, tarts implore ye.
The lighter troops of pastry shall fall before ye!
Confusion then, with wild uproar shall reign,
And all cry out—*Chaos is come again*!]

[ROGER.] [Zooks! he has set my mouth a-watering.]

[NEEDLE.] [I wish I was at it with all my soul.]

[FOOL.] [Are you content? For if you are not, nor gate nor wicket will be opened to you, and you may still cool your heels and suck your fingers 'till tomorrow morning. Speak ye murmuring tatterdemallions, are you content?]

[ALL.] [We are content. We are, bless our noble King and his wise Fool. To the wicket—to the wicket! Huzza! huzza! huzza!]

[*Exeunt.*]

The Procession
Ends the 2nd Act

PART THE THIRD.

SCENE [I], *St. George's Hall.*

Where the Knights are discovered feasting at the *Round Table.*
[Music during the banquet

Then an Entry of Warriors with a Grand March
As they march out
Enter in a hurry the King's Fool]

[FOOL.] [Peace, glory, and good fellowship forever attend the most illustrious Brotherhood. May one Fool be permitted among you for the sake of his intelligence, ordinary and extraordinary?]

[*The* King *nods.*]

[FOOL.] [A nod from his Majesty, like a word to the wise, is sufficient. Thus I proceed.

May it please your gartered glories all together! I come Ambassador from the mighty power the Mob *without*, who are somewhat impatient that they are not yet admitted here *within*. It is fitting, say they, (don't be offended if I am a little rough, for I am their representative) it is fitting, they allow, that the most honourable Knighthood should fill their lordly stomachs first. But as they are flesh and blood too, they say, flesh and blood cannot possibly bear to stay too long; for they urge (and their arguments are very keen) that by the villainy and imposition of your Majesty's graceless subjects of Windsor (for which every knave should be exalted upon his own signpost) they have thirsted and fasted for near seven hours by the clock. *Ergo*: they humbly hope that they may be graciously permitted to finish now what you have so nobly begun.—They likewise with most outrageous humility urge that they have your royal word, that in due time they should enter and fall to. That the due time is come they most hungerly conceive—they are indeed impatient.—My eloquence has hitherto curbed their passions, but as my rhetoric is run out, they are now ready to run in. And might a fool advise, I think it much better that they be permitted to enter, than that the old proverb should take effect—*vidilicet*—hunger will break down stone walls.]

[EDWARD.] [Most wisely has the fool advised us, lords.
My royal word was given, and shall be kept;
No subject shall upbraid my want of faith,
Their smallest rights are sacred as our own.
Let us retire, my Brothers, and give way
To this best guardian of my throne and kingdom,
Their honest liberty.—Now let 'em enter.]

[*Exeunt* King *and* Knights.]

[FOOL.] [Havoc's the word, and slaughter will ensue.]

[*Exit* Fool.]

[SCENE II], *After the different ceremonies, the scene closes, and the Comic Characters have a scene in another apartment near the hall.*

[*A great noise is heard. Enter several characters through a door, carrying away the various things of the feast.*]

[*After the noise and hurry, enter* Needle *and his* Wife, *she loaded with things and he fuddled.*]

[WIFE.] ['Tis a shame, Mr. Needle, that you would not assist me. Had you not taken to the liquor instead of loading yourself as I have done, we should have made a glorious jaunt of it!]

[NEEDLE.] [I have loaded myself, you fool, with the best too–sherry sack, Wife! I was the only gentleman among 'em all.]

[WIFE.] [When you are in liquor, Nat, you have no feeling for your wife and children.]

[NEEDLE.] [Because I'm a gentleman, I tell you, I despise gain, defy you, Wife, the flesh and the Devil, and that (*snaps his fingers*) for all the world.]

[WIFE.] [Yes, yes, you are not valiant, Nat, and so foul-mouthed in your cups that you would not mind speaking to the King (Heaven bless him!) if he came across you.]

[NEEDLE.] [I stay here on purpose. Edward the 3rd is a very good sort of a Majesty, and I'll give him a few hints to set all matters right. So go home, and I'll follow you.]

[WIFE.] [Dear Nat, don't be treasonous now. You'll get us all hanged if you approach his royal Majesty.]

[NEEDLE.] [I must have some alterations in the State. I will not get drunk for nothing.]

[WIFE.] [What will become of us? O dear, here comes his honour, Sir Dingle! Pray be advised by him.]

[NEEDLE.] [Indeed but I won't. When I am sober I am advised by everybody. When fuddled I'll be advised by nobody—there's the difference. Besides, he owes me money and I have a right to be saucy. 'Tis the way with gentlemen. Though he's a fool, I have as much sense as himself.]

[*Enter* Sir Dingle, *singing.*]

[SONG.]

[FOOL.] [If your lips you should smack
With old sherry sack,
Let your cares in a bumper be drowned O!
Let no sorrow stick
Circulation be quick
'Till your noddles like windmills turn round O!]

[What, my magnanimous *Needle*! with his most beauteous *thimble*. Won't you thread the castle gate, my boy, help to line the Windsor caravan, and sit cross legged to London? Ha, my little buckram and canvas!]

[NEEDLE.] [I won't sit cross legged for you, nor thread my needle, nor wear my thimble, nor line your head that wants it so much; so you may get your buckram and canvas elsewhere, Mr. Cap and Bells. He that lives by your custom must fast seven days a week. And there's a bob for you, Mr. Dingle.]

[FOOL.] [What, my flea rampant! Thou bitest in earnest. Hast thou been sucking the blood of the grape, as I have done, that thou skip'st about thus? What is the matter with thee, Needle, that thou stand'st tottering upon thy point as if thou hadst a loadstone in thy head?]

[NEEDLE.] [Sherry and sack is the best friend I have at Court. I owe him much, and other folks owe *me* much, and I wish they would pay me or fight me. And now it's out.]

[FOOL.] [What, is my tailor's goose turned a bird of prey and honest cabbage turned hemlock to poison his friend Dingle?]

[WIFE.] [Law, Sir Dingle, don't mind him. He's mad when he's drunk and contradicts *me*. He'll cry like a babe in a few minutes.]

[NEEDLE.] [I'm a gentleman and demand satisfaction!]

[FOOL.] [What, Bully Bodkie, would you make eyelit holes in me? What satisfaction, my most valiant Nit?]

[NEEDLE.] [Satisfaction of a gentleman —]

[FOOL.] [I have not paid you your bill, nor ever intend it. Is not that the satisfaction of a gentleman, and of a fine gentleman? You have my love, Needle, and that is worth a million. (*Strikes him on the shoulder.*)]

[NEEDLE.] [I am overcome with tenderness and I overflow with tears.]

[WIFE.] [Now he's maudlin and comes round again, he'll soon grow sick and repent.]

[NEEDLE.] [Though you owe me money and never intend to pay me, though the clothes upon your back are mine, and the money in your pocket *ought* to be mine—yet I love you (*sobs*), Sir Dingle, I am a true friend. I should die if I was to kill you. (*Cries.*)]

[FOOL.] [And so should I, Nat, if you was. But come, dry up your tears, my generous creditor, and let us completely finish what we have so deliciously begun. I have some heavenly liquor in my cellar, fit for the god Mars and the Queen of Beauty, fit for my magnanimous Needle and his unparalleled thimble, all animosities shall be drowned—take a new lease of friendship, bespeak some new clothes, and never think of paying for 'em. (*Taking him under one arm, and his wife under the other.*)]

[NEEDLE.] [I am for the satisfaction of a gentleman. (*Very drunk.*)]

[WIFE.] [I am for any satisfaction, Sir Dingle.]

[FOOL, *singing.*] [And you both shall have it. Come, my good friend, and thou his bosom blessing, let us thus proceed to my cellar and drown all animosities.

I am thy friend, Needle–
I'd leave the world for him that loves good sherry,
Sherry the fountain of all human bliss!
What mighty good have not been done by sherry?
What made great Alexander conqueror
Of the world? Why, sherry–what makes my Needle
As great as Alexander's self–Why, sherry –
Delectable, delicious, dainty sherry.
Sherry can rouse the tame–and warm the cold –
Make prudes to smile, and even tailors bold –
Melt the hard hearts of misers till they whimper,
Makes old men wanton and old maidens simper,
Can reconcile poor mortals to their fetters,
Husbands to wives and creditors to debtors,
Can jarring discord in sweet-concord bind,
Moisten, make maudlin, and unite mankind.]

[SCENE III], *Then the scene changes to a garden. Soft music is heard at a distance. The Genius of England leads on* King Edward.

KING EDWARD. What art thou, stranger, and why thus apart
With looks of sweet benevolence and love,
To these delightful shades, with which my eyes,
If mem'ry fails not, ne'er were charmed before;
Draw'st thou our steps by some resistless pow'r?

GENIUS. Behold the guardian Genius of this isle,
Descending from the realms of cloudless day!
Invisible, I've watched thy glorious deeds,
But on this solemn day I have vouchsafed
To manifest my presence; to declare,
Not in those whispers which have often spoke
Peace to thy conscious heart, but audibly,
And evident to all, th' assent of heav'n
To the great business which hath gathered here
This troupe of worthies from all nations round.
Know that those actions which are great and good
Receive a nobler sanction from the free
And universal voice of all mankind,
Which is the voice of heav'n, than from the highest,

The most illustrious act of regal pow'r.
This noble sanction, Edward, in the name
Not of this age alone but latest time,
Here do I solemnly annex to each
Of thy great acts, but chief to this most wise,
Most virtuous institution, which extends
Wide as thy fame, beyond your empire's bound,
A prize of virtue published to the world.
Ye registers of heav'n record the deed!

[A Chorus of Bards, Druids and Spirits *unseen, repeat it.*]
Ye registers of heav'n record the deed!

KING EDWARD. 'Tis wondrous all! my heart expands beyond
Its mortal bounds to more than earthly bliss!
GENIUS. More wonders are prepared for thee, O King!
Behold what precious fruit the tree shall bear,
Thy hand has planted in this happy isle!
Visions of glory strike his raptured sight!
Ye unborn ages, crowd upon his soul!
Spirits, attend! Unfold futurity!
Now, Edward, taste that bliss which ever flows
From royal virtues, has flowed, and shall flow
From thee, Friend, Guardian, Father of thy people.

[*Here a* Vision.]

KING EDWARD. This is too much for human strength to bear.
Hold, hold, my heart, th' excess of joy o'erwhelms me.
GENIUS. Now reascend the skies, immortal spirits.
Th' important act that drew you down to earth
Is finished. Spare we now his mortal sense,
That cannot long endure th' unshrouded beam
Of higher natures. Let him, undisturbed
But not unaided by the heav'nly pow'rs,
Complete th' illustrious work which future kings,
Struck with the beauty of the noble plan,
Shall emulously labor to maintain:

And may thy spirit, Edward, be their guide,
In ev'ry chapter thou henceforth preside,
In ev'ry breast infuse thy virtuous flame,
And teach them to respect their country's fame.

The SCENE *changes.*

GENIUS. Astonishment seals up his lips; his heart
Runs o'er with gratitude. Thy God-like mind
Exalts thee, Edward, above human-kind;
And from the realms of everlasting day
Calls down celestial bards thy praise to sing;
Calls a bright troop of spirits to survey
Thee, the great miracle on earth, a patriot king!

Enter Bards, Druids, and Spirits, who all join Chorus.

Hail! mighty nation, ever famed in war!
Lo, heav'n descends, thy festivals to share;
Celestial bards in living lays shall sing
Britannia's glories and her matchless king.

End of the Masque.

The following EXTRACTS *from* Selden's Titles of Honor, *and* Ashmole's Order of the Garter, *are inserted to show the authority upon which we have founded some part of our* Installation.

And so much the rather also, because we know by others of our own country, that in the selfsame year, a solemn and great meeting of Knights was appointed by the King at Windsor Castle, for the setting up of his *Round Table* there, *etc.*

And it seems that out of the plot and purpose of this *Round Table* at Windsor, erected in the same year wherein the Order of the New Garter was instituted and appointed to be celebrated on St. George's day of the same year, as we may collect out of Froissart also, the Order itself had chief part at least of its original. And the other traditions touching the Garter of the Queen, or of the Countess of Kent and Salisbury, may well stand with this, thus far, that the word and the use of the Garter, began as the traditions suppose, but that the Order was raised chiefly out of this of the *Round Table* of that time, as out of a Seminary. For the *Round Table* was in special use in those ages, for the drawing together of the braver Knights and Ladies, *etc.*

Froissart likewise says, *Et ordonna* (Edward the Third) *que d'an en an le jour Saint Gregore, s'en feroit la feste dedans le chateau de Vindesore, le quell chateau le Roy Artur avoit fait faire autreffois edifier et in icelui tenir la noble table ronde, etc.*

Selden, edit. 1672, pag. 658.

King Edward the Third having designed to restore the honor of the *Round Table*, held a juste at Windsor, in the 18th year of his REIGN, (but there is an old manuscript chronicle that has these words: King Edward in his 19th year begun his *Round Table*, and ordained the day annually to be kept there at Whitsuntide) and this meeting, in truth, occasioned the foundation of the most noble Order of the Garter, as shall be noted by and by.

Ashmole, edit. 1672, pag. 96.

He (Edward the Third) did thereupon first design (as being invited thereto by its ancient fame) the restoration of King Arthur's *Round Table*, which he exhibited with magnificent hastiludes and general justs, to invite hither the gallant and active spirits from abroad; and upon discovery of their courage and ability in the exercise of arms, to draw them to his party, and oblige them to himself.

Though King Edward so far advanced the honor of a Garter, as that the Order did derive its title and denomination from it; yet it is most evident, that he founded this more famous Order, not to give reputation to, or perpetuate an effeminate occasion, but to adorn martial virtue with honor, rewards, and splendor; to increase virtue and valor in the hearts of his nobility; or, as Andrew de Chesne saith, to honor military virtue with some glorious favors and rewards; that so true nobility (as is noted in the preface to the black book of the Order) after long and hazardous adventures, should not enviously be deprived of that honor which it hath really deserved; and that active and hardy youth might not want a spur in the profession of virtue, which is to be esteemed glorious and eternal.

Upon these grounds no doubt does our learned Selden affirm, that this Order was raised chiefly out of the *Round Table* of that time (the Knights thereof being in the flower of that age) as out of a seminary.

Ashmole, page 182.

Finis

The Irish Widow

1772

THE

IRISH WIDOW.

IN TWO ACTS:

AS IT IS PERFORMED AT THE

THEATRE ROYAL

IN

DRURY-LANE.

LONDON.

Printed for T. BECKET in the Strand.

MDCCLXXII.

[Price One Shilling.]

Facsimile title page of the First Edition.
Folger Shakespeare Library.

To Mrs. Barry

Madam,

After returning my thanks to the performers of this farce, for the great justice they have done me, I must beg leave to address myself in particular to you.

As your wishes produced the piece, and your performance has raised it into some consequence, to whom can it be so properly addressed? You were before ranked in the first class of our theatrical geniuses, and now you have the additional merit of transforming the *Grecian Daughter* into the *Irish Widow*, that is, of sinking to the lowest note from the top of the compass!

Permit me, Madam, like other coxcombs, to boast some favors I have received. You perform the principal character, some newspapers have criticized the farce, and the audiences have laughed heartily. Were not I as sensible as the severest critic of them all, that it is a trifle not worth the owning, I should subscribe my real name, instead of

Madam,
Your great admirer,
And humble servant,
The AUTHOR.

Dramatis Personae

Sir Patrick O'Neale	Mr. *Moody*.
Whittle	Mr. *Parsons*.
Nephew	Mr. *Cautherly*.
Bates	Mr. *Baddeley*.
Kecksy	Mr. *Dodd*.
Thomas	Mr. *Weston*.
Footman	Mr. *Griffith*.
Widow Brady	Mrs. *Barry*.

The Irish Widow

ACT I.

SCENE I, Whittle's *house*.
Enter Bates *and* Servant.

BATES. Is he gone out? His card tells me to come directly. I did but lock up some papers, take my hat and cane, and away I hurried.

SERVANT. My master desires you will sit down; he will return immediately. He had some business with his lawyer and went out in great haste, leaving the message I have delivered. Here is my young master.

Exit Servant.

Enter Nephew.

BATES. What, lively Billy! Hold. I beg your pardon, melancholy William, I think. Here's fine revolution. I hear your uncle who was last month all gravity and you all mirth have changed characters. He is now all spirit, and you are in the dumps, young man.

NEPHEW. And for the same reason. This journey to Scarborough will unfold the riddle.

BATES. Come, come, in plain English, and before your uncle comes, explain the matter.

NEPHEW. In the first place, I am undone.

BATES. In love I know. I hope your uncle is not undone too. That would be the devil.

NEPHEW. He has taken possession of him in every sense. In short, he came to Scarborough to see the lady I had fallen in love with.

BATES. And fell in love himself?

NEPHEW. Yes, and with the same lady.

BATES. That is the devil indeed.

NEPHEW. Oh, Mr. Bates, when I thought my happiness complete and wanted only my uncle's consent to give me the independence he so often has promised me, he came to Scarborough for that purpose and wished me joy of my choice. But in less than a week his approbation turned into a passion for her. He now hates the sight of me and is resolved with the consent of the father to make her his wife directly.

BATES. So he keeps you out of your fortune, won't give his consent, which his brother's foolish will requires, and he would marry himself the same woman, because right, title, conscience, nature, justice, and every law divine and human, are against it.

NEPHEW. Thus he tricks me at once both of wife and fortune, without the least want of either.

BATES. Well said, friend Whittle. But it can't be, it shan't be, and it must not be. This is murder and robbery in the strongest sense, and he shan't be hanged in chains to be laughed at by the whole town if I can help it.

NEPHEW. I am distracted, the widow is distressed, and we both shall run mad.

BATES. A widow, too! 'Gad a mercy, three score and five!

NEPHEW. But such a widow! She is now in town with her father, who wants to get her off his hands. 'Tis equal to him who has her, so she is provided for. I hear somebody coming. I must away to her lodgings, where she waits for me to execute a scheme directly for our delivery.

BATES. What is her name, Billy?

NEPHEW. Brady.

BATES. Brady! is not she daughter to Sir Patrick O'Neale?

NEPHEW. The same. She was sacrificed to the most senseless, drunken profligate in the whole country. He lived to run out his fortune, and the only advantage she got from the union was he broke that and his neck, before he had broke her heart.

BATES. The affair of marriage is in this country put upon the easiest footing. There is neither love or hate in the matter; necessity brings them together. They are united at first for their mutual convenience and separated ever after for their particular pleasures. Oh rare matrimony! Where does she lodge?

NEPHEW. In Pall Mall, near the hotel.

BATES. I'll call in my way and assist at the consultation. I am for a bold stroke, if gentle methods should fail.

NEPHEW. We have a plan, and a spirited one, if my sweet widow is able to go through it. Pray let us have your friendly assistance; ours is the cause of love and reason.

BATES. Get you gone with your love and reason. They seldom pull together nowadays. I'll give your uncle a dose first, and then I'll meet you at the widow's. What says your uncle's privy counseller, Mr. Thomas, to this?

NEPHEW. He is greatly our friend and will enter sincerely into our service. He is honest, sensible, ignorant, and particular, a kind of half coxcomb, with a thorough good heart. But he's here.

BATES. Do you go about your business and leave the rest to me.

Exit Nephew.

Enter Thomas.

Mr. Thomas, I am glad to see you. Upon my word, you look charmingly. You wear well, Mr. Thomas.

THOMAS. Which is a wonder, considering how the times go, Mr. Bates. They'll wear and tear me, too, if I don't take care of myself. My old master has taken the nearest way to wear himself out and all that belong to him.

BATES. Why surely this strange story about town is not true, that the old gentleman is fallen in love.

THOMAS. Ten times worse than that.

BATES. The devil!

THOMAS. And his horns—going to be married.

BATES. Not if I can help it.

THOMAS. You never saw such an altered man in your born days. He's grown young again. He frisks and prances and runs about as if he had a new pair of legs. He has left off his brown camlet surtout, which he wore all summer, and now with his hat under his arm he goes open breasted, and he dresses and powders and smirks so, that you would take him for the mad Frenchman in Bedlam, something wrong in his upper story. Would you think it, he wants me to have a pig-tail!

BATES. Then he is far gone indeed.

THOMAS. As sure as you are there, Mr. Bates, a pig-tail. We have had sad work about it. I made a compromise with him, to wear these ruffled shirts which he gave me. But they stand in my way. I am not so listless with them. Though I have tied up my hands for him, I won't tie up my head, that I am resolute.

BATES. This it is to be in love, Thomas?

THOMAS. He may make free with himself; he shan't make a fool of me. He has got his head into a bag, but I won't have a pig-tail tacked to mine, and so I told him.

BATES. What did you tell him?

---

93. have] *O1*, *O2*, *O3*, *O4*, *D1*, *D2*; wear *O5*.

94. Then] than in all editions.

THOMAS. That as I, and my father, and his father before me, had wore their own hair as heaven had sent it, I thought myself rather too old to set up for a monkey at my time of life and wear a pig-tail. He, he, he! He took it.

BATES. With a wry face, for it was wormwood.

THOMAS. Yes, he was frumped and called me old blockhead and would not speak to me the rest of the day. But the next day he was at it again. He then put me into a passion, and I could not help telling him that I was an Englishman born and had my prerogative as well as he, and that as long as I had breath in my body, I was for liberty and a straight head of hair.

BATES. Well said, Thomas. He could not answer that.

THOMAS. The poorest man in England is a match for the greatest, if he will but stick to the laws of the land and the statute books as they are delivered down from us to our forefathers.

BATES. You are right. We must lay our wits together and drive the widow out of your old master's head and put her into your young master's hands.

THOMAS. With all my heart; nothing can be more meritorious. Marry at his years! What a terrible account would he make of it, Mr. Bates. Let me see—on the debtor side sixty-five, and *per contra* creditor a buxom widow of twenty-three. He'll be a bankrupt in a fortnight. He, he, he!

BATES. And so he would, Mr. Thomas. What have you got in your hand?

THOMAS. A pamphlet my old gentleman takes in. He has left off buying histories and religious pieces by numbers, as he used to do, and since he has got this widow in his head he reads nothing but the Amorous Repository, Cupid's Revels, Call to Marriage, Hymen's Delights, Love Lies a Bleeding, Love in the Suds, and such like tender compositions.

BATES. Here he comes with all his folly about him.

THOMAS. Yes, and the first fool from vanity-fair. Heaven help us! Love turns man and woman topsy-turvy.

Exit Thomas.

WHITTLE (*without*). Where is he? Where is my good friend?

Enter Whittle.

Ha! Here he is. Give me your hand.

BATES. I am glad to see you in such spirits, my old gentleman.

125. sixty-five] 65 in all editions.
126. twenty-three] 23 in all editions.

WHITTLE. Not so old neither. No man ought to be called old, friend Bates, if he is in health, spirits, and –

BATES. In his senses–which I should rather doubt, as I never saw you half so frolicsome in my life.

WHITTLE. Never too old to learn, friend. And if I don't make use of my philosophy now, I may wear it out in twenty years. I have been always bantered as of too grave a cast. You know, when I studied at Lincoln's Inn they used to call me Young Wisdom.

BATES. And if they should now call you Old Folly it will be a much worse name.

WHITTLE. No young jackanapes dares call me so while I have this friend at my side. (*Touches his sword.*)

BATES. A hero too! What in the name of common sense is come to you, my friend? High spirits, quick honor, a long sword and a bag–you want nothing but to be terribly in love and sally forth Knight of the Woeful Countenance. Ha, ha, ha!

WHITTLE. Mr. Bates, the ladies, who are the best judges of countenances, are not of your opinion; and, unless you'll be a little serious, I must beg pardon for giving you this trouble, and I'll open my mind to some more attentive friend.

BATES. Well, come unlock then, you wild, handsome, vigorous young-dog, you. I will please you if I can.

WHITTLE. I believe you never saw me look better, Frank, did you?

BATES. Oh yes, rather better forty years ago.

WHITTLE. What, when I was at Merchant Tailor's School?

BATES. At Lincoln's Inn, too.

WHITTLE. It can't be. I never disguise my age, and next February I shall be fifty-four.

BATES. Fifty-four! Why I am sixty, and you always licked me at school, though I believe I could do as much for you now. And, ecod, I believe you deserve it, too.

WHITTLE. I tell you I am in my fifty-fifth year.

BATES. Oh, you are? Let me see–we were together at Cambridge, Anno Domini '25, which is near fifty years ago. You came to the college indeed surprisingly young, and, what is more surprising, by this calculation you went to school before you was born. You was always a forward child.

WHITTLE. I see there is no talking or consulting with you in this humor. And so, Mr. Bates, when you are in temper to show less of your wit and more of your friendship, I shall consult with you.

BATES. Fare you well, my old boy–young fellow, I mean. When you have done sowing your wild oats and have been blistered into your

173. fifty-fifth] 55th in all editions.

right senses; when you have half killed yourself with being a beau and return to your woolen caps, flannel waistcoats, worsted stockings, cork soles, and galochys, I am at your service again. So, bon jour to you, Monsieur Fifty-four, ha, ha!

Exit.

WHITTLE. He has certaiunly heard of my affair. But he is old and peevish; he wants spirit and strength of constitution to conceive my happiness. I am in love with the widow and must have her. Every man knows his own wants. Let the world laugh and my friends stare. Let 'em call me imprudent and mad, if they please. I live in good times and among people of fashion, so none of my neighbors, thank heaven, can have the assurance to laugh at me.

Enter Old Kecksy.

KECKSY. What, my friend Whittle. Joy, joy to you, old boy. You are going, a going, a going! A fine widow has bid for you and will have you, ha, friend? All for the best. There is nothing like it. Hugh, hugh, hugh! A good wife is a good thing, and a young one is a better, ha? Who's afraid? If I had not lately married one I should have been at death's door by this time. Hugh, hugh, hugh! (*Coughs.*)

WHITTLE. Thank, thank you, friend. I was coming to advise with you. I am got into the pound again—in love up to the ears. A fine woman, faith, and there's no love lost between us. Am I right, friend?

KECKSY. Right! Aye, right as my leg, Tom. Life's nothing without love. Hugh, hugh! I'm happy as the day's long. My wife loves gadding and I can't stay at home, so we are both of a mind. She's every night at one or other of the garden places; but, among friends, I am a little afraid of the damp. Hugh, hugh, hugh! She has got an Irish gentleman, a kind of cousin of hers, to take care of her, a fine fellow, and so goodnatured. It is a vast comfort to have such a friend in a family. Hugh, hugh, hugh!

WHITTLE. You are a bold man, cousin Kecksy.

KECKSY. Bold? Aye, to be sure. None but the brave deserve the fair. Hugh, hugh, hugh! Who's afraid?

WHITTLE. Why, your wife is five feet ten.

KECKSY. Without her shoes. I hate your little shrimps; none of your lean meagre French frogs for me. I was always fond of the majestic. Give me a slice of a good English sirloin, cut and come again. Hugh, hugh, hugh! That's my taste.

---

214. Hugh, hugh, hugh!] *O*1, *O*2, *O*3, *D*1, *D*2; Hugh! hugh! *O*4, *O*5.

Mrs. Barry and Wm. Parsons in *The Irish Widow.*
Harvard Theatre Collection

WHITTLE. I'm glad you have so good a stomach. And so you would advise me to marry the widow directly?

KECKSY. To be sure. You have not a moment to lose. I always mind what the poet says,

'Tis folly to lose time,
When man is in his prime.

Hugh, hugh, hugh!

WHITTLE. You have an ugly cough, cousin.

KECKSY. Marriage is the best lozenge for it.

WHITTLE. You have raised me from the dead. I am glad you came. Frank Bates had almost killed me with his jokes, but you have comforted me, and we will walk through the Park and I will carry you to the widow in Pall Mall.

KECKSY. With all my heart. I'll raise her spirits and yours too. Courage, Tom! come along. Who's afraid?

Exeunt.

SCENE [II], *the* Widow's *lodgings.*
Enter Widow, Nephew, *and* Bates.

BATES. Indeed, madam, there is no other way but to cast off your real character and assume a feigned one. It is an extraordinary occasion and requires extraordinary measures. Pluck up a spirit and do it for the honor of your sex.

NEPHEW. Only consider, my sweet Widow, that our all is at stake.

WIDOW. Could I bring my heart to act contrary to its feelings, would not you hate me for being a hypocrite, though it is done for your sake?

NEPHEW. Could I think myself incapable of such ingratitude?

WIDOW. Don't make fine speeches. You men are strange creatures. You turn our heads to your purposes and then despise us for the folly you teach us. 'Tis hard to assume a character contrary to my disposition. I cannot get rid of my unfashionable prejudices till I have been married in England some time and lived among my betters.

NEPHEW. Thou charming, adorable woman! What shall we do then? I never wished for a fortune till this moment.

WIDOW. Could we live upon affection, I would give your fortune to your uncle and thank him for taking it. And then –

NEPHEW. What then, my sweet Widow?

WIDOW. I would desire you to run away with me as fast as you can. What a pity it is that this money, which my heart despises, should hinder its happiness, or that for want of a few dirty acres, a poor woman must be made miserable and sacrificed twice to those who have them.

NEPHEW. Heaven forbid! These exquisite sentiments endear you more to me and distract me with the dread of losing you.

BATES. Young folks, let an old man who is not quite in love, and yet will admire a fine woman to the day of his death, throw in a little advice among your flames and darts.

WIDOW. Though a woman, a widow, and in love too, I can hear reason, Mr. Bates.

BATES. And that's a wonder. You have no time to lose. For want of a jointure you are still your father's slave. He is obstinate and has promised you to the old man. Now, madam, if you will not rise superior to your sex's weakness, to secure a young fellow instead of an old one, your eyes are a couple of hypocrites.

WIDOW. They are a couple of traitors, I'm sure, and have led their mistress into a toil from which all her wit cannot release her.

NEPHEW. But it can, if you will but exert it. My uncle adored and fell in love with you for your beauty, softness, and almost speechless reserve. Now, if amidst all his rapturous ideas of your delicacy you would bounce upon him a wild, ranting, buxom widow, he will grow sick of his bargain and give me a fortune to take you off his hands.

WIDOW. I shall make a very bad actress.

NEPHEW. You are an excellent mimic. Assume but the character of your Irish female neighbor in the country, with which you astonished us so agreeably at Scarborough, you will frighten my uncle into terms and do that for us which neither my love nor your virtue can accomplish without it.

WIDOW. Now for a trial. (*Mimicking a strong brogue.*) Fait and trot, if you will be after bringing me before the old jontleman, if he loves music, I will trate his ears with a little of the brogue, and some dancing too into the bargain, if he loves capering. Oh, bless me! My heart fails me and I am frightened out of my wits. I can never go through it. (Nephew *and* Bates *both laugh.*)

NEPHEW (*kneeling and kissing her hand*). Oh, 'tis admirable! Love himself inspires you, and we shall conquer. What say you, Mr. Bates?

BATES. I'll ensure your success. I can scarce believe my own ears. Such a tongue and a brogue would make Hercules tremble at five-and-twenty. But away, away, and give him the first broadside in the Park. There you'll find him hobbling with that old cuckold, Kecksy.

WIDOW. But will my dress suit the character I play?

NEPHEW. The very thing. Is your retinue ready and your part got by heart?

WIDOW. All is ready. 'Tis an act of despair to punish folly and reward merit. 'Tis the last effort of pure, honorable love. And if every woman would exert the same spirit for the same out-of-fashion rarity, there would be less business for Doctors Commons. Now let the critics laugh at me if they dare.

Exit with spirit.

NEPHEW. Brava! Bravissima! Sweet widow!

Exit after her.

BATES. Huzza! Huzza!

Exit.

SCENE [III], *the Park.*

Enter Whittle *and* Kecksy.

WHITTLE. Yes, yes, she is Irish, but so modest, so mild, and so tender, and just enough of the accent to give a peculiar sweetness to her words, which drop from her in monosyllables, with such a delicate reserve that I shall have all the comfort without the impertinence of a wife.

KECKSY. There our taste differs, friend. I am for a lively, smart girl in my house, hugh, hugh! to keep up my spirits and make me merry. I don't admire dumb waiters, not I. No still-life for me. I love their prittle prattle, it sets me to sleep, and I can take a sound nap while my Sally and her cousin are running and playing about the house like young cats.

WHITTLE. I am for no cats in my house. I cannot sleep with a noise. The widow was made on purpose for me. She is so bashful, has no acquaintance, and she never would stir out of doors if her friends were not afraid of a consumption, and so force her into the air. Such a delicate creature! You shall see her. You were always for a tall, chattering, frisky wench. Now for my part I am with the old saying,

Wife a mouse,
Quiet house;
Wife a cat,
Dreadful that.

KECKSY. I don't care for your sayings. Who's afraid?

8. I love their] *O*1, *O*2, *O*3, *O*4, *D*1, *D*2; I love the *O*5.

WHITTLE. There goes Bates. Let us avoid him; he will only be joking with us. When I have taken a serious thing into my head, I can't bear to have it laughed out again. This way, friend Kecksy. What have we got here?

KECKSY. Some fine, prancing wench, with her lovers and footman about her. She's a gay one by her motions.

WHITTLE. Were she not so flaunting, I should take it for—No, it is impossible; and yet is not that my nephew with her? I forbade him speaking to her. It can't be the widow; I hope it is not.

Enter Widow *followed by* Nephew, *three footmen and a black boy.*

WIDOW. Don't bother me, young man, with your darts, your cupids, and your pangs. If you had half of 'em about you that you swear you have, they would have cured you by killing you long ago. Would you have me faitless to your uncle, hah? young man? Was I not faitful to you till I was ordered to be faitful to him? But I must know more of your English ways, and live more among the English ladies, to learn how to be faitful to two at a time. And so there's my answer for you.

NEPHEW. Then I know my relief, for I cannot live without you.

Exit.

WIDOW. Take what relief you plase, young jontleman; what have I to do with dat? He is certainly mad or out of his sinses, for he swears he can't live without me, and yet he talks of killing himself. How does he make out dat? If a countryman of mine had made such a blunder, they would have put it into all the newspapers, and Falkner's Journal beside; but an Englishman may look over the hedge, while an Irishman must not stale a horse.

KECKSY. Is this the widow, friend Whittle?

WHITTLE. I don't know (*half sighing*) it is, and it is not!

WIDOW. Your servant, Mr. Whittol. I wish you would spake to your nephew not to be whining and dangling after me all day in his green coat like a parrot. It is not for my reputation that he should follow me about like a beggarman, and ask me for what I had given him long ago, but have since bestowed upon you, Mr. Whittol.

WHITTLE. He is an impudent beggar, and shall be really so for his disobedience.

WIDOW. As he can't live without me, you know, it will be charity to starve him. I wish the poor young man dead with all my heart, as he thinks it will do him a grate dale of good.

27.1. Stage direction inserted: KECKSY (*looking out*). O3, O4, O5.

KECKSY (*to* Whittle). She is tender, indeed, and I think she has the brogue a little. Hugh, hugh!

WHITTLE (*staring*). 'Tis stronger today than ever I heard it.

WIDOW. And are you now talking of my brogue? Is is always the most fullest when the wind is aesterly; it has the same effect upon me as upon stammering people. They can't spake for their impediment, and my tongue is fixed so loose in my mouth I can't stop it for the life of me.

WHITTLE. What a terrible misfortune, friend Kecksy!

KECKSY. Not at all. The more tongue the better, say I.

WIDOW. When the wind changes I have no brogue at all, at all. But come, Mr. Whittol, don't let us be vulgar and talk of our poor relations. It is impossible to be in this metropolis of London and have any thought but of operas, plays, masquerades, and panteons to keep up one's spirits in the winter, and Ranelagh, Vauxhall, and Marybone fireworks to cool and refresh one in the summer. (*Sings.*) La, la, la!

WHITTLE. I protest she puts me into a sweat; we shall have a mob about us.

KECKSY. The more the merrier, I say. Who's afraid?

WIDOW. How the people stare, as if they never saw a woman's voice before. But my vivacity has got the better of my good manners. This, I suppose, this strange gentleman, is a near friend and relation, and as such, notwithstanding his appearance, I shall always trate him, though I might dislike him upon a nearer acquaintance.

KECKSY. Madam, you do me honor. I like your frankness and I like your person, and I envy my friend Whittle, and if you were not engaged and I were not married I would endeavor to make myself agreeable to you, that I would. Hugh, hugh!

WIDOW. And indeed, sir, it would be very agraable to me; for if I should hate you as much as I did my first dare husband, I should always have the comfort that, in all human probability, my torments would not last long.

KECKSY. She utters something more than monosyllables, friend; this is better than bargain. She has a fine, bold way of talking.

WHITTLE. More bold than welcome. I am struck all of a heap.

WIDOW. What, are you low spirited, my dare Mr. Wittol? When you were at Scarborough and winning my affections you were all mirth and gaiety; and now you have won me, you are as thoughtful about it as if we had been married some time.

WHITTLE. Indeed, madam, I can't but say I am a little thoughtful. We take it by turns. You were very sorrowful a month ago for the loss

97. Mr. Wittol] *O*1, *O*2, *D*1, *D*2; Mr. Whittol *O*3, *O*4, *O*5.

of your husband, and that you could dry up your tears so soon naturally makes me a little thoughtful.

WIDOW. Indeed, I could dry up my tears for a dozen husbands, when I were sure of having a tirteenth like Mr. Wittol. That's very natural, sure, both in England, and Dublin too.

KECKSY. She won't die of a consumption; she has a fine full-toned voice, and you'll be very happy, Tom. Hugh, hugh!

WHITTLE (*aside*). Oh yes, very happy.

WIDOW. But come, don't let us be melancholy before the time. I am sure I have been moped up for a year and a half I was obliged to mourn for my first husband, that I might be sure of a second; and my father kept my spirits in subjection as the best receipt (he said) for changing a widow into a wife. But now I have my arms and legs at liberty, I must and will have my swing. Now I am out of my cage I could dance two nights togeder, and a day too, like any singing bird. And I'm in such spirits that I have got rid of my father, I could fly over the moon without wings and back again before dinner. Bless my eyes, and don't I see there Miss Nancy O'Flarty and her brother, Captain O'Flarty? He was one of my dying Strephons at Scarborough. I have a very grate regard for him and must make him a little miserable with my happiness (*curtsies*). Come along, Skips (*to the servants*), don't you be gostring there. Show your liveries and bow to your master that is to be, and to his friend, and hold up your heads and trip after me as lightly as if you had no legs to your feet. I shall be with you again, jontlemen, in the crack of a fan. [*Singing.*] Oh, I'll have a husband, ay marry.

Exit singing.

KECKSY. A fine buxom widow, faith! No acquaintance, delicate reserve, mopes at home, forced into the air, inclined to a consumption,—what a description you gave of your wife! Why, she beats my Sally, Tom.

WHITTLE. Yes, and she'll beat me if I don't take care. What a change is here! I must turn about, or this will turn my head. Dance for two nights together, and leap over the moon! You shall dance and leap by yourself, that I'm resolved.

KECKSY. Here she comes again. It does my heart good to see her. You are in luck, Tom.

WHITTLE. I'd give a finger to be out of such luck.

Enter Widow, *etc.*

---

106. Mr. Wittol] *O*1, *O*2, *D*1, *D*2; Mr. Whittol *O*3, *O*4, *O*5.
137. I'm resolved] *O*1, *O*2, *O*3, *O*4, D1, *D*2; I am *O*5.

WIDOW. Ha, ha, ha! The poor captain is marched off in a fury. He can't bear to hear that the town has capitulated to you, Mr. Wittol. I have promised to introduce him to you. He will make one of my danglers, to take a little exercise with me when you take your nap in the afternoon.

WHITTLE. You shan't catch me napping, I assure you. What a discovery and escape I have made! I am in a sweat with the thoughts of my danger.

KECKSY. I protest, cousin, there goes my wife and her friend Mr. MacBrawn. What a fine, stately couple they are! I must after 'em and have a laugh with them–now they giggle and walk quick, that I mayn't overtake 'em. Madam, your servant. You're a happy man, Tom. Keep up your spirits, old boy. Hugh, hugh! Who's afraid?

Exit.

WIDOW. I know Mr. MacBrawn extremely well. He was very intimate at our house, in my first husband's time. A great comfort he was to me, to be sure! He would very often leave his claret and companions for a little conversation with me. He was bred at the Dublin Univarsity and, being a very deep scholar, has fine talents for a tate a tate.

WHITTLE. She knows him too! I shall have my house overrun with the MacBrawns, O'Shoulders, and the blood of the Backwells. Lord have mercy upon me!

WIDOW. Pray, Mr. Wittol, is that poor spindle-legged crater of a cousin of yours lately married? Ha, ha, ha! I don't pity the poor crater his wife, for that agraable cough of his will soon reward her for all her sufferings.

WHITTLE (*aside*). What a delivery! a reprieve before the knot was tied.

WIDOW. Are you unwell, Mr. Wittol? I should be sorry you would fall sick before the happy day. Your being in danger afterwards would be a great consolation to me, because I should have the pleasure of nursing you myself.

WHITTLE. I hope never to give you that trouble, madam.

WIDOW. No trouble at all, at all. I assure you, sir, from my soul, that I shall take great delight in the occasion.

WHITTLE. Indeed, madam, I believe it.

WIDOW. I don't care how soon, the sooner the better and the more danger the more honor. I spake from my heart.

WHITTLE (*sighs*). And so do I from mine, madam.

WIDOW. But don't let us think of future pleasure and neglect present satisfaction. My mantua-maker is waiting for me to choose my clothes, in which I shall forget the sorrows of Mrs. Brady in the joys of Mrs. Wittol. Though I have a fortune myself, I shall bring a tolerable one to you, in debts, Mr. Wittol, and which I will pay you tinfold in tinderness; your deep purse and my open heart will make us the envy of the little grate ones and the grate little ones, the people of quality with no souls and grate souls with no cash at all. I hope you'll meet me at the Panteon this evening. Lady Rantiton and her daughter, Miss Nettledown, and Nancy Tittup, with half a dozen Maccaroonies and two savory vivers, are to take me there, and we propose a grate dale of chat and merriment, and dancing all night, and all other kind of recreations. I am quite another kind of a crater, now I am a bird in the fields. I can junket about for a week together; I have a fine constitution, and am never molested with your nasty vapors. Are you ever troubled with vapors, Mr. Whittol?

WHITTLE. A little now and then, madam.

WIDOW. I'll rattle 'em away like smoke. There are no vapors where I come. I hate your dumps and your nerves and your megrims; and I had much rather break your rest with a little racketting than let anything get into your head that should not be there, Mr. Whittol.

WHITTLE. I will take care that nothing shall be in my head but what ought to be there. (*Aside.*) What a deliverance!

WIDOW (*looking at her watch*). Bless me! How the hours of the clock creep away when we are plased with our company. But I must lave you, for there are half a hundred people waiting for me to pick your pocket, Mr. Wittol. And there is my own brother, Lieutenant O'Neale, is to arrive this morning, and he is so like me you would not know us asunder when we are together. You will be very fond of him, poor lad. He lives by his wits, as you do by your fortune, and so you may assist one another. Mr. Wittol, your obadient, 'till we meet at the Panteon. Follow me, Pompey; and Skips do you follow him.

POMPEY. The Baccararo whiteman no let blacky boy go first after you, missis; they pull and pinch me.

FOOTMAN. It is a shame, your ladyship, that a black negro should take place of English Christians. We can't follow him, indeed.

WIDOW. Then you may follow one another out of my sarvice. If you follow me you shall follow him, for he shall go before me. Can't I make him your superior, as the laws of the land have made him your aqual? Therefore resign as fast as you plase, you shan't oppose government and keep your places too. That is not good politics in England or Ireland either, so come along Pompay, be after going before me. Mr. Whittol, most tinderly yours.

Exit.

WHITTLE (*mimics her*). Most tinderly yours! 'Ecod I believe you are, and anybody's else. Oh, what an escape have I had! But how shall I clear myself of this business? I'll serve her as I would bad money, put her off into other hands. My nephew is fool enough to be in love with her, and if I give him a fortune he'll take the good and the bad together. He shall do so or starve. I'll send for Bates directly, confess my folly, ask his pardon, send him to my nephew, write and declare off with the Widow, and so get rid of her tinderness as fast as I can.

Exit.

End of the First Act.

ACT II.

A room in Whittle's *house.*
Enter Bates *and* Nephew.

NEPHEW (*taking him by the hand*). We are bound to you forever, Mr. Bates. I can say no more; words but ill express the real feelings of the heart.

BATES. I know you are a good lad, or I would not have meddled in the matter. But the business is not yet completed till *Signatum & Sigillatum.*

NEPHEW. Let me fly to the Widow and tell her how prosperously we go on.

BATES. Don't be in a hurry, young man. She is not in the dark, I assure you, nor has she yet finished her part. So capital an actress should not be idle in the last act.

NEPHEW. I could wish that you would let me come into my uncle's proposal at once, without vexing him farther.

BATES. Then I declare off. Thou silly young man, are you to be duped by your own weak good nature and his worldly craft? This does not arise from his love and justice to you, but from his own miserable situation. He must be tortured into justice; he shall not only give up your whole estate, which he is loath to part with, but you must now have a premium for agreeing to your own happiness. What, shall your widow, with wit and spirit that would do the greatest honor to our sex, go through her task cheerfully, and shall your courage give way and be outdone by a woman's? Fie, for shame!

NEPHEW. I beg your pardon, Mr. Bates. I will follow your directions, be as hard-hearted as my uncle, and vex his body and mind for the good of his soul.

BATES. That's a good child. And remember that your own and the Widow's future happiness depends upon your both going through this business with spirit. Make your uncle feel for himself, that he may do justice to other people. Is the Widow ready for the last experiment?

NEPHEW. She is; but think what anxiety I shall feel while she is in danger.

BATES. Ha, ha, ha! She'll be in no danger. Besides, shan't we be at hand to assist her? Hark! I hear him coming. I'll probe his callous heart to the quick, and if we are not paid for our trouble, say I am no politician. Fly—now we shall do!

Exit Nephew.

Enter Whittle.

[WHITTLE]. Well, Mr. Bates, have you talked with my nephew? Is not he overjoyed at the proposal?

BATES. The demon of discord has been among you and has untuned the whole family. You have screwed him too high. The young man is out of his senses, I think. He stares and mopes about and sighs; looks at me, indeed, but gives very absurd answers. I don't like him.

WHITTLE. What is the matter, think you?

BATES. What I have always expected. There is a crack in your family, and you take it by turns. You have had it, and now transfer it to your nephew, which, to your shame be it spoken, is the only transfer you have ever made him.

WHITTLE. But am I not going to do him more than justice?

BATES. As you have done him much less than justice hitherto, you can't begin too soon.

WHITTLE. Am not I going to give him the lady he likes, and which I was going to marry myself?

BATES. Yes, that is, you're taking a perpetual blister off your own back to clap it upon his. What a tender uncle you are!

WHITTLE. But you don't consider the estate which I shall give him.

BATES. *Restore* to him, you mean. 'Tis his own, and you should have given it up long ago. You must do more, or Old Nick will have you. Your nephew won't take the Widow off your hands without a fortune. Throw him ten thousand into the bargain.

WHITTLE. Indeed, but I shan't. He shall run mad and I'll marry her myself rather than do that. Mr. Bates, be a true friend and soothe my nephew to consent to my proposal.

BATES. You have raised the fiend and ought to lay him. However, I'll do my best for you. When the head is turned, nothing can bring it right again so soon as ten thousand pounds. Shall I promise for you?

WHITTLE. I'll sooner go to Bedlam myself.

Exit Bates.

Why, I am in a worse condition than I was before! If this widow's father will not let me be off without providing for his daughter, I may lose a great sum of money, and none of us be the better for it. My nephew half-mad, myself half-married, and no remedy for either of us!

Enter Servant.

[SERVANT]. Sir Patrick O'Neale is come to wait upon you. Would you please to see him?

WHITTLE. By all means, the very person I wanted. Don't let him wait.

Exit Servant.

I wonder if he has seen my letter to the Widow. I will sound him by degrees, that I may be sure of my mark before I strike the blow.

Enter Sir Patrick.

SIR PATRICK. Mr. Whizzle, your humble sarvent. It gives me grate pleasure that an old jontleman of your property will have the honor of being united with the family of the O'Neale's. We have been too much jontlemen not to spend our estate, as you have made yourself a kind of jontleman by getting one. One runs out one way and t'other runs in another, which makes them both meet at last and keeps up the balance of Europe.

WHITTLE. I am much obliged to you, Sir Patrick. I am an old gentleman, you say true; and I was thinking –

SIR PATRICK. And I was thinking if you were ever so old, my daughter can't make you young again. She has as fine rich tick blood in her veins as any in all Ireland. I wish you had a swate crater of a daughter like mine, that we might make a double cross of it.

WHITTLE (*aside*). That would be a double cross indeed!

SIR PATRICK. Though I was miserable enough with my first wife, who had the devil of a spirit and the very model of her daughter, yet a brave man never shrinks from danger, and I may have better luck another time.

WHITTLE. Yes, but I am no brave man, Sir Patrick, and I begin to shrink already.

SIR PATRICK. I have bred her up in great subjiction. She is as tame as a young colt and as tinder as a sucking chicken. You will find her a true jontlewoman, and so knowing that you can tache her nothing. She brings everything but money, and you have enough of that if you have nothing else, and that is what I call the balance of things.

WHITTLE. But I have been considering your daughter's great deserts and my great age.

SIR PATRICK. She is a charming crater. I would venture to say that, if I was not her father.

WHITTLE. I say, sir, as I have been considering your daughter's great deserts, and as I own I have great demerits –

SIR PATRICK. To be sure you have, but you can't help that. And if my daughter was to mention anything of a fleering at your age or your stinginess, by the balance of power but I would make her repate it a hundred times to your face to make her ashamed of it. But mum, old gentleman, the devil a word of your infirmities will she touch upon. I have brought her up to softness and to gentleness, as a kitten to new milk. She will spake nothing but "No" and "Yes," as if she were dumb. And no tame rabbit or pigeon will keep house or be more inganious with her needle and tambourine.

WHITTLE. She is vastly altered then since I saw her last, or I have lost my senses; and in either case we had much better, since I must speak plain, not come together –

SIR PATRICK. 'Till you are married, you mean–with all my heart; it is the more gentale for that, and like our family. I never saw Lady O'Nale, your mother-in-law, who poor crater is dead and can never be a mother-in-law again, 'till the week before I married her, and I did not care if I had never seen her then, which is a comfort too in case of death or other accidents of life.

WHITTLE. But you don't understand me, Sir Patrick, I say –

SIR PATRICK. I say, how can that be, when we both spake English?

WHITTLE. But you mistake my meaning and don't comprehend me.

SIR PATRICK. Then you don't comprehend yourself, Mr. Whizzle, and I have not the gift of prophecy to find out after you have spoke what never was in you.

WHITTLE. Let me intreat you to attend to me a little.

SIR PATRICK. I do attend, man; I don't interrupt you. Out with it.

WHITTLE. Your daughter –

SIR PATRICK. Your wife that is to be. Go on.

WHITTLE. My wife that is *not* to be! Zounds, will you hear me?

SIR PATRICK. To be or *not* to be, is that the question? I can swear too, if it wants a little of that.

WHITTLE. Dear Sir Patrick, hear me. I confess myself unworthy of her. I have the greatest regard for you, Sir Patrick. I should think myself honored by being in your family, but there are many reasons –

SIR PATRICK. To be sure there are many reasons why an old man should not marry a young woman; but as that was your business and not mine –

WHITTLE. I have wrote a letter to your daughter which I was in hopes you had seen and had brought me an answer to it.

SIR PATRICK. What the devil, Mr. Wizzle, do you make a letter-porter of me? Do you imagine, you dirty fellow with your cash, that Sir Patrick O'Nale would carry your letters? I would have you know that I despise letters and all that belong to 'em, nor would I carry a letter to the king, heaven bless him, unless it came from myself.

WHITTLE. But, dear Sir Patrick, don't be in a passion for nothing.

SIR PATRICK. What, is it nothing to make a penny postman of me? But I'll go to my daughter directly, for I have not seen her today, and if I find that you have written anything that I won't understand, I shall take it an affront to my family; and you shall either let out the noble blood of the O'Nales or we will spill the last drop of the red puddle of the Wizzels. (*Going and returns.*) Harkee, old Mr. Wizzle, Whezzle, Whistle, what's your name? You must not stir till I come back. If you offer to ate, drink, or sleep, till my honor is satisfied, 'twill be the worst male you ever took in your life. You had better fast a year and die at the end of six months than dare to lave your house. So now, Mr. Weezle, you are to do as you plase.

Exit.

WHITTLE. Now the devil is at work indeed. If some miracle don't save me, I shall run mad like my nephew and have a long Irish sword through me into the bargain. While I am in my senses I won't have the woman; and therefore he that is out of them shall have her, if I give half my fortune to make the match. Thomas!

Enter Thomas.

Sad work, Thomas!

THOMAS. Sad work, indeed. Why would you think of marrying? I knew what it would come to.

WHITTLE. Why, what has it come to?

THOMAS. It is in all the papers.

WHITTLE. So much the better; then nobody will believe it.

THOMAS. But they come to me to enquire.

WHITTLE. And you contradict it.

THOMAS. What signifies that? I was telling Lady Gabble's footman at the door just now that it was all a lie, and your nephew looks out of the two-pair-of-stairs window, with eyes all on fire, and

163. Harkee, old] *O1*, *O2*; Harkee, you *O3*, *O4*, *O5*, *D1*, *D2*.

tells the whole story. Upon that, there gathered such a mob.

WHITTLE. I shall be murdered, and have my house pulled down into the bargain.

THOMAS. It is all quiet again. I told them the young man was out of his senses and that you were out of town, so they went away quietly and said they would come and mob you another time.

WHITTLE. Thomas, what shall I do?

THOMAS. Nothing you have done, if you will have matters mend.

WHITTLE. I am out of my depth, and you won't lend me your hand to draw me out.

THOMAS. You were out of your depth to fall in love. Swim away as fast as you can, you'll be drowned if you marry.

WHITTLE. I'm frightened out of my wits. Yes, yes, 'tis all over with me. I must not stir out of my house, but am ordered to stay to be murdered in it for aught I know. What are you muttering, Thomas? Prithee, speak out and comfort me.

THOMAS. It is all a judgment upon you. Because your brother's foolish will says the young man must have your consent, you won't let him have her but will marry the Widow yourself. That's the dog in the manger; you can't eat the oats, and won't let those who can.

WHITTLE. But I consent that he shall have both the Widow and the fortune, if we can get him into his right senses.

THOMAS. For fear I should lose mine, I'll get out of Bedlam as soon as possible. You must provide yourself with another servant.

WHITTLE. The whole earth conspires against me! You shall stay with me till I die, and then you shall have a good legacy. And I won't live long, I promise you.

Knocking at the door.

THOMAS. Here are the undertakers already.

Exit.

WHITTLE. What shall I do? My head can't bear it. I will hang myself for fear of being run through the body.

Thomas *returns with bills.*

THOMAS. Half a score of people I never saw before, with these bills and draughts upon you for payment signed Martha Brady.

WHITTLE. I wish Martha Brady was at the bottom of the Thames. What an impudent, extravagant baggage to begin her tricks already! Send them to the devil and say I won't pay a farthing.

THOMAS (*going*). You'll have another mob about the door.

WHITTLE. Stay, stay, Thomas. Tell them I am very busy and they must come tomorrow morning. Stay, stay, that is promising payment. No, no, no—tell 'em they must stay till I am married, and so they will be satisfied and tricked into the bargain.

THOMAS (*aside*). When you are tricked we shall all be satisfied.

Exit.

WHITTLE. That of all dreadful things I should think of a woman, and that woman should be a widow, and that widow should be an Irish one—*quem deus vult perdere*. Who have we here? Another of the family, I suppose. (Whittle *retires.*)

Enter Widow *as Lieutenant O'Neale, seemingly fluttered and putting up his sword,* Thomas *following.*

THOMAS. I hope you are not hurt, Captain.

WIDOW. Oh not at all, at all. 'Tis well they run away, or I should have made them run faster. I shall teach them how to snigger and look through glasses at their betters. These are your Maccaroons, as they call themselves; by my soul but I would frightened their hair out of buckle, if they would have stood still till I had overtaken them. These whipper-snappers look so much more like girls in breeches than those I see in petticoats, that, fait and trot, it is a pity to hurt 'em. The fair sex in London here seem the most masculine of the two. But to business, friend; where is your master?

THOMAS. There, Captain. I hope he has not offended you.

WIDOW. If you are impartinent, sir, you will offend me. Lave the room.

THOMAS (*aside to his master*). I value my life too much not to do that. What a rawboned tartar! I wish he had not been caught and sent here.

Exit.

WHITTLE [*aside*]. Her brother, by all that's terrible, and as like her as two tigers! I sweat at the sight of him. I'm sorry Thomas is gone; he has been quarreling already.

WIDOW. Is your name Wittol?

WHITTLE. My name is Whittle, not Wittol.

WIDOW. We shan't stand for trifles. And you were born and christened by the name of Thomas?

WHITTLE. So they told me, sir.

WIDOW. Then they told no lies, fait; so far, so good. (*Takes out a letter.*) Do you know that handwriting?

234–35. frightened . . . if they would] *O1*, *O2*, *O3*, *D1*, *D2*; deleted in *O4*, *O5*—"I would have stood, *etc.*"

250. not Wittol] *O1*, *O2*, *D1*, *D2*; not Whittol *O3*, *O4*, *O5*.

WHITTLE. As well as I know this good friend of mine, who helps me upon such occasions. (*Showing his right hand and smiling.*)

WIDOW. You had better not show your teeth, sir, 'till we come to the jokes. The handwriting is yours.

WHITTLE. Yes, sir, it is mine. (*Sighs.*)

WIDOW. Death and powder! What do you sigh for? Are you ashamed or sorry for your handiworks?

WHITTLE. Partly one, partly t'other.

WIDOW. Will you be plased, sir, to rade it aloud, that you may know it again when you hare it?

WHITTLE (*takes his letter and reads*). Madam –

WIDOW. Would you be plased to let us know what madam you mean? for women of quality, and women of no quality, and women of all qualities, are so mixed together, that you don't know one from t'other, and are all called *madams.* You should always rade the subscription before you open the letter.

WHITTLE. I beg your pardon, sir. (*Aside.*) I don't like this ceremony. "To Mrs. Brady in Pall Mall."

WIDOW. Now prosade. Fire and powder, but I would –!

WHITTLE. Sir! What's the matter?

WIDOW. Nothing at all, Sir; pray go on.

WHITTLE (*reads*). "Madam–as I prefer your happiness to the indulgence of my own passions –

WIDOW. I will not prefer *your* happiness to the indulgence of my passions–Mr. Wittol, rade on.

WHITTLE. "I must confess that I am unworthy of your charms and virtues –

WIDOW. Very unworthy indeed; rade on, Sir.

WHITTLE. "I have for some days had a severe struggle between my justice and my passion –

WIDOW. I have had no struggle at all. My justice and passion are agreed.

WHITTLE. "The former has prevailed, and I beg leave to resign you, with all your accomplishments, to some more deserving though not more admiring, servant than your most miserable and devoted, Thomas Whittle."

WIDOW. And miserable and devoted you shall be to the postscript. Rade on.

WHITTLE. "Postscript: Let me have your pity but not your anger."

WIDOW. In answer to this love epistle, you pitiful fellow, my sister presents you with her tinderest wishes and assures you that you have, as you desire, her pity, and she generously throws her contempt too into the bargain.

WHITTLE. I'm infinitely obliged to her.

WIDOW. I must beg lave in the name of all our family to present the same to you.

WHITTLE. I am ditto to all the family.

WIDOW. But as a brache of promise to any of our family was never suffered without a brache into somebody's body, I have fixed upon myself to be your operator. And I believe that you will find that I have as fine a hand at this work, and will give you as little pain, as any in the three kingdoms. (*Sits down and loosens her knee-bands.*)

WHITTLE. For heaven's sake, Captain, what are you about?

WIDOW. I always loosen my garters for the advantage of lunging. It is for your sake as well as my own, for I will be twice through your body before you shall feel me once. (*She seems to practice.*)

WHITTLE (*aside*). What a bloody fellow it is! I wish Thomas would come in.

WIDOW. Come, sir, prepare yourself. You are not the first by half a score that I have run through and through the heart before they knew what was the matter with them.

WHITTLE. But, Captain, suppose I will marry your sister.

WIDOW. I have not the laste objection, if you recover of your wounds. Callagon O'Conner lives very happy with my great aunt, Mrs. Deborah O'Nale, in the county of Galloway—except a small asthma he got by my running him through the lungs at the Currough. He would have forsaken her, if I had not stopped his perfidy by a famous family kiptic I have here. Oho, my little old boy, but you shall get it. (*Draws.*)

WHITTLE. What shall I do? Well, sir, if I must—I must. I'll meet you tomorrow morning in Hyde Park, let the consequences be what it will.

WIDOW. For fear you might forget that favor, I must beg to be indulged with a little pushing now. I have set my heart upon it, and two birds in hand is worth one in the bushes, Mr. Wittol. Come, sir.

WHITTLE. But I have not settled my matters.

WIDOW. Oh, we'll settle 'em in a trice, I warrant you. (*Puts himself in a position.*)

WHITTLE. But I don't understand the sword. I had rather fight with pistols.

WIDOW. I am very happy it is in my power to oblige you. There, sir, take your choice. (*Offers pistols.*) I will plase you if I can.

WHITTLE [*aside*]. Out of the pan into the fire; there's no putting him off. If I had chosen poison I dare swear he had arsenic in his pocket. —Lookee, young gentleman, I am an old man, and you'll get no

322. kiptic] *O1*, *O2*, *D1*, *D2*; stiptic *O3*, *O4*, *O5*.
331. *himself*] *O1*, *O2*, *D1*, *D2*; herself *O3*, *O4*, *O5*.

credit by killing me. But I have a nephew as young as yourself, and you'll get more honor in facing him.

WIDOW. Aye, and more pleasure too! I expect ample satisfaction from him, after I have done your business. Prepare, sir.

WHITTLE. What the devil, won't one serve your turn? I can't fight and I won't fight. I'll do anything rather than fight; I'll marry your sister; my nephew shall marry her; I'll give him all my fortune. What would the fellow have? Here, nephew! Thomas! Murder, murder! (*He flies and she pursues.*)

Enter Bates *and* Nephew.

NEPHEW. What's the matter, uncle?

WHITTLE. Murder, that's all. That ruffian there would kill me and eat me afterwards.

NEPHEW. I'll find a way to cool him. Come out, sir; I am as mad as yourself. I'll match you, I warrant you. (*Going out with him.*)

WIDOW. I'll follow you all the world over. (*Going after him.*)

WHITTLE. Stay, stay, nephew; you shan't fight. We shall be exposed all over the town, and you may lose your life, and I shall be cursed from morning to night. Do, nephew, make yourself and me happy. Be the olive-branch and bring peace into my family. Return to the Widow. I will give you my consent and your fortune, and a fortune for the Widow, five thousand pounds! Do persuade him, Mr. Bates.

BATES. Do, sir, this is the very critical point of your life. I know you love her; 'tis the only method to restore us all to our senses.

NEPHEW. I must talk in private first, with this hot young gentleman.

WIDOW. As private as you plase, sir.

WHITTLE. Take their weapons away, Mr. Bates, and do you follow me to my study to witness my proposal. It is all ready and only wants signing. Come along, come along.

Exit.

BATES. Victoria! Victoria! Give me your swords and pistols, and now do your worst, you spirited loving young couple. I could leap out of my skin!

Exit.

THOMAS (*peeping in*). Joy, joy to you, ye fond charming pair! The fox is caught, and the young lambs may skip and play. I leave you to your transports!

Exit.

NEPHEW. Oh, my charming Widow! What a day have we gone through!

WIDOW. I would go through ten times as much to deceive an old amorous rogue like your uncle, to purchase a young one like his nephew.

NEPHEW. I listened at the door all this last scene; my heart was agitated with ten thousand fears. Suppose my uncle had been stout and drawn his sword?

WIDOW. I should have run away as he did. When two cowards meet, the struggle is who shall run first; and sure I can bate an old man at anything.

NEPHEW. Permit me thus to seal my happiness, (*Kisses her hand.*) and be assured that I am as sensible as I think myself undeserving of it.

WIDOW. I'll tell you what, Mr. Wittol, were I not sure you deserved some pains, I would not have taken any pains for you. And don't imagine now, because I have gone a little too far for the man I love, that I shall go a little too far when I'm your wife, indeed I shan't. I have done more than I should before I am your wife because I was in despair. But I won't do as much as I may, when I am your wife, though every Irish woman is fond of imitating her English betters.

NEPHEW. Thou divine, adorable woman! (*Kneels and kisses her hand.*)

Enter Whittle *and* Bates. Whittle *stares.*

BATES (*aside*). Confusion!

WHITTLE (*turning to Bates*). Hey day! I am afraid his head is not right yet! He was kneeling and kissing the Captain's hand. (*Aside to* Bates.)

BATES (*aside to* Whittle). Take no notice; all will come about.

WIDOW. I find, Mr. Whittol, your family loves kissing better than fighting. He swears I am as like my sister as two pigeons. I could excuse his raptures, for I had rather fight the best friend I have than slobber and salute him *a la françoise.*

Enter Sir Patrick O'Neale.

SIR PATRICK. I hope, Mr. Whizzle, you'll excuse my coming back to give you an answer, without having any to give. I hear a grate dale of news about myself, and came to know if it be true. They say my son is in London, when he tells me himself by letter here that he's at Limerick. And I have been with my daughter to tell her the news, but she would not stay at home to receave it. So I am

---

377. rogue] *O1*, *O2*, *D1*, *D2*; spark *O3*, *O4*, *O5*.
383. bate] *O1*, *O2*; beat *O3*, *O4*, *O5*, *D1*, *D2*.
387. Mr. Wittol] *O1*, *O2*; Mr. Whittle *D1*, *D2*; Sir *O3*, *O4*, *O5*.
393–94. her English betters] *O1*, *O2*, *D1*, *D2*; English fashions *O3*, *O4*, *O5*.

come—*O gra ma chree my little din ousil craw*, what have we got here? A piece of mummery! Here is my son and daughter too, fait. What, are you waring the breeches, Pat, to see how they become you when you are Mrs. Weezel?

WIDOW. I beg your pardon for that, sir. I wear them before marriage, because I think they become a woman better than after.

WHITTLE. What, is not this your son?

SIR PATRICK. No, but it is my daughter, and that is the same thing.

WIDOW. And your niece. sir, which is still better than either.

WHITTLE. Mighty well! And I suppose *you* have not lost your wits, young man!

BATES. I sympathize with you, sir. We lost 'em together and found 'em at the same time.

WHITTLE. Here's villainy! Mr. Bates, give me the paper. Not a farthing shall they have 'till the law gives it 'em.

BATES. We'll cheat the law and give it them now. (*Gives* Nephew *the paper.*)

WHITTLE. He may take his own, but he shan't have a sixpence of the five thousand pounds I promised him.

BATES. Witness, good folks, he owns to the promise.

SIR PATRICK. Fait, I'll witness dat, or anythink else in a good cause.

WHITTLE. What, am I choused again?

BATES. Why should not my friend be choused out of a little justice for the first time? Your hard usage has sharpened your nephew's wits; therefore beware, don't play with edgetools—you'll only cut your fingers.

SIR PATRICK. And your trote too, which is all one. Therefore, to make all asy, marry my daughter first and then quarrel with her afterwards. That will be in the natural course of things.

WHITTLE. Here, Thomas! Where are you?

Enter Thomas.

Here are fine doings! I am deceived, tricked, and cheated!

THOMAS. I wish you joy, sir; the best thing could have happened to you. And as a faithful servant I have done my best to check you.

WHITTLE. To check me?

THOMAS. You were galloping full speed and down hill too, and if we had not laid hold of the bridle, being a bad jockey, you would have hung by the horns in the stirrup, to the great joy of the whole town.

WHITTLE. What, have *you* helped to trick me?

THOMAS. Into happiness. You have been foolish a long while; turn

429. anythink] *O*1, *O*2; anything *O*3, *O*4, *O*5, *D*1, *D*2.
445. by the horns] *O*1, *O*2, *D*1, *D*2; by your horns *O*3, *O*4, *O*5.

about and be wise. He has got the woman and his estate. Give them your blessing, which is not worth much, and live like a Christian for the future.

WHITTLE. I will if I can, but I can't look at 'em. I can't bear the sound of my voice nor the sight of my face. Look ye, I am distressed and distracted, and can't come to yet. I will be reconciled, if possible, but don't let me see or hear from you, if you would have me forget and forgive you. I shall never lift up my head again!

Exit.

WIDOW. I hope, Sir Patrick, that my preferring the nephew to the uncle will meet with your approbation; though we have not so much money, we shall have more love. One mind and half a purse in marriage are much better than two minds and two purses. I did not come to England, nor keep good company, till it was too late to get rid of my country prejudices.

SIR PATRICK. You are out of my hands, Pat. So, if you won't trouble me with your afflictions, I shall sincerely rejoice at your felicity.

NEPHEW. It would be a great abatement of my present joy, could I believe that this lady should be assisted in her happiness, or be supported in her afflictions, by anyone but her lover and her husband.

SIR PATRICK. Fine notions are fine tings, but a fine estate gives everyting but idaas, and them too, if you'll appale to those who help you to spend it. What say you, Widow?

WIDOW. By your and their permission I will tell them to this good company. And for fear my words should want ideas too, I will add an Irish tune to 'em that may carry off a bad voice and bad matter.

SONG.

A Widow bewitched with her passion,
Tho' Irish, is now quite ashamed,
To think that she's so out of fashion,
To marry and then to be tamed:
'Tis love the dear joy,
That old fashioned boy,
Has got in my breast with his quiver;
The blind archin he,
Struck the *Cush la maw cree*,
And a husband secures me forever!
Ye fair ones I hope will excuse me,
Though vulgar pray do not abuse me;

452. of my face] *O*1, *O*2, *D*1, *D*2; of my own face *O*3, *O*4, *O*5.
470. tell them] *O*1, *O*2, *D*1, *D*2; tell my mind *O*3, *O*4, *O*5.

I cannot become a fine lady,
O love has bewitched Widow Brady.

II.

Ye critics to murder so willing,
Pray see all our errors with blindness;
For once change your method of killing,
And kill a fond Widow with kindness!
If you look so severe,
In a fit of despair,
Again I will draw forth my steel, Sirs,
You know I've the art,
To be twice through your heart,
Before I can make you to feel, Sirs:
Brother soldiers I hope you'll protect me,
Nor let cruel critics dissect me;
To favor my cause be but ready,
And grateful you'll find Widow Brady.

III.

Ye leaders of dress and the fashions,
Who gallop post haste to your ruin,
Whose taste has destroyed all your passions,
Pray, what do you think of my wooing?
You call it damn low,
Your heads and arms so, (*mimics them.*)
So listless, so loose, and so lazy:
But pray what can you,
That I cannot do?
O fie, my dear craters, be azy:
Ye patriots and courtiers so hearty,
To speach it and vote for your party,
For once be both constant and steady,
And vote to support Widow Brady.

IV.

To all that I see here before me,
The bottom, the top, and the middle,
For music we now must implore you,
No wedding without pipe and fiddle:
If all are in tune,
Pray let it be soon,
My heart in my bosom is prancing!
If your hands should unite,
To give us delight,

O that's the best piping and dancing!
  Your plaudits to me are a treasure,
  Your smiles are a dow'r for a lady;
  O joy to you all in full measure,
  So wishes, and prays Widow Brady.

Finis.

A Christmas Tale

A New Dramatic Entertainment

1773

A NEW

DRAMATIC ENTERTAINMENT,

CALLED

A Christmas Tale.

IN FIVE PARTS.

AS IT IS PERFORMED AT THE

THEATRE-ROYAL

IN

DRURY-LANE.

Embellished with an Etching, by Mr. *Loutherbourg*

LONDON:
Printed for T. BECKET, in the Strand.
MDCCLXXIV.

[Price One Shilling and Six-pence.]

Facsimile title page of the First Edition.
Folger Shakespeare Library.

Advertisement

The writer of the following Tale begs leave to make his acknowledgments to the public, for their very favorable reception of it. He hopes that the success attending this attempt, so well supported by the Scenery, Music, and Performers, will excite superior talents to productions of the same kind, more worthy of their approbation.

Prologue

Music plays, and several persons enter with different kind of dishes. After them Mr. Palmer, *in the character of* Christmas.

Go on—prepare my bounty for my friends,
And see that mirth with all her crew attends:

To the AUDIENCE.

Behold a personage well known to fame;
Once loved and honored—Christmas is my name!
My officers of state my taste display;
Cooks, scullions, pastry-cooks, prepare my way!
Holly and ivy round me honors spread,
And my retinue show I'm not ill-fed.
Minced pies by way of belt my breast divide,
And a large carving knife adorns my side;
'Tis no fop's weapon, 'twill be often drawn;
This turban for my head is collar'd brawn!
Tho' old and white my locks, my cheeks are cherry,
Warmed by good fires, good cheer, I'm always merry:
With carol, fiddle, dance, and pleasant tale,
Jest, gibe, prank, gambol, mummery and ale,
I, English hearts rejoiced in day of yore;
For new strange modes, imported by the score,
You will not sure turn Christmas out of door!
Suppose yourselves well-seated by a fire,
(Stuck close, you seem more warm than you desire)
Old Father Christmas now in all his glory,
Begs with kind hearts you'll listen to his story.
Clear well your minds from politics and spleen,
Hear my Tale out—see all that's to be seen!

Take care, my children, that you well behave;
You, Sir, in blue, red cape—not quite so grave.
That critic there in black—so stern and thin,
Before you frown, pray let the Tale begin —
You in the crimson capuchin, I fear you;
Why, Madam, at this time so cross appear you?
Excuse me, pray—I did not see your husband near you.
Don't think, fair ladies, I expect that you
Should hear my Tale—you've something else to do.
Nor will our beaux old English fare encourage;
No foreign taste could e'er digest plumb-porridge.
I have no sauce to quicken lifeless sinners,
My food is meant for * honest hearty grinners!
For you—you spirits with good stomachs bring;
O make the neighb'ring roof with rapture ring;
Open your mouths, pray swallow everything!
Critics beware, how you our pranks despise;
Hear well my Tale, or you shan't touch my pies;
The proverb change—be merry, but not wise.

* To the upper gallery.

Dramatis Personae

Men

Bonoro, *Good Magician*	Mr. *Bannister*,
Floridor, *his Son*	Mr. *Vernon*,
Tycho, *his 'Squire*	Mr. *Weston*,
Faladel, *Gentleman-Usher*	Mr. *Parsons*,
Nigromant, *Bad Magician*	Mr. *Champness*,
Radel	Mr. *Dimond*,
Messengers	Mr. *Griffith*, Master *Blanchard*.

Women

Camilla	Mrs. *Smith*,
Robinette	Mrs. *Wrighten*.

Good and Evil Spirits, *in various Characters, by*

Mr. *Hurst*,	Mr. *Ackman*,	Mr. *W. Palmer*,
Mr. *Wright*,	Mr. *Wrighten*,	Mr. *Courtney*,
Miss *Platt*,	Mrs. *Johnston*,	Mrs. *Bradshaw*,
Mrs. *Millidge*,	Mrs. *Scott*, &c. &c. &c.	

Dances

By Sig. Como	Mr. *Atkins*,	Mr. *Georgi*,
Signora Crespi	Mrs. *Sutton*,	Mrs. *Georgi*, &c.

The Scenery *invented by* Mr. De Loutherbourg.

Musick, by Mr. Dibdin

A Christmas Tale

PART I.

SCENE I, *A beautiful Landskip.*
Enter Robinette.

ROBINETTE. Tycho, Tycho! where are you Tycho? Sure the fellow has taken me at my word and gone to hang or drown himself. He threatened both. Lovers are great bullies and swear a thousand things they never intend to perform. If the poor woman shows any fear the bullies rave the more, and she gives up at once that noblest privilege of the sex, making the wisest fools and the stoutest miserable. I have a tongue to be sure that moves quick, and by outrunning my wit sometimes may encourage young coxcombs to hope too much. But then my heart all the while, poor thing, knows nothing of the matter and feels no more than my shoe knots.

SONG.

My eyes may speak pleasure,
Tongue flow without measure,
Yet my heart in my bosom lies still;
Thus the river is flowing,
The mill-clapper going,
But the miller's asleep in his mill.
Though lovers surround me,
With speeches confound me,
Yet my heart in my bosom lies still;
Thus the river is flowing,
The mill-clapper going,
But the miller's asleep in his mill.
The little God eyes me,

0.3. *Landskip*] *O1*, *O2*, *O3*, *O4*; *Landscape D1*.

And thinks to surprise me,
But my heart is awake in my breast;
Thus boys slyly creeping,
Would catch a bird sleeping,
But the linnet's awake in his nest.

Where can this Tycho have hid himself? I'm sure he went this way. Stay, is not that my gentleman creeping along the side of the canal? It is either he, my other lover, Faladel, or the monkey in his new livery. I must give him a little more hope, or we shall have no more sport with him.

Exit Robinette.

TYCHO (*peeping out of a tree*). There's a hard-hearted she-devil for you. Do I look like a monkey in a new livery? I don't know how love may have altered me, but I know a few weeks ago that I had the best face in this island, or my glass is a deceiver of youth. If I had not so much tenderness in my composition, I would play the devil among these petticoats. But here she comes again, and I can't say boo to her for the life of me.

Re-enter Robinette.

ROBINETTE. It was the monkey. And a very pretty fellow he is, now that he is well dressed. (Tycho *sighs in the tree*.) La, what's that? Did not I hear somebody sigh? It must be my lover. Tycho! Where are you, Tycho?

TYCHO (*in the tree and out of sight*). Here am I! (*Sighing*.)

ROBINETTE. Where?

TYCHO (*sighing*). Here.

ROBINETTE. Where, I say? Pray show your sweet face.

TYCHO (*peeping out*). Here it is. When you lose this, you won't get a better.

ROBINETTE. Not 'till I buy a gingerbread one. What are you doing there?

TYCHO. I was going to hang myself for love. But having left the cord behind me, I fell asleep 'till you wakened me. Pray lend me your garters, for I will not live, that I am resolved. (*Sighing*.)

ROBINETTE. Come down and I'll lend you anything. (*Aside*.) What can I possibly do with this strange animal?

Enter Tycho.

TYCHO. Here am I.

ROBINETTE. What is it you want?

---

41. that] *O*1, *O*2, *O*3, *O*4; that omitted *D*1.

TYCHO. Death or you. I must have one of you.

ROBINETTE. Have not I told you often, and I will now repeat it, that I can't leave Camilla. Let but Floridor, your friend, get the consent of Camilla, my friend, then I Robinette, her friend, take you Tycho, his friend. What would the fellow have?

TYCHO (*muttering*). *Your* friend and *my* friend and *his* friend and *her* friend! Then all are friends. Isn't it so?

ROBINETTE. To be sure. Now go about your business.

TYCHO. O bless me, now I am come to myself. I must send Floridor immediately to his father upon special matters. I thought to make away with myself and quite forgot it.

ROBINETTE. Floridor is as violent in love as you are melancholy. You must both mend your manners or Camilla and I shall look out for others. No more melancholy, Tycho, if you love and would win me.

TYCHO (*sighing*). Am I too melancholy for you?

ROBINETTE. Too melancholy? Your face seems preparing for a funeral instead of looking out for a wedding. I hate melancholy and all melancholy people. A cloudy face betokens a cloudy heart, and I will have neither. Never will I sail to the port of matrimony but with a smiling sea and a clear sky. That's the way to make a good voyage of it.

TYCHO. And so it is, faith. He, he, he! My face will become smiles as well as a great deal of thinking. I have studied myself into melancholy, but I'll burn my books and be as merry as you please to make me. He, he, he!

ROBINETTE. Now you dance about my heart and will certainly run away with it.

TYCHO. He, he, he! But where's Faladel, Robinette?

ROBINETTE. Perhaps sleeping in some tree for love of me as you did.

TYCHO (*sighing*). If he would do the other thing for you I should be very happy.

ROBINETTE. Melancholy and jealous too! I declare off. Fye, for shame! A man, a young man of person, parts, address and conversation, to be jealous of an old simpering, swaggering, rhyming gentleman usher, who is as dry as a mummy and talks of love, has no strength and talks of fighting giants, has no wit and thinks to gain me. O, fye, for shame!

TYCHO. It is indeed both a sin and a shame. I'll know myself better and be afraid of nobody but you, Robinette. I would say more, but it is time for me to laugh, he, he, he! is it not?

ROBINETTE. Now you show yourself to advantage. But look at the lovers there. They have had a fresh quarrel, I suppose. Go and end it, and take the hot fool home to his father to cool him.

TYCHO. I'll be melancholy no more. To please you, Robinette, I will dance when I am sad, be pert and merry though I have nothing to say like other young gentlemen. I'll be quite in the mode, more of the monkey and less of the man. Tol, lol, lol. Will that do? 'Bye, Robinette. Tol, lol, lol. Heigho!

Dances off and sighs.

ROBINETTE. I do like this fellow a little, though I plague him so. And perhaps I plague him because I like him. He's a strange creature, and yet I like him. I'm a strange creature too, and he likes me. He has a hundred faults. Hold, hold, Signora Robinetta, have not you a little fault or two in the corner of your heart, if your neighbors could come at them? O woman, woman! What an agreeable, whimsical, fanciful, coy, coquettish, quick-sighted, no-sighted, angelical, devilish jumble of agreeable matter art thou.

SONG.

O the freaks of womankind!
As swift as though we breed 'em:
No whims will starve in woman's mind,
For vanity will feed 'em;
Teasing ever,
Steady never,
Who the shifting clouds can bind?
O the freaks of womankind! *&c.*

Quick of ear and sharp of eye,
Others faults we hear and spy,
But to our own,
Alone,
We are both deaf and blind.
O the freaks of womankind! *&c.*

Exit Robinette.

SCENE II, Camilla's *magnificent garden.*
Enter Floridor, Camilla, *and* Tycho.

CAMILLA. I cannot bear your jealousy.

FLORIDOR. My jealousy would have merit with you if you loved as I did. But I have done, Madam, and have nothing more to say.

111. Signora Robinetta] *O1*, *O2*, *O3*, *O4*; Signora Robinette *D1*.
112. two] *O1*, *O2*, *O3*, *O4*; too *D1*.

Mr. Weston as Tycho in *A Christmas Tale*. By P. J. De Loutherbourg.
Harvard Theatre Collection

TYCHO. Then go to your father, who has something to say to you.

FLORIDOR (*walks about in disorder*). I'll follow you, Tycho.

TYCHO. What do you stay for, if you have no more to say?

FLORIDOR. I will say but three words, and then I'll come.

TYCHO. If you have three words the lady will have three thousand, which, at about two hundred and fifty words a minute, will just take up—I know my time and will be with you again.

Exit Tycho.

CAMILLA. Pray go to your father. I have told you my mind, Floridor. Why will you press me to change it? Don't let an ill opinion of your sex mislead you and injure me. I am resolved. You have my heart, I confess it. 'Tis ungenerous to urge me farther when you know my greatest distress is to refuse you anything.

FLORIDOR. My suspicions, Camilla, are the strongest proofs of my passion.

CAMILLA. Can you suspect me of such falsehood as to pretend a passion for you and secretly indulge one for another?

FLORIDOR. Nigromant, though a wicked, is a powerful magician, and his frequent visits might alarm a heart less sensible than mine.

CAMILLA. My pride will not let me answer an accusation that reflects the greatest dishonor both upon you and myself.

FLORIDOR. How can you suffer me to be tortured with jealousy, when you might—

CAMILLA. Stop, Floridor! When I might—what? Scorn a father's commands given me with his last breath and blessing?

FLORIDOR. With his last breath and blessing?

CAMILLA. Upon his deathbed he enjoined me with tears in his eyes not to give my hand but to him who could give me proofs of what this enchanted laurel would unfold.

FLORIDOR. And what are they? I conjure you, tell me.

CAMILLA. See and behold!

The laurel unfolds and discovers the words Valor, Constancy *and* Honor, *in letters of gold.*

You have proved your love to me by its unfolding at your request. Now read what is more expected from you.

FLORIDOR. Valor, Constancy and Honor! Can the son of Bonoro, and your lover, be suspected?

CAMILLA. I must not hear you, Floridor. Can you love me and refuse me these proofs? Marriage, my father added, was too great a stake to venture upon common security. If your passion is a true one, you'll convince me by your obedience. If it is a common one, I am too proud to accept it and too grateful to disobey my father.

SONG.

Woman should be wisely kind,
Nor give her passion scope;
Just reveal her inclination,
Never wed without probation,
Nor in the lover's mind,
Blight the sweet blossom, hope.

Youth and beauty kindle love,
Sighs and vows will fan the fire;
Sighs and vows may traitors prove,
Sorrow then succeeds desire;
Honor, faith, and well-earned fame,
Feed the sacred lasting flame!

FLORIDOR. You shall have the proofs from me you desire, and in return I will exact but one from you.

CAMILLA. If in my power, you shall command it.

FLORIDOR. Never see that cursed magician, Nigromant, more.

CAMILLA. Do you keep him from me then. How can I avoid him? He is crafty and powerful. Should I enrage him he would destroy our happiness forever.

FLORIDOR. You have spells to protect us.

CAMILLA. You have valor to protect us. It is you, Floridor, must deliver me from him. Valor, Constancy and Honor may subdue all evil spirits. And it is by them alone you can only reach the summit of your wishes.

FLORIDOR. Then I will prepare for the trial.

SONG.

'Tis beauty commands me, my heart must obey;
'Tis honor that calls me, and fame leads the way!
From the soft silken fetters of pleasure I fly,
With my love I must live, or with honor will die.
I wake from my trance,
Bring the sword, shield and lance,
My name shall be famous in story;
Now danger has charms,
For love sounds to arms,
And love is my passion and glory!

CAMILLA. Stay, Floridor. I have something yet to do.

Exit Camilla.

---

47. Nor] *O1*, *O2*, *O3*, *O4*; For *D1*.
70. silken] *O1*, *O2*, *O3*, *O4*; silent *D1*.
78.1. *Exit* Camilla] *O1*, *O2*, *O3*, *O4*; (*going*) *D1*.

FLORIDOR (*amazed*). What can this mean? What new trial for a heart so devoted to the object of its passion that every trifling circumstance hurries the spirits to it, as if alarmed by approaching danger.

Re-enter Camilla (*with a wreath of flowers*).

SONG.

O take this wreath my hand has wove,
The pledge and emblem of my love;
These flowers will keep their brightest hue,
Whilst you are constant, kind and true.

But should you false to love and me,
Wish from my fondness to be free,
Foreboding that my fate is nigh,
Each grateful flower will droop and die!

End of the first Part.

PART II

SCENE I, Bonoro's *Cell, with prisons round it.*
Chorus of Evil Spirits, *from the prisons.*

Mighty master, hear our sighs!
    Let thy slaves be free!
With folded hands and lifted eyes
    We call to thee!
    O end the strife!
    You grant us life;
Grant us still more–sweet liberty.

BONORO.
Wretched, base and blind,
    Evil spirits peace!
    Your clamors cease;
    By guilt confined,
    In vain the mind
Pants for freedom's happy hour;
    In pity to your pains,
    I loosed your chains,
But circumscribed your power,
    In pity to mankind.

What can be the meaning my son is not yet arrived? Love is his

89.1. End . . . Part] *O1*, *O2*, *O3*, *O4*; omitted *D1*.

master now, and his father must wait 'till superior commands are obeyed. Tycho! Tycho!

Enter Tycho.

TYCHO. Here am I!

BONORO. Where is my son Floridor?

TYCHO. Where I left him, at the old place.

BONORO. With Camilla?

TYCHO. To be sure.

BONORO. Did you tell him I wanted him?

TYCHO. I did.

BONORO. What said he?

TYCHO. That he would say but three words and follow me. I heard him say a hundred and sing a thousand. Lovers are bad arithmeticians.

BONORO. Why did not you return sooner?

TYCHO. I waited for him, to be sure.

BONORO. Have a care, Tycho. I will sooner forgive your weakness than your falsehood. Tell me the truth. Robinette detained you.

TYCHO. I was a little love bound, I must confess.

BONORO. Confess the truth always, nor ever be ashamed of the most natural if not the noblest passion.

TYCHO (*sighing*.) I am half dead with it, I'm sure. But I must never be melancholy again, and that it is that makes me so merry. He, he, he! (*Sighing*.) Heigh-ho!

BONORO. Let no passion raise your mind beyond its proper bounds. I knew of your foolish intentions. Such actions are the effects either of vice, cowardice, or poor paltry, mistaken philosophy.

TYCHO. You must not throw away your lessons upon me. I am in spirits now and always a-laughing. He, he, he!

BONORO. That may be as foolish the other way. Silly minds have no medium.

TYCHO. There's no pleasing some folks, full or fasting.

BONORO. I pity your weakness and am a friend to your honest simplicity.

TYCHO. I wish you would give me some love powder for Robinette.

BONORO. She is forward enough without it. If her blood rises above temperate you may repent the experiment. Here's my son. Leave us.

TYCHO. With all my heart. I'll go write to Robinette.

Enter Floridor.

(*Aside to* Floridor.) I wish you had made a little more haste with your three words.

Exit.

46. have] printed twice in *O1*, *O2*, *O3*, *O4*.

BONORO. No excuses for your delay, Son. Your mistress detained you and your father ought to wait.

FLORIDOR. I am ashamed of my neglect.

BONORO. I excuse it. I know the noble resolutions you have made which have more than half performed my commands. Camilla is an honor to her sex. Deserve her, Son, by your virtues, and my blessing shall attend your union.

FLORIDOR (*kneeling*). Thus let me show my thanks, duty, gratitude and love. (*Kissing his hand.*)

BONORO. Rise, Son, and attend to me. Some uncommon act of valor is expected from you. Before I obtained your mother's hand, I conquered and imprisoned these evil spirits (*pointing to the Dens*) who molested the world in various characters. You are now upon your trial. What can so strongly demand your valor as the destruction at once of your rival Nigromant, and the leader of these evil spirits?

FLORIDOR. Nothing. May I prove myself the son of such a father!

BONORO. Valor is best attended by faithfulness and simplicity. Tycho shall be your squire. I will myself with the proper ceremony dip the shield and sword in the lake of vapors. But these incantations will not do alone. Valor, Constancy and Honor must render all my charms effectual.

AIR VII.

Though strong your nerves to poise the spear,
Or raise the massy shield;
Though swift as lightning through the air
The sword of death you wield;
'Tis from the heart the power must flow,
To conquer and forgive the foe.

Though edged by spells and magic charms
Your sword may reap renown,
'Tis honor consecrates your arms
And gives the laurel crown.
'Tis from the heart the power must flow,
To conquer and forgive the foe.

FLORIDOR. As I feel your lessons, 'tis the best earnest of my executing them. But Sir, Father, I find you are informed that I am enjoined by Camilla to give proofs –

BONORO. I am. Her father, the good Bianco, was my friend. His power now possessed by his daughter was a limited one. He was oppressed at the end of his life by the superior arts of the wicked Nigromant

83. foe] *O1*, *O2*, *O3*, *O4*; goe *D1*.

for refusing him her hand. Now what object can at once so warmly bring forth the proofs required of you as so formidable a rival and detested a monster?

FLORIDOR. My heart pants for the contest.

BONORO. If you conquer, my Son, you gain glory and Camilla. If you are vanquished—come to my arms—(*Embraces him.*) I shall have that melancholy consolation that you gave the best proofs of your virtues.

FLORIDOR. Your words melt me and exalt me above myself!

BONORO. I must away to the lake with the sword and shield.

FLORIDOR. Shall I attend you, Sir?

BONORO. No, I must be alone. Now mark me, Son. Stay you here. And in my absence be a guardian of these evil spirits. This wand, should they be riotous or endeavor to tear off the talismans from their dens, will defeat their projects. (*Gives him the wand.*) To secure your wand, sleep must not close your eyes 'till my return. A drowsy watchman is the robber's best friend. Evil spirits have power only over thoughtless, lazy minds.

Exit Bonoro.

SONG.

FLORIDOR.
Tho' honor loudly strikes my ear,
The softer notes of love prevailing,
Every sense assailing,
Swell with hope or sink with fear.
Who for the goal of glory start,
To love as honor true,
Would ne'er forbid this trembling heart
To sigh a last adieu.
I go—my faith and truth to prove,
Valor ne'er was foe to love;
I will, I must, obey the call,
Love's triumphant over all.

Tycho!

Enter Tycho.

TYCHO. Here am I.

FLORIDOR. Approach, my Squire.

TYCHO. Your father has told me of my advancement, and if a man of honor may be said to know himself, I will venture to say that you are not very unfortunate in a Squire.

FLORIDOR. I am convinced of it. And the first duty I shall put you upon is to guard these evil spirits in my absence. I shall return directly, but I must see Camilla again.

TYCHO. To speak three words more.

FLORIDOR. I have something to say to her, which unsaid would damp the glory of any action I might achieve, and which when said will lighten and strengthen my heart for any adventure.

TYCHO. The moment your father has pardoned one fault you commit another. You keep his good nature in fine exercise.

FLORIDOR. I will never again give him the least cause of complaint. I must speak with Camilla, and directly.

TYCHO. I have three words too for Robinette.

FLORIDOR. Don't be a fool, but mind what I say to you.

TYCHO. A knight may plunge over head and ears while the poor squire must not wet his feet.

FLORIDOR. No talking. But mark me, should these evil spirits dare to be turbulent, this wand will control them. One caution above all is not to sleep upon any pretense whatsoever. Should the wand drop from your hand, we are undone. Be wise, active and vigilant!

Exit Floridor.

TYCHO. The young sinner preaches well. I am forbid talking and sleeping. I wonder he did not add eating and drinking too. 'Tis very hard that I may not take one look at Robinette. I am flesh and blood as well as he, am as personable as he, as jealous as he, have as fine passions and am as much beloved as he. To divert my melancholy I will show myself fit for my office (it is not every fool in office can do that) and examine these culprits, sinners and evil spirits. I will not get too near 'em though for fear of their laying a claw upon me. (*He speaks loud and with an affected air.*) Who are you in this lob's pound here?

FIRST SPIRIT. Save you, sweet Signior.

TYCHO. Well, well, none of your palaver. Answer my questions directly and keep your paws in your den. (*Raps his knuckles.*) What are you?

JESUIT. I am a Jesuit.

TYCHO. The devil you are! And how came you here?

JESUIT. Having some cardinal virtues, and making larger strides than they said became me, they have laid me by the heels, and it is impossible for me to do any good here.

TYCHO. No, nor anywhere else. So draw your beak, cormorant. And who are you with your sharp looks and your claws?

ATTORNEY. I am an attorney, at your service.

TYCHO. Not at mine, I beg of you. Are you in for your virtues too?

ATTORNEY. A little mistake in practice only.

TYCHO. Then for fear of more mistakes you shall stay where you are, Mr. Attorney.

POET. Signior Tycho, I beg your ears a moment.

TYCHO. What, have you lost your own?

POET. I am a poetical spirit. And here's a satire upon your neighbors and a panegyric upon yourself.

TYCHO. I'll touch nothing that belongs to you. I love my neighbors and I hate abuse. So keep in your fingers. (*Strikes them.*) But who are you that swell and look so big?

STATESMAN. I am a political spirit. I had a soul of fire that overleaped all laws and considerations. I was a statesman!

TYCHO. It was time to cool you a little, and spoil your leaping by keeping your soul under lock and key. Who are you, friend? And what are those rattles in your hand?

GAMESTER. A box and dice to divert us in our retirement.

TYCHO. Gamesters, I suppose. Pray, gentlemen, what brought you here?

GAMESTER. We lost good fortunes by keeping bad company. And to retrieve a little –

TYCHO. Became bad company yourselves.

GAMESTER. We did take an advantage, I must confess.

TYCHO. So they took an advantage of you and put you where you are. I wish all your family was with you, brothers, sisters and all!

ACTRESS. Turn your eyes this way, beautiful Sir, and look upon me with an eye of pity.

TYCHO. O, the females have found me out at last! What are you, a *bon* Jesuit?

ACTRESS. I was an actress some months ago.

TYCHO. An actress? What spirit's that?

ACTRESS. A spirit to entertain the public. But quitting that for private practice –

TYCHO. As you like private practice, I wish you joy of your situation.

ACTRESS. If you would permit me to come forth and approach you, I would amuse you with my history.

TYCHO. Many thanks, fair lady. But as I know nothing of acting, we are both much better as we are. Pray who are you, licking your lips and with your mouth open?

GLUTTON. I am a luxurious spirit. I loved eating and drinking a little too much.

TYCHO. O, a city spirit! I hope, friend, there is no great sin in a little eating and drinking?

GLUTTON. If I was out, good Sir, I would place such savory dainty dishes before you,

---

180. panegyric] *O*1, *O*2, *O*3, *O*4; panegyrick *D*1.
199–200. a *bon* Jesuit] *O*1, *O*2, *O*3, *O*4; a hen Jesuit *D*1.
215. Such] *Q*1, *O*2, *O*3, *O*4; omitted *D*1.

TYCHO. Hold your tongue, Sirrah; no bribery and corruption! He sets my mouth a watering already. This fellow shall be my cook, if I should ever get a good government.

WOMAN OF QUALITY. Turn to me, Signior. I have a right to be heard first.

TYCHO. Then don't lose your right, I beg you. Who are you, Madam?

WOMAN OF QUALITY. A spirit of quality.

TYCHO. And what are you in there for, Madam?

WOMAN OF QUALITY. For being a woman of quality.

TYCHO. A woman of bad qualities, you mean. Fie upon you! Who ever heard of a bad woman of quality? This is *scandalum magnatum horrendissinum*! You are a foul weed and ought to be plucked out from the fair garden of nobility. (*Aside.*) I wish Robinetta had heard me say that.

A voice is heard accompanied with a guitar.

What, have you singers and musicians among you?

ACTRESS. O yes, and dancers, actors, authors and managers too. We could entertain you, sweet Sir, if we were at liberty.

TYCHO. No, no, you'll sing better in your cage, my pretty birds. Come, let me hear you. (*He sits down.*) Whistle away. (*Aside.*) This is almost more than flesh and blood can bear. Such sweet looking spirits sure could never hurt one. Come, come, whistle away, my sweet canary birds.

DUETTE.

O hear me, kind and gentle swain,
  Let love's sweet voice delight you;
The ear of youth should drink each strain,
  When beauty's lips invite you.

As love and valor warm your heart,
  And faith and honor guard you;
From wounded breasts extract the dart,
  And beauty will reward you.

Our tear-stained eyes their wish disclose,
  Can cruel you refuse 'em?
O wipe the dew from off the rose,
  And place it in your bosom.

As they are singing, Tycho *by degrees falls asleep.*

TYCHO (*half asleep*). This is melting indeed! Bravo, bravo! Softly, my angel; not so loud, I beseech you. Sweet Robinetta! Encore, encore.

252. Robinetta] *O1*, *O2*, *O3*, *O4*; Robinette *D1*.

Sing again, or I'll—"As love and valor" (*Sings in his sleep.*) "and beauty's lips." Toll, lol, lal, lal! Robinetta—obinetta—binetta—netta—etta—ta—a —

Falls asleep and drops his wand; upon which is thunders. The dens burst open and various evil spirits of both sexes enter promiscuously and riotously express their joy.

Chorus of Evil Spirits.

'Tis done! 'tis done! 'tis done!
We break the galling chain.
We fly, we sink, and run,
From tyranny,
To liberty!
To liberty—again!
Revel, riot, dance and play,
Folly sleeps and Vice keeps holiday!

End of the Second Part.

PART III.

SCENE I, Camilla's *magnificent garden.*
Enter Camilla *and* Floridor.

CAMILLA. Why would you distress me thus and doubly wound me by this rash action? Your father will be incensed at your disobedience and hate me as the cause of it. Tycho may be worked upon by the evil spirits and undo us. My heart forebodes, too —

FLORIDOR. Can your heart be mine and conceive any doubts of me?

CAMILLA. Why should I imagine that I have charms powerful enough to fix you mine forever. Change of place may occasion change of sentiment. New objects may erase former impressions.

FLORIDOR. Indulge not these false alarms. Thou art queen of my heart and shalt reign there forever and alone.

CAMILLA. My fancy teems with a thousand apprehensions. All my senses are in disorder. I heard, or thought I heard, strange noises in the air. Even now my eyes are deceived, or this garden, the trees, the flowers, the heavens change their colors to my sight and seem to say something mysterious which is not in my heart to expound.

The objects in the garden vary their colors.

255.1. *upon which is*] *O1*, *O2*, *O3*, *O4*; upon which it *D1*.
263.1. End . . . Part] *O1*, *O2*, *O3*, *O4*; omitted *D1*.

FLORIDOR. These are the phantoms of love and fear.

CAMILLA. O, Floridor! You have taught me love, and love has taught me fear.

DIALOGUE SONG.

She.

Look round the earth, nor think it strange
To doubt of you when all things change;
The branching tree, the blooming flower,
Their form and hue change every hour;
While all around such change I see,
Alas, my heart must fear for thee.

He.

Blighted and chilled by cruel frost,
Their vigor droops, their beauty's lost;
My cheek may fade by your disdain,
To change my heart, all power is vain;
Look round the earth, the flower and tree
To nature's true as I to thee.

She.

Look up to heav'n—nor think it strange,
To doubt of you when all things change;
Sun, moon and stars, those forms so bright,
Are changing ever to the sight.
While in the heav'ns such change I see,
Alas, my heart must fear for thee.

He.

Clouded or bright, the moon and sun
Are constant to the course they run;
So gay or sad, my heart as true,
Rises and sets to love and you.
Look in the heav'ns, each star you see,
True to its orb as I to thee.

Enter Bonoro *hastily*.

He stops short and looks steadfastly upon Floridor, *who starts confounded, while* Camilla *appears distressed.*

BONORO (*after a pause*). Well you may start and be confounded, Son.

---

26. beauty] *O*1, *O*2, *O*3, *O*4; beauty's *D*1.
31–42. "These two verses omitted in representation" *D*1.

CAMILLA (*kneeling*). I am the cause of his disobedience. Let me be punished.

BONORO. Rise, excellent woman! (*Raises her.*) Your virtues are the best excuses for his disobedience, which will become its own punishment. His labors are trebled by it.

FLORIDOR. My father!

BONORO. Tycho has been overcome by the evil spirits. They have broken their chains and fled to your rival and enemy, Nigromant. Mischief is abroad.

CAMILLA. Then I am wretched indeed!

FLORIDOR. Doubt not of my valor or my love. Increase of danger makes me more worthy of Camilla.

BONORO. Your spirit charms me and disarms my anger. I have disenchanted from sleep and forgiven the poor penitent Squire. His was an error of judgment, yours of passion. But it is past and forgot. Tycho waits for you with your sword and shield in the grove by the enchanted lake. Begone. Remember the words of this divine oracle:

> May Valor, Constancy and Honor guide you. Let no pleasures entice you, no terrors daunt you. When once you see him, never lose sight of your foe. Follow him wherever he leads you. The greatest dangers are only the rugged paths which will lead you to renown (*pointing to* Camilla.) in the arms of innocence and beauty.

TRIO.

BONORO. May heav'ns blessing blend with mine!
To crown thy deeds at virtue's shrine,
Be love's best gift, Camilla, thine.

CAMILLA. May every sigh that's heaved by me,
And every wish that's breathed for thee,
Be prosp'rous gales on fortune's sea.

FLORIDOR. O when my bark, the tempest o'er,
With pilot love shall gain the shore,
Ambition cannot ask for more.
Of every blessings love's the source,
Valor but an empty name,
A roving, wild, destructive flame,
Till love and justice guide its course,
And then it mounts to fame.

Exeunt.

Enter Robinette.

ROBINETTE. So, so all matters are made up again, and the confusion which my poor, simple, melancholy lover, Tycho, occasioned is all kindly settled by the benevolence of Bonoro. I could not help listening to his fine sayings, not out of curiosity, but it really does one's heart good to hear a fine preacher of morality, and which is wonderful, see him practice it too. But the lovers, I see, (*looking out.*) are taking their last leave. The good man can scarce part them. Their lips are glued together. They'll never be got asunder. It makes my eyes and my mouth water. I'll look at 'em no more.

SONG.

ROBINETTE. Through all our hearts philosophers have taught
A subtle vapor flies,
Warmed in the veins, it kindles quick as thought
And sparkles in the eyes.

Be warned, ye fair, and retire,
Fly far from the flash,
You'll repent if you're rash,
O never play with fire.

If a youth comes with a grace and a song,
Like Phoebus decked in rays,
Then to your heart the fiery atoms throng,
And set it in a blaze.
Be warned, ye fair, *&c.*

But should the youth come with honor and truth,
Fly not your lover's rays.
His heart in a flame, let yours be the same,
And make a mutual blaze.

From him we need not retire,
When such can be found,
We may stand our ground,
O then we may play with fire.

I don't know what's the matter with me today. I am full of mischief, I believe. I am afraid these evil spirits that are got abroad again are a little busy with me. It can't be the loss of Tycho sure that affects me. I don't love him so well as that, neither. No matter what it is, why don't my loving cousin come back? O this love! this love! She can't leave her dying swain. Why should not I go after mine too?

89–90. makes my eyes] *O1*, *O2*, *O3*, *O4*; makes both my eyes *D1*.

Though I am not dying for him, he is for me. I'll go towards Bonoro's cell, I'm resolved. As I have less passion, I shall appear more generous by looking after my lover in his present situation. I never knew till this moment that I was half so good a creature as I really am.

Exit Robinette.

SCENE II, *the outside of* Bonoro's *cell.*
Enter Camilla.

CAMILLA. Farewell, O farewell, my Floridor. Thou seest but can'st not hear with what reluctance I am separated from thee. He too with unwilling steps moves slow along and turns his head this way to show that duty and inclination cannot yet be reconciled. Now he stands still, and with his eyes and one hand raised to Heaven, pressing his bosom with the other he seems to swear eternal love. I will ratify that vow and make it mutual. Now he seems distressed and hurries down the hill. And now he's gone—and now—I'm wretched. Heigh ho!

Enter Robinette.

ROBINETTE. Heigh ho! Why he'll come again, Cousin, depend upon it.

CAMILLA. May I depend upon his coming again as he goes away, constant and faithful. His father warned him to let no pleasure entice him. Is not that alarming?

ROBINETTE. What, is it your turn to be jealous?

CAMILLA. Can one love much and not be jealous a little?

ROBINETTE. Can you be long in doubt and have supernatural powers to assist you?

CAMILLA. The passion of love counteracts all operations of magic and levels us with the weakest. We can try gold but we can't make it. It is concealed by nature from the wisest of us.

ROBINETTE. Make a trial of his affections then, by assuming a form, if possible, handsomer than your own.

CAMILLA. That is not in my power. I can assume a form less agreeable, if possible, than my own. And with that and some other circumstance I am now going upon the trial.

ROBINETTE. I will attend you.

CAMILLA. No. I shall dispense with your company for some time. I leave you mistress of my garden and my castle. See whom you please and do what you please. Make yourself happy, while I perhaps am seeking to be miserable. (*Sighs.*)

SONG.

CAMILLA. O how weak will power and reason
To this bosom tyrant prove,
Every act is fancied treason,
To the jealous sovereign Love.

Passion urged the youth to danger,
Passion calls him back again;
Passion is to peace a stranger,
Seek I must my bliss or bane.

So the fevered minds that languish,
And in scorching torments rave,
Thus to end or ease their anguish,
Headlong plunge into the wave.

Exit Camilla.

ROBINETTE. Poor creature. I would not have her cares for all her magic and her grandeur. Mirth has got such possession of my heart that I defy all the handsome fellows in the world to take more of it than I please to give them. I have two lovers which I keep as two monkeys to divert me. I make 'em play me a thousand tricks, can change the very nature of 'em. If they grow mischievous I punish 'em. If all monkeys were served so, there would be less impertinence in the world. But mum! One of 'em is here. This is too old and too lively. I must make him melancholy or turn him off.

Enter Faladel.

FALADEL. Signora Robinette, I have followed you to say half a dozen kind words to you and vanish. He, he, he! By my faith and wand, I will not encroach upon you.

ROBINETTE. By my faith and fardingale, you may vanish before you have said the kind words to me, if you please. (*Mimics him.*) He, he, he! Well, what do you follow me for?

FALADEL. I could not help it. I knew where you was going. I followed you. And the following little ode came along with me and is at your service.

ODE.

Alack-a-day!
You would not stay.
I followed gay,
Like faithful Tray
With you to play,
Or here to stay,
At feet to lay.

For by my say,
I will obey
Whate'er you say
By night or day,
Whilst I am clay,
For ever aye.
Take pity, pray.

ROBINETTE. Upon my word that's very pretty and very moving.

FALADEL. Indeed and alack-a-day! I shall certainly die soon if you don't cure me with kindness. He, he, he! I shall indeed for ever and for aye. He, he!

ROBINETTE. What is your disorder, pray?

FALADEL. Alack-a-day! I'm troubled with the Tycho. Signora Robinette, do you understand me? He, he! By my faith I am!

ROBINETTE. Jealousy, I protest. And of poor Tycho.

FALADEL. Poor or rich, I am troubled with the Tycho. And I must either take steel myself or make my rival take it. Do you understand me? He, he, he! (*Claps his hand upon his sword.*) It is a serious matter, I do assure you. He, he, he! There must be blood shed. He, he, he! By my faith and wand, there must.

ROBINETTE. I wish you would make it a serious matter, and not be grinning so to spoil one of the handsomest faces in the Island.

FALADEL. Alack-a-day! I can't help laughing for the life of me. I was born so, though I'm unhappy all the while to desperation. He, he, he! By my faith and wand, I am!

ROBINETTE. By my faith too. My heart shall never be a prize for the best grinner. You must show your love to me by wearing a face of desperation, indeed.

FALADEL. What kind of face is that?

ROBINETTE. Thus, your eyes thus, looking about as it were thus—or thus—(*She puts on different faces.*)

FALADEL. Looking about for what, my sweet, cruel queen of hearts? He, he, he!

ROBINETTE. For a tree or a canal, to be sure, to put an end to your despair.

FALADEL. To dangle or float upon! I understand you. He, he, he! By my faith, I'll hit your taste or die for it. Will this do? Or this, or this? He, he, he!

SONG.

By my faith and wand,
Gracing now my hand,

105.1. "This song is omitted since the first night" *D1*.

I'm at your command.
  For ever and for aye.
Heart within my breast
Never shall have rest
Till of yours possessed.
  Heigh ho—alack-a-day.
Do you want a knight
Ready, brisk and tight,
Foes and fiends to fight,
  Forever and for aye?
If you want a slave
Whom you will not save,
Send me to my grave.
  I'm dead. Alack-a-day!

I'll stand by my song forever and aye.

ROBINETTE. You're at your grinning again.

FALADEL. Alack-a-day! and so I am. I can't stop it. My features run away with me. But I'll go and practice a little by myself and return again directly quite a new creature. By my faith, I will!

Exit.

ROBINETTE. Ha, ha, ha! If every woman before marriage would but train up her lovers to her inclination, as she does her birds or her dogs, we never should have an unhappy marriage. To be too much in love and to give men their way spoils everything. But what have we here? My lover, Tycho, and prepared for battle. Like master like man, he comes to take his last adieu. He seems very sad and thoughtful. But he sees me and brightens up into unnatural smiles. Ah, Signior Cavaliero Tycho!

Enter Tycho, *armed as* Floridor's *squire.*

TYCHO. Here am I, as merry as my situation will permit me. I have leave to kiss your fair hand and away. Though I am made a squire, I have had sad luck since I saw you. (*Looking grave, but recollecting himself.*) But it is all over and I don't mind it now. He, he, he!

ROBINETTE. If I had not taught you to laugh at misfortunes, your last adventure with the evil spirits would have broke your heart.

TYCHO. There was the devil to do. I have not recovered my fright yet, I am sure, though I put a good face upon it. He, he, he!

ROBINETTE. Sad work indeed. But how was it?

TYCHO. Two she devils throwed me into a trance, and as I could not

137. luck] *O1*, *O2*, *O3*, *O4*; look *D1*.

help myself in my sleep, they helped themselves out of their prisons and left me to pay the reckoning.

ROBINETTE. And a long one it was.

TYCHO. It was indeed. But our kind old gentleman gave me a sour look, a long speech, pitied my weakness and forgave me. 'Tis a good old soul.

ROBINETTE. Sad work indeed, Tycho.

TYCHO. It was horrible, horrible, and most horrible. He, he, he!

ROBINETTE. But how was it?

TYCHO. You must know I love music vastly, though I don't sing a note. And two she angel-devils sung me so out of my senses that I fell fast asleep.

ROBINETTE. Ay, ay, your old disorder. But I am sorry you can't sing. Your rival, Faladel, who was here just now, sings very prettily.

TYCHO. Yes, he may sing. But he can't write as I can. I have wrote a song upon you, and who knows but you may teach me to sing as you have taught me to laugh. He, he, he! (*Endeavors to sing.*)

ROBINETTE. O pray let's hear it.

TYCHO (*sings*). Sweet Robinette,
Your eyes are jet.

Your eyes are grey, but no matter for that. Poets may suppose anything.

Sweet Robinette,
Your eyes are jet,
And teeth are lily white –

You have a fine set of teeth, and if you had not I was resolved to give 'em to you. I don't love by halves.

Your cheeks are roses,
Lips are posies
And your nose is
Wond'rous bright.

Let my rival do that if he can. I wrote it and set it myself.

ROBINETTE. I don't doubt it. But, Tycho, I don't know if a *bright* nose is any compliment.

TYCHO. Why not? You must have something bright about you. But I don't want for words. You may alter it to *wond'rous right*, or *white*, or *light*, or *tight*. A tight nose is no bad thing as times go. He, he, he! Here comes my rival. Shall I hansel my maiden sword and lay him dead at your feet?

ROBINETTE. By no means. Kill him with jealousy. See how melancholy he is. He has lost all his spirit.

TYCHO. And I have got it. He, he, he! (*Aside to* Robinette.) What a dismal piece of mortality it is. I am quite ashamed now that ever I wore such a face as his.

ROBINETTE. Now for a curious scene.

Enter Faladel.

FALADEL. I hope I have conquered my foolish nature, Robinette, internally and externally forever and aye. (*Seeing* Tycho.) But there's my rival. Shall I sacrifice him to your beauty and my passion? (*Claps his hand to his sword.*)

ROBINETTE (*aside to* Faladel). O, by no means. Draw your wit upon him. Cut him up with that.

FALADEL. You command me. What a simple fellow it is, grinning like an idiot without ideas.

ROBINETTE (*aside to* Faladel). Did not I tell you so? A smirking face gives me the heartburn.

TYCHO (*aside to* Robinette *and grinning*). What a poor melancholy fool it is. He has done for himself, I see. Look at old miserable, Robinette. He, he, he!

ROBINETTE (*aside to* Tycho). What a figure from top to toe. Attack him, Tycho.

TYCHO. Your servant, Signior Faladel. I am sorry for your misfortune. He, he, he!

FALADEL. What misfortune, pray, Mr. Merry Andrew?

ROBINETTE (*aside to* Faladel). Attack his grinning, Faladel. (*Aside to* Tycho.) Attack his melancholy, Tycho.

TYCHO. I verily thought, Don Faladel, that you had put your face into mourning for some family misfortune. Ha, ha, ha!

FALADEL. How can I help being melancholy when I see how contemptible your grinning has made you? What a superlative happiness. I would laugh now if I durst. (*Begins to laugh and stops.*)

ROBINETTE. As you are both my friends, and one of you something more –

TYCHO (*aside*). A great deal more, I believe.

FALADEL (*aside*). I thought so, poor soul.

ROBINETTE. Pray let me introduce you to know each other better.

TYCHO. I have no objection. He, he, he!

FALADEL. I can have none to your commands.

ROBINETTE. Take hands, then. You must not be rivals (for I can but love one of you) and therefore be friends.

Each of 'em winks at Robinette, *which she returns as they are taking hands.*

FALADEL (*aside*). What a fool she makes of the poor man.

TYCHO (*aside*). How she shows Dismal off.

ROBINETTE. Thank you, gentlemen. I need not say which is my choice.

BOTH (*both nodding at her*). No, no.

FALADEL. It is too plain.

TYCHO. Half an eye may see it.

ROBINETTE. I must therefore now take my leave first of you, Signior Tycho. Distressed damsels, imprisoned knights and various adventures attend you. Don't be jealous, Signior Faladel, if I conduct this redoubted and magnanimous squire a little on his way.

FALADEL. Not in the least. (*Aside.*) How she jeers him.

ROBINETTE. Come, Don Tycho, the sword is drawn, the lance is couched, and the knight is impatient.

TYCHO. Donna Robinette, my sword is thine, my valor thine, my heart is thine, my blood is thine, and at my return my body shall be thine. Signior Dismallo, farewell. I wish your body joy of its wooden head. He, he, he!

Exit laughing with Robinette.

FALADEL. By my faith and wand, if I had not been commanded to the contrary, I would have divided his body and spoiled his grinning. But she hates and detests him for it, as she adores me for the contrary.

SONG.

FALADEL.

Once as merry as the lark
I mounted to the sky,
But now I'm grown a sober spark,
And like an owl,
The wisest fowl,
Will roll a dismal eye.
For Robinette will have it so,
And what she will shall be,
I therefore take to ho, ho, ho!
And turn off he, he, he!

Once as merry as the kid,
I frisked it o'er the ground,
But since I am to laugh forbid,
An ass I am,
A sheep, a lamb,
Shut up in dismal pound.
For Robinette will have it so,
And what she will shall be,
I therefore take to ho, ho, ho!
And turn off he, he, he!

243.1.–263. "Omitted in the representation" *O*1, *O*2, *O*3, *O*4, *D*1.

Enter Robinette.

ROBINETTE. Poor foolish fellow, he is gone. He'll be a breakfast for some giant. I begin to pity him.

FALADEL. Alack-a-day! He does not know his own weakness and has such a contemptible figure that he is below your pity. By my faith, he is.

ROBINETTE. I like his spirit of knight errantry. It becomes him.

FALADEL. Do you? I have a prodigious quantity of it myself. And, by my faith and wand, say but a word and I will be among the dragons, monsters, giants and hobgoblins tomorrow morning.

ROBINETTE. Will not that be depriving Camilla of the most complete gentleman usher that ever bore a wand?

FALADEL. Alack-a-day! All titles and services shall be given up for that of being your most humble servant and obedient knight forever and for aye.

ROBINETTE. If you will go, I shall present you with a scarf. Come on, Sir Faladel.

DUETTE.

BOTH.
O the delight,
To be an errant knight!

ROBINETTE.
O'er mountain, hill and rock,
In rain, and wind and snow,
All dangers he must mock
And must with pleasure go.
Quivering and quaking,
Shivering and shaking,
Dismal nights,
Horrid sprites,
Lions roaring,
Monsters snoring,
Castles tumbling,
Thunder grumbling,

BOTH.
O the delight,
To be an errant knight!

ROBINETTE.
Damsels squeaking,
Devils shrieking,
Clubs and giants,
Hurl defiance,
Night and day,
Lose the way,
Spirits sinking,
Nothing drinking,
Beat and beating,

Little eating,
Broken bones,
Beds of stones,
BOTH. O the delight,
To be an errant knight!

End of the Third Part.

PART IV.

SCENE I, *A dark wood.*
Enter Floridor *in great distress.*

SONG.

FLORIDOR. Cruel fiends pursue me,
Torment and undo me.
My rising hopes are crossed,
My sword and shield are lost.
My breast with valor glowed,
Fame her temple showed,
Fiends have interposed,
The gates are ever, ever closed!
Away with despair to the wind,
Nothing daunts the noble mind.
Crowned with these flowers I'll take the field,
My foes with this charm I will face,
Love alone shall supply the place
Of helmet, sword and shield.

What a series of distresses, since they broke their prisons, have these evil spirits prepared for me. They have conveyed my sword and shield from Tycho, have by their mischievous arts disturbed and intoxicated his mind. And all my fair prospect of renown and possession of the highest earthly bliss with Camilla is vanished and gone. What can I say to her? What can I plead to my father?

TYCHO (*within*). Signior Don Floridor, the lost sheep is found.

FLORIDOR. Here comes again the unhappy, intoxicated wretch. Where are you, Tycho?

Enter Tycho, *drunk.*

TYCHO. Here am I.

FLORIDOR. Have you recovered my sword and shield?

309.1. End . . . Part] omitted *D*1.

TYCHO. No, but I have recovered a better thing—hic—my understanding.

FLORIDOR. I wish I could see proof of it.

TYCHO. I wish you had found yours, and then you would not be in such a passion.

FLORIDOR. Tycho, collect yourself and answer a few questions.

TYCHO. Do you have all your senses about you, or shall I be too hard for you?

FLORIDOR. Prith'ee, peace. In the first place, at what time did you perceive yourself disordered?

TYCHO. As soon as I found that I had lost my senses.

FLORIDOR. How came you to lose your senses?

TYCHO. As other people do, by seeing a fine woman.

FLORIDOR. What, Robinette?

TYCHO. Much handsomer.

FLORIDOR. What did she do? Answer quickly.

TYCHO. Don't be in such a passion. Thus it is. "Don Tycho," says she (looking with such sweetness as I do now), "I have long admired you, loved or adored you." I forget which.

FLORIDOR. No matter which.

TYCHO. I must be—hic—exact. Looking sweetly, as I said before, she stretched out the whitest arm with the taperest fingers. Thus. "Here, Don Tycho, take this. Whenever you find yourself distressed in mind, taste it and be yourself again." She gave it me, sighed, wept much, and took to her heels. I had just parted with Robinette, who, with tears in her eyes, gave me this scarf. I, seeing the poor creature so tender-hearted about me, I grew tender-hearted about her, found myself low spirited, very low spirited, tapped the elixir of life, and was enchanted as you saw me.

FLORIDOR. Drunk, you mean, as I now see you.

TYCHO. No, enchanted.

FLORIDOR. Enchanted?

TYCHO. Yes, I say enchanted. I speak plain sure. I know what drunkenness is, well enough. Here is the enchanted vial. (*Shows it.*)

FLORIDOR. It was an evil spirit that deluded you.

TYCHO (*turns up the vial*). Good or evil spirit, it is gone.

FLORIDOR. It was one of the evil spirits your folly set at liberty that met you, tempted and overcame you. And the consequences have undone us.

TYCHO. I shall know the traitress again when I see her. But don't fret about your sword and shield. You shall have mine. And I'll stand by, if I can, and see fair play.

29. yours] *O*1, *O*2, *O*3, *O*4; your's *D*1.

FLORIDOR. I shall go distracted with my misfortunes.

TYCHO. Here is the evil spirit. Hold, hold! If it is, she is vastly altered since I saw her.

Enter Camilla *as an old woman.*

CAMILLA. Hold your peace, you intoxicated fool, or you'll repent your presumption.

TYCHO. I am not intoxicated with your person, Madam Nose and Chin.

FLORIDOR. Cease your ribaldry, Tycho. Forgive his folly. He is not himself or he would not have given his tongue such licence.

CAMILLA. Young Knight, civility should always be rewarded. What is the matter with you? Can I be of service?

FLORIDOR. Impossible, impossible! My mind will burst with agony.

TYCHO (*to the old woman*). I know you have a charm for the toothache and a spell for the ague. But can you dischant or unconjure my brains. That is, can you with witch elm, crooked pins, a dry toad, or any of your family receipts, make me as sensible as I was before?

CAMILLA. Very easily. Drink of the water of yonder brook, plentifully, and rest yourself upon the bank till you are called for, and the vapors of your brain will disperse and you'll be sober again.

TYCHO. As I'm a little thirsty and a little sleepy, I'll take your prescription. And if I was not already over head and ears in love, I would take you too, kind old lady, yours. Harkee, if you are his friend too, give the knight a little advice and bid him take mine if he would go through life as he ought to do.

Exit Tycho, *staggering.*

CAMILLA (*to* Floridor, *who walks about distractedly*). Vexation, young man, will never find your sword and shield.

FLORIDOR. Tormenting me will never cure my vexation. Why will you torment me when you can't assist me?

CAMILLA. Young Knight, you don't know what I might do with kind usage.

FLORIDOR. Unavailing pity as it wounds our pride doubles our distress.

CAMILLA. Passion blinds you and you can't see your friends.

SONG.

Young man, young man,
Be this your plan,
Wisdom get where'er you can.
　See, see,
　The humble bee,
Draws wealth from the meanest of flowers,
　Then hies away

With his precious prey,
No passion his prudence sours.

Young man, young man,
Be this your plan,
Wisdom get where'er you can.
Wild youth,
Passion and truth,
So opposite never agree.
Be prudent, sage,
Draw wit from old age,
And be wise as the humble bee.
Young man, young man,
Be this your plan,
Wisdom get where'er you can.

FLORIDOR. Pardon me, venerable lady. You have cooled my heated imagination and my folly is a convert to your wisdom.

CAMILLA. I will show my wisdom by asking beforehand what reward you will give me to recover your sword and shield.

FLORIDOR. You shall command my services and everything in my power.

CAMILLA. Shall I?

FLORIDOR. By my sword and honor of knighthood.

SOLEMN AIR.

By my shield and my sword,
By the chaplet that circles my brow,
By a knight's sacred word,
Whatever you ask,
How dreadful the task,
To perform it 'fore heav'n I vow.

CAMILLA. Will you as pledge of our compact give me those trifling flowers that are tied round your head?

FLORIDOR. Trifling flowers, and give them to you? You should sooner take my head from my body, or tear my heart from my bosom, than have the smallest bud of my sweet Camilla's chaplet.

CAMILLA. O love's extravagance. I may command everything in your power but what you don't choose to part with.

FLORIDOR. Ask my life and you shall have it. This wreath is dearer to me than my life.

CAMILLA. Well, well, I'll take you at your word.

---

127. and my sword] *O*1, *O*2, *O*3, *O*4; and by my sword *D*1.

"Whatever I ask,
How dreadful the task,
To perform it 'fore heaven, you vow."

Behold what charms there are in a young hero's services.

She waves her stick, the wood opens and discovers his sword and shield hung upon the stem of a tree.

FLORIDOR (*runs and takes them down*). How delightful to my eyes are these instruments of my fame and glory. Now task my service and my gratitude.

CAMILLA. I am not in haste for my reward. Other cares demand your services. I shall call upon you in my turn.

FLORIDOR. To whom am I bound in gratitude forever?

CAMILLA. Grinnelda is my name.

DUETTE.

Remember, young knight, remember,
Remember the words that I say,
Don't laugh at my age,
Nor scorn at my rage,
For though I have past my May,
I'm not frozen up in December.

Remember, I will remember,
Remember the words that you say.
I honor your age,
Nor scorn at your rage,
And though you are past your May,
Your heart is still warm in December.

SCENE II, *The outside of* Bonoro's *cell.*
Enter Bonoro *in great distress.*

BONORO. My heart is agitated and distressed. The various accidents which have befallen my son make me tremble for his youth and inexperience. I am unhappy and perplexed in spite of supernatural powers. The feelings of the father rise superior to everything. Radel, my spirit! Radel!

Enter Radel.

154. Remember . . . remember] lines designated *She* D1.
160. Remember . . . remember] lines designated *He* D1.

RADEL. Here my lord and master.

BONORO. Fly to my son with a troop of my spirits, that he may not be surrounded and overcome by the evil ones in his conflict with Nigromant.

RADEL. With the power and virtue you have given me I fly to execute your commands.

BONORO. Be swift as my wishes.

SONG.

No power can calm the storm to rest,
No magic charm the father's breast,
Which beats with doubts and fears.
No more for active scenes I burn,
My power and strength to weakness turn,
My manhood melts to tears.
I will not doubt, through stormy skies
My son shall break his way;
Shall cloudless o'er his errors rise,
And fame shall hail the day.

Exit Bonoro.

SCENE III, *A prospect of rocks.*
Enter Tycho *and* Floridor.

TYCHO. Heaven bless her for it, say I. You have got your sword and shield and I my senses. We are both beholden to her and should both do our best to be grateful. She might certainly have had me, had not Robinette engaged me beforehand. But what strange, fine, tremendous, diabolical, grand palace have we here?

FLORIDOR. This is the domain of Nigromant. Tycho, should the demons come upon you, remember they are but phantoms and will be dispersed by one gleam of your sword, as vapors before the sun. If free from guilt, you may defy and despise them.

TYCHO. Then I am their man.

FLORIDOR. Here will I plant my laurels or mix my ashes with the dust.

TYCHO. And I as your squire will take a slip of your laurels or slip into the next world as other rash squires have done before me.

FLORIDOR. Should I fall and you survive, Tycho, take this chaplet to Camilla. Tell her that my love never yielded, though my body did.

TYCHO. And if your unworthy Squire drops and you survive (which heaven forbid), tell Robinette that Tycho was true to the last. Tell her—that—. But as I hope I shall be able to carry the message myself, let us to business and put our loves in our pockets till we have done fighting.

FLORIDOR. Approach the castle gates, Tycho, and sound the horn of defiance. Call forth the black magician, the wicked Nigromant, to single combat.

TYCHO. To single combat. You're right, your commands shall be obeyed.

Tycho *sounds the horn. It thunders. The rocks split and discover the castle of* Nigromant *and the fiery lake.*

I have waked his devilship and blown all his castle about his ears.

NIGROMANT (*within*). Floridor, son of Bonoro, I come!

FLORIDOR. Nigromant, son of darkness and mischief, I attend thee!

NIGROMANT (*within*). Floridor, son of Bonoro, I abhor thy father's virtues. I hate thee and thy race. I call to thee and defy thee, and thou shall feel my vengeance.

TYCHO (*aside to Floridor*). I don't like the sound of his voice.

FLORIDOR. Come forth, thou foul son of darkness! I have experienced the mischievous hatred of thee and thy crew. Come forth from thy lurking places, face me like an open foe, and I'll forgive thee!

NIGROMANT (*appears in the fiery lake*). Here I am.

TYCHO. This must be the cock-devil of 'em all.

SONG.

NIGROMANT. Stripling traitor, victim of my rage!
Stripling traitor, offspring of sedition!
Dar'st thou with Nigromant engage?
Nothing shall my wrath assuage
But vengeance and perdition.

Triumphant joy my bosom swells.
Vain are your magic charms and spells.
Revenge that ne'er could sleep
Her crimson standard rears
Here on this fiery flood.
Revenge shall soon her laurels steep
In the son's blood
And in the father's tears.

FLORIDOR. Thy terrors, threats and boasts are vain,
Phantoms of a heated brain.
Let all thy fiends surround thee,
The elements conspire,
Through water, earth and fire
I'll follow and confound thee.

On the whirlwind if you ride,
Through all your spells I'll break,
Confound your guilt and pride,
And plunge into the fiery lake,
With virtue for my guide.

It thunders, and Floridor *plunges into the fiery lake.*

TYCHO. A good journey, good master. Your feathers will be singed at least. And if I had followed him I should have been ready roasted for the magician's table. (*A flourish of instruments.*) Here come the demons! But free from guilt, I defy and despise 'em!

Here a Dance of Demons.

During the dance, as often as the demons approach Tycho, *he claps his hand to his sword and cries out*: "I defy you and despise you!" *When they vanish he assumes an important air.*)

I have done their business. (*A rumbling noise is heard in the air.*) Here is more work for me. What have we here, a feathered monster?

Enter Faladel *as a large owl.*

TYCHO. Evil spirit, approach me not. If you will fight as a gentleman ought and come with a sword by your side, I am your man. (*Retiring.*) But I am no match for your beak and claws. Therefore keep off!

FALADEL (*clapping his wings*). Hoo! Hoo! Hoo!

TYCHO. I don't understand you, Mr. Owl.

FALADEL. I am no evil spirit but your rival Faladel.

TYCHO. Faladel!

FALADEL. By my faith and my wand, I am.

TYCHO. Faladel! Ha, ha, ha! And they have made an owl of you. Ha, ha, ha! I knew what your melancholy would come to. Ha, ha, ha! But how came you so altered for the better?

FALADEL. I went a knight-erranting by the command of Robinette, and the evil spirits belonging to this castle would not fight me, but, alack-a-day, changed me into this shape to divert the ladies of the seraglio forever and for aye.

TYCHO. And a very comical, diverting devil you must be. Ha, ha, ha! I would not have Robinette see you thus. She will like you ten times better than before. Such creatures as you in your human shapes (if they may be called so), are neither fish, flesh or fowl. But now you are something. You look wise at least, have a handsomer face, a finer shape and a much better pair of legs. Ha, ha, ha!

FALADEL. What, you have not left off your grinning, I see, though Robinette hates it so.

Enter Messenger *hastily.*

MESSENGER. Are you Don Tycho, squire to the victorious and magnanimous Floridor, son of Bonoro?

TYCHO. And is he victorious?

MESSENGER. He has conquered and bound Nigromant. And by the assistance of his father's good spirits all the evil ones are in chains.

FALADEL. Hoo! hoo! hoo!

MESSENGER. The conqueror has called for his squire to attend his triumphal entry into the palace and seraglio.

TYCHO. My heart is with him already, and the rest of my body shall follow as soon as my legs will permit it.

MESSENGER. I fly to let him know it.

Exit Messenger.

FALADEL. Hoo! hoo! hoo!

TYCHO. What makes you so merry?

FALADEL. One touch of the sword that has vanquished Nigromant will restore me. Be a generous rival and present me to him.

TYCHO. Upon my soul, you had better take my advice and stay as you are. But if you will be restored again from your being something to your former nothingness, I will present you to him. Give me a tip of your wing and I'll hand you to your restoration. Come along.

FALADEL. Hoo! hoo! hoo!

He claps his wings with joy, and Tycho *leads him off.*

SCENE IV, *The castle gates.*

The triumphal entry of Floridor *to martial music, with* Nigromant *and* Evil Spirits *in chains. Then enter* Tycho, *attended with the female* Evil Spirits.

TYCHO. Come along, come along. You are once more in my clutches, and I'll take care that you shall never catch me napping again.

SECOND WOMAN. Magnanimous Don Tycho!

TYCHO. O you couple of she devils with your sweet lullabies. It was your string-tickling and quavering that undid me. None of your hypocritical side-looks at me. (*They offer to play.*) Dare not to touch those deluding strings, that poison to the ears of honest men, or I shall forget your sex and drag you at my chariot wheels.

BOTH. Have pity upon us, most gracious Squire.

TYCHO. I will not be gracious. I have no pity, and I will be a severe though upright judge. Foul as you are, you shall have a fair trial. And be assured (for all your ogling and smiling) that I shall find better employment for your fingers than tinkling men of virtue asleep, that hell may break loose and the devils have a holiday.

THIRD WOMAN. I have a petition to deliver.

TYCHO. Justice is blind and can't read it. When I am a governor, all my judges shall be without eyes, ears, hands or pockets—no eyes to read petitions, no ears to hear 'em, no hands to take bribes, and no pockets to hold them. I am an upright judge myself who will not be bribed and, what is still more wonderful, am not worth a doit. Silence, ye fiends!

Say not a word. I've said, and said is done.
Stop all your tongues and let the court go on.

Exeunt.

End of the Fourth Part.

PART V.

SCENE I, *A grand apartment in the seraglio.*
Eunuchs *enter singing the following chorus.*

Touch the thrilling notes of pleasure,
Let the softest, melting measure,
Calm the conqueror's mind.
Let myrtle be with laurel twined,
Beauty with each smiling grace,
The sparkling eye and speaking face,
Attended by the laughing loves,
Around the hero play.
The toil and danger valor proves,
Love and beauty will repay.

Enter Floridor *and* Tycho.

TYCHO. What a fine refreshment this is after the hard labor of fighting and trying causes.

FLORIDOR. Tycho, has Faladel received the benefit he expected from the touch of my sword?

TYCHO. It was wonderfully efficacious. He moulted so fast that, though he made all the haste he could to his apartment, he left as many feathers in the way as if he had been plucked for the spit. The moment he is picked clean from the owl, he will resume the monkey

23.2. End . . . Part] omitted *D*1.

again and appear before Your Honor to pick a quarrel with me. The old bone of contention—Robinette.

FLORIDOR. We shall cool his courage. Bring before us the unhappy beauties who have been forced away and confined for the tyrant's pleasures.

TYCHO (*goes to the door and calls*). Open the female apartments and let their treasures be poured down at the feet of the conqueror. Those that belong to the Squire I shall visit privately and dispose of by private contract.

The chorus is sung again, during which many women of the seraglio enter veiled, and at last Camilla (*who is in chains*) *and* Robinette. *They throw up their veils.*

FLORIDOR (*starting*). Earth and heaven! Camilla!

TYCHO. Hell and the devil! Robinette!

FLORIDOR. All my laurels are blasted.

TYCHO. Mine are in a sad pickle too.

CAMILLA (*running to Floridor*). My life, my love, my Floridor! All my sorrows vanish in these arms. (*As she runs to* Floridor *he turns away*.) What, cold and regardless of me?

FLORIDOR. Can I see you here in the seraglio of Nigromant and not have cause to lament in the midst of my triumph?

CAMILLA. Can you see me here, and in chains, and not find cause for a greater triumph than that which you have gained? Unjust and ungrateful Floridor! We were seized upon by the magician, conveyed here to be the slaves of his pleasure. But my heart was engaged, my mind was free. I resisted his passion, scorned his power, and I triumphed in these chains. Unjust and ungrateful Floridor!

FLORIDOR. Then I have conquered indeed. And thus I seize the brightest reward that ever conquest was crowned withal.

After embracing her, he takes off her chains.

TYCHO. Where are your chains, Robinette?

ROBINETTE. I left 'em behind me.

TYCHO. I believe they slipped easily off. But did you resist too, Robinette?

ROBINETTE. I won't satisfy you. Don't think that I am like Camilla, to be suspected one moment and hugged the next.

TYCHO. Only say to satisfy my honor that you came here against your will, and I'll pass over the consequences.

ROBINETTE. Your honor! I prefer one feather of my favorite owl I have here to your whole mind and body.

---

27. of] *O1*, *O2*, *O3*, *O4*; off *D1*.

TYCHO. Oho, Signora Robinette, have I caught you. What, do you prefer that owl, Faladel, to me?

ROBINETTE. To all the world at present. I did like monkeys some time ago. My mind is changed. I hate grinning and folly. I am for wisdom and gravity. And so, follow *your* inclinations as I shall *mine*.

Exit Robinette.

TYCHO. And so I will, for my inclinations are to follow you. She shall either take me round the neck directly or I'll wring her owl's neck off before her face. She has taught me to be merry, and I won't be made miserable again, if I can help it. I have not conquered the evil spirits for nothing.

Exit Tycho *after* Robinette.

Floridor *and* Camilla *come forward.*

SONG in DIALOGUE.

CAMILLA. The storm shall beat my breast no more,
The vessel safe, the freight on shore,
No more my bark shall tempt the sea,
'Scaped from the rock of jealousy.

FLORIDOR. Bright are the flowers which form this wreath,
And fresh the odors which they breathe.
Thus ever shall our loves be free,
From cruel blights of jealousy.

BOTH. With roses and with myrtles crowned,
The conqueror, Love, smiles all around,
Triumphant reigns by heav'n's decree,
And leads in chains grim jealousy.

At the end of the song a Messenger *enters.*

MESSENGER (*delivers a letter*). For the conqueror, Floridor.

FLORIDOR (*reads*). "By my assistance you recovered your sword and shield by which you have conquered Nigromant and are possessed of his treasures. You are now worthy of my love, and therefore I demand yours.

Whatever you ask,
How dreadful the task,
To perform it 'fore heav'n I vow.
Grinnelda."

What a spiteful old hag! (Floridor *stands confounded.*)

CAMILLA. Whence comes that letter, Floridor, which distresses and confounds you so? I beg to see it. What's the matter? You alarm me.

FLORIDOR. Don't be alarmed. Indeed it is nothing.

CAMILLA. Then let me see this nothing. What, more confounded? O Floridor, false, false Floridor!

FLORIDOR. To convince you how little I value the writer and regard the contents, thus I destroy at once her vanity and your apprehensions.

He tears the letter. It thunders and grows dark. Flames of fire are seen through the seraglio windows. All but Floridor *quit the place, shrieking.*

Is heaven and earth in league against me? What have I done to provoke this war of elements?

Enter Tycho *terrified.*

TYCHO. The devils are got loose again. O, Signior Floridor, what have we done? The palace is on fire, the ladies have lost their senses, and I have lost both the ladies and my senses, for I saw –

FLORIDOR. What, what? Where is Camilla?

TYCHO. I thought I saw her carried through the air by the kind old witch who sobered me and recovered your sword and shield. But away—for the flames are coming upon us. I am no salamander as you are, and therefore I shall get into a colder climate.

Exit Tycho *running.*

FLORIDOR. I will brave it all.

The seraglio breaks to pieces and discovers the whole palace in flames.

SONG.

Let the loud thunder rattle,
  Flash lightning round my head,
Place me in the front of battle,
  By rage and horror led,
Though death in all her ghastly forms appear,
My heart, that knows no crime, can know no fear.

The flames and the ruins of the castle vanish away and discover a fine moonlight scene.

What can all this mean? By what offence unknown to me have I brought this complicated distress upon me?

Enter Tycho *frightened.*

TYCHO. What a dreadful combustion is this. Where my knight is, I

102. away—for] *O*1, *O*2, *O*3, *O*4; away, see *D*1.

can't tell. And where I am and how I got here the fiends alone who brought me here can tell.

FLORIDOR. Hark! Did I not hear a voice? Who's there?

TYCHO. I hear a voice too. I am afraid no friendly one. I expect every moment to feel feathers upon my skin and a crooked beak instead of a nose.

FLORIDOR. Who is muttering there? Art thou a good or evil spirit?

TYCHO. I am neither at present. And how you, Signior Floridor, can speak with so clear a tone of voice in such place as this, and in your condition, puzzles my philosophy.

FLORIDOR. My conscience upbraids me with nothing, and why should I fear?

TYCHO. My conscience is not quite asleep. But I hope my playing at hide-and-seek with the seraglio girls a little cannot be any great offence, after Robinette had discarded me.

Enter Camilla *as an old woman.*

CAMILLA. Joy to you, Floridor. Joy to myself. Now I have caught you near my own premises, I shall not let you go till you have fulfilled your engagements with me.

FLORIDOR. Where is Camilla, pray?

CAMILLA. I have her safe, and very safe—a pledge for your fulfilling the conditions of our treaty.

FLORIDOR. My sword is ready to obey your commands.

CAMILLA. Pooh, pooh! I want no assistance of your *sword*, not I. I must have your *love*, young man, and in return you shall have my maiden affections, for they were never yet bestowed upon anyone.

FLORIDOR. What can I do or say to her while my Camilla is in danger?

TYCHO. (*aside to* Floridor). Tell her you'll have her. She can't live long, and then Camilla may be yours.

CAMILLA. What are you muttering to him?

TYCHO. I was only wishing him joy of his good fortune, of which he does not seem quite so sensible as he ought.

CAMILLA. His joy perhaps is so great he wants words to express it.

TYCHO. What will become of us? Pray, if I may be so bold, what tomb is that? Your late husband's?

CAMILLA. No, no, fool! I am yet a virgin. That tomb is intended to bury any ungrateful lover that may chance to come in my way. Do you see that house there (*Pointing behind the scenes.*)

TYCHO. I see that—house do you call it? (*Aside.*) I have seen a handsomer pigsty.

CAMILLA. Aye, that house and all its furniture are mine. Go you there and prepare for our approaching nuptials.

TYCHO. She's mad. I can't stand upright in the house unless I put my head out of the chimney.

CAMILLA. Why don't you do as I order you?

TYCHO. I'll bring it here, if you please.

CAMILLA. If you are insolent I shall take another course with you. Do as I bid you, or –

TYCHO. You'll make me. I am gone.

Exit Tycho.

DUETTE.

CAMILLA. Take my hand, my heart is thine.
FLORIDOR. My hand and heart they are not mine.
CAMILLA. May love and all its joys be thine.
FLORIDOR. Ye gods above!
Are these the promised joys of love?
CAMILLA. These are the raptures called divine.
FLORIDOR. My hand and heart they are not mine.
CAMILLA. May love for many, many years,
Without its doubts, its cares and fears,
Each moment of our life control.
FLORIDOR. What anguish tears my tortured soul.
CAMILLA. Let me, sweet youth, thy charms behold,
And in these arms thy beauties fold.
FLORIDOR. I cannot hold, I cannot hold.
CAMILLA. No more can I, no more can I.
I blush for shame. O fie, O fie!
FLORIDOR. I am all on fire.
CAMILLA. And so am I, and so am I.
FLORIDOR. It burns, destroys.
What can I do?
CAMILLA. I feel it too.
O let's retire
And hide our loves.
FLORIDOR. Ye gods above!
Are these the promised joys of love?

CAMILLA. Come along, come along. I must compel you to be happy. Give me satisfaction, or you will repent it. (*Takes hold of his hand.*)

FLORIDOR. Draw me, tear me to pieces with wild horses, my last breath shall sigh Camilla. For I am her's and her's alone.

The stage grows light, and Camilla *quitting at once the form of the old woman, assumes her real character and dress.*

CAMILLA. And I am Floridor's and Floridor's alone. (Floridor *starts and stands astonished.*) Behold the reward of thy valor, constancy and honor! The fire has tried and proved the value of the metal. Come to my arms, my hero!

FLORIDOR. Was Grinnelda Camilla? Wonderful heaven! Let me first return my thanks there (*kneels*) for inspiring me with that valor, constancy and honor that has borne me up against every trial and completed my glory and happiness in the arms of my Camilla. (*Runs and embraces her.*)

CAMILLA. I resign my power, fortune, everything to love and be beloved by thee. (*Music is heard.*)

Bonoro *descends in a cloud.*

But see your father to perfect our union.

SONG.

BONORO.
Clouds that had gathered o'er the day,
Now leave the heav'ns more bright,
Vice before virtue's powerful ray,
Sinks to the shades of night.

These evil spirits that late rushed forth,
Are now in darkness bound;
While beauty, valor, matchless worth,
Spread wide their sunshine round.

Enter Tycho *frighted.*

TYCHO. Am I asleep or awake, or neither? or both? It must be a dream.

CAMILLA. I forgot poor Tycho. Have you prepared for the nuptials?

TYCHO. I had almost prepared for a long voyage in the air. I was luckily out of the hut to survey it, when a wind took it up like a boy's kite and it was soon out of sight. I wish the old hag had been in it.

FLORIDOR. I must not hear you say a word against Grinnelda. 'Tis through her that I am in possession of Camilla.

TYCHO. Then heaven bless her for it, say I. But I see I must be through somebody to be in possession of Robinette, and now is the time. (*Draws.*)

Enter Robinette *and* Faladel.

FALADEL. By my faith and wand, there is my rival. And he that will not die for you ought not to live. And so let the stoutest heart take you forever and for aye. (*Draws.*)

TYCHO. You owl, you! Come on. I will soon make you look more dismal than you are.

206. These] *O1*, *O2*, *O3*, *O4*; Those *D1*.

FALADEL. You monkey, you! I will spoil your grinning and settle your features in a moment. By my knighthood, I will.

ROBINETTE. Valiant Dons, a word with both of you before you fight for that which you can never obtain. Be assured, whatever liberties I may have taken with your folly, that I can never give my heart to an owl.

TYCHO. That's some comfort. He, he, he!

ROBINETTE. Nor a monkey.

FALADEL. I am satisfied forever and for aye. (*Turns off.*)

TYCHO. Here, take your scarf again (*pulling it off*). I won't stay to be laughed at. If your love-stomach for me returns, you know where to send for some plum cake this holiday time. And so, your servant.

Exit Tycho.

Bonoro *waves his wand. The cloud ascends and discovers a fine distant prospect of the sea and a castle at a distance, with the sun rising.*

BONORO.
Ye once most wretched of mankind,
By tyrant power and lust confined,
From vice and slavery free,
Come join our sports and this way move,
To celebrate their virtuous love
And your own liberty.

Enter the different characters of the seraglio, Men *and* Women, *and join in*
A GRAND DANCE.

Bonoro, Floridor, Camilla, Robinette, *&c. &c. come forward.*

SONG.

BONORO.
Honor is to beauty plighted,
Hearts with hands shall be united,
Hymen comes, his torch is lighted.
Honor, truth, and beauty call,
Attend the nuptial festival.

FLORIDOR.
Love in my breast, no storm blowing,
Feels each tide is fuller growing,
And in grateful strains o'erflowing,
Honor, truth, *&c.*

ROBINETTE.
Love in my breast, though a rover,
Calmly sporting with each lover,
Will today with joy run over.
Honor, truth, *&c.*

CAMILLA. Love in my breast knows no measure,
Swells and almost bursts with pleasure,
Here to share its boundless treasure.

FLORIDOR. / CAMILLA. Love in my breast, *&c.*

GRAND CHORUS.

Let the written page,
Through ev'ry age,
Record the wond'rous story;
'Tis decreed from above,
Her virtue should be crowned with love,
And his with love and glory.

Finis.

The Meeting of the Company; or, Bayes's Art of Acting

1774

Collated
&
Perfect.
J.L. 1800.

Sir

If the following little Piece call'd The Meeting of the Company or Bayes's Art of Acting, meets the approbation of the Lord Chamberlain we shall have it perform'd at the Theatre Royal in Drury Lane

5th Septr 1774 —

D. Garrick
for Mr Lacy &
himself

The managers' letter to the Lord Chamberlain for licensing, preceding the manuscript play in the Larpent Collection. The Huntington Library, San Marino, California.

Dramatis Personae

Phill, *the carpenter*	Mr. *Wright*.
Prompter, William Hopkins	Mr. *Ackman*.
Ballet Master	Mr. *Grimaldi*.
Singer	
Parsons	Mr. *Parsons*.
Miss Platt	Miss *Platt*.
Weston	Mr. *Weston*.
Patent	Mr. *Aickin*.
Hurst, a tragedy actor	Mr. *Hurst*.
Bayes	Mr. *King*.
Bransby	Mr. *Bransby*.
Baddeley	Mr. *Baddeley*.

Other members of the Drury Lane company
representing all walks of stage life.

The Meeting of the Company; or, Bayes's Art of Acting

The curtain rises and discovers the stage full of different people at work, painters, gilders, carpenters, etc., singers singing, dancers dancing, actors and actresses saluting each other, and all seem busy.

Enter Phill, *the carpenter.*

PHILL. Upon my word, Gentlemen and Ladies, if you won't clear the stage we can never be ready to open the house tomorrow.

Enter Prompter.

PROMPTER. What's the matter, Phill? Always a scolding.

PHILL. We shall never be ready if you don't give up the stage to us. Lower the clouds there, Rag, and bid Jack Trundle sweep out the thunder-trunk. We had very slovenly storms last season. Mr. Hopkins, did you ever see such a litter and hear such a noise?

PROMPTER. Yes, very often. Indeed Ladies and Gentlemen, you must practice your singing and dancing elsewhere, or we shan't ever be ready.

BALLET MASTER. Come along then, Gentlemen and Ladies, we'll go below.

Dancing off.

SINGER. And we'll practice in the Greenroom.

Exit singing and books.

PHILL. We shall do pretty well now. What with coronations, installations, Portsmouth Reviews, masquerades, Jubilees, Fete Champetres and the devil, we have no rest at all. Master's head is always at work, and we are never idle. If they want the perpetual motion let 'em come to our theatre. Come bustle, my lads. Clear away there.

Exit.

Enter Parsons.

PARSONS. How do you Master Prompter? Lame still I find. You have no enemy but the gout.

PROMPTER. And is not that enough? I have tried everything and nothing will do. My body is starved with abstinence and my pocket picked by the leige doctor, and this is my reward. (*Showing his foot.*) I am too poor to be made a fool of. My betters can afford it.

PARSONS. Ay, that leige doctor undertook for about ten thousand pounds to set a number of gouty folks a dancing in a twelve month. But before the time, he danced off with the money, and death danced off with him the year after.

PROMPTER. With the gout in his stomach. But what has recovered you so well. If you are as plump in the pocket as you are in the face, you have made a good campaign and the country agrees with you.

PARSONS. Pretty well, Mr. Hopkins. We set out heavily but we mended our pace, lived very well, paid our debts, had some bad houses, some indifferent and many very good ones, a few quarrels, an intrigue or two, and indispositions as usual.

Enter some actresses.

How do you, Ladies? You are welcome to town again. (*Salutes them.*) Miss Platt, the managers desire you will be ready in this part by tomorrow night. 'Tis very short and very easy study.

MISS PLATT. I have been harrassed all the summer, and now I must sit up all night to study this dab of a thing. Managers never consider the wear and tear of a constitution.

Exit peevishly.

PARSONS. Now the old work begins. Jingle jangle from September to June.

PROMPTER. I shall now get things ready for the rehearsal.

Exit.

Enter Weston.

PARSONS. What, little Tom Weston. Give me your hand, boy.

WESTON. As tall as yourself, goodman Parsons the Giant.

PARSONS. Come, come, we won't dispute about a quarter of an inch. You are a new man, so sleek, so clear, and the end of your nose as fair as the rest of your face. What have you been doing, boy?

WESTON. Turned over a new leaf.

PARSONS. In some tavern book, I suppose.

WESTON. No, no, the leaves there were quite full. I was obliged to reform, having no money. I am taking care of my constitution.

PARSONS. Reform! I should be glad to hear what you call reformation.

WESTON. Why, what other folks call reformation. I live soberly when I am ill in order to get well. And when I am well, I live a little pleasantly to get ill again. There would be no variety without it.

PARSONS. None of your variety for me.

WESTON. Besides, *there's a pleasure in being ill which none but actors know*.

PARSONS. I don't understand you.

WESTON. It vexes a manager and pays him in kind. I love to pay my debts when I am able. But talk of the manager and he is here.

Enter Patent, *performers meeting him.*

PATENT. Gentlemen and Ladies, your servant. All meet me with cheerful smiling faces. What a pity it is that they should grow cold and cloudy with the winter. Mr. Parsons, your servant. Tom Weston, your hand. All in spirits, I hope, and ready to take the field.

PARSONS. The army catches spirit from the general. I rejoice to see you so well. We were damp'd by the newspapers.

PATENT. Ay, ay, they killed me one day and revived me the next. Newspaper life, like real life, is chequered, a mixture of good and evil. What they took away yesteday they'll give again tomorrow, sometimes dead, sometimes alive. Now praise, now blame, make holes and darn 'em again, can anything be more impartial?

WESTON. What, may any man who gives me a plaister have liberty to break my head?

PATENT. Break your vanity's head, you mean, Tom. If the fools of our profession would have more sensibility upon the stage and less off it, they might strut their hour without fretting. Let 'em never play the fool but when they ought to do it, be as fine gentlemen as they can in their business and never assume the character out of it, and the newspapers won't hurt 'em.

PARSONS. But to be always in fear of a cat-o'-nine-tails?

PATENT. This paper police may go a little too far sometimes, and so will Constables and Justices of the Peace, and therefore would you have none? Come, come, if we and our betters were not well watched, the state and the stage would both suffer for it. But, mum! This is only among ourselves. Now let us prepare for action.

WESTON. We'll do our best, General. Good pay and well paid is the nerves of war. Had I the salary of a general, I could command an army as well as the best.

A tragedy actor comes from the rest.

TRAGEDY ACTOR. With submission, Mr. Weston, what did you mean by saying you could command an army?

WESTON. I meant to say that I could play tragedy as well as the best of you.

ALL. Ha, ha, ha!

PATENT. Well said, Tom. Ha, ha, ha!

WESTON. And I would do it too. Who's afraid?

TRAGEDY ACTOR. Don't imagine, Sir, because you can make an audience laugh in Jerry Sneak, Dr. Last, *etc.*, that you can speak heroic verse and touch the passions. (*Struts about.*)

WESTON. Why not? I can set my arms so, take two strides, roar as well as the best of you, and look like an owl.

TRAGEDY ACTOR (*with contempt*). Is there nothing else requisite to form a tragedian?

WESTON. O, yes, the perriwig maker to make me a bush, a tailor a hoop petticoat, a carpenter a truncheon, a shoemaker high heels and cork soles. And as for strange faces and strange noises I can make them myself.

PATENT. Pray, gentlemen, don't quarrel about nothing, and before the season begins.

TRAGEDY ACTOR. About nothing, Mr. Patent?

PATENT. Dear Mr. Hurst, don't put on a tragedy face to me. Mr. Bayes will be here directly, and he'll prove to us all that there is nothing in acting tragedy or comedy.

WESTON. He proves there is nothing in writing them?

PATENT. You may jest if you please, but Mr. Bayes is very serious.

PARSONS. Not the less foolish for that.

PATENT. As you shall see by his letter. There, read it. (*Gives the letter.*)

WESTON. How do you know that I can? I'll try whether I have not forgot. (*They get about him while he reads.*) "Sir, though you and your players used me and my play very ill, I will see you and your players again."

PARSONS. A very good reason that.

WESTON (*reading*). "Though you and your players have deprived me of my just rights and profits, I will nevertheless be the making of you both."

PATENT. There's a good Christian for you.

WESTON (*reads*). "I have discovered a method to make the worst actors equal to the best. As you have plenty to work upon –"

PARSONS. We are much obliged to him.

WESTON (*reads*). "If you will promise to perform my play, I will instruct your players directly. As they are a kind of smoky chimneys, I'll undertake 'em. No cure no pay; say ay or no. Yours, if you are wise—Bayes." We are smoky chimneys, are we? We shall smoke him, I believe, if he comes.

BAYES (*without*). Pray take my cloak, young man, and show me to the manager.

PATENT. Here he comes. Tom, don't be too riotous, but listen to him and learn.

WESTON. Rather too old for that.

Enter Bayes.

BAYES. Mr. Patent, your humble servant. Gentlemen and Ladies, I may be your friend if you are not your own enemies. Let all past mistakes be forgotten and let us begin a new score.

WESTON. I always do, wherever I can.

BAYES. I hope you have all had a successful summer. I dare say you have all filled your pockets. The poor people in the country know no better.

TRAGEDY ACTOR. There are very good judges in country towns, Mr. Bayes.

BAYES. And you are a very good actor in a country town, Mr. Hurst. You roar and they clap. 'Tis all very well. One man's meat is another man's poison. We must all live, Mr. Hurst. I wish you joy of your country judges and your country judges joy of you, with all my heart. What, my old friend Mr. Bransby? I sincerely wish you joy. I heard of your fame in the country.

BRANSBY (*roughly*). I have not been in the country.

BAYES. I mean, Mr.—when you were in the country.

BRANSBY. I have not been there for many years.

BAYES. So much the better. Between you and me, you are much in the right on't.

Enter Baddeley.

Mr. Baddeley, your hand. I regard you as a brother author. Your Magic Lantern has bewitched everybody. What, have you produced some ridiculous characters?

BADDELEY. Very ridiculous indeed.

BAYES. I hope you will lash the bad poets, ha?

BADDELEY. I have not yet, but in my next edition I have such a character of a poet.

BAYES. I rejoice to hear it. Tell me a little. Is he ridiculous?

BADDELEY. O yes, a conceited old fool whose vanity makes him ridiculous even to the lamplighters of the theatre.

BAYES (*chuckles*). Good, good. Go on.

BADDELEY. Though old, there is not an infirmity of the mind which he has not. To crown the whole, with a face as rough as mine and a wig like yours, he fancies himself a *beau garçon* and gallants the ladies.

BAYES. What an old fool it must be. Work him and jerk him, I beg of you. (*Both laugh.*)

BADDELEY. Never fear me.

BAYES. But, Mr. Baddeley, when you speak of him again, don't make any comparisons between your face and my wig, I beg of you. Take that hint from me, and I wish your performance a continuance of public favor.

BADDELEY. Neither your heir or mine will be much the richer for our scribbling, Mr. Bayes.

Exit.

BAYES. *Scribbling? Our scribbling!* How we apples swim! A word with you, Mr. Patent. As I came through the hall, there were some of your actors to whom I gave a very proper salute (careless indeed, but civil), to which they made little or no return.

PATENT. Indeed.

BAYES. One in particular, dressed in red, with a cocked hat, black beard, and a cane dangling upon his wrist, looked full in my face and laughed at me.

PATENT. It was Tom King. I am sure he meant nothing.

BAYES. I know that very well. I don't expect meaning from them, but submission and civility. Your players appear to me rather more conceited than they were. Indeed there was little room for any addition in that particular.

PATENT. The matter is this, Mr. Bayes, being just returned from the country, where they play kings and heroes, and they can't be lowered immediately. In a few days, by good discipline and walking them from their dreams of royalty, they'll be very civil again and very good subjects.

BAYES. Poor fellows. Their weak heads are easily turned. But we'll fix 'em. Do you about your business, Mr. Patent, and I'll to mine. When I have given 'em a lecture or two, you shall hear them.

PATENT. I will prepare matters for opening the season, and you for carrying it on successfully.

Exit.

BAYES. Leave that to me. If I don't chip your blocks into some shape, say I am no workman. (*Pulls out his book.*)

WESTON. Are you a carpenter, Mr. Bayes?

BAYES. Figurative, Mr. Weston. I am fond of figures and make a good one whenever I can.

PARSONS (*looking at him from top to toe*). I see you do.

BAYES. Gentlemen and Ladies, oblige me with your attention. As music is said to have charms "To sooth the savage beast, to soften rocks and bend the knotted oak," I shall convey my instructions to you in very musical numbers. It will indeed be the only way to break through and soften that strong, rocky, knotty, crusty matter which nature has (as I may say) enveloped you with. I shall convince the world in this instance as I have in others that I will always oppose nature, that I am above her and despise her. But to business. Here is the grand specific. Surround me; my good patients take your medicines kindly. To ascertain my right to the invention and secure my property, for these are thievish times, I call it *Bayes's Art of Acting*; or, *The Worst Equal to the Best.* A very comfortable remedy for you, my good friends, so take it without loss of time. I will not only make the worst equal to the best, but the tragedians, comedians, and vice verso.

WESTON. Vice versy? What's that, pray?

BAYES. That is, I will make the comedians tragedians.

WESTON. That's good news, Parsons, that vice versy.

PARSONS. Who knows but you and I may play Brutus and Cassius.

BAYES. Silence, I beseech you. Who among you is the least fit to be either the hero in tragedy or fine gentleman in comedy? Let him come forward. To show the force of my art, I will begin with him first. Not a soul of 'em will stir.

WESTON. Mr. Bayes, put it the other way and ask who is most fit for a hero and fine gentleman and try the effect of it.

BAYES. Thank you. Any gentleman, I say, that is most fit for the characters of a hero or fine gentleman may begin the experiment. (*They all come forward.*)

WESTON. I told you so, Mr. Bayes. All heroes and fine gentlemen. Now, gentlemen, you may go back again, for I'll be the man. I'm not ashamed to own that I am the least fit.

BAYES. And therefore the most fit. You shall both be a hero and fine gentleman, and you won't be the first little man who has tried at both.

ALL. Ha, ha, ha! Now for it, Tom!

BAYES. Before I begin, I must tell you that I intend to extend my scheme to Poetry, Painting and Music, and will in a few years make genius of as little consequence in this nation as a fine complexion,

THE

THEATRES.

A

POETICAL DISSECTION.

By Sir NICHOLAS NIPCLOSE, Baronet.

THE SECOND EDITION.

Behold the Muses ROSCIUS sue in Vain,
Taylors & Carpenters usurp their Reign.

LONDON:
PRINTED FOR JOHN BELL, NEAR EXETER-EXCHANGE, IN THE STRAND;
AND C. ETHERINGTON, AT YORK.
M.DCC.LXXII.

Title Page from *The Theatres. A Poetical Dissection* by Sir Nicholas Nipclose. Victoria and Albert Museum

which you know, ladies, is to be bought of any French milliner in the Bills of Mortality. Pray be silent. You'll never have such another opportunity.

He reads.

"Of giving life to clods I make profession,
Grace to the lame and to the blind expression.
In me the dullest mortal finds a friend,
I beg you all for your own sakes attend.
Whither your bias be,
To skip and grin in Comedy,
Or rant and roar in Tragedy,
It is all one to me."

WESTON. That we do verily believe.

BAYES. When I come to some striking forcible lines, you must all by way of a Greek Chorus repeat and act them. I wish that some scholars and gentlemen of the university were here. It would give 'em great pleasure.

Shakespeare has said—a silly, empty creature!
"Never o'erstep the modesty of nature."
I say you *must*. To prove it I engage
Whate'er your sex or character or age,
No modesty will do upon the stage.

WESTON. Ladies, pray mind what the gentleman says to you.

BAYES. And pray mind the following string of similes, if you love good writing.

WESTON (*aside*). I wish I could return the favor with another string.

BAYES. "Genius a gem, search all the kingdom round,
Is not on ev'ry dunghill to be found.
Therefore in charity I come to tell
How *Bristol Stones*, well set, will do as well."

PARSONS. Brethren of the Bristol Company, there is some comfort for us.

BAYES. I'll comfort you all, man, woman and child, before I have done with you. (*Reads.*)

"Nature's a bird, and every fool will fail
Who hopes to lay some salt upon her tail.
In vain to seize the wanton, boobies watch her,
They've neither eyes, legs, hands or heads to catch her."

Ergo, 'tis not worth your while to run after her.

WESTON. I'll try a little for all that.

BAYES (*reads*). "Gold is a scarce commodity –

WESTON. So it is.

BAYES. Don't interrupt me. (*Reads.*)

"Gold is a scarce commodity—but brass,
Of which no scarcity, as well may pass."

WESTON. There's comfort again for us. These hard times –

BAYES. That I may not burden your minds too much, which may be overloaded already, I shall comprise the Art of Acting comedy and tragedy in a few lines. You have heard of the Iliad in a Nutshell. Here it is. (*Shows the paper.*)

WESTON. Crack away and give us the kernel.

BAYES (*reads*). "First, gentlemen, turn nature out of door,
Then rant away 'till you can rant no more.
Walk, talk and look as none walked, talked and looked before."

PARSONS. We can all do that.

WESTON. And have done it a hundred times.

BAYES. Silence, or you are undone.

WESTON. Mum!

BAYES (*reads*). "Would you in tragedy extort applause,
Distort *yourselves*—now rage, now start, now pause.
Beat breast, roll eyes, stretch nose, up brows, down jaws.
Then strut, stride, stare, goggle, bounce and bawl,
And when you're out of breath, pant, drag and drawl."

There's a picture for you, Gentlemen and Ladies.

WESTON. And a devilish ugly one.

BAYES. Repeat it after me and act it.

WESTON. "Would you in tragedy *etc.*"

BAYES (*reads*). "Be in extremes in Buskin or in Sock,
In action wild, in attitude a block.
From the spectator's eye your faults to hide,
Be either whirlwind or be petrified."

Exampli—Gratis—mind, Gentlemen and Ladies.

(*He reads.*) "I thurst for vengeance, bring me, fiends, a cup
Large as my soul, that I may drink it up."

WESTON. That I may drink it up. That's good. (*Licks his lips.*)

BAYES. But you must not drink it up with joy, Mr. Weston.

WESTON. I can't help it. You must alter the figure.

BAYES. Not for all the wine in the kingdom. Mind me. (*He reads.*)

" 'Tis only blood can quench me. Thus I draw
My droughty dagger, and thus slake it. Ha!"

(*Starts into an attitude.*) There's start, pant, pause, drag and drawl for you. Now Chorus all. " 'Tis only blood, *etc.*"

They all chorus.

" 'Tis only blood *etc.*"

BAYES. Are you all blocked in attitude? Tell me, somebody, for I can't stir.

PARSONS (*in an attitude*). Nor I.

WESTON. Block and all. Block, I assure you, Mr. Bayes, from one end to the other.

BAYES. Thank ye, Gentlemen. But to proceed.

"To heighten terror–be it wrong or right,
Be black your coat, your handkerchief be white,
Thus pull your hair to add to your distress.
What your face cannot, let your wig express."

I have seen a Romeo so expeditious that he has been dressed like a bridegroom in one scene, and in the next slap he has a complete suit of mourning made and dresses himself in it from top to toe before the tailor could finish a single buttonhole. (*He reads.*)

"Your author's words, or lengthen 'em or lop 'em,
Stretch 'em in tragic scenes, in comic chop 'em.
On tragic rack first stretch the word and tear,
Crack nerves, burst brain, rivet me despa-a-re."

Crack nerves, burst brain. *There's a tear for you.* Rivet me despa-a-a-air *and there's a stretch for you.* Mind and mark all your r'rs too, or you won't outstep the modesty of nature.

"Cr'rck–bur'rst–ner'rves–brain–rivet despa-a-a-air,"

I'll make a word of two syllables two and twenty, if I please. I shall reach their hearts one way or another.

WESTON. If you have a receipt for men as well as words, I wish you would stretch me and Parsons a little.

BAYES. You may have your wish sooner than you expect, Gentlemen. Though I can't make tall men of you, I'll make great men of you, which is a better thing. (*He reads.*)

"Observe in comedy to frisk about.
Never stand still. Jerk, work; fly in, fly out,
Your faults conceal in flutter and in hurry,
And with snip, snap, the poet's meaning worry,
Like bullies hide your wants in bounce and vapor.
If mem'ry fails, take snuff, laugh, curse and caper.
Hey, Jack! what!—damn it! ha, ha! Cloud, dull, sad,
Cuss it! Hell devil! Woman, wine, drunk, mad!"

Now get into the road as fast as you can and drive away.

"Life's a postchaise. Oil it with pleasure, Boy.
Smooth run the wheels when they are greased with joy."

(*Capers.*) You should always caper off here.
"Smooth run the wheels *etc.*"

WESTON. With all my heart.
"Life's a postchaise *etc.*"

They all caper off repeating the lines, and he on the other side.

BAYES. Very well on all sides. Let me see an audience that won't be moved with that. (*He turns, and seeing them gone stares and drops his voice.*) They are moved indeed. Where the devil are they? (*He turns to the other side.*) Now Mr. Weston, mind and caper in again repeating
"Life's a postchaise *etc.*"

WESTON (*without*). I'll caper no more.

BAYES (*approaching the side scene*). What do you say?

Enter Weston.

WESTON. I'll caper no more, I tell you.

BAYES. You won't caper anymore? But I'll make you caper, and to some tune. Where's the manager?

WESTON. You had better keep your passion for your next tragedy. It is thrown away upon me. I'll caper no more, I tell you.

BAYES. I'll appeal to the town and make you caper.

WESTON. So will I, and make you both curse and caper.

BAYES. You don't know what I have to say to them.

WESTON. I can say something to 'em too.

BAYES. That you may not run your head against a wall (which perhaps would not hurt you), I will tell you what I'll say to them.

WESTON. Come along. I'll answer it.

BAYES (*addressing himself to the house*). Ladies and Gentlemen. (I wish from my heart there was somebody in the house to hear me.) Ladies and Gentlemen –

WESTON. So far I am with you. "*Ladies and Gentlemen*"

BAYES. Here's a very silly fellow of an actor.

WESTON. Of an author I say –

BAYES. Who can scarce read

WESTON. Who can't write –

BAYES. and knows nothing of his profession.

WESTON. No–nothing of his profession.

BAYES. If you will suffer such a pigmy, insignificant fellow to laugh at me, and not take it ill

WESTON. I am often laughted at and never take it ill.

BAYES. I say, Gentlemen and Ladies, if you will not drive such a little blockhead from the stage, you will not have a single author of merit to write for you.

WESTON. And I say, Gentlemen and Ladies, if you will not drive such a great blockhead from the stage, you will not have a single author of merit to write for you. If nature is to be turned out of doors, there will be nothing but ranting and roaring in tragedy and capering and facemaking in comedy. The stage will go to ruin, the public will go to sleep, and I shall go to jail, and there will be an end of poor Johnny Pringle and his pig.

Exit.

BAYES. Johnny Pringle and–what am I reduced to! Very fine, very fine. And so here I am left to cool my heels by myself again. This is a settled and determined plan to affront me. I will keep down my bile if possible. (*Whistles and walks about.*) It won't do. The devil has got the better, and I must leave my curses behind me. May this house be always as empty as it is now. Or if it must fill, let it be with fine ladies to disturb the actors, fine gentlemen to admire themselves, and fat citizens to snore in the boxes. May the pit be filled with nothing but crabbed critics, unemployed actors, and managers' orders. May places be kept in the green boxes without being paid for, and may the galleries never bring good humor or horse laughs with them again. If I ever honor this place with my wit and presence again, may I for my folly be doomed to be an actor here in the winter and get money by tumbling and rope-dancing in the summer. Now my mind's easy. (*Sighs.*) *Sic transit gloria mundi.*

Exit.

Finis.

Bon Ton; or, High Life above Stairs

1775

BON TON;

OR,

High Life above Stairs.

A

COMEDY.

IN TWO ACTS.

AS IT IS PERFORMED AT THE

THEATRE ROYAL,

IN

DRURY-LANE.

LONDON:

Printed for T. BECKET, the Corner of the Adelphi, in the Strand. 1775.

[PRICE ONE-SHILLING.]

Facsimile title page of the First Edition.
Folger Shakespeare Library.

Advertisement

This little Drama, which had been thrown aside for many years, was brought out last season, with some alterations, for the benefit of MR. KING, as a token of regard for one, who, during a long engagement, was never known, unless confined by real illness, to disappoint the Public, or distress the Managers—The Author is sincerely apprehensive that the excellence of the performance upon the stage, will greatly lessen its credit with the readers in the closet.

Prologue

Written by GEORGE COLMAN
Spoken by Mr. King

Fashion in ev'ry thing bears sov'reign sway,
And words and periwigs have both their day:
Each have their *purlieus* too, are modish each
In stated districts, wigs as well as speech.
The *Tyburn* scratch, thick club, and *Temple* tie,
The parson's feather-top, frizz'd broad and high!
The coachman's cauliflower, built tiers on tiers!
Differ not more from bags and brigadiers,
Than great St. George's, or St. James's styles,
From the broad dialect of Broad St. Giles.
What is *Bon Ton*?—"Oh, damme," cries a buck—
Half drunk—"ask me, my dear, and you're in luck!
"Bon Ton's to swear, break windows, beat the watch,
"Pick up a wench, drink healths, and roar a catch.
"Keep it up, keep it up! damme, take your swing!
"Bon Ton is Life, my boy; Bon Ton's the thing!"
"Ah! I loves life, and all the joys it yields"—
Says Madam Fussock, warm from Spital-fields.
"*Bone Tone's* the space 'twixt Saturday and Monday,
"And riding in a one-horse chair o' Sunday!
" 'Tis drinking tea on summer afternoons
"At Bagnigge-Wells, with china and gilt spoons!
" 'Tis laying by our stuffs, red cloaks, and pattens,
"To dance cow-tillions, all in silks and satins!"
"Vulgar!" cries Miss. Observe in higher life
The feather'd spinster, and thrice-feather'd wife!
"The *Club's Bon Ton. Bon Ton's* a constant trade
"Of rout, *Festino*, Ball and Masquerade!
" 'Tis plays and puppet-shows; 'tis something new!
" 'Tis losing thousands ev'ry night at loo!

"Nature it thwarts, and contradicts all reason;
" 'Tis stiff French stays, and fruit when out of season!
"A rose, when half a guinea is the price;
"A set of bays, scarce bigger than six mice;
"To visit friends you never wish to see;
"Marriage 'twixt those, who never can agree;
"Old dowagers, dressed, painted, patch'd, and curl'd;
"This is *Bon Ton*, and this we call *the world!*"
* ["True," says my Lord; and thou my only son,
"Whate'er your faults, ne'er sin against *Bon Ton!*
"Who toils for learning at a public school,
"And digs for Greek and Latin is a fool.
"French, French, my boy's the thing! *jasez!* prate, chatter!
"Trim be the mode, whipt-syllabub the matter!
"Walk like a Frenchman! for on English pegs
"Moves native awkwardness with two left legs.
"Of courtly friendship form a treacherous league;
"Seduce men's daughters, with their wives intrigue;
"In sightly semicircles round your nails;
"Keep your teeth clean—and grin, if small talk fails –
"But never *laugh*, whatever jest prevails!
"Nothing but nonsense e'er gave laughter birth,
"That vulgar way the vulgar show their mirth.
"Laughter's a rude convulsion, sense that justles,
"Disturbs the cockles, and distorts the muscles.
"Hearts may be black, but all should wear clean faces;
"The Graces, boy! the Graces, Graces, Graces!"]
Such is *Bon Ton!* and walk this city through
In building, scribbling, fighting, and virtù,
And various other shapes, 'twill rise to view.
Tonight our *Bayes*, with bold, but careless tints,
Hits off a sketch or two, like Darly's prints.
Should connoisseurs allow his rough draughts strike 'em,
'Twill be Bon Ton to see 'em and to like 'em.

* The Lines between Crotchets are omitted in the Theatre.

Dramatis Personae

Men.

Lord Minikin	Mr. *Dodd.*
Sir John Trotley	Mr. *King.*
Colonel Tivy	Mr. *Brereton.*
Jessamy	Mr. *La Mash.*
Davy	Mr. *Parsons.*
Mignon	Mr. *Burton.*

Women.

Lady Minikin	Mrs. *King.*
Miss Tittup	Mrs. *Abington.*
Gymp	Miss *Platt.*

Bon Ton; or, High Life Above Stairs

ACT I. SCENE I.

Enter Lady Minikin *and Miss* Tittup.

LADY MINIKIN. It is not, my dear, that I have the least regard for my Lord; I had no love for him before I married him, and you know, matrimony is no breeder of affection; but it hurts my pride, that he should neglect me, and run after other women.

MISS TITTUP. Ha, ha, ha, how can you be so hypocritical, Lady Minikin, as to pretend to uneasiness at such trifles: but pray have you made any new discoveries of my Lord's gallantry?

LADY MINIKIN. New discoveries! why, I saw him myself yesterday morning in a hackney-coach, with a minx in a pink cardinal; you shall absolutely burn yours, Tittup, for I shall never bear to see one of that color again.

MISS TITTUP. Sure she does not suspect me. (*Aside.*) And where was your Ladyship, pray, when you saw him?

LADY MINIKIN. Taking the air with Colonel Tivy in his *vis-à-vis*.

MISS TITTUP. But, my dear Lady Minikin, how can you be so angry that my Lord was hurting your pride, as you call it, in the hackney-coach, when you had him so much in your power in the *vis-à-vis*?

LADY MINIKIN. What, with my Lord's friend, and my friend's lover! (*Takes her by the hand.*) O fie, Tittup!

MISS TITTUP. Pooh, pooh, Love and Friendship are very fine names to be sure, but they are mere visiting acquaintance; we know their names indeed, talk of 'em sometimes, and let 'em knock at our doors, but we never let 'em in, you know. (*Looking roguishly at her.*)

LADY MINIKIN. I vow, Tittup, you are extremely polite.

MISS TITTUP. I am extremely indifferent in these affairs, thanks to my education.—We must marry, you know, because other people of fashion marry; but I should think very meanly of myself, if after I was married, I should feel the least concern at all about my husband.

LADY MINIKIN. I hate to praise myself, and yet I may with truth aver that no woman of quality ever had, can have, or will have, so consummate a contempt for her Lord, as I have for my most honorable and puissant Earl of Minikin, Viscount Perriwinkle, and Baron Titmouse.—Ha, ha, ha!

MISS TITTUP. But is it not strange, Lady Minikin, that merely his being your husband, should create such indifference; for certainly, in every other eye, his Lordship has great accomplishments.

LADY MINIKIN. Accomplishments! thy head is certainly turned; if you know any of 'em, pray let's have 'em; they are a novelty, and will amuse me.

MISS TITTUP. Imprimis, he is a man of quality.

LADY MINIKIN. Which, to be sure, includes all the cardinal virtues—poor girl!—go on!

MISS TITTUP. He is a very handsome man.

LADY MINIKIN. He has a very bad constitution.

MISS TITTUP. He has wit.

LADY MINIKIN. He is a Lord, and a little goes a great way.

MISS TITTUP. He has great good nature.

LADY MINIKIN. No wonder—he's a fool.

MISS TITTUP. And then his fortune, you'll allow —

LADY MINIKIN. Was a great one—but he games, and if fairly, he's undone; if not, he deserves to be hanged—and so, Exit my Lord Minikin.—And now, let your wise uncle, and my good cousin Sir John Trotley, Baronet, enter: Where is he, pray?

MISS TITTUP. In his own room, I suppose, reading pamphlets and newspapers, against the enormities of the times; if he stays here a week longer, notwithstanding my expectations from him, I shall certainly affront him.

LADY MINIKIN. I am a great favorite, but it is impossible much longer to act up to his very righteous ideas of things.—Isn't it pleasant to hear him abuse everybody and everything, and yet always finishing with a—*You'll excuse me, Cousin*?—Ha, ha, ha!

MISS TITTUP. What do you think the Goth said to me yesterday? One of the knots of his tie hanging down his left shoulder, and his fringed cravat nicely twisted down his breast, and thrust through his gold button hole, which looked exactly like my little Barbet's head in his gold collar—"*Niece Tittup*," cries he, drawing himself up, "*I protest against this manner of conducting yourself, both at home and abroad*."—"What are your objections, Sir John?" answered I, a little pertly.—"*Various and manifold*," replied he. "*I have no time to enumerate particulars now, but I will venture to prophesy, if you keep whirling round in the vortex of Pantheons, Operas, Fes-*

tinos, Coteries, Masquerades, and all the Devilades in this town, your head will be giddy, down you will fall, lose the name of Lucretia, and be called nothing but Tittup ever after—You'll excuse me, Cousin!"—And so he left me.

LADY MINIKIN. O, the barbarian!

Enter Gymp.

GYMP. A card, your Ladyship, from Mrs. Pewitt.

LADY MINIKIN. Poor Pewitt!—If she can be but seen at public places, with a woman of quality, she's the happiest of plebeians. (*Reads the Card.*) "Mrs. Pewitt's respects to Lady Minikin, and Miss Tittup; hopes to have the pleasure of attending them, to Lady Filligree's ball this evening.—Lady Daisey sees masks."—We'll certainly attend her.—Gymp, put some message cards upon my toilet, I'll send an answer immediately; and tell one of my footmen, that he must make some visits for me today again, and send me a list of those he made yesterday: he must be sure to call at Lady Pettitoes, and if she should unluckily be at home, he must say that he came to inquire after her sprained ankle.

MISS TITTUP. Ay, ay, give our compliments to her sprained ankle.

LADY MINIKIN. That woman's so fat, she'll never get well of it, and I am resolved not to call at her door myself, till I am sure of not finding her at home.—I am horridly low spirited today; do send your Colonel to play at chess with me. Since he belonged to you, Titty, I have taken a kind of liking to him; I like everything that loves my Titty. (*Kisses her.*)

MISS TITTUP. I know you do, my dear Lady. (*Kisses her.*)

LADY MINIKIN. That sneer I don't like; if she suspects, I shall hate her. (*Aside.*) Well, dear Titty, I'll go and write my cards, and dress for the masquerade, and if that won't raise my spirits, you must assist me to plague my Lord a little.

Exit Lady Minikin.

MISS TITTUP. Yes, and I'll plague my Lady a little, or I am much mistaken: my Lord shall know every tittle that has passed: what a poor, blind, half-witted, self-conceited creature, this dear friend and relation of mine is! And what a fine spirited gallant soldier my Colonel is! My Lady Minikin likes him, he likes my fortune; my Lord likes me, and I like my Lord; however, not so much as he imagines, or to play the fool so rashly as he may expect; she must be very silly indeed, who can't flutter about the flame without burning her wings. What a great revolution in this family in the space of fifteen months! —We went out of England a very awkward, regular, good English family. But half a year in France, and a winter passed in the warmer climate of Italy, have ripened our minds to every refinement of ease, dissipation and pleasure.

Enter Colonel Tivy.

COLONEL TIVY. May I hope, Madam, that your humble servant had some share in your last reverie?

MISS TITTUP. How is it possible to have the least knowledge of Colonel Tivy and not make him the principal object of one's reflections?

COLONEL TIVY. That man must have very little feeling and taste, who is not proud of a place in the thoughts of the finest woman in Europe.

MISS TITTUP. O fie, Colonel! (*Curtsies and blushes.*)

COLONEL TIVY. By my honor, Madam, I mean what I say.

MISS TITTUP. By your honor, Colonel! why will you pass off your counters to me? Don't I know that you fine gentlemen regard no honor but that which is given at the gaming table; and which indeed ought to be the only honor you should make free with.

COLONEL TIVY. How can you, Miss, treat me so cruelly? Have I not absolutely forsworn dice, mistress, everything, since I dared to offer myself to you?

MISS TITTUP. Yes, Colonel, and when I dare to receive you, you may return to everything again, and not violate the laws of the present happy matrimonial establishment.

COLONEL TIVY. Give me but your consent, Madam, and your life to come –

MISS TITTUP. Do you get my consent, Colonel, and I'll take care of my life to come.

COLONEL TIVY. How shall I get your consent?

MISS TITTUP. By getting me in the humor.

COLONEL TIVY. But how to get you in the humor?

MISS TITTUP. O, there are several ways; I am very good-natured.

COLONEL TIVY. Are you in the humor now?

MISS TITTUP. Try me.

COLONEL TIVY. How shall I?

MISS TITTUP. How shall I!—you a soldier, and not know the art military? how shall I?—I'll tell you how;—when you have a subtle, treacherous, politic enemy to deal with, never stand shilly-shally and lose your time in treaties and parlies, but cock your hat, draw your sword;—march, beat drum—dub, dub, a-dub—present, fire, piff-pauff—'tis done! they fly, they yield—Victoria! Victoria! –

Running off.

COLONEL TIVY. Stay, stay, my dear, dear angel! – (*Bringing her back.*)

MISS TITTUP. No, no, no. I have no time to be killed now; besides, Lady

Minikin is in the vapors and wants you at chess, and my Lord is low spirited and wants me at picquet; my uncle is in an ill humor and wants me to discard you and go with him into the country.

COLONEL TIVY. And will you, Miss?

MISS TITTUP. Will I!—no, I never do as I am bid; but you ought—so go to my Lady.

COLONEL TIVY. Nay, but Miss.

MISS TITTUP. Nay, but Colonel, if you won't obey your commanding officer, you shall be broke, and then my maid won't accept of you; so march, Colonel! Look'ee, Sir, I will command before marriage, and do what I please afterwards, or I have been well educated to very little purpose.

Exit.

COLONEL TIVY. What a mad devil it is!—now, if I had the least affection for the girl, I should be damnably vexed at this.— but she has a fine fortune, and I must have her if I can.—Tol, lol, lol, —

Exit singing.

Enter Sir John Trotley *and* Davy.

SIR JOHN TROTLEY. Hold your tongue, Davy, you talk like a fool.

DAVY. It is a fine place, your Honor, and I could live here forever!

SIR JOHN TROTLEY. More shame for you—live here forever!—what, among thieves and pickpockets! What a revolution since my time! The more I see, the more I've cause for lamentation; what a dreadful change has time brought about in twenty years! I should not have known the place again, nor the people; all the signs that made so noble an appearance, are all taken down;—not a bob or tie-wig to be seen. All the degrees from the parade in St. James's Park to the stool and brush at the corner of every street, have their hair tied up—the mason laying bricks, the baker with his basket, the postboy crying newspapers, and the doctor prescribing physic, have all their hair tied up; and that's the reason so many heads are tied up every month.

DAVY. I shall have my head tied up tomorrow. Mr. Wisp will do it for me—your honor and I look like Philistines among 'em.

SIR JOHN TROTLEY. And I shall break your head if it is tied up; I hate innovation;—all confusion and no distinction!—The streets now are as smooth as a turnpike-road! No rattling and exercise in the hackney-coaches; those who ride in 'em are all fast asleep; and they have strings in their hands, that the coachman must pull to waken 'em, when they are to be set down—what luxury and abomination!

DAVY. Is it so, your honor? 'feckins, I liked it hugely.

Mr. Emery as Davy in *Bon Ton.*
Folger Shakespeare Library

SIR JOHN TROTLEY. But you must hate and detest London.

DAVY. How can I manage that, your honor, when there is everything to delight my eye, and cherish my heart.

SIR JOHN TROTLEY. 'Tis all deceit and delusion.

DAVY. Such crowding, coaching, carting, and squeezing, such a power of fine sights, fine shops full of fine things, and then such fine illuminations all of a row! and such fine dainty ladies in the streets, so civil and so graceless.—They talk of country girls,—these here look more healthy and rosy by half.

SIR JOHN TROTLEY. Sirrah, they are prostitutes, and are civil to delude and destroy you: they are painted Jezebels, and they who hearken to 'em, like Jezebel of old, will go to the dogs; if you dare to look at 'em, you will be tainted, and if you speak to 'em you are undone.

DAVY. Bless us, bless us!—how does your honor know all this!—were they as bad in your time?

SIR JOHN TROTLEY. Not by half, Davy.—In my time, there was a sort of decency in the worst of women;—but the harlots now watch like tigers for their prey; and drag you to their dens of infamy—see, Davy, how they have torn my neckcloth. (*Shows his neckcloth.*)

DAVY. If you had gone civilly, your honor, they would not have hurt you.

SIR JOHN TROTLEY. Well, we'll get away as fast as we can.

DAVY. Not this month, I hope, for I have not had half my belly full yet.

SIR JOHN TROTLEY. I'll knock you down, Davy, if you grow profligate; you shan't go out again to-night, and to-morrow keep in my room, and stay till I can look over my things, and see they don't cheat you.

DAVY. Your honor then won't keep your word with me! (*Sulkily.*)

SIR JOHN TROTLEY. Why, what did I promise you?

DAVY. That I should take sixpen'oth of one of the theatres to-night, and a shilling place at the other to-morrow.

SIR JOHN TROTLEY. Well, well, so I did: is it a moral piece, Davy?

DAVY. O yes, and written by a clergyman; it is called the *Rival Cannanites, or the Tragedy of Braggadocia.*

SIR JOHN TROTLEY. Be a good lad, and I won't be worse than my word; there's money for you—(*Gives him some.*) but come straight home, for I shall want to go to bed.

DAVY. To be sure, your honor—as I am to go so soon, I'll make a night of it.

Aside, and exit.

SIR JOHN TROTLEY. This fellow would turn rake and maccaroni if he was to stay here a week longer—bless me, what dangers are in this town at every step! O, that I were once settled safe again at Trotley Place!—nothing but to save my country should bring me back again; my niece Lucretia, is so be-fashioned and be-devilled, that nothing, I fear, can save her; however, to ease my conscience, I must try: but what can be expected from the young women of these times, but sallow looks, wild schemes, saucy words, and loose morals!—They lie a-bed all day, sit up all night; if they are silent, they are gaming, and if they talk, 'tis either scandal or infidelity; and that they may look what they are, their heads are all feather, and round their necks are twisted rattle-snake tippets—*O Tempora, O Mores*!

Exit.

SCENE II.

Lord Minikin *discovered in his powdering grown, with* Jessamy *and* Mignon.

LORD MINIKIN. Prithee, Mignon, don't plague me any more; dost think a nobleman's head has nothing to do but be tortured all day under thy infernal fingers! give me my clothes.

MIGNON. Ven you loss your monee, my Lor, you no goot humor, the devil may dress your *cheveux* for me!

Exit.

LORD MINIKIN. That fellow's an impudent rascal, but he's a genius, so I must bear with him. Our beef and pudding enriches their blood so much, that the slaves, in a month, forget their misery and soup-maigre—O, my head!—a chair, Jessamy!—I must absolutely change my wine-merchant: I can't taste his champagne, without disordering myself for a week!—heigh-ho!—(*Sighs.*)

Enter Miss Tittup.

MISS TITTUP. What makes you sigh, my Lord?

LORD MINIKIN. Because you were so near me, child.

MISS TITTUP. Indeed! I should rather have thought my Lady had been with you—by your looks, my Lord. I am afraid Fortune jilted you last night.

LORD MINIKIN. No, faith; our champagne was not good yesterday, and I am vapored like our English November; but one glance of my Tittup can dispel vapors like—like —

MISS TITTUP. Like something very fine to be sure; but pray keep your simile for the next time;—and hark'ee—a little prudence will not be amiss; Mr. Jessamy will think you mad, and me worse. (*Half aside.*)

JESSAMY. O, pray don't mind me, Madam.

LORD MINIKIN. Gadso, Jessamy, look out my domino, and I'll ring the bell when I want you.

JESSAMY. I shall, my Lord;–Miss thinks that everybody is blind in the house but herself.

Aside and exit.

MISS TITTUP. Upon my word, my Lord, you must be a little more prudent, or we shall become the town-talk.

LORD MINIKIN. And so I will, my dear; and therefore to prevent surprise, I'll lock the door. (*Locks it.*)

MISS TITTUP. What do you mean, my Lord?

LORD MINIKIN. Prudence, child, prudence; I keep all my jewels under lock and key.

MISS TITTUP. You are not in possession yet, my Lord. I can't stay two minutes. I only came to tell you that Lady Minikin saw us yesterday in the hackney-coach; she did not know me, I believe; she pretends to be greatly uneasy at your neglect of her; she certainly has some mischief in her head.

LORD MINIKIN. No intentions, I hope, of being fond of me?

MISS TITTUP. No, no, make yourself easy; she hates you most unalterably.

LORD MINIKIN. You have given me spirits again.

MISS TITTUP. Her pride is alarmed that you should prefer any of the sex to her.

LORD MINIKIN. Her pride then has been alarmed ever since I had the honor of knowing her.

MISS TITTUP. But, dear my Lord, let us be merry and wise; should she ever be convinced that we have a *tendre* for each other, she certainly would proclaim it, and then –

LORD MINIKIN. We should be envied, and she would be laughed at, my sweet cousin.

MISS TITTUP. Nay, I would have her mortified too–for though I love her Ladyship sincerely, I cannot say but I love a little mischief as sincerely: but then if my Uncle Trotley should know of our affairs, he is so old-fashioned, prudish, and out of the way, he would either strike me out of his will, or insist upon my quitting the house.

LORD MINIKIN. My good cousin is a queer mortal, that's certain; I wish we could get him handsomely into the country again–he has a fine fortune to leave behind him –

MISS TITTUP. But then he lives so regularly, and never makes use of a physician, that he may live these twenty years.

LORD MINIKIN. What can we do with the barbarian?

MISS TITTUP. I don't know what's the matter with me, but I am really in fear of him; I suppose reading his formal books when I was in the country with him, and going so constantly to church, with my elbows stuck to my hips, and my toes turned in, has given me these foolish prejudices.

LORD MINIKIN. Then you must affront him, or you'll never get the better of him.

Sir John Trotley

(*Knocking at the door.*)

SIR JOHN TROTLEY. My Lord, my Lord, are you busy?

(*My Lord unlocks the door softly.*)

MISS TITTUP. Heav'ns! 'tis that detestable brute, my uncle!

LORD MINIKIN. That horrid dog, my cousin!

MISS TITTUP. What shall we do, my Lord? (*Softly.*)

SIR JOHN TROTLEY (*at the door*). Nay, my Lord, my Lord, I heard you; pray let me speak with you?

LORD MINIKIN. Ho, Sir John, is it you? I beg your pardon, I'll put up my papers and open the door.

MISS TITTUP. Stay, stay, my Lord, I would not meet him now for the world; if he sees me here alone with you, he'll rave like a madman; put me up the chimney,—anywhere.

LORD MINIKIN (*aloud*). I'm coming, Sir John! here, here, get behind my great chair; he shan't see you, and you may hear all; I'll be short and pleasant with him.

(*Puts her behind the chair, and opens the door.*)

Enter Sir John.

During this Scene, my Lord turns the chair as Sir John *moves to conceal* Tittup.

SIR JOHN TROTLEY. You'll excuse me, my Lord, that I have broken in upon you? I heard you talking pretty loud; what, have you nobody with you? What were you about, cousin? (*Looking about.*)

LORD MINIKIN. A particular affair, Sir John; I always lock myself up to study my speeches, and speak 'em aloud for the sake of the tone and action —

SIR JOHN TROTLEY. Ay, ay, 'tis the best way; I am sorry I disturbed you;—you'll excuse me, cousin!

LORD MINIKIN. I am rather obliged to you, Sir John;—intense application to these things ruins my health; but one must do it for the sake of the nation.

SIR JOHN TROTLEY. May be so, and I hope the nation will be the better for't—you'll excuse me!

LORD MINIKEN. Excuse you, Sir John, I love your frankness; but why won't you be franker still? We have always something for dinner, and you will never dine at home.

SIR JOHN TROTLEY. You must know, my Lord, that I love to know what I eat;—I hate to travel where I don't know my way; and since you have brought in foreign fashions and figaries, everything and everybody are in masquerade; your men and manners too are as much frittered and fricasseed, as your beef and mutton; I love a plain dish, my Lord.

MISS TITTUP (*peeping*). I wish I was out of the room, or he at the bottom of the Thames.

SIR JOHN TROTLEY. But to the point;—I came, my Lord, to open my mind to you about my niece Tittup; shall I do it freely?

MISS TITTUP. Now for it!

LORD MINIKIN. The freer the better; Tittup's a fine girl, cousin, and deserves all the kindness you can show her.

(*Lord* Minikin *and* Tittup *make signs at each other.*)

SIR JOHN TROTLEY. She must deserve it, though, before she shall have it; and I would have her begin with lengthening her petticoats, covering her shoulders, and wearing a cap upon her head.

MISS TITTUP (*aside*). O, frightful!

LORD MINIKIN. Don't you think a taper leg, and falling shoulders, and fine hair, delightful objects, Sir John?

SIR JOHN TROTLEY. And therefore ought to be concealed; 'tis their interest to conceal 'em; when you take from the men the pleasure of imagination there will be a scarcity of husbands;—and then taper legs, falling shoulders and fine hair may be had for nothing.

LORD MINIKIN. Well said, Sir John; ha, ha!—your niece shall wear a horseman's-coat, and jack-boots to please you.

SIR JOHN TROTLEY. You may sneer, my Lord, but for all that, I think my niece in a bad way; she must leave me and the country, forsooth, to travel and see good company and fashions; I have seen 'em too, and wish from my heart that she is not much the worse for her journey. You'll excuse me!

LORD MINIKIN. But why in a passion, Sir John? —

(*My Lord nods and laughs at Miss* Tittup, *who peeps from behind.*)

Don't you think that my Lady and I shall be able and willing to put her into the right road?

SIR JOHN TROTLEY. Zounds! my Lord, you are out of it yourself; this comes of your travelling; all the town knows how you and my Lady live together; and I must tell you—you'll excuse me!—that my niece suffers by the bargain; prudence, my Lord, is a very fine thing.

LORD MINIKIN. So is a long neckcloth nicely twisted into a buttonhole, but I don't choose to wear one;—you'll excuse me!

SIR JOHN TROTLEY. I wish that he who first changed long neckcloths, for such things as you wear, had the wearing of a twisted neckcloth that I would give him.

LORD MINIKIN. Prithee, Baronet, don't be so horridly out of the way; prudence is a very vulgar virtue, and so incompatible with our present ease and refinement, that a prudent man of fashion is now as great a miracle as a pale woman of quality; we got rid of our *mauvais honte*, at the time that we imported our neighbors' rouge, and their morals.

SIR JOHN TROTLEY. Did you ever hear the like! I am not surprised, my Lord, that you think so lightly, and talk so vainly, who are so polite a husband; your lady, my cousin, is a fine woman, and brought you a fine fortune, and deserves better usage.

LORD MINIKIN. Will you have her, Sir John? She is very much at your service.

SIR JOHN TROTLEY. Profligate!—What did you marry her for, my Lord?

LORD MINIKIN. Convenience!—Marriage is not now-a-days, an affair of inclination, but convenience; and they who marry for love, and such old-fashioned stuff, are to me as ridiculous as those that advertise for an agreeable companion in a post chaise.

SIR JOHN TROTLEY. I have done, my Lord; Miss Tittup shall either return with me into the country, or not a penny shall she have from Sir John Trotley, Baronet.

(*Whistles and walks about.*)

MISS TITTUP (*aside*). I am frightened out of my wits!

(*Lord* Minikin *sings and sits down.*)

SIR JOHN TROTLEY. Pray, my Lord, what husband is this you have got for her?

LORD MINIKIN. A friend of mine; a man of wit, and a fine gentleman.

SIR JOHN TROTLEY. May be so, and yet make a damned husband for all that. You'll excuse me!—What estate has he, pray?

LORD MINIKIN. He's a Colonel; his elder brother, Sir Tan Tivy, will certainly break his neck, and then my friend will be a happy man.

SIR JOHN TROTLEY. Here's morals!—a happy man when his brother has broke his neck!—a happy man. Mercy on me!

LORD MINIKIN. Why he'll have six thousand a year, Sir John —

SIR JOHN TROTLEY. I don't care what he'll have, nor I don't care what he is, nor who my niece marries; she is a fine lady and let her have a fine gentleman; I shan't hinder her; I'll away into the country tomorrow, and leave you to your fine doings; I have no relish for 'em, not I; I can't live among you, nor eat with you, nor game with you; I hate cards and dice, I will neither rob nor be robbed; I am contented with what I have, and am very happy, my Lord, though my brother has not broke his neck;—you'll excuse me!

Exit.

LORD MINIKIN. Ha, ha, ha! Come, fox, come out of your hole! Ha, ha, ha!

MISS TITTUP. Indeed, my Lord, you have undone me; not a foot shall I have of Trotley Manor, that's positive!—but no matter, there's no danger of his breaking his neck; so I'll e'en make myself happy with what I have, and behave to him, for the future, as if he was a poor relation.

LORD MINIKIN (*kneeling, snatching her hand, and kissing it*). I must kneel and adore you for your spirit; my sweet, heavenly Lucretia!

Re-enter Sir John.

SIR JOHN TROTLEY. One thing I had forgot. (*Starts.*)

MISS TITTUP. Ha! he's here again!

SIR JOHN TROTLEY. Why, what the devil;—heigh-ho! my niece, Lucretia, and my virtuous Lord, studing speeches for the good of the nation. —Yes, yes, you have been making fine speeches, indeed, my Lord; and your arguments have prevailed, I see. I beg your pardon, I did not mean to interrupt your studies—you'll excuse me, my Lord!

LORD MINIKIN (*Smiling, and mocking him.*). You'll excuse me, Sir John!

SIR JOHN TROTLEY. O yes, my Lord, but I'm afraid the devil won't excuse you at the proper time.—Miss Lucretia, how do you, child! You are to be married soon—I wish the gentleman joy, Miss Lucretia; he is a happy man to be sure, and will want nothing but the breaking of his brother's neck to be completely so.

MISS TITTUP. Upon my word, Uncle, you are always putting bad constructions upon things; my Lord has been soliciting me to marry his friend—and having that moment extorted a consent from me —he was thanking and wishing me joy—in his foolish manner. (*Hesitating.*)

SIR JOHN TROTLEY. Is that all! but how came you here, child?—did you fly down the chimney, or in at the window? For I don't remember seeing you when I was here before.

MISS TITTUP. How can you talk so, Sir John?—You really confound me with your suspicions;—and then you ask so many questions, and I have so many things to do, that— that—upon my word, if I don't make haste, I shan't get my dress ready for the ball; so I must run.—You'll excuse me, Uncle!

Exit running.

SIR JOHN TROTLEY. A fine hopeful young Lady that, my Lord.

LORD MINIKIN. She's well-bred and has wit.

SIR JOHN TROTLEY. She has wit and breeding enough to laugh at her relations, and bestow favors on your Lordship; but I must tell you plainly, my Lord—you'll excuse me—that your marrying your Lady, my cousin, to use her ill, and sending for my niece, your cousin, to debauch her—

LORD MINIKIN. You're warm, Sir John, and don't know the world, and I never contend with ignorance and passion; live with me some time, and you'll be satisfied of my honor and good intentions to you and your family; in the meantime command my house;—I must attend immediately Lady Filligree's masquerade, and I am sorry you won't make one with us;—here, Jessamy, give me my domino, and call a chair; and don't let my uncle want for any thing; you'll excuse me, Sir John, tol, lol, derol,—

Exit singing.

SIR JOHN TROTLEY. The world's at an end! here's fine work; here are precious doings! this Lord is a pillar of the state too; no wonder that the building is in danger with such rotten supporters;—heigh-ho!—and then my poor Lady Minikin, what a friend and husband she is blessed with!—Let me consider!—Should I tell the good woman of these pranks, I may only make more mischief, and mayhap, go near to kill her, for she's as tender as she's virtuous;—poor Lady! I'll e'en go and comfort her directly, endeavor to draw her from the wickedness of this town into the country, where she shall have reading, fowling, and fishing, to keep up her spirits, and when I die, I will leave her that part of my fortune, with which I intended to reward the virtues of Miss Lucretia Tittup, with a plague to her.

Exit.

SCENE III, *Lady* Minikin's *apartments.* *Lady* Minikin *and Colonel* Tivy *discovered.*

LADY MINIKIN. Don't urge it, Colonel; I can't think of coming home from the masquerade this evening. Though I should pass for my niece, it would make an uproar among the servants; and perhaps from the mistake break off your match with Tittup.

COLONEL TIVY. My dear Lady Minikin, you know my marriage with your niece is only a secondary consideration; my first and principal object is you—you, Madam!—therefore, my dear Lady, give me your promise to leave the ball with me; you must, Lady Minikin; a bold young fellow and a soldier as I am, ought not to be kept from plunder when the town has capitulated.

LADY MINIKIN. But it has not capitulated, and perhaps never will; however, Colonel, since you are so furious, I must come to terms, I think.—Keep your eyes upon me at the ball,—I think I may expect that,—and when I drop my handkerchief, 'tis your signal for pursuing; I shall get home as fast as I can, you may follow me as fast as you can; my Lord and Tittup will be otherwise employed; Gymp will let us in the back way—no, no, my heart misgives me!

COLONEL TIVY. Then I am miserable!

LADY MINIKIN. Nay, rather than you should be miserable, Colonel, I will indulge your martial spirit; meet me in the field; there's my gauntlet. (*Throws down her glove.*)

COLONEL TIVY (*seizing it*). Thus I accept your sweet challenge; and if I fail you, may I hereafter, both in love and war, be branded with the name of coward. (*Kneels and kisses her hand.*)

Enter Sir John, *opening the door.*

SIR JOHN TROTLEY. May I presume, cousin.

LADY MINIKIN. Ha! (*Squalls.*)

SIR JOHN TROTLEY. Mercy upon us, what are we at now? (*Looks astonished.*)

LADY MINIKIN. How can you be so rude, Sir John, to come into a lady's room, without first knocking at the door? You have frightened me out of my wits!

SIR JOHN TROTLEY. I am sure you have frightened me out of mine!

COLONEL TIVY. Such rudeness deserves death!

SIR JOHN TROTLEY. Death indeed! for I shall never recover myself again! All pigs of the same sty! all studying for the good of the nation!

LADY MINIKIN. We must soothe him, and not provoke him. (*Half aside to the Colonel.*)

COLONEL TIVY. I would cut his throat if you'd permit me. (*Aside to Lady Minikin.*)

SIR JOHN TROTLEY. The Devil has got his hoof into the house, and has corrupted the whole family; I'll get out of it as fast as I can, lest he should lay hold of me too. (*Going.*)

LADY MINIKIN. Sir John, I must insist upon your not going away in a mistake.

SIR JOHN TROTLEY. No mistake, my Lady, I am thoroughly convinced —mercy on me!

LADY MINIKIN. I must beg you, Sir John, not to make any wrong constructions upon this accident; you must know, that the moment you was at the door—I had promised the Colonel no longer to be his enemy in his designs upon Miss Tittup—this threw him into such a rapture that upon my promising my interest with you—and wishing him joy—he fell upon his knees, and—and—(*Laughing.*) ha, ha, ha!

COLONEL TIVY. Ha, ha, ha! yes, yes, I fell upon my knees, and—and —

SIR JOHN TROTLEY. Ay, ay, fell upon your knees and—and,—ha! ha! a very good joke, faith; and the best of it is, that they are wishing joy all over the house upon the same occasion: and my Lord is wishing joy, and I wish him joy and you with all my heart.

LADY MINIKIN. Upon my word, Sir John, your cruel suspicions affect me strongly; and though my resentment is curbed by my regard, my tears cannot be restrained; 'tis the only resource my innocence has left.

Exit crying.

COLONEL TIVY. I reverence you, Sir, as a relation to that Lady, but as her slanderer I detest you. Her tears must be dried, and my honor satisfied; you know what I mean; take your choice;—time, place, sword or pistol; consider it calmly, and determine as you please; I am a soldier, Sir John.

Exit.

SIR JOHN TROTLEY. Very fine, truly! and so between the crocodile and the bully, my throat is to be cut; they are guilty of all sort of iniquity, and when they are discovered, no humility and repentence;—the ladies have resource to their tongues or their tears, and the gallants to their swords.—That I may not be drawn in by the one, or drawn upon by the other, I'll hurry into the country while I retain my senses, and can sleep in a whole skin.

Exit.

End of the First Act.

ACT II. SCENE I.

Enter Sir John *and* Jessamy.

SIR JOHN TROTLEY. There is no bearing this! what a land are we in! Upon my word, Mr. Jessamy, you should look well to the house; there are certainly rogues about it: for I did but cross the way just now to the Pamphlet-shop, to buy a touch of the times, and they have taken my hanger from my side; ay, and had a pluck at my watch too, but I heard of their tricks, and had it sewed to my pocket.

JESSAMY. Don't be alarmed, Sir John; 'tis a very common thing, and if you will walk the streets without convoy, you will be picked up by privateers of all kinds; ha, ha!

SIR JOHN TROTLEY. Not be alarmed when I am robbed!—why, they might have cut my throat with my own hanger; I shan't sleep a wink all night; so pray lend me some weapon of defence, for I am sure if they attack me in the open street, they'll be with me at night again.

JESSAMY. I'll lend you my own sword, Sir John; but be assured there's no danger; there's robbing and murder cried every night under my window; but it no more disturbs me, than the ticking of my watch at my bed's head.

SIR JOHN TROTLEY. Well, well, be that as it will, I must be upon my guard; what a dreadful place this is! But 'tis all owing to the corruption of the times; the great folks game, and the poor folks rob; no wonder that murder ensues; sad, sad, sad!—well, let me but get over this night, and I'll leave this den of thieves to-morrow; how long will your Lord and Lady stay at this masking and mummery before they come home?

JESSAMY. 'Tis impossible to say the time, Sir; that merely depends upon the spirits of the company and the nature of the entertainment: for my own part, I generally make it myself till four or five in the morning.

SIR JOHN TROTLEY. Why, what the devil, do you make one at these masqueradings?

JESSAMY. I seldom miss, Sir; I may venture to say that nobody knows the trim and small talk of the place better than I do; I was always reckoned an incomparable mask.

SIR JOHN TROTLEY. Thou art an incomparable coxcomb, I am sure. (*Aside.*)

JESSAMY. An odd, ridiculous accident happened to me at a masquerade three years ago; I was in tip-top spirits, and had drank a little too freely of the champagne, I believe.

SIR JOHN TROTLEY. You'll be hanged, I believe. (*Aside.*)

JESSAMY. Wit flew about. In short, I was in spirits; at last, from drinking and rattling, to vary the pleasure, we went to dancing: and who do you think I danced a minuet with? he! he! Pray guess, Sir John?

SIR JOHN TROTLEY (*half aside*). Danced a minuet with.

JESSAMY. My own lady, that's all; the eyes of the whole assembly were upon us; my lady dances well, and, I believe, I am pretty tolerable.

After the dance I was running into a little coquetry and small talk with her.

SIR JOHN TROTLEY. With your lady? (*Aside.*) Chaos is come again!

JESSAMY. With my lady—but upon my turning my hand thus— (*Conceitedly.*) egad, she caught me; whispered me who I was; I would fain have laughed her out of it, but it would not do. "No, no, Jessamy," says she, "I am not to be deceived. Pray wear gloves for the future; for you may as well go bare-faced as show that hand and diamond ring."

SIR JOHN TROTLEY (*aside*). What a sink of iniquity!—Prostitution on all sides! from the lord to the pickpocket.—Pray, Mr. Jessamy, among your other virtues, I suppose you game a little, eh, Mr. Jessamy?

JESSAMY. A little whist or so;—but I am tied up from the dice; I must never touch a box again.

SIR JOHN TROTLEY (*aside*). I wish you were tied up somewhere else; I sweat from top to toe!—Pray lend me your sword, Mr. Jessamy; I shall go to my room; and let my Lord and Lady and my niece Tittup know that I beg they will excuse ceremonies, that I must be up and gone before they go to bed; and that I have a most profound respect and love for them, and—that I hope we shall never see one another again as long as we live.

JESSAMY. I shall certainly obey your commands; what poor ignorant wretches, these country gentlemen are!

Aside and exit.

SIR JOHN TROTLEY. If I stay in this place another day, it would throw me into a fever! Oh I wish it was morning—this comes of visiting my relations!

Enter Davy, *drunk.*

SIR JOHN TROTLEY. So, you wicked wretch you—where have you been, and what have you been doing?

DAVY. Merry-making, your honor,—London for ever!

SIR JOHN TROTLEY. Did I not order you to come directly from the play, and not be idling and raking about?

DAVY. Servants don't do what they are bid in London.

SIR JOHN TROTLEY. And did not I order you not to make a jackanapes of yourself, and tie your hair up like a monkey?

DAVY. And therefore I did it—no pleasing the ladies without this—my Lord's servants call you an old out-of-fashioned codger, and have taught me what's what.

SIR JOHN TROTLEY. Here's an imp of the devil! He is undone, and will poison the whole country.—Sirrah, get everything ready, I'll be going directly.

DAVY. To bed, Sir!—I want to go to bed myself, Sir.

SIR JOHN TROTLEY. Why how now—you are drunk too, Sirrah.

DAVY. I am a little, your honor, because I have been drinking.

SIR JOHN TROTLEY. That is not all—you have been in bad company, Sirrah!

DAVY. Indeed, your honor's mistaken, I never kept such good company in all my life.

SIR JOHN TROTLEY. The fellow does not understand me—where have you been, you drunkard?

DAVY. Drinking, to be sure, if I am a drunkard; and if you had been drinking too, as I have been, you would not be in such a passion with a body—it makes one so good-natured —

SIR JOHN TROTLEY. This is another addition to my misfortunes! I shall have this fellow carry into the country as many vices as will corrupt the whole parish.

DAVY. I'll take what I can, to be sure, your Worship.

SIR JOHN TROTLEY. Get away, you beast you, and sleep off the debauchery you have contracted this fortnight, or I shall leave you behind, as a proper person to make one of his Lordship's family.

DAVY. So much the better—give me more wages, less work, and the key of the ale-cellar, and I am your servant; if not, provide yourself with another. (*Struts about.*)

SIR JOHN TROTLEY. Here's a reprobate!—this is the completion of my misery! But hark'ee villain—go to bed—and sleep off your iniquity, and then pack up the things, or I'll pack you off to Newgate, and transport you for life.

Exit.

DAVY. That for you, old codger. (*Snaps his fingers.*)—I know the law better than to be frightened with moonshine! I wish that I was to live here all my days!—this is life indeed! A servant lives up to his eyes in clover; they have wages, and board-wages, and nothing to do, but to grow fat and saucy—they are as happy as their master, they play for ever at cards, swear like emperors, drink like fishes, and go a-wenching with as much ease and tranquility, as if they were going to a sermon! Oh! 'tis a fine life!

Exit reeling.

SCENE II, *A Chamber in Lord* Minikin's *House.*

Enter Lord Minikin, *and Miss* Tittup, *in masquerade dresses, lighted by* Jessamy.

LORD MINIKIN. Set down the candles, Jessamy, and should your Lady come home let me know—be sure you are not out of the way.

JESSAMY. I have lived too long with your Lordship, to need the caution. Who the Devil have we got now? But that's my Lord's business, and not mine.

Exit.

MISS TITTUP (*pulling off her mask*). Upon my word, my Lord, this coming home so soon from the masquerade is very imprudent, and will certainly be observed. I am most inconceivably frightened, I can assure you. My Uncle Trotley has a light in his room; the accident this morning will certainly keep him upon the watch. Pray, my Lord, let us defer our meetings till he goes into the country. I find that my English heart, though it has ventured so far, grows fearful and awkward to practice the freedoms of warmer climates. (*My Lord takes her by the hand.*) If you will not desist, my Lord—we are separated forever—the sight of the precipice turns my head. I have been giddy with it too long, and must turn from it while I can—pray be quiet, my Lord, I will meet you to-morrow.

LORD MINIKIN. To-morrow! 'tis an age in my situation—let the weak, bashful, coyish whiner be intimidated with these faint alarms, but let the bold experienced lover kindle at the danger, and like the eagle in the midst of storms thus pounce upon his prey. (*Takes hold of her.*)

MISS TITTUP. Dear, Mr. Eagle, be merciful, pray let the poor pigeon fly for this once.

LORD MINIKIN. If I do, my Dove, may I be cursed to have my wife as fond of me, as I am now of thee. (*Offers to kiss her.*)

JESSAMY (*without, knocking at the door*). My Lord, my Lord! —

MISS TITTUP (*screams*). Ha!

LORD MINIKIN. Who's there?

JESSAMY (*peeping*). 'Tis I, my Lord, may I come in?

LORD MINIKIN. Damn the fellow! What's the matter?

JESSAMY. Nay, not much my Lord—only my Lady's come home.

MISS TITTUP. Then I'm undone—what shall I do?—I'll run into my own room.

LORD MINIKIN. Then she may meet you going to hers.

JESSAMY. There's a dark, deep closet, my Lord. Miss may hide herself there.

MISS TITTUP. For heaven's sake put me into it, and when her Ladyship's safe, let me know, my Lord.—What an escape have I had!

LORD MINIKIN. The moment her evil spirit is laid, I'll let my angel out. (*Puts her into the closet.*) Lock the door on the inside.—Come softly to my room, Jessamy —

JESSAMY. If a board creaks, your Lordship shall never give me a laced waistcoat again.

Exeunt.

Enter Gymp *lighting in Lady* Minikin *and Colonel* Tivy, *in masquerade dresses.*

GYMP. Pray, my Lady, go no farther with the Colonel; I know you mean nothing but innocence, but I'm sure there will be bloodshed, for my Lord is certainly in the house–I'll take my affadavy that I heard –

COLONEL TIVY. It can't be, I tell you; we left him this moment at the masquerade–I spoke to him before I came out.

LADY MINIKIN. He's too busy and too well employed to think of home –but don't tremble so, Gymp. There is no harm I assure you–the Colonel is to marry my niece, and it is proper to settle some matters relating to it–they are left to us.

GYMP. Yes, yes, madam, to be sure it is proper that you talk together,– I know you mean nothing but innocence,–but indeed there will be bloodshed.

COLONEL TIVY. The girl's a fool. I have no sword by my side.

GYMP. But my Lord has, and you may kill one another with that–I know you mean nothing but innocence, but I certainly heard him go up the backstairs into his room talking with Jessamy.

LADY MINIKIN. 'Tis impossible but the girl must have fancied this.– Can't you ask Whisp, or Mignon, if their master is come in?

GYMP. Lord, my Lady, they are always drunk before this, and asleep in the kitchen.

LADY MINIKIN. This frightened fool has made me as ridiculous as herself; hark!–Colonel, I'll swear there is something upon the stairs; now I am in the field I find I am a coward.

GYMP. There will certainly be bloodshed.

COLONEL TIVY. I'll slip down with Gymp this back way then. (*Going.*)

GYMP. O dear, my Lady, there is somebody coming up them too.

COLONEL TIVY. Zounds! I've got between two fires!

LADY MINIKIN. Run into the closet.

COLONEL TIVY (*Runs to the closet*). There's no retreat–the door is locked!

LADY MINIKIN. Behind the chimney-board, Gympy.

COLONEL TIVY. I shall certainly be taken prisoner. (*Goes behind the board.*) You'll let me know when the enemy's decamped.

LADY MINIKIN. Leave that to me.–Do you, Gymp, go down the backstairs, and leave me to face my Lord. I think I can match him at hypocrisy. (*Sits down.*)

Enter Lord Minikin.

LORD MINIKIN. What, is your Ladyship so soon returned from Lady Filigree's?

LADY MINIKIN. I am sure, my Lord, I ought to be more surprised at your being here so soon when I saw you so well entertained in a *tête-à-tête* with a lady in crimson. Such sights, my Lord, will always drive me from my most favorite amusements.

LORD MINIKIN. You find at least, that the Lady, whoever she was, could not engage me to stay, when I found your Ladyship had left the ball.

LADY MINIKIN. Your Lordship's sneering upon my unhappy temper, may be a proof of your wit, but is none of your humanity, and this behavior is as great an insult upon me, as even your falsehood itself. (*Pretends to weep.*)

LORD MINIKIN. Nay, my dear Lady Minikin; if you are resolved to play tragedy, I shall roar away too, and pull out my cambric handkerchief.

LADY MINIKIN. I think, my Lord, we had better retire to our apartments; my weakness and your brutality will only expose us to our servants. Where is Tittup, pray?

LORD MINIKIN. I left her with the Colonel—a masquerade to young folks upon the point of matrimony is as delightful as it is disgusting to those who are happily married and are wise enough to love home and the company of their wives. (*Takes hold of her hand.*)

LADY MINIKIN (*aside*). False man!—I had as lief a toad touched me.

LORD MINIKIN (*aside*). She gives me the *frison*—I must propose to stay, or I shall never get rid of her.—I am quite aguish tonight,—he—he—do, my dear, let us make a little fire here and have a family *tête-à-tête* by way of novelty. (*Rings a bell.*)

Enter Jessamy.

LORD MINIKIN. Let 'em take away that chimney-board and light a fire here immediately.

LADY MINIKIN (*aside*). What shall I do?—Here, Jessamy, there is no occasion. I am going to my own chamber, and my Lord won't stay here by himself.

Exit Jessamy.

LORD MINIKIN. How cruel it is, Lady Minikin, to deprive me of the pleasure of a domestic duetto (*Aside.*) A good escape, faith!

LADY MINIKIN. I have too much regard for Lord Minikin to agree to anything that would afford him so little pleasure. I shall retire to my own apartments.

LORD MINIKIN. Well, if your Ladyship will be cruel, I must still, like the miser, starve and sigh, though possessed of the greatest treasure. (*Bows.*) I wish your Ladyship a good night. (*He takes one candle and Lady* Minikin *takes the other.*) May I presume—(*Salutes her.*)

LADY MINIKIN. Your Lordship is too obliging. (*Aside.*) Nasty man!

LORD MINIKLN (*aside*). Disagreeable woman!

(*They wipe their lips and exeunt ceremoniously.*)

MISS TITTUP (*peeping out of the closet*). All's silent now and quite dark; what has been doing here I cannot guess. I long to be relieved. I wish my Lord was come—but I hear a noise! (*She shuts the door.*)

COLONEL TIVY (*peeping over the chimney-board.*) I wonder my Lady doest not come. I would not have Miss Tittup know of this—'would be ten thousand pounds out of my way, and I can't afford to give so much for a little gallantry.

MISS TITTUP (*comes forward*). What would my Colonel say to find his bride that is to be in this critical situation?

Enter Lord Minikin, *at one door in the dark.*

LORD MINIKIN. Now to relieve my prisoner. (*Comes forward.*)

Enter Lady Minikin, *at the other door.*

LADY MINIKIN. My poor Colonel will be as miserable, as if he were besieged in garrison; I must release him. (*Going towards the chimney.*)

LORD MINIKIN. Hist—hist! —

MISS TITTUP, LADY MINIKIN, AND COLONEL TIVY. Here! here! —

LORD MINIKIN. This way.

LADY MINIKIN. Softly.

(*They all grope about till Lord* Minikin *has got Lady* Minikin, *and the Colonel, Miss* Tittup.)

SIR JOHN TROTLEY (*speaks without*). Light this way, I say; I am sure there are thieves; get a blunderbuss.

JESSAMY. Indeed you dreamt it; there is nobody but the family.

(*All stand and stare.*)

Enter Sir John *in his cap, and with hanger drawn, with* Jessamy.

SIR JOHN TROTLEY. Give me the candle; I'll ferret 'em out I warrant; bring a blunderbuss, I say; they have been skipping about that gallery in the dark this half hour; there must be mischief.—I have watched 'em into this room—ho, ho, are you there? If you stir, you are dead men—(*They retire.*)—and (*Seeing the ladies.*) women too! —egad—ha! What's this? The same party again! and two couple they are of as choice mortals as ever were hatched in this righteous town.—You'll excuse me, cousins! (*They all look confounded.*)

LORD MINIKIN. In the name of wonder, how comes all this about?

SIR JOHN TROTLEY. Well, but hark'ee my dear cousins, have you not got wrong partners? Here has been some mistake in the dark; I am mighty glad that I have brought you a candle, to set all to rights again—you'll excuse me, gentlemen and ladies!

Enter Gymp, *with a candle.*

GYMP. What, in the name of mercy, is the matter?

SIR JOHN TROTLEY. Why the old matter, and the old game, Mrs. Gymp, and I'll match my cousins here at it, against all the world, and I say done first.

LORD MINIKIN. What is the meaning, Sir John, of all this tumult and consternation? May not Lady Minikin and I, and the Colonel and your niece, be seen in my house together without your raising the family, and making this uproar and confusion?

SIR JOHN TROTLEY. Come, come, good folks, I see you are all confounded. I'll settle this matter in a moment.—As for you, Colonel—though you have not deserved plain dealing from me, I will now be serious. You imagine this young lady has an independent fortune, besides expectations from me.—'Tis a mistake; she has no expectations from me. If she marry you, and I don't consent to her marriage, she will have no fortune at all.

COLONEL TIVY. Plain dealing is a jewel, and to show you, Sir John, that I can pay you in kind, I am most sincerely obliged to you for your intelligence, and I am, ladies, your most obedient humble servant. I shall see you, my Lord, at the club to-morrow?

Exit Colonel Tivy.

LORD MINIKIN. *Sans doute, mon cher Colonel*—I'll meet you there without fail.

SIR JOHN TROTLEY. My Lord, you'll have something else to do.

LORD MINIKIN. Indeed! what is that, good Sir John.

SIR JOHN TROTLEY. You must meet your lawyers and creditors to-morrow, and be told, what you have always turned a deaf ear to, that the dissipation of your fortune and morals, must be followed by years of parsimony and repentance—as you are fond of going abroad, you may indulge that inclination without having it in your power to indulge any other.

LORD MINIKIN (*aside*). The bumpkin is no fool, and is damned satirical.

SIR JOHN TROTLEY. This kind of quarantine for pestilential minds, will bring you to your senses, and make you renounce foreign vices and follies, and return with joy to your country and property again—read that, my Lord, and know your fate. (*Gives a paper.*)

LORD MINIKIN. What an abomination this is! that a man of fashion, and a nobleman, shall be obliged to submit to the laws of his country.

SIR JOHN TROTLEY. Thank heaven, my Lord, we are in that country!—You are silent, ladies. If repentance has subdued your tongues, I shall have hopes of you—a little country air might perhaps do well—as you are distressed, I am at your service—what say you, my Lady?

LADY MINIKIN. However appearances have condemned me, give me leave to disavow the substance of those appearances. My mind has been tainted, but not profligate—your kindness and example may restore me to my former natural English constitution.

SIR JOHN TROTLEY. Will you resign your Lady to me, my Lord, for a time?

LORD MINIKIN. For ever, dear Sir John, without a murmur.

SIR JOHN TROTLEY. Well, Miss, and what say you?

MISS TITTUP. Guilty, uncle. (*Curtsying.*)

SIR JOHN TROTLEY. Guilty! the devil you are! Of what?

MISS TITTUP. Of consenting to marry one, whom my heart could not approve, and coquetting with another, which friendship, duty, honor, morals, and everything but fashion, ought to have forbidden.

SIR JOHN TROTLEY. Thus then, with the wife of one under this arm, and the mistress of another, under this, I sally forth a Knight Errant, to rescue distressed damsels from those monsters, foreign vices and *Bon Ton*, as they call it; and I trust that every English hand and heart here, will assist me in so desperate an undertaking.—*You'll excuse me, Sirs?*

The End.

May-Day; or, The Little Gipsy 1775

MAY-DAY:

OR, THE

LITTLE GIPSY.

A MUSICAL FARCE,

OF ONE ACT.

TO WHICH IS ADDED THE

THEATRICAL CANDIDATES.

A MUSICAL PRELUDE.

AS THEY ARE BOTH PERFORMED AT THE

THEATRE-ROYAL, in DRURY-LANE.

LONDON:

Printed for T. BECKET, the Corner of the Adelphi, in the Strand. 1775.

Facsimile title page of the First Edition.
Folger Shakespeare Library.

Advertisement

The author of this musical farce, begs leave to inform the readers, if there should be any, that it was merely intended to introduce the *Little Gipsy* to the public, whose youth and total inexperience of the stage, made it necessary to give as little dialogue to her character as possible, her success depending wholly upon her singing. This reason added to another, which is, that the piece was produced at an early part of the season, when better writers are not willing to come forth, is the best apology the author can make for its defects.

Advertisement] omitted *D*1.

Dramatis Personae

Men.

Furrow, *a rich farmer*	Mr. *Parsons.*
William, *his son*	Mr. *Vernon.*
Clod, *his servant*	Mr. *Bannister.*
Dozey	Mr. *Weston.*
Cryer	Mr. *Wrighten.*

Women.

Little Gipsy	Miss *Abrams.*
Dolly	Mrs. *Wrighten.*

Country Lads and Lasses.

1. Parsons] *O*1, *O*2; Mr. Parker *D*1.
2. Vernon] *O*1, *O*2; Mr. Webster *D*1.
3. Bannister] *O*1, *O*2; Mr. Ryder *D*1.
4. Weston] *O*1, *O*2; Mr. O'Keefe *D*1.
5. Wrighten] *O*1, *O*2; Mr. Stanton *D*1.
6. Miss Abrams] *O*1, *O*2; Miss Potter *D*1.
7. Mrs. Wrighten] *O*1, *O*2; Mrs. Thompson *D*1.

May-Day; or, The Little Gipsy

SCENE I.

Enter William *and* Dolly.

WILLIAM. Go on, dear sister Dolly. And so my sweet girl was brought to the Widow Gadly's, as a relation of hers from Shropshire, and went by the name of Belton?

DOLLY. Yes, yes. You had not been gone to London two days before your father and she met in the Widow's garden. I was with him. He was very inquisitive, indeed, and was struck with her lively manner. I could hardly get him home to dinner.

WILLIAM. Why, this is beyond expectation. And so, Dolly –

DOLLY. Yes, his liking went much beyond my expectation or your wishes. In a week he fell in love with her and is at this time a very dangerous rival.

WILLIAM. I am sure to have some mischief happen in all my schemes.

DOLLY. Her singing and twenty little agreeable fooleries she puts on have bewitched him. Her mimicking the gipsies has so enchanted him that he has prevailed upon her to come to the Maypole today among the holiday lads and lasses and tell their fortunes. She has dressed up herself often and been among 'em without their knowing who she is. In short, she has bewitched the whole village. I am to be there too, as her mother. My father will have it so.

WILLIAM. So much the better. While you are telling fortunes, I may talk to her without being observed. Send but a fortune-teller or a mountebank among country people, and they have no eyes and ears for anything else. Where is my father now?

DOLLY. Upon some knotty point with Roger Dozey, the clerk. I must go and prepare for the frolic. Don't be melancholy, Will. The worst that can happen is to marry the girl without your father's consent, turn gipsy with your wife, and send your children to steal his poultry.

WILLIAM. But harkee, Dolly, who is to have Mr. Goodwill's Mayday legacy? A hundred pounds is a tolerable foundation to build upon. What is become of George, Dolly?

DOLLY. I have not time to tell you. He is a rogue like the rest of you. But as I have a heart that can make an honest man happy that possesses it, so it has a spirit within it to despise a knave or a coxcomb.

Would women do as I do,
With spirit scorn dejection;
The men no arts could fly to,
They'd keep 'em in subjection.
But if we sigh or simper,
The love-sick farce is over;
They'll bring us soon to whimper,
And then goodnight the lover.

Would women do as I do,
No knaves or fools could cheat 'em;
They'd passion bid goodby to,
And trick for trick would meet 'em.
But if we sigh or simper,
The love-sick farce is over;
They'll bring us soon to whimper,
And then goodnight the lover.

WILLIAM. Well said, Dolly, but I am afraid in my situation I must give up all hope.

DOLLY. Then you'll give up the best friend you have. Make much of her, or with a true female spirit like mine she'll leave you the moment you seem to neglect her.

Exit.

WILLIAM. How can my heart rest, when I see from the land,
Fanny's arms opened wide to receive me?
If hope cast her anchor to fix on the sand,
The winds and the waves both deceive me.

My love to its duty, still constant and true,
Though of fortune and tempest the sport,
Shall beat round the shore, the dear object in view,
'Till it sinks, or is safe in the port.

SCENE, *a hall in* Furrow's *house.*
Enter Furrow *and* Dozey.

FURROW. Well, but Dozey, think a little and hear a little before you speak, and understand my question.

DOZEY. Put it.

FURROW. You know that Walter Goodwill, Esq., left a legacy of one hundred pounds to the couple who shall be married upon certain conditions in this parish on the first of May.

DOZEY. I have 'em in my hand here, a true copy.

FURROW. You told me so before.

DOZEY. Truth may be told at any time.

FURROW. Zounds! Hold your tongue, or we shall keep talking all day.

DOZEY. Keep your temper, which is a better thing.

FURROW. But I can't if you won't hear me.

DOZEY (*twirling his thumbs*). I say nothing and will say nothing.

FURROW. I know you are my friend, Dozey, and I have been your friend. I found you a good companion and a scholar and got you raised from sexton to clerk.

DOZEY. Necessity! There was but one person more in the parish beside myself who could read, and he stammered.

FURROW. Well, well, no matter; we shall never come to the point.

DOZEY. Never, if you travel out of the way so.

FURROW. I say then –

DOZEY. And I am silent.

FURROW. I am over head and ears in love.

DOZEY. You had better be over head and ears in your horse pond, for that might cool you. Put no more upon an old horse than he can bear. An excellent saying!

FURROW. You put more upon me than I can bear. I want no advice but your opinion. If I marry Fanny Belton, may I demand Squire Goodwill's hundred pound legacy?

DOZEY (*searching for his spectacles*). I will read it.

FURROW. Zounds, I have read it a thousand times; and the bellman cries it all about the parish.

DOZEY. Are you her free choice?

FURROW. To be sure I am, as she is mine.

DOZEY. What age has she?

FURROW. About twenty.

DOZEY. Has she her senses perfect?

FURROW. To be sure.

DOZEY. I doubt it. A girl of twenty marry three-score and five, a free choice and in her senses, it can't be.

FURROW. You are grown old and stupid.

DOZEY. She must be young and stupid, which is worse.

FURROW. May I claim the legacy if I marry her?

DOZEY. You say the choice is free?

FURROW. I do.

DOZEY. But is it not *fit*, another of the conditions. The choice must be both *free* and *fit*. Ergo, I say you can't have a penny of it.

FURROW. Why will you vex me so, Roger Dozey? I am always helping you out of scrapes and difficulties, and why won't you assist me?

DOZEY. I am getting you out of a scrape now by preventing your marrying.

FURROW. I'll tell you what, Roger. There is something so perverse about you that, though I am your friend, you are always thwarting me.

DOZEY. Because you're always wrong. You are so blinded with passion that you would thrust your hand in the fire, if I did not take care that you should not burn your fingers.

FURROW. Well, but dear Dozey, you are the fore-horse of this parish and can lead the rest of the team as you please. Pray now, con over this matter by yourself. You shall sit in my little smoking room and have a bottle of my best October to help your study, and when you have finished the bottle and settled your mind with a dram afterwards, meet me at the maypole and give your opinion. I shall be there by that time to claim the girl and the legacy. If it is mine, a good large fee out of it shall be yours. Remember that.

Exit.

DOZEY. It is the only thing you have said worth remembering. Let me see. A large fee and a good bottle of October will do wonders. And yet to make the union of one and twenty with sixty-five *fit* will require more fees than his purse can furnish, and more October than ever was or ever will be in his cellar. However, not to be rash, I'll drink the bottle and consider the case.

Exit.

SCENE II, *A country prospect, A village and a Maypole with a garland. Lads and lasses are discovered dancing, while others are playing on the ground. After the dance they surround the Maypole and sing the following Chorus.*

O lovely sweet May!
The first of sweet May!

Spring opens her treasure
Of mirth, love, and pleasure.
The earth is dressed gay,
We see all around, and we hear from each spray,
That nature proclaims it a festival day.

CLOD. Well sung, my lasses. Which of you all will have Squire Goodwill's legacy? I don't believe that any of you are in the right road to it. It must be turned over to the next year, and then I shall marry one of you out of pity and get double by it.

BETTY. I'll assure you, Goodman Clod, I would not have you for double and double and double –

CLOD. The grapes are sour, Betty.

NANCY. What a sin and a shame it is that a poor girl should miss such a fine fortune for want of a sweetheart.

BETTY. It's a sin and a shame that there's no young fellow to be had for love or money. The devil is in 'em, I believe.

NANCY. They are like their betters in London. They marry, as they would do anything, for money. But then they yawn and had rather let it alone.

CLOD. What the duce, have we got any macaronies in the country?

BETTY. Macaronies? What are them, Clod?

CLOD. Tho'f I saw a power of 'em when I was up among 'em, yet I hardly know what to make of 'em.

BETTY. What, were they living creters?

CLOD. Yes, and upon two legs, too, such as they were.

NANCY. What, like Christians?

CLOD. Ecod, I don't know what they're alike, not I. They look like something, and yet they are nothing. I heard a person say I sat next to at the show play (for I would see everything) that these macaronies say themselves they have no souls, and I say they have no bodies, and so we may well say that they look like something and are nothing, ecod.

BETTY. Come, prithee, Clod, let's hear all about what you saw in London, and about the fine ladies too. What did they look like, pray?

CLOD. Like a hundred things all in one day, but my song that I got there will tell you better all about it than I can.

I.

What's a poor simple clown,
To do in the town,

22. macaronies] *O*1; macatonies *O*2, *D*1.
23. macaronies] *O*1, *D*1; macatonies *O*2.
32. macaronies] *O*1, *D*1; macatonies *O*2.

Of their freaks and fagaries I'll none,
The folks I saw there,
Two faces did wear,
An honest man ne'er has but one.

CHORUS.

Let others to London go roam,
I love my neighbor,
To sing and to labor,
To me there's nothing like country and home.

II.

Nay, the ladies, I vow,
I cannot tell how,
Were now white as curd, and now red;
Law! how would you stare,
At their huge crop of hair,
'Tis a haycock o'top of their head!

CHORUS. Let others, *etc.*

III.

Then 'tis so dizened out,
An with trinkets about,
With ribbons and flippets between;
They so noddle and toss,
Just like a fore horse,
With tossels and bells in a team.

CHORUS. Let others, *etc.*

IV.

Then the fops are so fine,
With lank wasted chine,
And a little skimp bit of a hat;
Which from sun, wind, and rain,
Will not shelter their brain,
Though there's no need to take care of that.

CHORUS. Let others, *etc.*

V.

'Would you these creatures ape,
'In looks and their shape,
'Teach a calf on his hind legs to go;
'Let him waddle in gait,
'A skim-dish on his pate,
'And he'll look all the world like a beau.

CHORUS. Let others, *etc.*

VI.

'To keep my brains right,
'My bones whole and tight,
'To speak nor to look would I dare;
'As they bake they shall brew,
'Old Nick and his crew,
'At London keep Vanity Fair.

CHORUS. Let others, *etc.*

ALL. Well sung, Clod.

BETTY. But tell us, Clod, how did young Will Furrow behave in London? He raked it about, I suppose, and that makes him so scornful to us.

CLOD. Poor lad! He was more moped than I was. He's not scornful. His father, shame upon him, crossed him in love, and he sent him there to forget it.

NANCY. And he ought to be crossed in love. What does he mean by taking his love out of the parish? If he has lost one there, he may find another here, egad. And I had liked to have said a better.

CLOD. Aye, but that's as he thinks. If he loves lamb he won't like to be crammed with pork. Ha, ha, ha!

BETTY. His father would send him to the market town to make a schollard of him, which only gave him a hankering to be proud, to wear a tucker and despise his neighbors.

CLOD. Here he comes, and let him speak for himself. He looks as gay as the best of us.

Enter William.

WILLIAM. My sweet lasses, a merry May to you all. I must have the privilege of the day. Kisses and the first of May have ever gone together in our village, and I hate to break though a good old custom. (*Kisses them.*)

BETTY. Old customs are good all the year round, and there can't be a better than this. (*Curtsies and kisses him.*)

The tabor and pipe is heard.

CLOD. Come, come, adon with your kissing, for here comes the Crier to proclaim Squire Goodwill's legacy.

Enter Crier, *tabor and pipe playing.*

CRIER. O yes! O yes! O yes! Be it known to all lads and lasses of this village of Couplewell, that George Goodwill, Esq., late of Bounty Hall in this county, has made the following bequest. You, my lads, open your ears, and you, my lasses, hold your tongues, and hear his worship's legacy.

CLOD. Silence! Silence!

CRIER (*reads*). "Is there a maid, and maid she be,
But how to find her out, who knows?"

CLOD. Who knows, indeed!

CRIER. Silence, and don't disturb the court. (*Reads.*)

"Is there a maid, and maid she be,
But how to find her out, who knows?
Who makes a choice that's *fit* and *free*,
To buy the wedding clothes;
If such rare maid and match be found,
Within the parish bound,
The first of May
Shall be the day,
I give this pair a hundred pound.
God save the King!"

Exit Crier, *the lads and lasses huzzaing.*

WILLIAM. Well, my good girls, and which of you is to have the hundred pound legacy?

NANCY. Any of us, if you will give us a right and title. What say you to that, Mr. William? The money ought not to go out of the parish.

BETTY. Aye, come now, here are choice. You must be very nice indeed, if one of us and a hundred pound won't satisfy you.

CLOD (*aside*). Ecod, but he knows a trick worth two of that.

BETTY. Well, what say you, Mr. Will?

WILLIAM. I like you all so well that I can't find in my heart to take one of you without the others.

NANCY. What, would you make a great Turk of us and live like a heathen in a serallery?

WILLIAM.

I.

Yes, I'll give my heart away
To her will not forsake it.
Softly, maidens, softly pray,
You must not snatch,
Nor fight nor scratch,
But gently, gently take it.

---

143. not forsake] *O*1, *O*2; nor forsake *D*1.

II.

Ever constant, warm and true,
  The toy is worth the keeping,
'Tis not spoiled with fashions new;
    But full of love,
    It will not rove –
The corn is worth the reaping.

III.

Maidens, come, put in your claim,
  I will not give it blindly.
My heart a lamb, though brisk is tame;
    So let each lass
    Before me pass,
Who wins, pray use it kindly.

IV.

All have such bewitching ways,
  To give to one would wrong ye;
In turns to each my fancy strays;
    So let each fair
    Take equal share,
I throw my heart among ye.

CLOD. You may as well throw your hat among 'em, Master William. These lasses cannot live upon such slender fare as a bit of your heart.

WILLIAM (*aside*). Then they must fast, Clod; for I have not even a bit of my heart to give them.—What in the name of May, neighbors, comes tripping through Farmer Danby's gate and looks like May from top to toe?

CLOD. As I hope to be married, 'tis the Little Gipsy that has got a bit of your father's heart; aye, and a good bit, too, and holds it fast.

JENNY. I'll be hanged if she's not going to the Grange now. Your father casts a sheep's eye at her. He hinders his own son from wedding lawfully, while he is running after this Little Gipsy. I hope she'll run away with his silver tankard.

WILLIAM. Upon my word, I think my father has a good taste. How long has she been amongst you? Who is she? What is she? And whence comes she?

JENNY. That we neither know nor can guess. She always comes out of Squire Grinly's copse, but nobody knows how she gets there. Clod dogged her t'other night, but she took care to throw something in his eyes that struck fire and half blinded him.

CLOD. Aye, feath, did she. And while I was rubbing 'em she vanished away and left me up to my middle in a bog.

WILLIAM. Poor Clod, you paid dearly for peeping.

BETTY. I wish she would sing! She is a perfect nightingale.

WILLIAM. Hush! Hark, I hear something. Let's go back, or she may be shame-faced. She's very young and seems very modest. True merit is always bashful and should never want for encouragement. She comes this way. Let us keep back a little. (*They retire.*)

Enter Little Gipsy.

GIPSY.
Hail, Spring! whose charms make nature gay,
O breathe some charm on me,
That I may bless this joyful day,
Inspired by love and thee!

O Love! be all thy magic mine,
Two faithful hearts to save;
The glory as the cause be thine,
And heal the wounds you gave.

What a character am I obliged to support! I shall certainly be discovered. The country folks I see are retired to watch me, and my sweetheart among 'em. I am more afraid of a discovery from these than from wiser people. Cunning will very often overshoot the mark, while simplicity hits it. I must rely upon my dress and manner. If I can but manage to tell other people's fortune, though but falsely, I may really make my own.

CLOD. She mutters something to herself. I wish I could hear what she is maundering about.

WILLIAM. Fortune-tellers always do so. The devil must be always talked to very civilly and not loud, or he won't be at their elbow.

CLOD. Lord bless her, there's no harm in her. I wish I was the devil to be so talked to.

GIPSY. What a frolic have I begun! Should I succeed, our present distress will double our succeeding happiness.

The country people come forward.

Your servant, pretty maids, and to you also young men, if you are good; for naughtiness, they say, has found its way into the country. I hope none of you have seen it.

WILLIAM. Oh, yes, I have seen enough of it; it hangs about one like a pest. And for fear my clothes should be infected, I ordered that they should be burned before I left London.

CLOD. Aye, aye, wickedness there sticks to a body like pitch.

GIPSY. Then I'll fly away from the infection. (*Going.*)

Harriet Abrams as Silvia in *Cymon*.
Harvard Theatre Collection

WILLIAM. No, no, you Little Gipsy, that won't do. We must hear that sweet voice again and have our fortunes told before you go away.

They lay hold upon her.

JENNY. I vow, neighbors, I think I have seen this face before.

GIPSY. It is not worth looking upon a second time.

WILLIAM. Indeed, but it is. I could look at it forever.

CLOD. Ecod, and so could I, and buss it into the bargain.

BETTY. Law, don't make such a fuss with the poor girl, as if nobody was worth killing but a gipsy. Sing away, child, and don't mind 'em.

GIPSY. No more I will, mistress. (*Curtsies.*)

I.

O spread thy rich mantle, sweet May, o'er the ground,
Drive the blasts of keen winter away;
Let the birds sweetly carol, thy flow'rets smile round,
And let us with all nature be gay.

II.

Let spleen, spite, and envy, those clouds of the mind,
Be dispersed by the sunshine of joy;
The pleasures of Eden had blessed human kind,
Had no fiend entered there to destroy.

III.

As May with her sunshine can warm the cold earth,
Let each fair with the season improve;
Be widows restored from their mourning to mirth,
And hard-hearted maids yield to love.

IV.

With the treasures of spring, let the village be dressed,
Its joys let the season impart;
When rapture swells high and o'erflows from each breast,
'Tis the May of the mind and the heart.

WILLIAM. Now you have charmed our ears one way, my sweet Gipsy, delight our hearts by telling us our fortunes.

CLOD. Here are fine cross doings in my hand. (*Showing it.*)

JENNY. Pray look into mine first. (*Cleaning her hand.*)

DOLLY. Here's a hand for you, Gipsy. (*Showing hers.*)

GIPSY. I never saw a worse in all my life. Bless me, here it is; it frights me to see it!

DOLLY. Then I am sure it will fright me to hear it, so I'll stay till another time.

WILLIAM. Little, pretty Gipsy, what say you to mine?

GIPSY (*looking into his hand*). You have a dozen lasses in love with you, and are in love with none of 'em.

CLOD. There's a little witch for you.

WILLIAM. There you are out, Gipsy. I do love one truly and sincerely.

GIPSY. As much as you love me. Don't believe him, lasses. Come, come, let me see your hand again. By the faith of a gipsy, you are in love, and the lass that you love –

ALL (*getting about her*). Who is she?

GIPSY. She is in this parish, and not above twenty yards from the Maypole.

CLOD. The dickens she is! Who, who is it? (*All looking out.*)

WILLIAM. Say no more, Gipsy. You know nothing at all of the matter. You should be whipped for fibbing.

CLOD. And I'll be the constable. But, ecod, I would not hurt her.

GIPSY. Aye, but I do know, and she is about my size. (*They all measure with her.*)

WILLIAM. Hold your tongue, I say. Here comes your mother, I suppose.

Enter Dolly, *like an old gipsy.*

DOLLY. What, did you run away from me, you little baggage? Have I not warned you from wandering in the fields by yourself these wicked times?

GIPSY. Pray, Mother, don't be angry. The morning was so fine, the fields so charming, and the lads and lasses so merry, I could not stay at home; and I knew you'd come limping after.

DOLLY. Hussy, hussy! Have not I told you that when the kid wanders from its dam the fox will have a breakfast?

CLOD. Ecod, and a good breakfast, too. It makes my mouth water.

DOLLY. I don't much like the company you are in. Who is that young rake there?

WILLIAM. One that hates kid, mother, and is only giving your daughter a little good advice.

DOLLY. Indeed, the young fellows of this age are not so rampant as they were in my days. Well, my lads and lasses, who among you longs to know their fortunes? I am the oldest and the best fortune-teller under the sun. (*They all gather about her.*)

WILLIAM. Now, my dear Little Gipsy, you must tell me my fortune.

(*They retire, and the rest get about* Dolly.)

JENNY. Now for it, Mother.

DOLLY. Young maids and young swains, if you're curious to know,
What husbands you'll have and what wives;

From above I can know what you'll do here below,
And what you have done all your lives:
Don't blush and don't fear,
As I'm old I am wise,
And I read in your eyes –
I must whisper the rest in your ear.
If you, a false man, should betray a fond maid,
I'll read what the stars have decreed;
If you, a fond maid, should be ever betrayed,
You'll be sorry that page I should read.
Don't blush and don't fear, *etc.*
If youth weds old age,though it wallows in gold,
With satins and silks and fine watch;
Yet when for base gold youth and beauty is sold,
The devil alone makes the match.
Don't blush and don't fear, *etc.*
If an old man's so rash to wed a young wife,
Or an old woman wed a young man;
For such husband and wife I read danger and strife,
For nature detests such a plan.
Don't blush and don't fear, *etc.*

CLOD. There's a slap o'the chops for old measter; ecod, I wish he was here to take it.

JENNY. But now, come to particulars, Goody Gipsy.

NANCY. Aye, aye, to particulars. We must have particulars.

CLOD. Aye, zooks, let's understand your gibberish.

DOLLY. Let me sit down upon the bench under yonder tree and I'll tell you all I know.

CLOD. And he that desires to know more is a fool. Come along, Dame Deal-devil.

They retire with Dolly, *and then* William *and* Gipsy *come forward.*

WILLIAM. May heaven prosper what love has invented; and may this joyful day finish our cares forever.

DUETTO.
William *and* Gipsy.

Passion of the purest nature,
Glows within this faithful breast,
While I gaze on each loved feature,
Love will let me know no rest.

Thus the ewe her lamb carressing,
Watches with a mother's fear,

While she eyes her little blessing,
Thinks the cruel wolf is near.

FURROW (*without*). Where is the Gipsy? Where is my Little Gipsy, I say?

WILLIAM. The wolf is near indeed, for here comes my father.

GIPSY. What shall we do?

Enter Furrow.

FURROW. Where are the lads and lasses, and what are you two doing here alone?

WILLIAM. Had I my will, we should not long have been here alone. I would have put her into the hands of the constable and sent her to her parish. (Gipsy *looks grave.*)

FURROW (*aside*). She has cheated him too. That's excellent! This is a rare frolic, faith.—You send her to the constable, you booby? I should have put you in the stocks if you had, Sirrah. Don't be grave, my little pretty Gipsy, that bumpkin shan't hurt you. (*Aside.*) What a fine May-game this is! I love her more than ever. I'll marry her today and have the hundred pounds too.

LITTLE GIPSY (*going*). I'll go home directly. I can't bear to see that young man look so cross.

FURROW. You shall go to my home, my dainty, sweet Gipsy, and make him look crosser.

WILLIAM. I wonder, Father, you are not ashamed of yourself, to be imposed upon by such a little pilfering creature. She ought to be whipped from village to village and made an example of.

FURROW (*aside*). How the fool is taken in! I'm out of my wits.—I'll make an example of you, rascal, if you don't speak more tenderly to that lady.

WILLIAM. Lady! A fine lady, ha, ha, ha!

LITTLE GIPSY. Don't put yourself into a rage with him. He is mad, they say, mad for love.

FURROW. So am I, too! I am his father and have more right to be mad than he has.

WILLIAM. A lady! A gipsy lady! Ha, ha, ha!

FURROW. And what is more, Mr. Impudence, she shall be my lady; and then what will you say to that, rascal?

WILLIAM. That you have got a fine lady.

FURROW. Have I given you a good education, you ungrateful whelp, you, to laugh at me? Get out of my sight, or I'll spoil your mummery, I will. (*Holding up his stick.*)

WILLIAM. I am gone, Sir. One word, if you please. You have prevented me from being happy with the choice of my heart, and to one superior to her sex in every quality of the mind, and now without the excuse of youth on your part or the least merit on hers. As you have made me miserable with great cruelty, you are going to make yourself so without reason. And so, Sir, I am yours and that fair lady's very humble servant. Ha, ha, ha!

Exit.

FURROW. If I had not resolved not to be in a passion this first of May, the festival of our village, I should have sent him to the bottom of our horsepond. But I can't help laughing, neither; you have done it so featly. How the poor boy was taken in, he, he, he! Fine frolic, faith! And now, Miss, I will open my mind more to you. Why should we lose a hundred pounds? I'll marry you today. The better day, the better deed. What say you, my Little Gipsy?

GIPSY. It will make a great noise.

FURROW. I love a noise. What is anybody good for without noise? Besides, we shall be the happiest couple for a hundred miles round.

GIPSY. Not while your son is miserable. Make him happy first, and then nobody can blame you.

FURROW. What a sweet creature you are! Don't trouble your head about such a fellow. I'll turn him out of the house to seek his fortune, and so he'll be provided for.

GIPSY. If he is not happy, I shall be miserable; nor would I be a queen at the expense of another's happiness, for all the world.

FURROW. What a sweet creature you are! And how happy shall I be! The rascal shall know your kindness to him and how little he deserves it. It shall be done, and the village shall know it is all your doings. And here they come. Now for it! I am ten times happier than I was this morning.

Enter all the lads and lasses.

Come, where is my son? Where is the scapegrace?

CLOD. Here, Master William!

Enter William.

Here's Scapegrace, Sir.

FURROW. Now you shall know what a fine lady this is, or rather how unlike a fine lady she is. This pilferer, wretch, baggage, and so on—she vows not to be made happy till you are so. And so, being prevailed upon by her and her alone, I give you my consent to marry the girl you were so fond of, or any girl of character, and before all my neighbors here on this joyful holiday, the first of May. And I likewise consent to give you the Bilberry farm to maintain her and my grandchildren.

WILLIAM. If you indulge my inclinations, I have no right to find fault with yours. Be my choice where it will, you will be satisfied?

FURROW. More than satisfied. I will rejoice at it and reward it. Name the party, Boy.

The girls stand all round with great seeming anxiety.

WILLIAM. I always did obey you, and will now. (*Looking at and passing by the other girls.*) This—this is my choice. (*Takes the* Little Gipsy *by the hand.*)

CLOD (*aside*). Zooks, here's a fine overturn in a horsepond.

FURROW. He's cracked, sure!

WILLIAM. I was, Sir, and almost broken hearted. But your kindness, consent, and generosity have made me a man again. And thus we thank you. (*They kneel to him.*)

FURROW. This is some May-game. Do you know her? And does she know you?

WILLIAM. We have known each other long. This is she, Father, I saw, loved, and was betrothed to. But your command separated us for a time. In my absence to London she was here under the name of Belton. You saw her often and liked her, nay loved her. It was our innocent device that you might see her merits and not think 'em unworthy of your son. You overrun our expectations, and we delayed the discovery till this, we hope, happy moment.

CLOD. You must forgive 'em, Measter.

ALL. To be sure.

FURROW. I can't. I am tricked and cheated. I can't recall the farm, but I can and I will – (*Walks about angrily.*)

CLOD. Be more foolish if you please. You have tricked and cheated yourself, Measter; but heaven has been kind to you and set all to rights again.

GIPSY (*addressing herself to* Furrow).

418.1. Here 8 speeches are added in *O2*:

WILLIAM. She is in this parish, Sir.

ALL THE GIRLS. Is she—(*They all get near.*)

FURROW. I'm glad on it—. Who is she?

BETTY. Name her.

CLOD. Now they are all agog—and so am I.

FURROW. But where is she, Will?

WILLIAM. In this parish—and in this company!

FURROW. The devil she is—stand around lasses. Now for it, Will—my consent—the Bilberry Farm and 'Squire Goodwill's legacy, shall go with your choice. Now, Boy, take her by the hand.

426. This . . . May-game] *O1*, *D1*; O ho! This . . . May-game *O2*.

433. merits] *O1*, *O2*; remits *D1*.

I.

Love reigns this season, makes his choice,
And shall not we with birds rejoice?
O calm your rage, hear nature say,
Be kind with me the first of May.

II.

Would you, like misers, hate to bless,
Keep wealth from youth you can't possess?
To nature hark, you'll hear her say,
Be kind with me the first of May.

III.

Oh! then be bounteous like the spring,
Which makes creation sport and sing,
With nature let your heart be gay,
And both be kind this first of May.

FURROW. I won't be sung out of my senses.

Enter Dozey, *drunk.*

DOZEY. Where is he? Where is the bridegroom? I have it, I have it. October has done it! It has inspired me! And the legacy shall be old George Furrow's or I will never taste October again. I have got you the money, old Boy! (*Claps him on the shoulder.*)

FURROW (*sulky*). You are got drunk, you old fool, and I don't want the money.

DOZEY. What, you are sick of marriage and don't want the wife, perhaps. Did not I tell you it was not fit? Was not I free enough to tell you so? It is not fit.

FURROW. This drunken old fool completes my misery.

DOZEY. Old fool! What, Mr. Pot, do you abuse your friend Kettle? Old fool, am I? Now judge, neighbors. I have been drinking October to make this a joyful May Day, and he wants to marry a young girls to turn it into sackcloth and ashes. Who's old fool now?

FURROW. Take him away.

DOZEY. I shall take myself away. Lasses, if any of you long for the legacy and are not engaged, I am your man. That old fellow there would have married a child in sober sadness; but I have been courting a good bottle of October, and now, having lost my senses, I am free and fit to marry anybody.

Exit reeling.

ALL. Ha, ha, ha!

FURROW. Where's Dolly? Was she in this plot?

WILLIAM. In that part of it you gave her. She performed the old Gipsy to a miracle, as these lasses can testify, and then went home to prepare the May feast.

FURROW (*sulky*). I will have no feast.

JENNY. Was she the old Gipsy?

BETTY. It is all a dream to me.

FURROW. I can't come to rights again.

The lads and lasses push the Gipsy *and* William *towards him, saying, "to him, to him."*

CLOD. Never was known such a thing as ill-nature and unkindness in our village on the first day of May for these ten thousand years.

FINALE.

CLOD.
Shall our hearts on May Day,
Lack and-a-well-a-day!
Want their recreation?
No, no, no, it can't be so,
Love with us must bud and blow,
Unblighted by vexation.

WILLIAM.
Shall a maid on May-Day,
Lack and-a-well-a-day!
Die of desperation?
No, no, no, for pity's sake,
To your care a couple take,
And give 'em consolation.

GIPSY.
Shall a youth on May Day,
Lack and-a-well-a-day!
Lament a separation?
No, no, no, the lad is true,
Let him have of love his due,
Indulge his inclination.

FURROW.
Shall my heart on May Day,
Lack and-a-well-a-day!
Refuse its approbation?
No, no, no, within our breast,
Rage, revenge, and such like guests,
Should ne'er have habitation.

WILLIAM *and* GIPSY.
We no more on May Day,
O, what a happy day!
Shall never know vexation.
No, no, no, your worth we'll sing,
Join your name to bounteous spring,
In kind commemoration.

GRAND CHORUS.

Cold winter will fly,
When spring's warmer sky,
The charms of young nature display;
When the heart is unkind,
With the frost of the mind,
Benevolence melts it like May.

End of May-Day.

The Theatrical Candidates 1775

THE

Theatrical Candidates:

A

MUSICAL PRELUDE,

UPON THE

OPENING AND ALTERATIONS

OF THE

THEATRE

Facsimile title page preceding the musical prelude.
Folger Shakespeare Library.

Dramatis Personae

Men.

Mercury	Mr. *Vernon.*
Harlequin	Mr. *Dodd.*

Women.

Tragedy	Mrs. *Smith.*
Comedy	Mrs. *Wrighten.*

Followers of Tragedy, Comedy, and Harlequin.

The Theatrical Candidates

Enter Mercury.

MERCURY. I, god of wits and thieves–birds of a feather,
(For wit and thieving often go together)
Am sent to see this house's transformation,
And, if the critics give their approbation,
Or as in other cases–"Yawn at alteration."
Old Lady Drury, like some other ladies,
To charm by false appearances whose trade is,
By help of paint, new bodice and new gown,
Hopes a new face to pass upon the town.
By such like art, stale toasts and Macaronies
Have made out many a Venus and Adonis.
To business now!–Two rival dames above
Have prayed for leave to quit their father Jove;
And hearing in the papers–we have there
Morning and *Evening* as you have 'em here;
Juno loves scandal as all good wives do,
If it be fresh, no matter whether true.
Momus writes paragraphs and I find squibs,
And Pluto keeps a press to print the fibs.
Hearing this house was now made good as new,
And thinking each that she was sure of you,
They came full speed, these rival petticoats,
To canvas for your int'rest and your votes.
They will not join, but sep'rate beg your favor,
To take possession and live here forever.
Full of their merits, they are waiting near.
Is it your pleasure that they now appear?
I'll call 'em in; and while they urge their claims,
And critics, you examine well the dames,

I'll to Apollo and beg his direction.
The god of wisdom's new at an election!

SONG.

Hark! the pipe, the trumpet, drum;
See the sister Muses come!
'Tis time to haste away!
When the female tongues begin,
Who has ears to bear the din,
And wings to fly, will stay?
I'll away, I'll away.

When the female tongues begin,
Who has ears to bear the din,
And wings to fly, will stay?

Runs off.

Enter Tragedy *and followers to a march.*

TRAGEDY. Britons, your votes and int'rest both I claim.
They're mine by right—Melpomene my name.

SONG.

If still your hearts can swell with glory,
Those passions feel your sires have known;
Can glow with deeds of ancient story,
Or beat with transport at your own!
Success is mine.
My rival must resign,
And here I fix my empire and my throne!

My nobler pow'rs shall Britons move,
If Britons still they are;
And softer passions melt the fair
To pity, tenderness and love.
My merits told, who dares contend with me?

Enter Comedy *and followers.*

COMEDY. I dare, proud dame! My name is Comedy!
Think you, your strutting, straddling, puffy pride,
Your rolling eyes, arms kimbo'd, tragic stride
Can frighten me?—Britons, 'tis yours to choose,
That murd'ring lady or this laughing muse.
Now make your choice. With smiles I'll strive to win ye.

36. to bear] *O1*, *D1*; to hear *O2*.
40. to bear] *O1*, *D1*; to hear *O2*.

Garrick between Comedy and Tragedy. Engraving by Corbett after Reynolds.
Harvard Theatre Collection

If you choose her, she'll stick a dagger in ye!

SONG.

'Tis wit, love, and laughter that Britons control,
Away with your dungeons, your dagger and bowl;
Sportive humor is now on the wing!
'Tis true comic mirth
To pleasure gives birth,
As sunshine unfolds the sweet buds of the spring.
No grief shall annoy,
Our hearts light as air,
In full tides of joy,
We drown sorrow and care.
Away with your dungeons, *etc.*

TRAGEDY. Such flippant flirts grave Britons will despise.
COMEDY. No, but they won't. They're merry and are wise.
TRAGEDY. You can be wise too, nay, a thief can be!
Wise with stale sentiments all stolen from me,
Which long cast off from my heroic verses
Have stuffed your motley, dull sententious farces.
The town grew sick!
COMEDY. For all this mighty pother,
Have you not laughed with one eye, cried with t'other?
TRAGEDY. In all the realms of nonsense can there be
A monster like your comic-tragedy?
COMEDY. Oh yes, my dear!—your tragic-comedy.

DUETTO.

TRAGEDY. Would you lose your power and weight,
With this flirt-gill laugh and prate?
COMEDY. Let this lady rage and weep;
Would you choose to go to sleep?
TRAGEDY. You're a thief, and whipped should be.
COMEDY. You're a thief, have stol'n from me.
BOTH. Ever distant will we be.
Never can or will agree.

TRAGEDY. I beg relief. Such company's a curse.
COMEDY. And so do I. I never yet kept worse.
TRAGEDY. Which will you choose?
COMEDY. Sour Her, or smiling Me?
There are but two of us.

Enter Harlequin, *etc.*

HARLEQUIN. Oh yes, we're three!
Your votes and int'rest, pray, for me! (*To the pit.*)

TRAGEDY. What, fall'n so low to cope with thee?
HARLEQUIN. Ouy, ouy!
COMEDY. Alas, poor We! (*Shrugs her shoulders and laughs.*)
HARLEQUIN. Though this maid scorns me, this with passion flies out,
Though you may laugh, and you may cry your eyes out,
For all your airs, sharp looks, and sharper nails,
Draggled you were till I held up your tails.
Each friend I have above, whose voice so loud is,
Will never give me up for two such dowdies.
She's grown so grave, and she so cross and bloody,
Without my help your brains will all be muddy.
Deep thought and politics so stir your gall,
When you come here you should not think at all.
And I'm the best for that. Be my protectors
And let friend Punch here talk to the electors.

I.

Should Harlequin be banished hence,
Quit the place to wit and sense,
What would be the consequence?
Empty houses,
You and spouses,
And your pretty children dear,
Ne'er would come,
Leave your home,
Unless that I came after;
Frisking here,
Whisking there,
Tripping, skipping, ev'rywhere,
To crack your sides with laughter.

II.

Though Comedy may make you grin,
And Tragedy move all within,
Why not poll for Harlequin?
My patched jacket
Makes a racket,
Oh, the joy when I appear!
House is full,
Never dull!
Brisk, wanton, wild and clever!
Frisking here,
Whisking there,
Tripping, skipping, everywhere,
Harlequin forever!

Enter Mercury, *out of breath.*

MERCURY. Apollo, god of wisdom and this isle,
Upon your quarrel, Ladies, deigns to smile,
With your permission, Sirs, and approbation,
Determines thus, this sister altercation.
You, Tragedy, must weep and love and rage,
And keep your turn, but not engross the stage.
And you, gay madam, gay to give delight,
Must not, turned prude, encroach upon her right.
Each sep'rate charm: you grave, you light as feather,
Unless that Shakespeare bring you both together;
On both by nature's grant that conq'ror seizes,
To use you when and where and how he pleases.
For you, Monsieur (*To* Harlequin.), whenever farce or song,
Are sick and tired, then you, without a tongue,
Or with one if you please, in Drury Lane,
As *locum tenens*, may hold up their train.
Thus spoke Apollo, but he added too,
Vain his decrees until confirmed by you. (*To the audience.*)

SONG AND CHORUS.

MERCURY. The muses may sing and Apollo inspire,
But fruitless their song and his lyre,
Till you shall their raptures proclaim.
'Tis you must decree,
For your praise is the key,
To open the Temple of Fame.
MELPOMENE. My thunders may roll, and my voice shake the stage;
But fruitless my tears and my rage,
Till you shall my triumphs proclaim!
'Tis you must decree, *etc.*
THALIA. Though poignant my wit, and my satire is true,
My fable and characters new;
'Tis you must my genius proclaim!
'Tis you must decree, *etc.*
HARLEQUIN. With heels light as air, though about I may frisk,
No monkey more nimble and brisk,
Yet you must my merits proclaim;
'Tis you must decree,
You may send me to be,
Tom Fool to the Temple of Fame.

Finis.

List of References
Commentary and Notes
Roster of Drury Lane Actors
Index to Commentary

List of References

In this edition references to works are given by short title only. This list of references does not include the newspapers and other periodicals of the time.

Anon. *Lethe Rehearsed; or, A Critical Discussion of the Beauties and Blemishes of that Performance, etc.* London, 1749.

Addison, Joseph. *The Drummer; or, The Haunted House.* London, 1716.

Allen, Ralph G. "A Christmas Tale, or Harlequin Scene Painter." *Tennessee Studies in Literature* (1974), 149–61.

Angelo, Henry. *Reminiscences of Henry Angelo.* 2 vols. London, 1828–30.

Ashmole, Elias. *The History of the Order of the Garter.* London, 1672.

Baker, David Erskine. *A Companion to the Playhouse.* 2 vols. London, 1764.

Baker, David Erskine, Isaac Reed, and Stephen Jones. *Biographia Dramatica.* London, 1812.

Baker, Thomas. *Tunbridge Walks.* London, 1703.

Barton-Ticknor Collection. Boston Public Library, Boston, Massachusetts.

Beatty, Joseph M. "Garrick, Colman, and *The Clandestine Marriage.*" *Modern Language Notes*, 36 (1921), 129–41.

Bergmann, Fredrick L. "David Garrick and *The Clandestine Marriage.*" *PMLA*, 67 (1952), 148–62.

Boaden, James, ed. *The Private Correspondence of David Garrick*, 2 vols. London, 1821–32.

Boswell, James. *Life of Samuel Johnson.* Edited by George Birbeck Hill; rev. L. F. Powell. 6 vols. London, 1934–50.

Burnim, Kalman A. *David Garrick, Director.* Pittsburgh, Pa., 1961.

Bushwell, John. *An Historical Account of the Knights of the Most Noble Order of the Garter.* London, 1757.

Cibber, Colley. *The Careless Husband.* London, 1705.

Colman, George (the Elder). *The English Merchant.* London, 1767.

Colman, George (the Younger). *Posthumous Letters from Various Celebrated Men.* London, 1820.

Cooke, J. *Lethe.* London, 1745.

Cozens-Hardy, Basil, ed. *The Diary of Sylas Neville, 1767–1788.* Oxford, 1950.

———. Typescript of the Neville MS. Microfilm in Folger Shakespeare Library, Washington, D.C.

Cradock, Joseph. *Literary and Miscellaneous Memoirs.* 4 vols. London, 1828.

Cross, Richard. MS Diary, 1747–60, 1760–68. Folger Shakespeare Library, Washington, D.C.

Dancourt, Florent Carton Sieur. *La Parisienne*. La Haye, 1694.

Davies, Thomas. *Memoirs of the Life of David Garrick*. 2 vols. London, 1808.

Deelman, Christian. *The Great Shakespeare Jubilee*. New York, 1964.

Dodsley, Robert. *A Collection of Poems*. London, 1748.

Doran, John. *Annals of the English Stage*. 3 vols. London, 1888.

England, Martha Winburn. *Garrick and Stratford*. New York, 1962.

Etherege, Sir George. *The Man of Mode*. London, 1676.

Fagan, Barthélemi-Christophe. *La Pupille*. Paris, 1758.

Fawcett, John. Commonplace Book of Clippings. Folger Shakespeare Library, Washington, D.C.

Fiske, Roger. *English Theatre Music in the Eighteenth Century*. Oxford, 1973.

Fitzgerald, Percy. *The Life of David Garrick*. 2 vols. London, 1868.

———. *A New History of the English Stage*. 2 vols. London, 1882.

Forster, John. *Life of Oliver Goldsmith*. London, 1848.

———. *Life and Times of Oliver Goldsmith*. 2nd ed. 2 vols. London, 1854.

Garrick, David. *The Poetical Works of David Garrick*. London, 1785.

Genest, John. *Some Account of the English Stage*. 10 vols. Bath, 1832.

Hedgcock, Frank A. *A Cosmopolitan Actor: David Garrick and His French Friends*. London, 1912.

Highfill, Philip H., Jr., Kalman A. Burnim, and Edward A. Langhans. *A Biographical Dictionary of Actors, Actresses, Musicians, Dancers, Managers, and Other Stage Personnel in London, 1660–1800*. Carbondale, Ill., 1973–.

Hogan, Charles Beecher. *The London Stage, Part 5: 1776–1800*. 3 vols. Carbondale, Illinois, 1968.

Hopkins, William. MS Diary, 1769–76. Folger Shakespeare Library, Washington, D.C.

Hughes, Leo. *A Century of English Farce*. Princeton, 1956.

Iacuzzi, Alfred. *The European Vogue of Favart*. New York, 1932.

Kelly, John A. *German Visitors to English Theaters in the Eighteenth Century*. Princeton, 1936.

Kinne, Willard Austin. *Revivals and Importations of French Comedies in England 1749–1800*. New York, 1939.

Knapp, Mary E. *A Checklist of Verse by David Garrick*. Charlottesville, Va., 1955 (revised 1974).

Knight, Joseph. *David Garrick*. London, 1894.

Lamb, Charles. *Dramatic Essays of Charles Lamb*. Edited by Brander Matthews. New York, 1892.

Lee, Sir Sidney. *A Life of William Shakespeare*. London, 1925.

Le Sage, Alain René. *Crispin, rival de son maître*. Paris, 1707.

Little, David Mason, George M. Kahrl, and Phoebe de K. Wilson, eds. *The Letters of David Garrick*. 3 vols. Cambridge, Mass., 1963.

Macmillan, Dougald. *Catalogue of the Larpent Plays in the Huntington Library*. San Marino, Calif., 1939.

———. *Drury Lane Calendar, 1747–1776*. Oxford, 1938.

Miller, James. *An Hospital for Fools.* London, 1739.
Molière, Jean-Baptiste. *The Dramatic Works of J. B. Poquelin-Molière.* Translated by Henri Van Laun. 6 vols. Edinburgh, 1878.
Motteux, Peter Antony. *The Novelty; or, Every Act a Play.* London, 1697.
Murphy, Arthur. *The Life of David Garrick.* 2 vols. London, 1801.
Nicoll, Allardyce. *British Drama.* New York, 1925.
———. *A History of Restoration Drama, 1660–1700.* Cambridge, 1923.
———. *A History of Early Eighteenth-Century Drama, 1700–1750.* Cambridge, 1929.
———. *A History of Late Eighteenth-Century Drama, 1750–1800.* Cambridge, 1937.
Otway, Thomas. *The Orphan.* London, 1680.
Oulton, W. C. *The History of the London Theatres.* 2 vols. London, 1796.
Page, E. R. *George Colman, The Elder.* New York, 1935.
Pedicord, Harry William. *The Theatrical Public in the Time of David Garrick.* New York, 1954.
Perrin, Michel. *David Garrick Homme de Theatre.* 2 vols. Dissertation. Universite de Lille, 1978.
Scouten, Arthur H. *The London Stage. Part 3: 1729–1747.* 2 vols. Carbondale, Ill., 1961.
Seldon, John. *Titles of Honor.* London, 1614.
Stein, Elizabeth P. *Three Plays by David Garrick.* New York, 1926.
———. *David Garrick, Dramatist.* New York, 1938.
Stone, George Winchester, Jr. *The London Stage. Part 4: 1747–1776.* 3 vols. Carbondale, Ill., 1962.
Swift, Jonathan. *Works.* Vol. III. Dublin, 1735.
Vanbrugh, Sir John. *The Provok'd Wife.* London, 1697.
Victor, Benjamin. *The History of the Theatres of London.* 3 vols. London, 1761–71.
Walpole, Horace. *Letters*, ed. Ms. Paget Toynbee. 16 vols. London, 1903–1905.
West, Gilbert. *The Institution of the Garter.* London, 1742.
Wilkinson, Tate. *Memoirs of His Own Life.* York, 1790.
———. *The Wandering Patentee.* London, 1795.
Wycherley, William. *The Country Wife.* London, 1675.

Commentary and Notes

Cymon. A Dramatic Romance

Cymon, that piece of "Garrick's gingerbread," as Horace Walpole aptly characterized it,[1] has never been cited for literary merit but has been somewhat grudgingly admired for its longevity. First produced on 2 January 1767 as a holiday offering to the Drury Lane patrons, Garrick's "dramatic romance," which is based on Dryden's poem "Cymon and Iphigenia," was still going strong in 1850, when it received the compliment of itself being adapted to the taste of an audience of nearly a century after its debut.[2] Garrick himself produced the spectacle sixty-four times in seven successive seasons beginning with that of 1766–67.

Although much deplored from the beginning, Garrick's spectacle brought playgoers in droves to Drury Lane. A contemporary bit of doggerel verse in the *Gentleman's Magazine* would lay the popularity of the offering to the nondiscriminating mob in the upper gallery:

> But now heave at your eyes and ears;
> The high-puff'd *Cymon* next appears:
> Earth, heav'n, and hell, are all united,
> The upper gall'ry, so delighted![3]

But Horace Walpole, writing five years after its initial performance, lays the cause for its popularity on persons of quality as well as on gallery-sitters; *Cymon*, he wrote, "delights the mob in the boxes as well as in the footman's gallery."[4] The prologue, written by Garrick and spoken by Thomas King, avows that the production was for the pleasure of the upper gallery,[5] and

1. Letter to the Countess of Upper Ossory, *Letters*, ed. Mrs. Paget Toynbee (London, 1903), XV, 102.
2. James Robinson Planché's one-act "lyrical, comical, pastoral" play *Cymon and Iphigenia*, produced at the Lyceum Theatre on 1 April 1850.
3. January 1767.
4. Letter to the Reverend William Cole, *Letters*, VIII, 141.
5. Lines 29–30. The Prologue was printed in the *Gentleman's Magazine* for January 1767 (p. 41) and appeared with the printed play beginning with the third edition (Becket and De Hondt, 1767).

Garrick himself referred, in a letter to John Wilkes, to his effort as "Trash."[6] The *Theatrical Monitor* agreed, dubbing the play "the stupidity of all stupid things" and later taking Garrick to task for the huge expenditures involved in producing "simple *Cymon*" at the expense of regular dramatic fare,[7] a charge strongly reminiscent of the one leveled against the producer / director in 1763, at the time of the advanced-price riots at Drury Lane, that had he not dressed his plays in such costly scenery, the higher prices would not have been necessary.[8]

Yet the public favored *Cymon* with good houses for twenty-eight performances during its first season (1766–67) and for from one to nine performances in each of the next six. After Garrick terminated his managership of Drury Lane the play continued to be acted—from one to seven times each during eight seasons between 1777 and 1789. Garrick's *Cymon* had the further distinction of being performed seven times during three seasons at Covent Garden between 1783 and 1787. *Cymon* as altered from Garrick took the Drury Lane stage for thirty-six performances during the 1791–92 season and was acted seven more times the following season. A new version was then offered at Covent Garden as an afterpiece for twenty performances in ten successive seasons between 1789 and 1799.

The longevity of *Cymon* is, quite naturally, tied in with the profits it brought the theater. During its first season the twenty-eight performances grossed £4,906/1/6, whereas Covent Garden records indicate an income of £4,854/5/0 for the same nights, giving Drury Lane an income of about £52 more than the rival house attained. But *Cymon*'s best night that season brought an income of only £228/13/0 (8 January), whereas the Covent Garden box office garnered more than that on three occasions: £241/3/0 for Richard Brome's *The Jovial Crew* (29 January), £244/14/6 for Colley Cibber's *Love Makes a Man* (21 May), and £230/18/6 for *Romeo and Juliet* (16 February). *Cymon*'s grosses on these three nights, according to the Treasurer's Account Books, were £207/1/6, £153/2/0, and £199/8/6 respectively. Yet the popularity of *Cymon* was such that it was selected for benefits again and again: three times during its second season, six times in 1769–70, three times the next season, four times the next, and again three times in 1772–73, or nineteen benefits in the six seasons following its first presentation.

The Monthly Review of January, 1767, stressed the native simplicity of the piece: "There is no species of dramatic composition wherein it is more difficult to succeed than works where the writer endeavours to represent native, genuine simplicity. Here, more than in any other pieces, it may be said, *artis est, celare artem*. The sallies of wit must be subdued, the flights of imagination restrained, and the author must remain under a sort of self-denial. Such are the simple graces that affect us most in this Dramatic Romance. The strokes of nature in Cymon and Sylvia and the easy cheerfulness of Linco have more power over us than the drolleries of Dorus, or even the magic of

6. 17 March [1767], *Letters*, II, 561.
7. 24 October 1767 and 19 December 1769.
8. *Theatrical Disquisitions; or a Review of the Late Riot at Drury Lane Theatre, on the 25th and 26th of January* (London, 1763).

Merlin and Urganda."[9] The writer cites Aristotle on the importance of music and scenery in tragedy and then takes Garrick to task for clouding the moral: "that there is no magic like virtue." Merlin acts too much from a spirit of revenge, "a passion unallied to pure virtue," says the writer. He approves of the songs.[10]

But *Cymon* is much more than simplicity and moral. It is, in addition, spectacle, magic, and music, elements calculated to delight large segments of the audience.

Spectacle it was predominantly, and Garrick went to a great deal of trouble in getting the spectacular effects and transformations he wanted, including a tower enveloped in flames before sinking to the ground. Professor Kalman Burnim speculates it was for *Cymon* that Garrick queried Jean Monnet, the French theater manager, on the torches which had been used in a Paris production of *Castor and Pollux*.[11] Monnet sent Garrick a sample torch, explaining that he was including "a little packet of the powder with which it is already filled, and which is called here licopocium; you will easily get it at London. To moisten the wick you need the strongest and best spirits of wine you can procure. You will take care, if you want the torch to act properly, not to fill it more than halfway; that is, up to the cross I have made on the tin."[12] To the burning tower Garrick added groves, a magnificent garden, Urganda's palace,[13] and the "dresses, dances, sinkings, flyings, scenes" that will "make you stare," in the words of Garrick's prologue.[14] As Tom Davies noted, "Mr. Garrick, in his Cymon and The Christmas Tale, embraced every occasion to treat the audience with fine scenes, splendid dresses, brisk music, lively dances, and all the ornaments which his plot would admit. The scene of the several orders of chivalry in Cymon was new, and finely imagined; and the whole piece is happily varied, very lively and entertaining."[15] Some years later the *Theatrical Review* indicated that "the Machinery is admirably calculated to *elevate* and *surprize*,"[16] and, indeed, it continued to be developed as the play went through season after season. Before the end of the century the extravaganza had grown to the point that, completely new in scenery, costume, decoration, and machinery, it concluded with "a Grand Procession of the Hundred Knights of Chivalry, and the Representation of an Ancient Tournament."[17] (Drury Lane at King's in the Haymarket, 31 December 1791.) *The Morning Post* for 3 January 1792 printed an account of the procession of more than a hundred persons: Anglo-Saxon knights, ancient British and Norman knights, Indians, Turks, Scythians, Romans, a dwarf, a giant,

9. Vol. 36 (1767), p. 71.
10. Ibid.
11. *David Garrick, Director* (Pittsburgh, 1961), p. 73.
12. *The Private Correspondence of David Garrick*, ed. James Boaden (London, 1831–32), II, 499.
13. Comments in Garrick's autograph notebook, Harvard Theatre Collection.
14. Lines 34–35.
15. *Memoirs of the Life of David Garrick* (London, 1808), II, 124.
16. (1772), II, 160.
17. Charles Beecher Hogan, *London Stage*, Part 5, II, 1416.

Hymen, piping fauns, bands of cupids, etc. And W. C. Oulton, in his *History of the Theatres of London*, tells of a jousting tournament on the stage in which three horses took part. He continues, "... the Prince of Wales' Highlander made one of the procession, and entered the lists as a champion, fighting with an enormous club; against him a small female warrior was opposed, by whom he was subdued. It was by far the grandest spectacle ever seen upon the stage."[18] Thereafter the spectacle continued to have horses, and the manager's book notes that "The unhorsing of St. James was dexterously performed. He fell so as to give the impression of reality to every heart. The rearing and plunging of the black horse was admirable."[19] Receipts for *Cymon* on 4 January 1792 (Drury Lane at King's in the Haymarket) were given in the account book as £582/15/6, "being the largest amount received at this theatre during its occupancy by the DL company."[20] So *Cymon* for its longevity depended more and more upon extravaganza for its popular appeal.

But not everyone was pleased with the play. Says Arthur Murphy, "When we have said that the orders of chivalry walked in procession, and that the music, scenes and decorations were superb, we shall have stated the whole merit of this extraordinary performance. Being the manager's production, it was cherished by his care, and to that was indebted for considerable success."[21] And Genest reports that "as a first-piece it is contemptible—if it had been brought out in 2 acts as a mere vehicle for songs, scenery, &c., it might have passed without censure."[22] In fact, John Hoadly had, in a letter to Garrick, prophesied failure if Garrick made it a five-act mainpiece: "The character and the scenery, etc., of the rest may support it through two or three acts at most; but surely nothing full of Urgandas and Merlins can be drawn out longer to keep a sensible audience pleased. Cymon, the natural Cymon, will be the hero, add what you please; and I could wish that he had none but natural things and objects about him; but as they are, take heed of bending the bow till it loses its elasticity. You are not apt to do that neither, but this struck me so strongly that I could not help *crying out*."[23] The doggerel verse quoted above from the *Gentleman's Magazine* continued,

They sing, they dance, they sink, they fly!
For *scenes*, *show*, *dresses*, all defy:
And then the wit and humour—stay—
We'll talk of *them* another day.

Elizabeth P. Stein observes that *Cymon*, *Harlequin's Invasion*, and *A Christmas Tale* "reveal Garrick as incapable of dealing with fantastic and supernatural themes and characters. Scenes in which these feature promi-

18. 1796 ed., II, 215; quoted in Hogan, *London Stage*, Part 5, II, 1416.
19. Hogan, *London Stage*, Part 5, II, 1417 (2 January 1792).
20. Ibid.
21. *Life of David Garrick* (London, 1801), I, 38–39.
22. *Some Account of the English Stage from the Restoration in 1660 to 1830* (Bath, 1832), V, 121.
23. *Private Correspondence*, I, 249.

nently are invariably cumbersome and heavy. On the other hand, those scenes into which Garrick introduces characters from every-day life are excellent in their realism, humor, and briskness of movement. These plays, then, confirm . . . that Garrick's natural aptitude as a dramatist was not serious but basically and thoroughly comic in its nature."[24] Yet the record shows a remarkable longevity for a fantastic and supernatural play so often sneered at as "gingerbread."

TEXTS

O1 1st edition. London: T. Becket and P. A. DeHondt, 1767.
O2 2nd edition. London: T. Becket and P. A. DeHondt, 1767.
O3 3rd edition. London: T. Becket and P. A. DeHondt, 1767.
O4 "A New Edition." London: T. Becket and P. A. DeHondt, 1768.
O5 "A New Edition." London: T. Becket and P. A. DeHondt, 1770.
D Dublin: W. and W. Smith, W. Wilson, J. Exshaw, H. Saunders, W. Sleater, D. Chamberlaine, J. Potts, J. Hoey, jun., J. Mitchell, S. Watson, J. Williams, and W. Colles, 1771.
O6 "A New Edition." London: T. Becket, 1778.

[TITLE PAGE]

Soli . . . Arcades] Arcadians, the only ones skilled at singing. (Virgil, *Eclogues* 10.32–33)

[PROLOGUE]

12. zodiac] a complete circuit; hence, the year.

18. itching palms] a sign of wanting money.

34. sinkings] scenic effects in which the scene sinks to the ground, as when a tower burns. flyings] the use of stage machinery to cause characters to fly from the scene.

42.1 *late accident*] After playing Tom in *The Conscious Lovers* on Friday, 16 May, King fell from his horse and broke his thigh. The performance for Saturday, 17 May, was cancelled.

[ACT I]

16. rakes] dissipated or immoral men of fashion.

25. Arcadia] traditional home of the shepherds in pastoral poetry and romance. Suggests rustic retirement and simplicity.

216. linnet] a small brown European songbird, *Acanthis cannabina*, so named because it feeds on linseeds.

[ACT II, i]

28. Marry come up] an expression of indignant or amused surprise or contempt.

63. among the willows] the willow symbolized grief for unrequited love.

---

24. *David Garrick, Dramatist* (New York, 1937), p. 156.

[ACT III, iii]

53. *tabor*] a small drum played by a fifer.

[ACT IV, ii]

16–17. reach the grapes] not achieving one's will, as in Aesop's fable "The Fox and the Grapes."

[EPILOGUE]

George Keate] (1729–97), F.R.S., a minor poet, naturalist, antiquary, and artist.

21. Bloods] rakes, roisterers.

22. Jonathan's] a coffee house favored by stockjobbers, in Exchange Alley.

23. new bush] to brush or tease a wig.

36. monkies] those who perform comical antics, mimics. Mab] Henry Woodward, the actor, wrote a popular pantomime called *Queen Mab*, first performed 26 December 1750. The characters were Italian grotesques. Dr. Faustus] Marlowe's play, probably mentioned here more for the sake of rhyme than anything else.

Linco's Travels. An Interlude

The success Garrick had experienced with *The Farmer's Return from London* in 1761, and the popularity of Thomas King's Linco in the musical play *Cymon* in 1767, prompted the writing of another interlude before the season's close to capitalize on King's comic success. The occasion was King's benefit on 6 April 1767, and the interlude was played between Shakespeare's *Cymbeline*, with King as Cloten, and the farce *The Deuce is in Him*. Billed for one night only, the little piece was played six times by popular demand that season and then became a staple for benefit performances, usually in March, April, and May of the seasons from 1767–68 through 1774–75. For the evening of 22 March 1770 it was advertised as given with "additions." What these were we have no way of knowing. The Larpent MS, according to Dougald MacMillan, is "practically identical" with the printed text.[1] Presumably the supplementary material was retained in subsequent performances. In all, *Linco's Travels* achieved a total of twenty-six performances at Drury Lane.

The interlude has no plot. The situation is the same as that employed for *The Farmer's Return from London*—Linco returns to his village after a period of travel and recounts his impressions to old Dorcas and other villagers in Arcadia. But the piece gave Garrick the opportunity to satirize briefly Frenchmen, Italians, Germans, before concentrating on his usual target, the Englishman returned from his Grand Tour utterly unfit to find a secure place in English society because of his affectations.

We are fortunate to find a first-nighter's report in the Neville MS Diary: "After the play, King in the character of Linco, with Dorcas and others of his neighbors, asking him questions, partly spoke and partly sang,

1. *Catalogue of the Larpent Plays.* MS No. 268, p. 46.

for this night only,—a new very humorous little piece called Linco's Travels, particularly in England. Glad I did not go to the other House, tho' I wished to see Macklin, who played there this night only for his daughter's benefit."[2] Music for the interlude was provided by Michael Arne, composer of the successful score for Garrick's *Cymon.* The songs were published by J. Fowler (London, 1767) as by Michael Arne and Joseph Vernon.

Linco's Travels was not published during Garrick's lifetime. It appears only in the second volume of *The Poetical Works of David Garrick, Esq.*, 1785.

[THE PLAY]

23. madding] raving.

127. green bags] barristers and lawyers. Bag of green material (now blue) used by barristers and lawyers for documents and papers.

A Peep Behind the Curtain; or, The New Rehearsal

A Peep Behind the Curtain, the first of the burlesque-rehearsal pieces written by Garrick, was produced on 23 October 1767 following a performance of Lillo's *The London Merchant.* It became an immediate hit and was played for twenty-five performances that first season. *The Theatrical Observer*, 23 October 1767, contained what might just possibly be a puff by the management, but nevertheless it sounded the general theme of approbation: "There is in this little piece a very extensive fund of humour, especially for those who are conversant with theatrical matters. Previous to the Burletta part, particularly in a scene between the two stage-sweepers, the entertainment it affords is exquisite; and in the Burletta, the music of which is masterly to an uncommon degree, the fine performance of Mr. Vernon and Mrs. Arne, is entitled to the highest approbation: Mr. Palmer and Mr. Dodd deserve much praise: Mrs. Clive is extremely capital: and not withstanding the great estimation in which every lover of the Drama holds Mr. King, it will not, perhaps, be going too far if we assert, he never played a character more entirely to the satisfaction of the public. Upon the whole, we venture to pronounce *A Peep behind the Curtain*, to be one of the most pleasing productions, in its kind, which the stage has ever exhibited, and the best proof which can be given to support the justice of our opinion is the universal applause with which it is received by the most crowded audiences."

Anti-Momus, writing in *The Theatrical Monitor*, however, was of a different mind and devoted space in three numbers (III, IX, XIV) to criticism of the piece. On Saturday, 7 November 1767, it was denounced as "a fresh attack on the public" exceeding "even Cymon in dullness." On Saturday, 19 December 1767, "His new farce of a Peep Behind the Curtain is only a bad imitation of a French piece called *La Repetition.*" Finally, on Saturday, 27 February 1768, when the piece was still attracting the crowds, a fulsome at-

2. Quoted in *The London Stage*, Part 4, II, 1234.

tack as follows: "I have in No. III, taken notice of the new Farce . . . that the *sweeping scene* is the only part that contains any Humour, if it can be allowed so. This piece . . . deserves a more particular criticism; not indeed, on account of its intrinsic merit, (for it is, to the last degree, contemptible . . .)" After criticizing Garrick for making fun of the bickering authors who have submitted scripts to Drury Lane, and ridiculing the constant jealousies harbored among his players, the writer continues: "The fourth or fifth design of the author in this new rehearsal is to contemn and sneer at the design of the Old Rehearsal by the Duke of Buckingham, which was to ridicule the unnatural taste of the poets and the managers, in introducing a variety of monsters in the course of the exhibition, by his introducing Patagonian puppets, dancing cows, sheep, goats, and Harlequin tricks to delude and dazzle the gaping multitude. Is it not surprising, that a man who disgusted us so last winter, with that most ridiculous and monstrous of all productions *Cymon*, should now have the impudence to introduce it this season again? . . . these low exhibitions and mimes are calculated to arouse the passions, and lay asleep reason for other particular purposes; to the private rehearsal or public representation of which, I would not more suffer my wife, my daughter, or my sister to go, than I would to enter a brothel."

Criticism notwithstanding, *A Peep Behind the Curtain* achieved a total of fifty-seven performances by the season 1776–77. Its popularity is also reflected in the fact that Becket published three editions in 1767 and another in 1772.

As a burlesque-rehearsal the play follows the standard pattern as created by earlier dramatists from Shakespeare's play-within-a-play *A Midsummer Night's Dream* to *The Rehearsal* by George Villiers, second Duke of Buckingham, and his associates. But Garrick added to the genre something entirely new—his play-within-a-play is a musical piece of the type called *burletta*, the burletta of *Orpheus*, with music especially composed by the violinist François Hippolite Barthélemon, internationally known instrumentalist and composer, a member of the Drury Lane orchestra and leader of the band at Vauxhall Gardens.

In the eighteenth century the burletta was the legal term for any piece of three acts which contained at least five songs. This was a ploy of the minor theatre managers to get away with adaptations and performance of legitimate theatre fare ordinarily forbidden by the Licensing Act of 1737. By the time of *A Peep Behind the Curtain* this concept had broadened somewhat, and the genre was to become closely allied to both burlesque and extravanganza in the nineteenth century. In his use of this form Garrick was able to give his audience a satiric display of stage business, the problems of authors and an acting company with unusual customs, and an unflattering look at itself as a motley group of spectators. In the burletta *Orpheus* he satirized once more the persistent patronage of Italian opera in London.

Despite the critics, Garrick's characterizations are well done. They represent what he himself termed the proper *vis comica*. The Fuz family appears to be cut from Molière's cloth, in particular the situation in *Les Femmes savantes*. Lady Fuz is the ludicrous dowager who savors romance but still manages a dutiful husband. Here is the familiar and vulgar portrait already drawn in Mrs. Riot (*Lethe*), Mrs. Snip (*Harlequin's Invasion*), and Mrs. Heidelberg (*The Clandestine Marriage*). She affects a taste for matters theatrical and pretends to be a critic. She is always looking for excuse to enact the theatre's famous love-scenes, in particular those in *Romeo and Juliet*. While she would prefer one of the young actors as Romeo, she is not above pressing her reluctant husband into the role. Sir Toby, despite his age, reluctantly agrees. Her genuine interest in things theatrical can be seen in her startling request to see such unusual stage mechanics as the thunder and lightning machines while she awaits the arrival of the author and the start of his rehearsal.

Sir Macaroni Virtu affects to be known as a dilettante composer. Actually he has composed two of the burletta's songs. But to our surprise, however, Garrick uses this outrageous character to express the manager's opinion of the depths to which contemporary comedy has sunk. Through Sir Macaroni and Glib, the dramatist Garrick ridicules sentimental comedy and also the ridiculous pretensions of contemporary theatre in the burletta of *Orpheus*.

To return to *Orpheus*, the reader is warned against dismissing this musical offering as the ridiculous affair it seems to be. Actually, the humor of this sketch has been undervalued. A closer study will afford the discerning reader delight in the lyrics provided for Barthélemon's music. Garrick's skill in light verse was never better than in these extravagantly humorous songs, especially the air:

> "Though she scolded all day, and all night did the same,
> Though she was too rampant, and I was too tame;
> Though shriller her notes than the ear-piercing fife,
> *I must and I will go to hell for my wife*."

With Thomas King brilliantly cast as the author Glib, a real "Bayes," and Kitty Clive as Lady Fuz, this little play captivated its audiences for fifty-seven performances.

TEXTS

O1 1st edition. London: T. Becket and P. A. De Hondt, 1767.
O2 2nd edition. London: T. Becket and P. A. De Hondt, 1767.
O3 3rd edition. London: T. Becket and P. A. De Hondt, 1767.
D1 Dublin: G. Faulkner, J. Exshaw, H. Saunders, W. Sleater, D. Chamberlaine, J. Potts, J. Mitchell, J. Williams, and W. Colles, 1767.
O4 London: T. Becket, 1772.
D2 Dublin: George Faulkner, 1777.
O5 London: Printed for Sadler and Co. [17—?].

[PROLOGUE]

13. Imprimis] In the first place.

19. Burletta] a drama in rhyme, which is entirely musical; legally—any piece in three acts including at least five songs. Music for this burletta *Orpheus* was composed by F. H. Barthélemon.

34. Malice prepense] deliberate intention and plan to do something unlawful.

[ACT I, i]

7. Exeter-Change] Exchange in Exeter Street, the Strand, near Covent Garden Market.

33. Polonius] see Shakespeare's *Hamlet*, III, ii, line 100.

68. the Tweed] a river in southern Scotland and England.

[ACT I, ii]

14. Negers] Negroes.

32.1. Hopkins] William Hopkins, Garrick's prompter from 1762 to 1776.

43. Saunders] head carpenter at Drury Lane.

74. *Cymon*] a Christmas spectacular produced at Drury Lane on 2 January 1767.

138. pinch of cephalic] a pinch of snuff.

170–71. *partie quarrée*] 4-part singing, a quartet.

185. "High life below stairs"] a farce by James Townley (Drury Lane 31 October 1759)

203. *in petto*] in secret.

264. fumet] game flavor.

329. Clive] Catherine or "Kitty" (1711–85), leading actress throughout Garrick's management.

[ACT II]

2–3. *caput mortuum*] dead head.

20.1. Johnston] boxkeeper and housekeeper at Drury Lane from 1761–62 through 1774–75.

185. *courante*] old, lively French dance with gliding or running steps.

309. *dégagé*] easy and free in manner.

313. Linco] see *Linco's Travels* (Drury Lane 6 April 1767), an interlude.

The Jubilee

On Monday, 8 May 1769, George Keate and Francis Wheler called at Garrick's house in Southampton Street. Their mission was to represent the Town Council and Corporation of Stratford-upon-Avon in presenting to the actor a box of mulberry wood containing the Freedom of Stratford. Such an honor was in response to Garrick's gift to Stratford's new Town Hall of a statue of Shakespeare and the actor's own portrait by Thomas Gainsborough. And on 9 May Garrick sent a press release to the London newspapers announcing a grand Jubilee in honor of Shakespeare to be held at Stratford sometime in the coming September.

On Thursday, 18 May, Garrick played Archer in Farquhar's *The Beaux' Strategem*, his last appearance for the season. At the evening's close he spoke the customary "Occasional Epilogue" and sent his audience away with these words of invitation:

My eyes, till then, no sights like this will see,
Unless we meet at *Shakespeare's Jubilee*!
On Avon's Banks, where flowers eternal blow!

Like its full stream our Gratitude shall flow!
There let us revel, show our fond regard,
On that lov'd Spot, first breath'd our matchless Bard;
To him all Honour, Gratitude is due,
To him we owe our all – to Him and You.[1]

The projected Jubilee took place on 6–9 September, just prior to the opening of the London theatre season. This Jubilee and the new season to follow made 1769 an outstanding year in English theatrical history. The story of the glories, absurdities and disasters of the events at Stratford that autumn has been told so many times that it is unnecessary to recount it here. Outstanding among the documented accounts are those of Martha Winburn England[2] and the late Christian Deelman,[3] both writers subscribing to the fact that Garrick lost some £2,000 in the Stratford venture.

Whatever plans Garrick may have had to recoup such a loss, immediate prompting came from the news that George Colman at Covent Garden was announcing a production of his own comedy, *Man and Wife; or, The Shakespeare Jubilee* on 7 October. George Winchester Stone, Jr., notes that "its first three performances brought houses of £234, £210, and £173 respectively. It had twelve performances in two months, and five more the same season when it was reduced to an afterpiece."[4] Seven days later Garrick brought out his *Jubilee*, not as a mainpiece but as an afterpiece, and achieved the record number of 88 performances, far greater than any other such production in London during the eighteenth century. The afterpiece was again played in the season 1760–61 for 26 performances, and it was revived in 1775–76 for 33 more, a grand total of 147 performances.

Garrick's reactions to Colman's challenge are gleefully reported long after *The Jubilee* had become a sensation at Drury Lane. Writing to the Reverend Evan Lloyd on 4 December 1769, when the afterpiece was at its 39th performance, Garrick said: "–What say You to our Jubilee?–ye Story of it is this–[word?] was brought me to Hampton, that Colman intended to Exhibit our Pageant in a 3 Act Comedy of his call'd Man & Wife–he did so, & has not got much credit by it–I set myself down to work, & in a day & a half produc'd our Jubilee–which has had more success than any thing I Ever remember–it is crowded [in] 15 Minutes after ye Doors are open'd, & will be play'd to morrow for ye 39th time–I have really given Such a true picture, I mean for resemblance of our Stratford Business, that You are in ye midst of it at Drury Lane playhouse–I wrote ye petite piece upon one Single Idea, which struck me at ye time, & Which has fortunately struck ye audience in y^{e}

1. Printed in an unsigned letter to *The Public Advertiser*, 23 May 1769. We are indebted to Professor Mary E. Knapp for this information. She also adds, "If the entire 'Address' was printed before Garrick's retirement, I have not seen it . . . how strange it is that the entire 'Address' didn't get into the papers and magazines until June 1776. I can't imagine how Garrick could have prevented it; but, obviously, he did!"
2. *Garrick and Stratford.*
3. *The Great Shakespeare Jubilee.*
4. *The London Stage*, Part 4, III, 1419.

Same Manner—it is this—I suppose an Irishman (excellently perform'd by Moody) to come from Dublin to See y[e] Pageant—he is oblig'd to lye in a post Chaise all Night—undergoes all kind of fatigue & inconvenience to see y[e] Pageant, but unluckily goes to Sleep as y[e] Pageant passes by; & returns to Ireland without knowing any thing of ye Matter—it occasions much laug[hter] but as Bayes says, you'll know it bett[er when] You see it —"[5]

The scenes developed underscore the Irishman's bewilderment. The afterpiece begins with a domestic situation involving Goody Benson, her neighbor Margery Jarvis, and the naïve countryman Ralph. These characters represent the town of Stratford unsettled by the invasion of fine folk from London and fearful of what the Jubilee will bring about—"a plot of the Jews and Papishes" to "ravish man, woman and child," or another Gunpowder Plot. Garrick then shifts attention to a street in Stratford to introduce his Irishman forced to bed down in a post chaise. Surrounded by fantastics, musicians, and singers, the Irishman wants to learn what a Jubilee is all about. By way of comic explanation Garrick introduces his own version of the satiric account given by Samuel Foote in his *Devil Upon Two Sticks*. Foote, a visitor to the Stratford Jubilee, had intended originally a savage burlesque of the whole business, but ultimately was persuaded to content himself with a humorous description. By introducing Foote's impressions into his own play, Garrick adroitly avoided antagonizing his rival author and manager and used the situation to his own purpose of bringing comic success out of what had been indeed a ludicrous disaster. A musician sings of a Jubilee

Crowded without company.
Riot without jollity, . . .
Music without melody
Singing without harmony . . .
Lodgings without bedding, Sir,
Beds as if they'd lead in, Sir, *etc.*[6]

From the street we are taken to the yard of the White Lion Inn and a scene of even greater confusion. People come and go with their baggage; some demand rooms and food, while frenzied waiters are trying to answer bells and fending off outraged patrons. Rival pedlars appear trying to sell articles made from Shakespeare's mulberry tree, only to be exposed as frauds. This occasions the song sung by Joseph Vernon as a ballad-singer, "O Rare Warwickshire!"

Then "with Bells ringing, fifes play[g], drums beating, & Cannon firing" the procession of Shakespeare's characters begins. In all, nineteen plays are represented, each with a particular and well-known scene. The characters pass in review from the top of the stage downward to the audience. Eight of Shakespeare's comedies are represented in the first part of the pageant—*As You Like It*, *The Tempest*, *The Merchant of Venice*, *Much Ado About Nothing*, *Two Gentlemen of Verona*, *Twelfth Night*, *A Midsummer Night's Dream*, and *The Merry Wives of Windsor*. An interval separates these come-

5. *Letters of David Garrick*, II, 675.
6. I, ii, lines 38–54.

dies from the tragedies, including a Pageant Chorus written by Isaac Bickerstaff to music of Charles Dibdin (who was responsible for the entire musical score) and the appearance of "the Statue of Shakespeare supported by the Passions and surrounded by the Seven Muses with their Trophies." After the interval, eleven tragedies and histories are represented—*Richard III*, *Cymbeline*, *Hamlet*, *Othello*, *Romeo and Juliet*, *Henry V*, *King Lear*, *Henry VIII*, *Macbeth*, *Julius Caesar*, and *Antony and Cleopatra*.[7]

Three scenes make up the second part. In the first, two country girls, Nancy and Sukey, continue the Stratford citizens' impressions of the Jubilee —Sukey tries to tell Nancy about having seen Shakespeare's plays at Birmingham and Coventry, especially *Romeo and Juliet*, until she is interrupted by the Irishman in his cups. In scene two that gentleman pursues the girls through a "landskip" until he learns from Roger that the pageant is over and that the visitors are crowding into the Rotunda. This brings an outburst of disappointed fury from the Irishman: "I came here three hundred miles to lie in a postchaise without Sleep, and to Sleep when I shou'd be awake, to get nothing to ate, and pay double for that—and now I must return back in the rain, as great a fool as those who hate to stay in their own Country, and return from their travels as much Improv'd as I myself shall when I go back to Kilkenny."[8] He follows Roger into "some corner of the round house" as the closing scene appears, a "magnificent transparent one—in which the Capital Characters of Shakespeare are exhibited at full length—with Shakespeare's Statue in Y^{e} Middle crown'd by Tragedy & Comedy, fairies and Cupids surrounding him, & all the Banners waving at Y^{e} Upper End." *The Jubilee* ends with a spectacular Chorus "during which the Guns fire, bells ring, etc., etc., and the Audience applaud."

In *The Jubilee* Garrick did more than provide a framework for the Shakespearean pageant. The afterpiece is remarkable for the realism with which he portrayed his comic characters and humorous situations. And the whole play is remarkable for the economy with which he provided a view of Stratford in recounting the adventures of his Shakespearean celebration. Each character has his own individuality and avoids the stereotype Garrick so often uses elsewhere—the two ancient crones, their friend Ralph, Nancy and Sukey, Roger, and especially the Irishman as acted by John Moody. And the madcap comedy of the scene in the White Lion Inn Yard anticipates the vitality of the opening of the second part of the American musical *Hello, Dolly*. It is little wonder that Garrick's public crowded to the performances and helped him recoup four times over his losses at Stratford. In producing a satire on his own Jubilee, Garrick "gave an impetus to the Shakespearean cult

7. See *The London Stage*, Part 4, I, cxxi–cxxii, for an account of James Messink's scenario for the "Pageant of *Shakespeare's Jubilee* in the year 1770." Professor Stone describes the manuscript at the Folger Library as differing frequently from the Huntington Library manuscript, "chiefly in the order to the plays, and the number of 'pageants.'" Messink's list was evidently drawn up as a suggestion to the management but was not used in its entirety, perhaps for economic reasons.

8. II, ii, lines 18–24.

at Stratford which thenceforth steadily developed into a national vogue, and helped to quicken the popular enthusiasm."[9]

Two manuscript copies of *The Jubilee* are extant. The Barton-Ticknor Collection in the Boston Public Library includes an incomplete copy in Garrick's handwriting. Fortunately, a complete manuscript in someone else's hand is the Drury Lane copy and survives in the Kemble-Devonshire Collection of the Huntington Library. Corrections and numerous production notes are in Garrick's hand, and a notation by John Phillip Kemble dated 1800 confirms that "the Manuscript Notes, as well as the Memoranda . . . are in Mr Garrick's Handwriting." Elizabeth P. Stein discovered both manuscripts and published the Huntington copy in *Three Plays by David Garrick*, New York, 1926. The present edition is again based on the Huntington manuscript with permission.

[DRAMATIS PERSONAE]

0.1. Cast of performers in *The Jubilee* at Drury Lane Theatre on 14 October 1769 taken from *The London Stage*, Part 4, III, 1429–30.

[FIRST PART, i]

43. fillip] a snap of the fingers.

47. College] name of the largest house in Stratford, built in 1353.

53. round house] the Rotunda, designed for eating and entertainment for spectators at the Jubilee.

67. his image] the bust memorial to Shakespeare in Stratford Church. show people paint] the importance of the Jubilee called for a new coat of paint on the bust.

72. the Steward] David Garrick.

77. the pipers] bagpipers.

[FIRST PART, ii]

18. first floor] floor of the vehicle, not its seating.

37–59. Garrick's poetical description of the Jubilee.

77. great big Inn] the White Lion Inn.

77–78. all the plays . . . doors] rooms were designated not by numbers but by the titles of Shakespeare's plays.

93. county] Professor Stein misread the manuscript and has printed "country" for "county."

[FIRST PART, iii]

0.1–2. A crowd of people . . . stage.] Garrick's manuscript note opposite this stage direction: "N.B. this is perhaps a Scene of ye most regular confusion that was Ever exhibited."

0.2. *Bar bell rings.*] Another "bar bell"—this time it is to represent the on-stage action of the White Lion Inn.

2. the Julius Caesar] the room designated after Shakespeare's tragedy.

28. the pageant] a feature of the second day at 11:00 A.M.

---

9. Quoted from Sir Sidney Lee, *A Life of William Shakespeare*, p. 601.

35. book customer] a credit customer.

87. oak plant] cudgel.

89. spalpeens] rascals.

93. shellalee] oak stick or cudgel.

94. Notified Porcupine Man] Porcupine Man, as advertised.

99. To ax a Tirteen] Irish silver shilling worth thirteen pence.

100.2. bills] handbills or playbills.

118. fringes] Garrick defined this word as "franchises," and it means the incidental sideshows and exhibitions permitted by the officials of the Jubilee.

119.2. Bannister *and* Vernon] Charles Bannister and Joseph Vernon.

119.3. *Mulberry Cup*] the cup presented to Garrick by the Mayor and the Stratford Corporation.

166.1. Kear] James Thomas Kear.

[THE PAGEANT]

0.4. Garrick's note: "N.B. in the procession Every Scene in ye different Plays represents some capital part of it in Action."

23. rick] in a stack, piled up.

36.1. *Midsummer Night's Dream*] Garrick's note reads: "Suppose Bottom & Q of F^{s} asleep in ye Chariot—& K. of F—drops her Eyes with ye Flower, turns out Bottom & takes his Place & She awakes Etc."

40.1. *Merry Wives of Windsor*] opposite this entry is a manuscript note in an unknown hand: "What is ye whim of having These particularly on Horseback? Cath^{e} & Petruchio, as describ'd by Grumio, w^{d} have had a fine Effect. I w^{d} introduce C & P. in this Manner & four Fellows sh^{e} bring in Sr John in ye Buck Basket, ye Wives on either Side covering him with foul Cloaths, & he endeavouring to get out."

64.1. *by Bickerstaff*] Isaac Bickerstaff, Garrick's house dramatist.

[SECOND PART, i]

1. Pagan] pageant.

2. Shakespur ribbon] multicolored ribbons purchased by the spectators. See Dr. Johnson's prologue for Drury Lane opening 15 September 1747: "Each change of many-color'd life he drew."

18. Birmingham] an important theatre on the provincial circuit.

62. Ample-Theatre] Amphitheatre.

[SECOND PART, ii]

15. *Rain behind.*] Garrick's stage direction was a provocative reminder of the torrential rains at Stratford.

[SECOND PART, iii]

10.4. Mrs. Baddeley] Sophia Snow Baddeley.

18.1. Miss Radley] Eleanor Radley, later Mrs. Fitzgerald.

The Institution of the Garter; or, Arthur's Roundtable Restored

Nine princes and nobility were duly installed as Knights of the Garter in ceremonies at Windsor Castle on 25 July 1771. This was the largest number to be honored in many years, the last ceremonies having elevated only three (6 May 1760), and two persons (25 September 1762). The prevailing mood in 1771 was one of excitement and curiosity, for those installed included: Adolphus Frederick, 4th Duke of Mechlingberg Strelitz; George August Frederick, Prince of Wales; Henry, Hereditary Prince of Brunswick Lunenburg; George Montagu Dunk, Earl of Halifax; George Keppel, Duke of Albemarle; Henry Frederick, Duke of Cumberland; George Spencer, Duke of Marlborough; August Henry Fitzroy, Duke of Grafton; Granville Leveson-Gower, second Earl Gower; and Frederick, Bishop of Oshaburg.[1]

Garrick was aware of the intense public interest in the ceremonies, but his particular interest was in honoring the current Lord Chamberlain, the second Earl Gower (1721–1803), who had been selected on 11 February 1771, and who a various times after 1754 was M.P. for Garrick's hometown of Lichfield. As early as 1766 Garrick was writing to his brother George, sojourning in Lichfield: "The Seat at Lichfield is too costly a one for Me—Lord G. has too much Interest, & tho' I may have half a Dozen Loving friends for Me, yet I sh[d] be oblig'd to sneak, with my tail between my Legs, out of y[e] Town Hall, up Bow-Street, & pass by the Free School as Miserable, as I once was Merry."[2] Now that the second Earl was made a Knight of the Garter, it was most proper that the Drury Lane patentee organize a theatrical celebration of the event honoring the Lord Chamberlain.

In his preparations for a masque befitting the occasion, Garrick turned to two standard reference works, *Titles of Honor* by John Seldon, 1614, and Elias Ashmole's *The History of the Order of the Garter*, 1672.[3] But his greatest assistance came from the work of Gilbert West (1703–56). West had published a dramatic poem called *The Institution of the Garter* in 1742, which was later reprinted in Dodsley's *A Collection of Poems*, 1748. In his advertisement to the Drury Lane masque as published, Garrick explained that this production was in response to "the eager and almost universal curiosity, which the late Installation . . . excited in the public," which "seemed in a manner to command our attention and justify our endeavours to exhibit a representation of it." Admitting the difficulty of transferring this "great solemnity" to the stage, he describes how he has taken West's poem, "impossible to bring it on the stage as it was originally written because, though rich in machinery, it was little more than a poem in dialogue without action," altered it, and added some "comic scenes." The result was a spectacular afterpiece which ran for thirty-three nights at Drury Lane, opening on 28 October 1771. And the success which Garrick met with prompted George Colman at Covent Garden to stage his own masque, compiled chiefly from Ben Jonson's *Oberon* and called *The Fairy Prince: With the Installation of the Garter*, which outran Garrick's piece by two performances that season.

---

1. MS addendum to John Buswell, *An Historical Account of the Knights of the Most Noble Order of the Garter*. In the possession of Harry William Pedicord.
2. *Letters*, II, 537.
3. See the *Extracts* Garrick published at the end of this text. He wished to demonstrate the "authority upon which we have founded some part of our Installation."

Despite the popularity of Garrick's production, a part of the public remained unimpressed. William Hopkins, Garrick's prompter, expressed concern on the opening night: "This Entertainment is got up at vast Expense both in Scenery & Dresses very great Applause. But I wish it may answer the expence."[4] The following night's performance inspired him to add: "The Serious part of the Entertainment Dull & Heavy."[5] The *Theatrical Review*, having reviewed and expressed displeasure from the beginning, commented specifically on 2 November 1771, while the performance was still fresh and playing to packed houses: "We were not a little pleased to observe this evening that Mr. King, in the character of Sir Dingle, omitted the parody on the lines with which the third act of Otway's *Orphan* concludes.[6] But we think the introducing of a chine of roast beef, decorated with a flag, to be carried off in triumph by the rabble, accompanied from the orchestra with music of the old song of that title is a pitiful addition to the performance, and intended only as a sacrifice to the caprice of the riotous inhabitants of the upper gallery. Had this Entertainment been exhibited at a French theatre it would have had some claim to merit. This seems to be a piece of stage policy, arising from a consciousness, that the whole performance is too contemptible to meet with countenance from any but the sons of riot, for which reason they are brib'd to support it, by this notable trick."

A critical reference to the comedy scenes which Garrick inserted into West's material calls for explanation at this point. All that has been published heretofore is *The Scenes, Choruses, and Serious Dialogue of the Masque Called the Institution of the Garter; or, Arthur's Round Table Restored*, London, 1771. For the comic scenes, which are included in this edition for the first time, we are indebted to Larpent MS 327 in the Huntington Library. Since Garrick omitted these scenes in the one and only printing of this work, it is proper to return them to the form in which the complete manuscript

4. George Winchester Stone, Jr., *The London Stage*, Part 4, III, 1579.
5. Ibid.
6. Compare Part III, ii, lines 116–30, with Otway's speech for Castalio in Act III of *The Orphan*:

I'd leave the world for him that hates a woman.
Woman, the fountain of all human frailty!
What mighty ills have not been done by woman?
Who was't betray'd the capitol? A woman!
Who lost Mark Antony the world? A woman!
Who was the cause of a long ten years' war,
And laid, at last, old Troy in ashes? Woman!
Destructive, damnable, deceitful woman!
Woman, to man first as a blessing given;
When innocence and love were in their prime,
Happy awhile in Paradise they lay;
But quickly woman long'd to go astray;
Some foolish, new adventure needs must prove,
And the first devil she saw, she chang'd her love:
To his temptations lewdly she inclin'd
Her soul, and for an apple damn'd mankind.

was submitted to the Lord Chamberlain. These scenes have been placed in brackets.

The first part of the masque consists of four serious scenes deriving for the most part from West's poem. Three Spirits, joined by a Chorus of Bards and Spirits, summon the Genius of England. That exalted personage descends to the stage to meet with a Druid band and the attendant Spirits; he orders them all to St. George's Chapel, Windsor, to guide King Edward's choice of his first colleagues. In the closing scene of Part I we see the Knights seated in their stalls in the Chapel as King Edward greets the Prince of Wales and confers upon him the Garter. A chorus of praise concludes Part I.

In the second part Garrick introduces his comic characters standing at a gate of Windsor Castle. Different lowlife persons, countrymen and their women, especially Roger, Nat Needle and his wife and son, are trying their best to find a way into the castle and to witness what they variously call the "Estallation" or the "Exhaltation." They appeal to the king's fool, Sir Dingle, and his companion Signior Catterwalins to secure entrance. But Sir Dingle reminds them that his duties lie in another direction: "I am poet laureate for the day, and this beardless fellow here, Signior Catterwalins, is my gentleman usher. And with my want of wit and his want of manhood, we are to throw into ecstacies half a score of duchesses, thirteen to the dozen of countesses, and uncountable numbers of inferior quality."[7]

When a woman complains that he has already promised to let them in, Sir Dingle replies: "I live in the land of promises, and I'll give you a hundred more. We give nothing else here. Besides, I am a wit and have a very short memory, and yesterday is an age. Do you think I am so vulgar, or so little a courtier, to remember what I promised yesterday? Fie, for shame."[8] Being dunned by Nat Needle, the tailor, for unpaid tailoring bills, Sir Dingle finally agrees to admit the folk as freebooters after the knights have satisfied their appetites. Upon this assurance the second part closes with a grand procession of the knights.

Part three opens with a scene in St. George's Hall, where the knights are seen feasting at the Round Table. Sir Dingle enters and confers with King Edward. He reminds the king of his obligations to "the mighty power the Mob without," and declares that "they are flesh and blood too, they say." The king agrees to admit the Mob, since they represent "this best guardian of my throne and kingdom, their honest liberty." The scene then shifts to another apartment adjacent to the Hall, and we are treated to the spectacle of folk carrying away the remainder of the feast. The scene is a noisy riot reminiscent of the one in the White Lion Inn Yard in scene 3 of the first part of *The Jubilee* (1769), with Mrs. Needle complaining loudly that Nat is drunk and can think only of the knights' liquor. Meanwhile, she herself is laden down with foodstuffs for the family larder. Nat grows maudlin and declares his love for Sir Dingle, even though he knows he'll go unpaid for Dingle's clothes bills. Sir Dingle ends the scene by carrying off Nat and Mrs. Needle, one under each arm, singing: "Husbands to wives and creditors to

7. Part II, i, lines 30–35.
8. Part II, i, lines 40–44.

debtors, / Can jarring discord in sweet-concord bind, / Moisten, make maudlin, and unite mankind."[9]

The final scene of part three takes place in a garden setting, where the Genius of England leads on King Edward, praises his great deeds, and promises that the Garter shall become a "prize of virtue published to the world." The masque closes with a final chorus acclaiming the triumphs of the British nation.

If, as William Hopkins confided, "The Serious part of the Entertainment [was] Dull & Heavy," Garrick pleased his customers in the upper gallery by his scenes of comic lowlife, permitted the gentry in the lower regions of the house to feel superior and identify more or less with the noble Knights of the Garter, and made an outrageous and effective appeal to the patriotism of the entire audience. No wonder that the critic of the *Theatrical Review* complained of a stage policy "arising from a consciousness, that the whole performance is too contemptible to meet with countenance from any but the sons of riot"—but the astute manager knew what he was about and filled his theatre for thirty-three nights that season.

We must not be surprised, however, to find Garrick publishing the so-called serious portions of this entertainment and omitting his comic scenes. Although the latter brought a semblance of liveliness to the evening, the characters in the comic scenes are not at all new. Nat Needle and his wife are merely copies of Tailor Snip and his wife of *Harlequin's Invasion* (1759), while Roger and the rest of the country folk are copies of Goody Benson, Margery Jarvis, and Ralph, the Stratford natives lampooned in *The Jubilee* (1769). All of these characters are fated to reappear again in the later afterpiece known as *May-Day; or, The Little Gipsy* (1775).

The only original characters are Sir Dingle and Signior Catterwalins. In the role of the king's fool, Garrick created another fine vehicle for his friend Tom King, an elegant comedian, who, while posing as a fool, is actually the spokesman for the playwright. The role of Signior Catterwalins (later to be changed to a female singing role named Squallini) once again allows Garrick to poke fun at the Italian opera.

If Garrick could not pleasure his audience with his serious scenes, his natural aptitude for the rustic comedy saved the evening's performance and assured a lengthy run for this afterpiece.

TEXTS

O London: T. Becket and P. A. De Hondt, 1771.
MS Larpent 9. S. (LA 327).

[ADVERTISEMENT]

1–2. the late Installation] 25 July 1771.

8. Mr. Gilbert West] Gilbert West, LL.D. (1705?–56), nephew of Sir Richard Temple, Lord Cobham.

9. *The Institution . . . Garter*] London, 1742.

9. Part III, ii, lines 128–30.

16–17. Edward the Third] 1312–77, king 1332–77.

26–27. The comic parts] herein published for the first time by permission of the Henry Huntington Library, Larpent 9. S. (LA 327).

39. the Black Prince] Edward, Prince of Wales, son of Edward III, so-called from the color of his armor.

[PART THE FIRST, i]

45. encomiasts] eulogists.

[PART THE FIRST, iii]

96. Cappadocian George] Prince of Cappadocia.

[PART THE SECOND, i]

3. Estallation] Installation.
13. loffat] laugh at.
24.1–2. Signior Catterwawlins] Squallini in the published *Dramatis Personae.*
32. gentleman usher] a court usher.
132. fardingales] farthingales, hooped petticoats.
141. pothooks] S-shaped hooks.
144. Deel] Devil.
159. *Imprimis*] In the first place. *Secundo*] Secondly.
188–89. tatterdemallions] ragamuffins.

[PART THE THIRD, i]

26. *vidilicet*] namely.
69. line] line up.
80. loadstone] something that attracts as a magnet.

[EXTRACTS]

0.1. Selden's] John Selden (1584–1654), *Titles of Honor* (1614).
0.2. Ashmole's] Elias Ashmole's *Order of the Garter* (1672).
8. St. George's day] April 23.
9. Froissart] Jean Froissart (1333?–1400?), historian and poet.
23. a juste] a joust or tournament.
27. Whitsuntide] the week beginning with Whitsunday, the 7th Sunday after Easter.
33. hastiludes] spear-play, tilts.

The Irish Widow

The Irish Widow was first performed at Drury Lane on 23 October 1772, following the mainpiece, *The Gamesters*, Garrick's alteration of James Shirley's *The Gamester.* Success was anticipated for this farce, even though Garrick deprecated the work to Sir William Young as having been composed "in less than a week."[1] Hopkins the prompter noted that it "was written on

1. *Letters*, II, 846.

purpose to shew Mrs. Barry in an Irish part,"[2] and Garrick indicates as much in the advertisement to the printed text. Despite mostly adverse criticism, the farce achieved twenty performances in the first season and fifty-seven performances from 1772 through 1776. No less than seven editions were called for during Garrick's lifetime—three in the first year! Writing to James Boswell, 17 November 1772, Garrick remarked that "a Farce call'd The Irish Widow has had great Success, & will I suppose if taken care of, make You laugh in Scotland."[3]

Hopkins reluctantly admitted in his *Diary* that Mrs. Barry "did not succeed so well in it as was expected, but upon the Whole the Farce was well perform'd and met with great Applause."[4] Most critics thought otherwise, and it is a wonder that the piece lasted as long as it did. *Town and Country Magazine* considered it "a very indifferent production, and, as it did not meet with the applause that was expected, no one has adopted the bantling; though many are of the opinion that Mr. Garrick had a hand in it, as it is got up to the best advantage, and a new dance is introduced between the acts to put the Audience in a good humour for the succeeding scenes. . . . The piece concludes with a song sung by Mrs. Barry, by way of epilogue, which we think was injudiciously allotted to her, as her *forte* does not consist in singing."[5] *Westminster Magazine* was even more severe: "This piece was full of those uncouth ramblings after novelty which men destitute of Genius and Taste may be supposed to produce. Short as it was, it proved that the Author was possessed of neither; and every Scene seemed to be a literary Monster which teemed with Errors against Nature."[6]

And yet the farce succeeded beyond all expectations. Writing to George Faulkner, 28 November 1772, Garrick said jokingly, "If you see at y^r^ return to Dublin any handsome Actress who can perform the part of the *Irish Widow* well, pray run away with her, & by that time you will be thoroughly sick of her, I will take her off y^r^ hands & make her Fortune reviving the Widow—for the Moment that Farce began to get ye managers profit & Credit, Mrs Barry found out ye Playing so late, & in breeches would kill her, so the Irish Widow was destroy'd in ye midst of her Triumph."[7]

In *The Irish Widow* Garrick returns to the plots of Molière for *Le Marriage forcé* and *L'Avare*. One of his favorite targets of satire is the older man who determines to rival a younger, his own son or nephew. He used the situation as early as *Miss in Her Teens* (1747), again in the Lord Chalkstone episode added to *Lethe* (1756), in *The Guardian* (1759), in *The Clandestine Marriage* (1766), and finally in *May-Day* (1775). For *The Irish Widow* he borrows from *L'Avare* the situation in which the older man rivals his nephew and resolves to make a marriage depriving the younger man of his inheritance. Bates, a family friend, contrives a plot whereby the

2. 23 October 1772.
3. *Letters*, II, 828.
4. 23 October 1772.
5. October 1772, *The Theatre*, 39, p. 546.
6. 1773, p. 33.
7. *Letters*, II, 833.

Widow will assist him in getting not only the estate but also a bonus of ten thousand pounds in order to extricate Old Whittle from obligations to the Widow.

From *Le Marriage forcé* Garrick takes the scene in which the aged Sganarelle is disillusioned by the coquette Dorimène when he hears her catalogue her diversions, her ideas of the marriage contract, and especially her fondness for much younger men. Young Whittle, in Garrick's play, is assisted by Bates and the Widow in deceiving Old Whittle and his friend Kecksy with an Irish harridan act which panics the old man into relinquishing his claims and willingly giving his rights in the Widow to his nephew. Also from *Le Marriage forcé* is taken the dueling scene in which Sganarelle is challenged by the heroine's brother. The situation is made more extravagant when Garrick has the Widow disguised as her brother to preserve the honor of the O'Neale family, and finally to persuade Old Whittle to give in writing his disavowal of all claims upon her and the estate, and the giving of a bonus to the young lady. Elizabeth Stein has suggested that Garrick probably took the situation in which the Widow disguises herself as her brother from his friend John Hoadly's *The Lady Her Own Champion* (1742?), which is also derived from *Le Marriage forcé*.[8]

The changes made by Garrick are chiefly those of characterization. The Molière types are not only Anglicized but also have their idiosyncrasies underscored, so that with his own stage business he intensifies the action and the pace is invariably quickened. The characters of the Widow Brady, Old Whittle, Young Whittle, and Sir Patrick O'Neale come from Molière indeed, but each is carefully established as English and Irish.

The Widow, having been forced into a first marriage with a scoundrel, finds herself at age twenty-three free to search for love in a second union. She is therefore incapable of the cold calculations of a Dorimène and anticipates a normally happy marriage with the young man of her choice. This prepares for the denouement, which is not as acerbic as Molière's, and which shows Garrick as a defender of morality rather than a scourge of manners. It would appear that Garrick also had in mind Jonson's *The Silent Woman* when the heroine suddenly changes from "almost speechless reserve" to a "Wild, ranting buxom widow," in order to discourage her preposterous suitor.

Old Whittle is more than Molière's aged Sganarelle. Not only does he wish to attract the Widow, but to do so he affects the dress and actions of youth. Thomas, his servant, is appalled at the sight of his employer—"He frisks, and prances, and runs about, as if he had a new pair of legs. He has left off his brown camlet surtout, which he wore all summer, and now with his hat under his arm, he goes open breasted, and he dresses, and powders and smirks so, that you would take him for the mad Frenchman in Bedlam."[9]

8. *David Garrick, Dramatist*, p. 98. Professor Stein reminds us that Hoadly had read his play to Garrick and Margaret Woffington "at breakfast at her lodgings." See John Hoadly's letter to Garrick, 21 May 1772, in Boaden, *Correspondence*, I, 466.

9. I, lines 87–91.

It takes the combined wits of all the conspirators to bring the old fool back to his senses and to take up his former way of life.

While Young Whittle remains much the same as Alcides in *Le Marriage forcé*, Sir Patrick O'Neale is a more animated and stronger person than Molière's Alcanter. He is the typical member of Irish nobility, poor but proud, who is determined to have his daughter marry money, even though it will be another marriage of convenience.

Garrick's original contributions to the comedy are the characters of Kecksy and Thomas, the house servant. We have seen an unfinished and tentative portrait of Kecksy in the character of Dizzy, Daffodil's unfortunate cousin in *The Male Coquette* (1757). Here he appears in all his comic glory—as old as Old Whittle but decidedly more infirm. He has married a young wife and is already the complaisant cuckold who, between seizures of coughing, recommends that his ancient friend take the young Widow to wife. Thomas, on the other hand, together with Bates, represents Garrick's commonsense philosophy. He delights in the subterfuge which ultimately returns his employer to his appropriate mode of living. He reminds Old Whittle of his foolishness: "You were galloping full speed and down hill too, and if we had not laid hold of the bridle, being a bad jockey, you would have hung by the horns in the stirrup, to the great joy of the whole town."[10]

The comedy concludes with the victory of the conspirators, the return of the old man to sanity, and a song. Garrick shrewdly anticipates criticism of this song "by way of epilogue" when he has Mrs. Barry introduce it with the words: "And for fear my words should want ideas too, I will add an Irish tune to 'em that may carry off a bad voice and bad matter."[11]

The Irish Widow earned its popularity. Garrick created a fine, fast-paced farce with sure-fire situations, sure-fire characterizations, and his customary brisk dialogue. Only Mrs. Barry's reluctance to continue the role curtailed its original record. With fifty-six performances during his management, the farce continued in the repertoire well into the early nineteenth century.

TEXTS

O1 1st edition. London: T. Becket, 1772.
O2 2nd edition. London: T. Becket, 1772.
O3 3rd edition. London: T. Becket, 1772.
O4 4th edition. London: T. Becket, 1772.
D1 Corke: Printed for the Company of Booksellers, 1773.
O5 5th edition. London: T. Becket, 1774.
D2 Dublin: Exshaw, Saunders, Sleater, Williams, 1774.

[DRAMATIS PERSONAE]

1. Moody] John Moody, veteran actor at Drury Lane, made his debut under Garrick as Thyreus in *Antony and Cleopatra*, 12 January 1759.

10. II, lines 443–45.
11. II, lines 471–72.

2. Parsons] William Parsons came to Drury Lane in the season 1762–63 and remained with Garrick through 1775–76.

3. Cautherly] Samuel Cautherly, a protegè of Garrick, made his adult debut at Drury Lane as George Barnwell on 26 September 1765. He remained with the company through Garrick's retirement.

4. Baddeley] Robert Baddeley (1733–94) made his debut at the Haymarket as Sir William Wealthy in Foote's *The Minor* on 28 June 1760. On 20 October 1760 he bowed at Drury Lane in the same role. His reputation was based on low comedy roles, especially that of Moses in Sheridan's *The School for Scandal* (1777).

5. Dodd] James William Dodd made his debut at Drury Lane as Faddle in Edward Moore's *The Foundling* on 3 October 1765 and continued as a member of the company for many years.

6. Weston] Thomas Weston first appeared as Dick in Foote's *The Minor* at the Haymarket in 1760. By the season of 1761–62 he had joined the Drury Lane company, with which he was to remain through 1766–67.

7. Griffith] a utility actor who joined Drury Lane in 1750–51.

8. Mrs. Barry] Ann, Mrs. Spranger Barry, known as the "York Heroine." She followed her husband to Drury Lane in 1767–68. Both removed to Covent Garden in the season 1774–75.

[TO MRS. BARRY]

9. *Grecian Daughter*] Arthur Murphy's tragedy produced at Drury Lane 26 February 1772.

[ACT I, i]

11. Scarborough] a resort town in Yorkshire.
91. Bedlam] St. Mary of Bethlehem Hospital for the mentally ill.
186. galochys] overshoes.

[ACT I, iii]

74. pantaons] pantheons.
112. moped up] dispirited.
124. gostring] swaggering.
190. Macaroonies] English dandies affecting foreign manners and fashions. savory vivers] tasty eatables.
195. vapors] depressed spirits, hypochondria.
215. Baccararo] gambler, cardsharp.

[ACT II]

5–6. *Signatum & Sigillatum*] signed and sealed.
113. fleering] sneering.
184. two-pair-of-stairs window] hall window.
228. *quem deus vult perdere*] whom the god would destroy.
322. kiptic] stiptic.
410. *O gra ma chree my little din ousil craw*] O love my heart my little deary.
431. choused] swindled, cheated.
481. *Cush la maw cree*] My dearest heart.

A Christmas Tale

Two days after Christmas, Monday, 27 December 1773, Garrick produced another of his spectacular pieces, a tale of love and magic wrapped in beautiful settings by Phillipe Jacques De Loutherbourg and interspersed with no less than thirty-two musical numbers in a score by Charles Dibdin. He called it *A Christmas Tale* and suggested by way of the Prologue that the audience receive this holiday extravaganza as children attending a Christmas party: "My food is meant for honest, hearty grinners! / For you–you spirits with good stomachs bring; / O make the neigh'bring roof with rapture ring; / Open your mouths, pray swallow everything."[1]

Although he cautioned the critics to "be merry but not wise," some of them heartily disliked what they saw. *The Westminster Magazine* commented on the production after it had been condensed into an afterpiece and still did not relish it: "Though greatly shortened, it still contains nothing; and we were sorry to see the genius and abilities of Mr. Loutherbourg so misemployed. The scenes and machines were all admirable; and we could not help wishing that the talents of this man, instead of being used to save paltry things from damnation, were united to those of a Shakespeare, to astonish or to enchant us into virtue."[2] Nevertheless, *A Christmas Tale* became the sensation of the London season, and seventeen performances were given. Two other performances were given in the following season, 1774–75.

The entertainment was an elaborate affair. It is in five parts and involves as principal actors ten men and two women. Six men and five women singers are listed as part of an even larger chorus, and six principal dancers led the ballet ensemble. Hopkins in his *Diary* remarked that "this piece was written by Mr. Garrick which he wrote in a hurry & on purpose to Show Some fine Scenes which were designed by Mon[s] De Loutherbourg particularly a Burning Palace *etc.* which was extremely fine and Novel. Mr. Weston Play'd very well. The Music by Mr. Dibdin, the worst he ever Compos'd. The Piece was very well receiv'd."[3] Such are the ingredients in creating a successful holiday entertainment, not only in Garrick's age but even in our own time.

Writing as Hopkins tells us "in a hurry" and with his scenes already established by the brush of De Loutherbourg, Garrick turned to another French confection, Charles Simon Favart's *La Fée Urgèle.* This is a fairy play which had appeared in France in 1765, and as light opera it relies upon lyrics to carry plot and dialogue with considerable success. While Garrick apparently modelled *A Christmas Tale* on the Favart piece, he changed the atmosphere carefully established by the Frenchman into a rather dull and didactic representation of the land of love and magic. According to custom, most Christmas entertainments were expected to present a moral lesson, and Garrick felt obliged to obey and to load the piece with fine examples of moral preachment not to be found in Favart.

1. Prologue, lines 38–41.
2. October 1776, pp. 539–40.
3. Monday, 27 December 1773.

Such a change in spirit may also be due to Garrick's familiarity with Chaucer's *Tale of the Wyf of Bathe* and Fletcher's *Women Pleased*, especially the situation involving Belvidere and Silvio after the latter's banishment. Garrick's heroine, Camilla, with the aid of magic turns herself into an aged crone to aid Floridor in retrieving his lost sword and shield. For this deliverance she asks his love, is refused by the hero as he vows eternal devotion to Camilla, and, as the stage lightens, reveals herself in "her real character and dress." Garrick will have none of the sentimental denouement of *La Fée Urgèle*, in which the heroine insists she's dying of a broken heart, nor of the Chaucer-Fletcher solution in which the heroine faces her lover with the alternatives of having her old and ugly but faithful, or young and fair and unpredictable, with the hero asked by the lady to decide. Garrick chooses a speedy if artificial way out, allowing Floridor's declaration of love for Camilla alone to decide the matter.

From Favart, Garrick borrows his characters for the secondary plot and with his usual artistry gives them a reality and humor not to be found in his principal roles. He obviously delights in these scenes of countryside frolic and lovemaking. Robinette is the saucy confidante wooed by Tycho and Faladel. In Favart Robinette finally marries her suitor, but Garrick in adding yet another would-be lover, Faladel, allows his soubrette to end the play without choosing one or the other. As often happens in musical plays, the low-comedy roles outshine the major characters.

As indicated by the prompter, however, the main attraction in *A Christmas Tale* was the remarkable work of De Loutherbourg. Although the use of transparencies had been a part of Garrick's stagecraft since his production of another Christmas entertainment, *Harlequin's Invasion*, in the season of 1759–60, the advent of De Loutherbourg refined and expanded scenic possibilities. *A Christmas Tale* was De Loutherbourg's debut at Drury Lane, and, as we have remarked, the collaboration with Garrick's expertise resulted in a scenic sensation.

Eight great scenes were painted and equipped with varied lighting effects. First, "a beautiful landskip"; then "Camilla's magnificent garden," with its "enchanted laurel" and flowers that in moments of stress "vary their colours"; Bonoro's Cell, with prisons around it which burst open when Tycho is put to sleep and the prisoners have obtained his magic wand; a Dark Wood which opens to reveal the castle of Nigromant and the bad magician in his fiery lake; the castle gates; and finally "A Grand Apartment in the Seraglio." Here wonder is piled on wonder as the entertainment reaches its close. Floridor receives a letter from the ancient "Grinnelda" (really Camilla in disguise) demanding his love in return for his victory over Nigromant. To show his disgust Floridor tears the letter in pieces. Thunder and darkness occur, and flames of fire appear through the seraglio windows. Then the seraglio breaks apart to discover the entire palace in flames. But after some moments all dissolves into "a fine moonlight scene" with Bonoro descending in a cloud. When the cloud ascends the audience is treated to a "fine distant prospect of the sea and a castle" at sunrise.

To accomplish all this scene enchantment De Loutherbourg was able to use the lighting system Garrick had imported from France after his visit there in 1764–65, especially two new reflecting lamps designed by Boquet. By the skillful handling of silk screens and drop curtains, with lights playing on them front and rear, the artist achieved phenomenal effects for his time, improving greatly upon the work of his predecessors, Thomas French and Henry Angelo, whose transparencies had beguiled spectators in *Harlequin's Invasion* (1759) and *The Jubilee* (1769).[4]

If *A Christmas Tale* was only the sensation of a season and soon forgotten, it had served Garrick and De Loutherbourg very well both in money and reputation. Its total of nineteen performances is phenomenal for an entertainment devoid of character development and even common sense. As spectacle, however, it bids for attention as a recipe for holiday glitter and nonsensical amusement.

TEXTS

O1 1st edition. London: T. Becket, 1774.
O2 2nd edition. London: T. Becket, 1774.
O3 3rd edition. London: T. Becket, 1774.
D1 Dublin: Lynch, Williams, Wilson, and Husband, 1774.
O4 4th edition. London: T. Becket, 1776. [In 3 acts.]

[PROLOGUE]

12. collar'd brawn] rolled roast of boar's meat.
30. capuchin] a woman's hooded cloak.

[PART I, i]

37. glass] mirror.
93–94. gentleman usher] a court usher.

[PART II, i]

109. talismans] magic charms.
159–60. lob's pound] lout's pound.
162. parlaver] palaver, to talk profusely.
170. cormorant] a large, voracious seabird.
227–28. *scandalum magnatum horrendissinum*] a great, frightful scandal.

[PART III, ii]

53. wand] a gentleman usher's staff.
55. fardingale] farthingale, hooped petticoat.
64. Tray] pet dog in the nursery rhyme.
182. hansel] handsel, to test or try.

[PART IV, i]

80. ague] fever.
128. chaplet] wreath for the head.

4. See Ralph G. Allen's discussion of De Loutherbourg's work in "A Christmas Tale, or, Harlequin Scene Painter," *Tennessee Studies in Literature*, 19, 149–61.

[PART IV, iii]

83. seraglio] harem.

[PART IV, iv]

20. doit] half of a farthing.

[PART V, i]

198. Draw] Cleave.

The Meeting of the Company

On 29 December 1771 one of Garrick's close friends, the Reverend John Hoadly, wrote in some puzzlement, "report says, you are reviving Bayes, with some additional Scene of your own. An hardy undertaking, my good Friend."[1] In his reply on 4 January 1772 Garrick assured the good Doctor that "Y^r^ Intelligence about a New Scene in ye Rehearsal is not exact–I had an intention of introducing my Art of Acting into y^r^ play, which I must have mentioned to You Some time or another: I suppose ye Manager has objections to Bayes's piece, the Poet to induce ye Manager to Accept it, promises, if he will perform it, to make his Actors (the bad ones) equal to ye best by a certain receipt he was master of, & had discover'd by long Study–the Manager agrees, the actors are call'd in, to be taught ye great Secret–Bayes then gives them his Art of Acting–which will shew all ye false manners of acting Tragedy & Comedy, wch I have collected in about 30 or 40 comical Verses–but I shall keep it for an Interlude–it will be too much for Me wth Bayes."[2]

When *The Meeting of the Company* finally appeared on Saturday evening, 17 September 1774, it was not as an interlude but as what was known as a Prelude. Taking the place of the customary "occasional prologue," it served to open the season of 1774–75 in the newly decorated house. It had originally been scheduled for 5 September, according to Garrick's application to the Lord Chamberlain.

Using the burlesque-rehearsal form, as he had done previously in *A Peep Behind the Curtain* (1767), Garrick relies upon the popularity of Buckingham's *The Rehearsal*, even to the naming of the leading character Bayes. His hero, however, unlike Buckingham's, is not interested in playwriting and *Drama Commonplaces* but in Bayes's *Art of Acting*. He claims the ability to change the acting technique of Garrick's company until he makes "the worst equal to the best." In his instructions to the assembled actors and his attempt at a rehearsal of the new method Garrick satirizes the absurdities in the contemporary acting of both tragedy and comedy.

Like Molière's *L'Impromptu de Versailles* (1663), Garrick allows the audience a candid look backstage at Drury Lane and gives the actors their own professional names for the most part. The prelude opens as a salute to the newly decorated theatre, and we see last-minute preparations for the

1. Boaden, I, 448.
2. *Letters*, II, 782.

opening of the new season. The technical staff is shown at work; singers and dancers rehearse; and the members of the acting company gradually arrive at the theatre after their summer's stint in the provinces. While the actors squabble and complain among themselves, they are united in resentment against a man who would presume to teach them how to perform.

With the appearance of Bayes to conduct his rehearsal, the company is first treated to his low opinion of their work in the provinces, and manager Patent must intervene so that Bayes can proceed wth his class instruction from Bayes's *Art of Acting; or, The Worst Equal to the Best.*

His basic principle is to rid the stage of what he calls Nature, and he is quick to belittle Shakespeare and that poet's respect for the "Modesty of Nature." He insists that "No Modesty will do upon the stage."

> Nature's a bird, and every fool will fail
> Who hopes to lay some salt upon her tail.
> In vain to seize the wanton, boobies watch her,
> They've neither eyes, legs, hands or heads to catch her.[3]

Reading from his acting manual, Bayes advises the actors to "Be in extremes in Buskin or in Sock, / In action wild, in attitude a block. / From the spectator's eye your faults to hide, / Be either whirlwind or be petrified."[4]

And finally, after many jibes at contemporary modes in the acting profession, Bayes tries to teach them all to caper in comedy and to keep on reciting as they leave the stage. The actors readily comply; but once offstage they refuse to continue, leaving the instructor alone. As he is about to share his complaints with the audience, the comedian Tom Weston returns to advise the public: "if you will not drive such a great blockhead from the stage, you will not have a single author of merit to write for you. If nature is to be turned out of doors, there will be nothing but ranting and roaring in tragedy and capering and face-making in comedy. The stage will go to ruin, the public will go to sleep."[5]

But Bayes insists on having the last word—and through his indignant complaint Garrick gives the audience a rather complete picture of itself and its usual behavior. "May this house be always as empty as it is now. Or if it must fill, let it be with fine ladies to disturb the actors, fine gentlemen to admire themselves, and fat citizens in the boxes. May the pit be filled with nothing but crabbed critics, unemployed actors, and managers' orders. May places be kept in the green boxes without being paid for, and may the galleries never bring good humor or horse laughs with them again . . . may I for my folly be doomed to be an actor here in the winter and get money by tumbling and rope-dancing in the summer."[6]

Although this prelude was disliked by the critic of *The Westminster Magazine*,[7] Hopkins commented in his *Diary*: "This new Prelude . . . is full

3. I, lines 286–89.
4. I, lines 319–22.
5. I, lines 415–20.
6. I, lines 426–36.
7. George Winchester Stone, Jr., see *The London Stage*, Part 4, III, 1833.

of fine Satyr & an Excellent Lesson to all performers, it was received with very great Applause and will be profitable to the Proprietors."[8] He was correct, of course, as indicated by its record of eleven performances in the season. After seven nights it was acted four more times "By particular desire."

The manuscript of *The Meeting of the Company* was discovered in the Kemble-Devonshire Collection of the Huntington Library by Elizabeth P. Stein and published in her *Three Plays by David Garrick* (New York, 1928). The present edition is again based upon the manuscript. A cast of characters is not given in the manuscript, nor does Professor Stein include one. To those actors already mentioned by name in the prelude it is now possible to add the other actors by reference to *The London Stage*, Part 4.[9]

[DRAMATIS PERSONAE]

0.1. No cast is listed in the original manuscript in the Huntington Library, HM 12, Kemble-Devonshire Collection, Vol. 332. The tentative cast has been assembled from the manuscript and from *The London Stage*, Part 4, III, 1833.

[THE PLAY]

6–7. Mr. Hopkins] William Hopkins, Garrick's prompter.

14–15. coronations . . . Champetres] spectacular reproductions of public events, such as the Coronation of George III and Queen Charlotte in 1761; *The Institution of the Order of the Garter* in 1771; Portsmouth Reviews, naval extravaganza; masquerades . . . Fete Champetres, outdoor entertainments.

31. a good campaign] a successful tour of the provincial theatres.

42–43. September to June] the theatre season for the Patent theatres.

101. Jerry Sneak, Dr. Last] Jerry Sneak, in Samuel Foote's *The Mayor of Garrat*; Dr. Last in Foote and Isaac Bickerstaff's *Dr. Last in His Chariot.*

164. Magic Lantern] *The Modern Magic Lanthorn* was first presented by Baddeley at Lebeck's Head on 5 September 1774, later at Panton Street, 10–15 April 1775, and at Marlebone Gardens from 30 May through 20 June 1775.

247. first little man] David Garrick.

254. Bills of Mortality] periodically published return of the deaths in particular districts.

281. Bristol Stones] transparent rock-crystals found in limestone near Bristol.

282. the Bristol Company] provincial theatre at Bristol.

417–21. Weston speech] Garrick's thoughts on actors and playwrights.

421. Johnny Pringle and his pig] a specialty act of Weston's.

426–33. Bayes speech] Garrick's criticism of audiences of the time.

Bon Ton; or, High Life above Stairs

Like *Lilliput* and *The Male Coquette*, *Bon Ton* is a miniature comedy of manners strongly reminiscent of Restoration comedy, an afterpiece which, according to William Hopkins was "Written 15 or 16 years ago. Mr. Gar-

8. Ibid. See also Macmillan, *Drury Lane Calendar*, p. 179.
9. III, 1833.

rick out of friendship for Mr. King gave it him to get up for his Benefit."[1] In the advertisement to the published text Garrick maintains that *Bon Ton* was written and then "thrown aside for many years." If prompter and manager are correct, then *Bon Ton* was composed at about the same time as *Lilliput* (1756) and *The Male Coquette* (1757)—nineteen years before its premiere. Certainly all three comedies are alike in tone and demonstrate Garrick's sophistication and his partiality for the Restoration mode of social satire. Were it not for the word of the prompter, however, we might suspect Garrick of dissimulation in regard to the date of this comedy and judge *Bon Ton* a product of a more mature period, it being generally considered one of the most polished and brilliant little pieces of the English theatre.

On 18 March 1775 Thomas King's benefit bill offered the public as mainpiece Shakespeare's *Measure for Measure*, followed by the first performance of *Bon Ton*. On that evening, according to Garrick, the little comedy was presented "with some alterations,[2] for the benefit of Mr. King, as a token of regard for one, who, during a long engagement, was never known, unless confined by real illness, to disappoint the Public, or distress the Managers." In his *Diary* for that night Hopkins noted that while "The Play was very Imperfect, . . . It was very well perform'd & received with the highest Applause."[3]

The prompter's account as to the play's being "Imperfect" is indeed confirmed by a letter from Garrick to George Colman soon after 18 March 1775, and certainly prior to its next performance on 27 March 1775. After thanking Colman for his "excellent Prologue," Garrick goes on to say that he "would wish to add to ye obligation by desiring him to look over the Farce & draw his Pencil thro' the parts his judgment would omit in ye next representation—Mr. Garrick not being present at ye representation, he likewise should be very happy if Mr Colman, would shew his regard to him, & take ye trouble which is wanting to make *Bon Ton* palatable."[4] At this late date it is impossible to say what Colman did to Garrick's text—this is not a problem such as we encounter with the Garrick-Colman *The Clandestine Marriage*.[5] But George Colman's pencil may account for some sixteen pages of manuscript included in the play when it was submitted for license which were not printed by Garrick.

The manager's tribute to the veteran actor explains in part why he entrusted the staging of this new piece to King rather than assume his customary responsibility. We should remember, however, that Garrick was in poor health at this time and intended to retire from the stage some fifteen months later. He must have given over his responsibility gladly. In fact, the manager, as we have noted, was not present on the night of the first performance. But Thomas King had enlisted under Garrick's management in the season 1749–

1. *MS Diaries of the Drury Lane Theatre.*
2. Dougald Macmillan, in the Larpent Catalogue, states: "a few deletions of text . . . a total of some 16 pages of MS not printed; other differences slight."
3. *MS Diaries of the Drury Lane Theatre.*
4. *Letters*, III, 997.
5. *The Plays of David Garrick*, I, 855–64.

50 and quickly proved a mainstay of the Drury Lane company until his retirement in 1802. Highlights of his lengthy career included the original Lord Ogleby in *The Clandestine Marriage* in 1766 and the original Sir Peter Teazle in Sheridan's *The School for Scandal* in 1777.

For a new play, *Bon Ton* was produced very late in the acting season and attained only eight performances before the house closed for the summer. In the same month the play was noticed by two London publications. *The London Chronicle*, 11–14 March, announced that *Bon Ton* was "said to be the production of the Author of the Maid of the Oaks. Certain it is, that Mr. Garrick hath revised, corrected, and altered it."[6] A highly negative review then appeared in the *Westminster Magazine*, also identifying the author as John Burgoyne and including the following opinion: "From this sketch our Readers will be able to form some opinion of the new Comedy of *Bon Ton*, which is asserted to be the production of the Author of the *Maid of the Oaks*, and appears to be a cut from the same cloth, ornamented with a little of Mr. Garrick's fringe. Without either originality of character or novelty of situation, it perhaps very justly depicts the manners and vices of the Great World; and to that very reason, probably, we are to ascribe its want of acumen, wit, and laughableness."[7]

The public, however, thought otherwise, and *Bon Ton* was performed before enthusiastic audiences for eighteen nights in the season 1775–76 and achieved a total of twenty-six performances before Garrick left the stage. Its brilliance must have been recognized very quickly, for it became one of the most popular afterpieces to remain in the standard repertoire well into the nineteenth century, both in England and America.

The London critics, although wrong in their attribution of authorship, could discern the distinctive hand of Garrick in the play. And the writer in the *Westminster Magazine*, while complaining of the lack of originality in characters and dramatic situations, was quick to admit that it "perhaps very justly depicts the manners and vices of the Great World." Throughout his life, as actor and manager, Garrick's preference for the astringency of Restoration comedy was as well known as his public role of moralist, especially in his defense of the institution of marriage.

In *Bon Ton* Garrick makes his points quite early. The Minikin family is determined to maintain its position in the world of fashion. Its members have traveled extensively—"half a year in France, and a winter passed in the warmer climate of Italy."[8] They have returned to England as hybrid creatures with what they assume to be continental manners, including a passion for drinking, gaming, and extra-marital love affairs on the part of Lord Minikin and his lady and her cousin, Lucretia Tittup. As the play begins, seduction is in the air. Lord Minikin has plans for Lucretia, while Lady Minikin wishes to retaliate against her husband by encouraging the attentions of Colonel Tivy, her young cousin's fiancé.

Into this situation comes Lucretia's uncle from the country, Sir John

6. Vol. 37, p. 248.
7. March 1775, p. 125.
8. I, i, lines 111–12.

Trotley, a determined moralist and spokesman for Garrick. Sir John has no liking for the fine world of fashion and determines to rescue his errant niece: "nothing, I fear, can save her; however, to ease my conscience, I must try: but what can be expected from the young women of these times, but sallow looks, wild schemes, saucy words, and loose morals!—They lie a-bed all day, sit up all night; if they are silent, they are gaming, and if they talk, 'tis either scandal or infidelity; and that they may look what they are, their heads are all feather, and round their necks are twisted rattle-snake tippets—*O Tempore, O Mores*!"[9] Sir John is shocked when Lord Minikin explains that his marriage is one of convenience: "Marriage is not now-a-days, an affair of inclination, but convenience; and they who marry for love, and such old-fashioned stuff, are to me as ridiculous as those that advertise for an agreeable companion in a post-chaise."[10]

When Sir John himself encounters London's pickpockets, and his own servant, young Davy, returns drunk from a night on the town, the country gentleman determines to take matters into his own hands. He breaks in upon the Lord and Lucretia to find the gentleman in a compromising position. When he goes to inform Lady Minikin of her husband's conduct, he discovers the lady receiving amorous attentions from Colonel Tivy. And when the Colonel suggests that entering without first knocking at a lady's door deserves death, Sir John replies, "Death indeed! for I shall never recover myself again! All pigs of the same sty! all studying for the good of the nation."[11] When he discovers the two couples in an embarrassing situation upon their return from a masquerade, Sir John disinherits his niece and carries her and Lady Minikin home to Trotley Place, where he earnestly hopes to reform them. He closes the comedy with a moral: "Thus then, with the wife of one under this arm, and the mistress of another, under this, I sally forth a Knight Errant, to rescue distressed damsels from those monsters, foreign vices and *Bon Ton*, as they call it; and I trust that every English hand and heart here, will assist me in so desperate an undertaking.—*You'll excuse me, Sirs*?"[12]

While the character of Sir John Trotley as commentator is borrowed from the Jonsonian humors comedies, the remaining characters are created in the finest tradition of Restoration comedy. Lord and Lady Minikin are familiar types, while Miss Lucretia recalls something of the *jeu d'esprit* of such heroines as Etherege's Harriet in *The Man of Mode*, or perhaps even a likeness to Congreve's Millamant in *The Way of the World*. Colonel Tivy is the typical well-born scoundrel who quickly deserts his dear Lucretia once she has been disinherited. Even the servants, especially Jessamy and Davy, are derived from the same tradition. Nowhere is the Restoration tone more evident than in the dialogue, replete with *double entendres*. Speaking of love and friendship as "mere visiting acquaintance," Miss Tittup goes on to say, "we know their names indeed, talk of 'em sometimes, and let 'em knock at our doors, but we never let 'em in, you know. (*Looking roguishly at*

9. I, i, lines 232–39.
10. I, ii, lines 156–59.
11. I, iii, lines 33–35.
12. II, ii, lines 210–15.

her.)"[13] Lady Minikin explains her desire for a game of chess with Colonel Tivy: "Since he belonged to you, Titty, I have taken a kind of liking to him; I like everything that loves my Titty. (*Kisses her.*)"[14]

As he did in his alterations of such Restoration plays as the Buckingham version of Fletcher's *The Chances* and Wycherley's *The Country Wife*, Garrick allows himself in *Bon Ton* to savor the bawdy qualities of Restoration comedy, and at the same time to maintain his audience's regard for the stage as a place for moral instruction in the leading character, Sir John Trotley. As played by Thomas King, we may be certain that the proper balance between the Restoration and his own age's taste was maintained. This explains the continuing popularity of *Bon Ton* into the next century.

TEXTS

O1 1st edition. London: T. Becket, 1775.
O2 2nd edition. London: Printed for Sadler and Co., 1776.

[ADVERTISEMENT]

3. Mr. King] Thomas King (1730–1804), Garrick's most trusted colleague as an actor at Drury Lane Theatre. King originated the roles of Sir Peter Teazle, Puff, and Sir Anthony Absolute in Sheridan's comedies.

[THE PROLOGUE]

3. *purlieus*] environs.

5. *Tyburn* scratch] a type of periwig short enough to let one scratch his head. thick club] hair worn at the back in a club-shaped knot or tail. *Temple* tie] a pigtail peculiar to some members of the legal profession.

10. Broad St. Giles] home of the Cockneys; *i.e.*, true Londoners.

18. Madam Fussock] a fat woman. Spital-fields] manufacturing district in London's East End.

22. Bagnigge-Wells] popular resort.

28. *Festino*] entertainment or feast.

30. loo] card game played for stakes and forfeits.

44. whipt-syllabub] whipped cream with wine or cider.

61. *Bayes*] character satirizing John Dryden in *The Rehearsal*, by George Villiers, second Duke of Buckingham.

62. Darly's] Mattias or Matthew Darly, caricaturist, designer, and engraver.

[ACT I. SCENE i]

0.2. Minikin] an affected darling. Tittup] a frolicsome, capering person.

9. cardinal] a woman's short cloak, usually hooded.

14. *vis-à-vis*] a carriage with facing seats.

40. Imprimis] first, in the first place.

62. Goth] uncouth barbarian.

71. *Pantheons*] buildings where famous dead of a nation are buried.

---

13. I, i, lines 21–23.
14. I, i, lines 93–95.

73. Lucretia] legendary Roman wife raped by Sextus, son of Tarquinius Superbus.

151. vapors] depressed spirits, hypochondria.

173. bob] short curl or knob of hair, a short haircut.

188. 'feckins] oath of astonishment.

227. maccaroni] a coarse, lewd fellow.

238. tippets] fur scarves.

[SCENE ii]

5. cheveux] hair.

8–9. soup maigre] soup not made from flesh or its juices.

24. domino] loose cloak, with hood and mask, for masquerades.

49. *tendre*] infatuation.

125. jack-boots] sturdy boots reaching above the knee.

147. *mauvais honte*] bashfulness or false shame.

[ACT II. SCENE i]

5. hanger] a short sword.

111. Newgate] a London prison.

[SCENE ii]

104. *frison*] chilliness, shivering.

May-Day; or, The Little Gipsy

Garrick's miniature comic opera, with music by Dr. Thomas Arne, was first produced at Drury Lane on the evening of Saturday, 28 October 1775, and managed sixteen performances before the close of the season. William Hopkins notes in his *Diary* that both the featured singer and the farce itself were well received. "This Musical Farce of one Act was wrote by Mr G on purpose to introduce Miss Abrams (a Jew) about 17 years old. She is very small, a Swarthy Complexion, has a very sweet Voice and a fine Shake, but not quite power enough yet—both the Piece and Young Lady were receiv'd with great Applause."[1]

In his advertisement to the printed text of *May-Day* Garrick anticipates criticism with his usual air of professional humility. He explains that the farce was produced at a time in the fall season when better writers were reluctant to show their work, and that the trifle served only to introduce Dr. Arne's young pupil, who was certainly inexperienced as an actress. Quite candidly he confesses that he has given the young lady as little spoken dialogue as possible.

Except for Garrick's customary ability to create stereotype scenes of low-comedy in village life, *May-Day* has little to recommend it. It is an artificial concoction using one of Garrick's favorite and, by this time, shop-worn

1. *The London Stage*, Part 4, III, 1923.

plots—a father and son who vie for the affections of a young woman. Elizabeth Stein remarks that "the humor of the play, too, is not in the usual vein. It is strained and lacks the sprightliness and spontaneity so characteristic of Garrick's work at its best . . . The play on the whole has not much of the vivacity and briskness of movement that we usually meet with in a Garrick farce. Moreover, the piece and the songs, although the time of action is the first day of May, have nothing in them of the spirit of May and the out-of-doors, but breathe rather something of the atmosphere of the Drury Lane Theatre."[2]

Reviews of the production show that it was to Dr. Arne that Garrick owed the success of this piece. *Town and Country Magazine* for November 1775 had this to say: "The chief recommendation of this production consists in the music, which has considerable merit, and it is well adapted to the airs; as to the fable it is simple, and not very interesting. A young lady, named Abrahams, and said to be a Jewess, made her first appearance in the Gipsy, and met with great applause, her voice being very melodious, and her taste for music very correct." Even the *Westminster Magazine* (November 1775), usually quite critical of Garrick productions, reluctantly admitted the charm of the evening's performance: "This Opera is evidently a theatrical trifle whipped up merely to introduce Miss Abrahams, a young Jewess, who performed the part of the *Little Gipsy*; it would therefore be uncandid and ridiculous to try it by the serious rules of dramatic criticism. For this reason we shall only observe, that the preparation is palatable, and that the hand of the preparer is discoverable from the affinity between the scene of *Roger* and the *Old Man*, and that of *Whittle* and *Thomas* in the *Irish Widow*, and from the resemblance which the description of London given in Mr. Bannister's song bears to *Linco's Travels*. The music of the Overture and the Finale were remarkably light and pretty: some of the Airs also did Dr. Arne credit." Roger Fiske confirms these critical remarks with a modern opinion of the score: "The libretto is hardly distinguished, but the music is full of charm, and as with all Arne's later operas, there are enough extra staves in the published score to provide most of the orchestral detail. The overture is usually good, and the first movement, with its engaging second subject, is about as near to conventional sonata form as Arne ever got. The Little Gipsy has some entrancing songs, and her friend Dolly has a 'winner' as well."[3]

May-Day may have been an impromptu exercise bolstered by Arne's melodious tunes, but the manager's astuteness is demonstrated in the sixteen performances he was able to obtain from such a slight piece in one season. *May-Day* appeared in no less than three editions printed by Becket in as many years.

TEXTS

O1 London: T. Becket, 1775.
O2 London: T. Becket, 1776.
D1 Dublin: Printed for Corcoran, Hoey, etc., 1777.

2. *David Garrick, Dramatist*, p. 154.
3. *English Theatre Music*, p. 368.

[SCENE ii]

22. macaronies] English dandies affecting foreign mannerisms.
41. fagaries] whims.
64. chine] spine.
88. moped] dispirited.
98. tucker] a detachable collar.
141. serallery] a seraglio.
210. maundering] grumbling.
385. featly] gracefully.

The Theatrical Candidates

When Garrick and James Lacy opened Drury Lane Theatre for their first season in 1747, Garrick spoke the prologue written for the occasion by Dr. Samuel Johnson. That prologue concluded with the hope that the audience and this new management could establish a decent stage.

'Tis yours, this night, to bid the reign commence
Of rescued Nature and reviving Sense;
To chase the charms of Sound, the pomp of Show,
For useful Mirth and salutary Woe;
Bid scene Virtue form the rising age,
And Truth diffuse her radiance from the stage.

Three years later at the opening of another season Garrick spoke a "New Occasional Prologue" in which he had to admit that his ambitious reform had not exactly succeeded.

Sacred to Shakespeare was this spot design'd,
To pierce the heart, and humanize the mind.
But if an empty House, the Actors curse,
Show us our Lears and Hamlet lose their force;
Unwilling we must change the nobler scene,
And in our turn present you Harlequin; . . .[1]

And throughout his career Garrick was to plead with his public for more discriminating taste.

When he opened his refurbished theatre in the fall of his final acting season, 1775–76, he saluted the elegant Adam interior and other improvements, not with another prologue but with a musical prelude, *The Theatrical Candidates* (23 September 1775). For a final time he instructed his public as to the purpose of the playhouse and an audience's power to determine future attractions at the box office. While this prelude is slight indeed in dramatic terms, its dialogue and songs were an appropriate gesture toward Garrick's lifetime philosophy of dramatic reform.

The occasion of the remodeling of Drury Lane inspired the representation of Comedy and Tragedy vying for the approval of theatre patrons, only

1. *Poetical Works of David Garrick*, I, 102.

to be challenged once more by Harlequin's putting a word in for Pantomime. The situation is much like that Garrick had used before in *Harlequin's Invasion*, 1750.

Mercury, who has been sent from above to view the altered theatre and its decorations, is well aware of the coming debate between Comedy and Tragedy and Harlequin, and promises to return with a final judgment in the case. Meanwhile, the three modes of entertainment have at each other, allowing Garrick to express again his long-standing criticisms. Comedy berates Melpomena for her presumption:

> Think you, your strutting, straddling, puffy pride,
> Your rolling eyes, arms kimbo'd, tragic stride
> Can frighten me? [2]

And Tragedy replies in kind.

> You can be wise too, nay, a thief can be!
> Wise with stale sentiments all stolen from me,
> Which long cast off from my heroic verses
> Have stuffed your motley, dull sententious farces.
> The town grew sick! [3]

And each has what she thinks is the last word. Tragedy cries, "In all the realms of nonsense can there be / A monster like your comic-tragedy?" to which Comedy replies, "Oh yes, my dear!—your tragic-comedy."[4]

Upon Harlequin's arrival the debate grows warmer still. His appeal for audience votes reminds everyone that

> Though you may laugh, and you may cry your eyes out,
> For all your airs, sharp looks, and sharper nails,
> Draggled you were till I held up your tails.
> Each friend I have above, whose voice so loud is,
> Will never give me up for two such dowdies.
> She's grown so grave, and she so cross and bloody,
> Without my help your brains will all be muddy.
> Deep thought and politics so stir your gall,
> When you come here you should not think at all.[5]

Finally Mercury arrives from Parnassus to announce the decision of Apollo concerning all three. Tragedy and Comedy must go their separate ways, except when they must join in the plays of William Shakespeare. Harlequin's place is to appear only in support of the two, and only when farce and musical entertainments fail to draw at the box office.

> For you, Monsieur, whenever farce or song,
> Are sick and tired, then you, without a tongue,

---

2. I, i, lines 57–59.
3. Ibid., lines 76–80.
4. Ibid., lines 83–85.
5. Ibid., lines 105–13.

Or with one if you please, in Drury Lane,
As *locum tenens*, may hold up their train.
  Thus spoke Apollo, but he added too,
Vain his decrees until confirmed by you. (*To the audience.*)[6]

The Theatrical Candidates had a musical score by William Bates. What part this composer had in the success of the prelude can be surmised by a report from *Town and Country Magazine* for September 1775: "This prelude is generally ascribed to Mr. Garrick, which breathes in many parts, original humour and satire, and is no discredit to his pen. The overture (which as well as the rest of the music, was set by Mr. Bates) was at least pretty, and several of the airs were much approved. The full chorus particularly met with great encomiums, the music being not only well adapted, but also well executed. Some of the pit were of opinion, that Mrs. Smith did not enter sufficiently into the spirit of her part, whilst Mrs. Wrighton greatly outréed hers. Upon the whole, however, it was well received by the generality of the audience."[7] *Westminster Magazine* (September 1775) had this to say about the production: "This *petite morceau* is evidently the production of Mr. Garrick; and though it neither teemed with the wit of a Chesterfield, nor the polished style of a Lyttelton, had a sufficient share of merit to recommend itself to the audience, who received it with applause. The only objection we have to offer on the occasion is, that there appeared something of the burlesque in Tragedy's asking our votes in a song; and this instance of the Ridiculous was heightened by the inanimate appearance of Mrs. Smith, who, though a pleasing figure, has it not in her power to express any of those passions which alarm, fire, and melt the soul, and which are the proper characteristics of Tragedy. The other parts were well supported. The music, which was composed by Mr. Bates, was sprightly and agreeable."[8]

The Theatrical Candidates was given sixteen nights in the season 1775–76, and Becket printed two editions of the prelude, combining it with *May-Day; or, The Little Gipsy*.

TEXTS

O1 London: T. Becket, 1775.
O2 London: T. Becket, 1776.
D1 Dublin: Printed for Corcoran, Hoey, etc., 1777.

[THE PLAY]

10. Macaronies] English dandies affecting foreign mannerisms.
18. Momus] sleepy god of the Greeks who carps at everything.
43. Melpomene] the muse of tragedy.
87. flirt-gill] a young woman of wanton or giddy character.
115. Punch] hero of *Punch and Judy*.
124. came after] the pantomime used as an afterpiece.
157. *locum tenens*] a temporary substitute.

6. Ibid., lines 154–59.
7. *The Theatre*, No. 65, p. 488.
8. Page 454.

Roster of the Drury Lane Company *

Abington, Francis Barton (1737–1815). Having begun her stage career as Miranda in Mrs. Centlivre's *The Busy Body* on 21 August 1755 with Theophilus Cibber's "Bayes's New-rais'd Company of Comedians" at the Haymarket, she joined the Drury Lane company in 1756, playing Lady Pliant in *The Double Dealer*. She remained with the house until 1782 and was one of its greatest stars. Richard Brinsley Sheridan created Lady Teazle in his *The School for Scandal* especially for her.

Abrams, Harriet (1760–1825?). A pupil of Dr. Thomas Arne, she was introduced at Drury Lane by Garrick at the age of fifteen as the Little Gipsy in *May Day*, an afterpiece written by Garrick especially to introduce her, according to William Hopkins. Garrick referred to her affectionately as "my little jew Girl." She was with the company as singer of leading roles and secondary parts from 1755 until 1780.

Ackman, Ellis (d. 1774). A utility actor at Drury Lane for twenty-five seasons, he made his debut as Lennox in *Macbeth* on 23 April 1750. His repertory was heavily Shakespearean, with minor or secondary roles in Garrick's revivals of the Bard. Other than these parts he played infrequently and mainly in the most minor roles.

Aickin, James (c. 1735–1803). Joined the Drury Lane company in 1767, making his debut there as Young Belmont in *The Foundling* on 6 November. He remained for his entire career, also playing most summers at the Haymarket. His forte was portraying "honest" men, eccentrics, and Irishmen, and he was useful to Garrick in both major and minor Shakespeare roles.

* For biographical information we are indebted to several standard sources, but we are most heavily indebted to *A Biographical Dictionary of Actors, Actresses, Dancers, Managers, and Other Stage Personnel in London, 1660–1800*, by Philip H. Highfill, Jr., Kalman A. Burnim, and Edward A. Langhans (Carbondale, Ill.: Southern Illinois University Press, 1973–). We are particularly in debt to Professors Highfill, Burnim, and Langhans for permission to consult their unpublished files on the stage personnel of the period.

Arne, Elizabeth Wright (1751?–69). Michael Arne's second wife, she sang leading roles in *Cymon* and *The Padlock*. Her first appearance was at the age of nine or ten as a fairy in *Edgar and Emmeline* at Drury Lane on 31 January 1761. Thomas Davies tells us that she died at the age of seventeen or eighteen.

Arne, Michael (c. 1740–86). Son of Dr. Thomas Augustine Arne, he was actor, singer, and composer of music for the theatre and a writer of popular songs. His work for Garrick included music for *Harlequin's Invasion* (31 December 1759), *Edgar and Emmeline* (31 January 1761), *A Midsummer Night's Dream* (23 November 1763), and *Cymon* (2 January 1767).

Arthur, John (1708?–72). Played a harlequin and minor dramatic roles for Rich at Covent Garden for three years before coming to Drury Lane for the 1741–42 season, returning to Rich after three years when Garrick became manager. He was author of a ballad-opera, *The Lucky Discovery; or, the Tanner of York* (C. G. 24 April 1738), built machines and other properties for Rich and for Garrick, and managed provincial theatres at Bath, Portsmouth, and Bristol.

Atkins, Charles (d. 1775). A dancer, acrobat, and actor of minor roles, he began his career presumably at Covent Garden in the 1748–49 season—at least a Mr. Atkins danced there through the 1750–51 season. Presumably he is the Atkins who danced in *Harlequin Ranger* at Drury Lane on 26 December 1751, remaining on the payroll through the 1760–61 season as dancer and bit player, chiefly in comic roles.

Baddeley, Robert (1733–94). Reputedly a pastry cook, he first appeared at Drury Lane on 20 October 1760 as Sir William Wealthy in Foote's *The Minor*, having made his stage debut in the same role in June of that year at the Haymarket. Noted for low comedy roles, he was the original Moses in Sheridan's *The School for Scandal* (1775) and played the part more than two hundred times. He was a member of "The School of Garrick," a society formed by actors after Garrick's death, fought a bloodless duel with George Garrick over the character of Baddeley's wife, and left his house for the use of indigent actors, stipulating that the interest from £100 be used annually to provide Twelfth Night cakes and ale to Drury Lane actors, a tradition which continues today.

Baddeley, Sophia Snow (1745?–86). The daughter of a serjeant-trumpeter to George II, she eloped with the actor Robert Baddeley about 1763 and joined the Drury Lane company in 1764, first playing Ophelia to Holland's Hamlet on 27 September. Her other famous Shakespeare roles were Desdemona and Imogen, and she played Polly in *The Beggar's Opera* and Fanny in *The Clandestine Marriage*. George III ordered Zoffany to paint her scene with King as Lord Ogleby. A marital rift took her from London for a time, and when she returned to Drury Lane she and her husband did not speak except when required to do so by their roles. She eventually left London to escape her creditors, playing in Dublin, York, and Edinburgh.

Baker, Miss Mary. *See* Mrs. Thomas King.

Bambridge, Mrs. (fl. 1731–54). After making her debut at Goodman's Fields on 11 October 1731 as Angelica in *The Constant Couple* and remaining there a few years, she and her husband played the fair booths, eventually returning to Goodman's Fields. Her last recorded appearances were with the Richmond and Twickenham summer companies in 1751.

Bannister, Charles (1741–1804). Early enamored of the stage, he applied at the age of eighteen to Garrick for a place at Drury Lane but was not hired. He worked for Rich a while and finally came to Drury Lane as Merlin in *Cymon* (22 September 1767). Bannister became a regular at Drury Lane through the 1786–87 season, then shifted back and forth from Garrick's house to Covent Garden, playing most summers at the Haymarket. He retired after the 1797–98 season, having been a leader in the founding of "The School of Garrick" club after the actor's death.

Bardin, Peter (d. 1773). The pseudonymous Mr. Johnston, his first recorded stage appearance is as Humphrey in *The Conscious Lovers* at Goodman's Fields on 22 January 1730. He played comic eccentrics, beaux, fops, and gallants. His roles included Kent and Albany in *King Lear*, Macheath in *The Beggar's Opera*, and Juan in *Rule a Wife and Have a Wife*.

Barry, Ann (1734–1801). The wife of Spranger Barry, the great Drury Lane actor, she began her career in the provinces, married William Dancer, an actor in the York company, moved with him to Dublin, where Spranger Barry undertook her instruction as an actress, and after the death of Dancer remained with Barry, eventually marrying him. Both moved to the Drury Lane company in 1767, where she opened as Sigismunda in *Tancred and Sigismunda* on 14 October. After continual disagreements with Garrick, both Barrys moved to Covent Garden for the 1774–75 season.

Barry, Mrs. William (1739–71). First employed by Spranger Barry, then joint manager of the Crow Street Theatre in Dublin, she made her debut as Juliet on 27 January 1759. She married Spranger's brother William in 1762, acted at Bristol in 1766, and made her Drury Lane debut as Juliet on 20 September of that year. She played Fanny in *The Clandestine Marriage* on 17 May 1770, regularly played summers at Bristol, and died at the age of thirty-one of unknown causes.

Beard, John (1716?–91). The most celebrated English singer in the middle of the century, he was a protégé of Handel and began his adult career at Covent Garden. He came to Drury Lane for the 1737–38 season, remained there (except for one season) until 1743, returned to Covent Garden until 1748, and then came again to Garrick's house to remain until his retirement in 1767.

Bennett, Elizabeth (1714–91). A spinster, she played in minor theatres until she joined Drury Lane in 1735–36 as a dancer. She advanced to minor comic roles beginning with the 1738–39 season and continued there for the next twenty-six years, specializing in roles of the pert maidservant, the gossip, the mistress.

Bensley, Robert (1742–1817). A leading actor in London theatres for thirty-one years, he made his debut as Pierre in *Venice Preserv'd* at Drury Lane on 2 October 1765, having been coached for the role by George Colman. In 1767 he went to Covent Garden but returned to Drury Lane in 1775–76 for Garrick's last year as manager, again appearing as Pierre. He remained there until his retirement in 1796.

Blakes, Charles (d. 1763). A journeyman actor, he began his career at the Haymarket on 27 May 1736, was acting at Goodman's Fields in 1740, worked at Covent Garden in 1741, and first played at Drury Lane in 1743, beginning his career there as the Bailiff in *The Committee* on 9 October. He remained at Drury Lane to the end of his career.

Blanchard, Master Thomas (1760–97). Son of the actor Thomas Blanchard, he first appeared with his father at Drury Lane on 13 October 1773 as Cupid in *A Trip to Scotland*. He was also a singer popular with the Bath and Bristol theatres.

Booth, Mr. (fl. 1762–71). One or more actors of this name played at the Haymarket beginning with the 1761–62 season and at Drury Lane from 1768–69 through 1770–71, doing bit parts.

Bradshaw, Mary (d. 1780). Probably the wife of Bradshaw the Drury Lane boxkeeper, she made her debut at Lincoln's Inn Fields on 7 January 1743 as Nell in *The Devil to Pay* and the next month played Lucy in *The Beggar's Opera* there. She joined the Drury Lane company for the 1743–44 season and remained, with some small exceptions, for thirty-seven years. She was famous as Garrick's wife in *The Farmer's Return from London*.

Bransby, Astley (d. 1789). A member of the Drury Lane company from Garrick's first season, 1747–48, he remained there throughout the management, playing minor supporting roles for some thirty-three years.

Brereton, William (1751–87). A handsome young man, Brereton had the advantage of an acquaintanceship, through his father, with Garrick and appeared on the Drury Lane stage at the age of seventeen as Douglas in John Home's play of that name (10 November 1768). He spent eighteen of his acting years at Drury Lane but was never greatly acclaimed.

Bridges, Mr. [William?] (fl. 1728–51). A Dublin actor from 1737 to at least 1740, he first appeared at Drury Lane on 7 April 1742 as Pinchwife in *The Country Wife*, picking up Garrick's role for two performances and, as a result, becoming a permanent member of the company the next season. He became a mainstay for Garrick in such roles as Syphax in *Cato*, Aesop in *Aesop*, and the Uncle in *The London Merchant*. Except for two seasons he remained at Drury Lane until his final appearance on the stage, 8 May 1751, as Balance in *The Recruiting Officer*.

Burton, John (d. 1797?). An actor and dancer, he was the son of Edward Burton, a Drury Lane player, and first appeared on that stage as Master Burton, the Page in *Love Makes a Man* (28 October 1762). He played similar child's roles until the 1767–68 season, when he began to be billed as J. Burton and played mature roles. He remained a utility actor there through the 1795–96 season.

Cape, Master (fl. 1768–79). Edward Cape Everard appeared at Drury Lane in the 1768–69 season. By 1777–78 he was known as Cape Everard and played the minor theatres through 1778–79.

Castle, Richard (d. 1779). A minor actor in theatres at Bath, Richmond, Twickenham, and Bristol, he opened at Covent Garden in 1757 as Jack

Meggot in *The Suspicious Husband* (18 November) but apparently returned to the provinces until he appeared as John in the first performance of *The Jealous Wife* at Drury Lane on 12 February 1761. He continued there for eleven years, playing fairly undistinguished utility roles and acting less and less frequently until his retirement.

Cautherley, Samuel (d. 1805). Rumored illegitimate son of Garrick and certainly his protégé, Cautherley made his debut at Drury Lane in a children's performance of *Miss in Her Teens* on 28 April 1755 and his adult debut as George Barnwell in Lillo's play ten years later (26 September 1765). For the years remaining to him as an actor his meager abilities confined him mostly to secondary roles, although he was allowed to play Hamlet with Mrs. Baddeley and Romeo with Mrs. Barry, both times to cool receptions. He last played at Drury Lane on 26 September 1776, exactly ten years after his first adult role there, as Rivers in *The Note of Hand.*

Champness, Samuel Thomas (d. 1803). Featured bass singer at Drury Lane between 1748 and 1774, he was famous for singing in Handel's oratorios. It was reputedly Handel who had given him a start as a boy, and the composer eventually wrote several songs expressly for him in the oratorio *Joseph and His Brethren* (C. G. 2 March 1744). When he retired from the stage at the end of the 1773–74 season Garrick played in *Zara* for his benefit (13 May).

Chapman, Thomas (c. 1683–1747). A player primarily at Lincoln's Inn Fields and Covent Garden, and at Richmond (where he was manager) and Bartholomew Fair in the summers, he displayed his versatility by playing two roles in two theatres on the same night: while playing the Beggar in *The Beggar's Opera* at Covent Garden on 1 January 1733, he ran, during his off-stage time, to Lincoln's Inn Fields to play Southampton in John Banks's *The Unhappy Favorite.*

Clive, Catherine Raftor (1711–85). A famous comedienne and Garrick's colleague throughout his career, Kitty Clive apparently made her debut as a page in *Mithridates, King of Pontus* in April 1728, and by the next season she began to be recognized for her comic genius. But she had other distinctions as well: Handel chose her to sing Dalila in his oratorio *Samson* in 1743, and she was a friend of Samuel Johnson. When Garrick became manager at Drury Lane she became the comedy mainstay of that house.

Clough, Thomas (d. 1770). An actor in minor theatres and fair booths, he joined the Drury Lane company in 1752–53, first appearing as Jeremy in *The Double Disappointment* (11 October). After a season of barnstorming, he returned to Drury Lane and remained for fifteen years, closing his career there on 5 June 1770 in *The Jubilee.* He is pictured by Zoffany as a watchman in the famous portrait of Garrick as Lord Brute in *The Provok'd Wife.*

Como, Antonio (fl. 1770–76). A dancer and ballet master, he first performed at Drury Lane on 30 September 1773 in a comic dance called *The Mountaineers.* He danced in *Alfred, A Christmas Tale*, and *Florizel and Perdita*, among others. He remained at Drury Lane through the 1775–76 season.

Courtney, Mr. (f. 1773–75). A singer and actor, he first played at the Haymarket in 1773 and went to Drury Lane that year as a regular member of the company. He played in *The Christmas Tale* and *Catherine and Petruchio.*

Crespi, Signora (fl. 1773–86). The dancing partner of Antonio Como, she first appeared at Drury Lane on 30 September 1773 in *The Mountaineers.* She performed solo and appeared with the ballet there for several seasons and also was a principal dancer at the King's Theatre. She left Drury Lane after the 1777–78 season.

Cross, Elizabeth (1707–81). Wife of Richard Cross, the Drury Lane prompter, she became a mainstay of the company in secondary roles from her first appearance on 18 April 1727 as Mrs. Chat in *The Committee* until her death on 29 June 1781. She appeared briefly at the Haymarket when Theophilus Cibber led the Drury Lane dissidents there in 1733, and for two seasons she appeared at Covent Garden (1739–40, 1740–41). She rarely played leading roles but concentrated on a few secondary ones which she considered her property.

Dagueville, Peter (fl. 1768–94). A dancer, ballet master, and choreographer, Peter D'Egville apparently made his Drury Lane debut on 1 November 1768 in a dance entitled *The Piedmontese Mountaineer.* He was "first dancer" and later also ballet master there. In addition he had his own dancing school in London. He was discharged by Garrick during the 1773–74 season.

De Loutherbourg, Phillipe Jacques (1740–1812). The most famous scene designer of the period, he first came to Garrick's aid in 1771 when he presented a proposal for the scenes, mechanics, and lighting of Drury Lane. Garrick engaged him, and he remained with the theatre through 1781. One of his notable designs was for *Alfred,* in which he included a grand naval review with "two Lines of Men of War . . . not painted flat upon the Scenes, but . . . made with all their Rigging, Masts &c." (*St. James's Chronicle,* 4–9 October 1773). He "invented and designed" the scenery for Sheridan's *A Monody On the Death of Garrick,* which was given at Drury Lane on 11 March 1779.

Dibdin, Charles (1745–1814). An actor, singer, composer, and dramatist, he performed and composed at Drury Lane from the 1767–68 season through that of 1775–76 and then moved to Covent Garden, where he was composer from 1778–79 through 1780–81. He achieved a brilliant success as Ralph in Bickerstaff's *The Maid of the Mill,* the play running more than fifty nights at Covent Garden. He said that while playing summers at Richmond Garrick taught him how to play Lord Ogleby in *The Clandestine Marriage.* He composed music for the Stratford Jubilee in 1769 and published it as *Shakespeare's Garland* that same year.

Dimond, William Wyatt (d. 1812). An actor and sometime theatre manager, Dimond made his Drury Lane debut as Romeo on 1 October 1772, being billed as a "young Gentleman, first appearance on any stage." He continued there through the 1773–74 season and then acted in minor theatres until his last appearance, at Bristol, on 1 July 1801 as Edgar in *King Lear.*

Dodd, James William (1740?–96). An actor, singer, and sometime manager,

Dodd made his debut at Drury Lane on 3 October 1776 as Faddle in Edward Moore's *The Foundling*, adding a new song to the part. He soon established himself as an actor of fops, beaux, and coxcombs and played such roles for thirty-one years. He remained a regular at Drury Lane until his death.

Dunstall, Mary (d. 1758). Wife of the actor John Dunstall, Mary made her debut at Goodman's Fields on 22 October 1740 as Melinda in *The Recruiting Officer*. She moved with her husband to Lincoln's Inn Fields and then to the Haymarket and Covent Garden. Her last recorded appearance was as Mrs. Peachum in *The Beggar's Opera* on 30 March 1758.

Fawcett, John (d. 1793). Having learned singing from Dr. Thomas Augustine Arne, to whom he was apprenticed, Fawcett first appeared at Drury Lane Theatre in the juvenile role of Filch in *The Beggar's Opera* on 23 September 1760. After a time at Covent Garden and the King's Theatre, he returned to Drury Lane on 23 September 1766 as Gildenstern in *Hamlet*. For thirty-three years a useful actor in supporting roles in the theatres, he played Dorilas in *Cymon* and Lennox in *Macbeth*.

Fox, Joseph (d. 1791). Having begun his career at Covent Garden as Fenton in *The Merry Wives of Windsor*, he spent some thirty-three years in the theatre, ending his career as a theatre owner in Brighton on 7 December 1791. He played journeyman roles at Drury Lane from 1758, having made hi debut as a slave in *Oroonoko* on 1 December and playing there every season (except 1765–66) through 1767–68. His roles included Rosencrantz in *Hamlet*, Burgundy in *King Lear*, and Mat in *The Beggar's Opera*. Later he played at Covent Garden and the Haymarket, was keeper of the Shakespeare Tavern and Coffee House in Bow Street, and leased and managed theatres at Brighton.

Giorgi, Signor (d. 1808). First appearing at Drury Lane in a dance called *The Italian Peasant* on 4 October 1757, he was a featured dancer at that theatre each season through 1776–77, often dancing with his wife, Signora Ann Giorgi. He danced in *The Enchanter*, *Cymon*, *Alfred*, *A Christmas Tale*, and *Florizel and Perdita*, among many others.

Giorgi, Signora Ann (d. 1809). Having first appeared on the London bills as a dancer with her husband, Signor Giorgi, in *Harlequin's Invasion* at Drury Lane on 31 December 1759, she danced in the chorus there each winter season through 1773–74. Her dances were included in *The Enchanter*, *Cymon*, *The Jubilee*, *King Arthur*, and *A Christmas Tale*.

Green, Mrs. Henry, née Jane Hippisley (1719–91). Daughter of the comedian John Hippisley, Jane made her debut at Drury Lane as Rose in *The Recruiting Officer* on 11 January 1740. She played Prince Edward in *Richard III* on 19 October 1741 when Garrick made his debut at Goodman's Fields, and as Jane Green she was among the company of seventy which Garrick assembled in his first season as manager of Drury Lane, 1747–48. She played Mrs. Tatoo in *Lethe*, Armelina in *Albumazar*, and Mrs. Heidelberg in *The Clandestine Marriage* (at Covent Garden), and was the original Mrs. Malaprop in Sheridan's *The Rivals* (17 January 1775).

Griffith, Richard (d. c. 1799). Son of the Irish actor Thomas Griffith, he first acted at Drury Lane as Barnwell in *The London Merchant* on 18 September 1750. After tours in the provinces and at Covent Garden, he returned to Drury Lane on 18 September 1764 as Archer in *The Beaux' Strategem.* He played Lord Foppington in *The Careless Husband*, Lord Trinket in *The Jealous Wife*, the Gentleman Usher in *King Lear*, and Young Clackit in *The Guardian.*

Grimaldi, Giuseppe (d. 1788). Father of the well-known clown Joseph Grimaldi (1778–1837), Giuseppe first performed at Drury Lane in a dance called *The Millers* on 12 October 1758. He danced in *Harlequin's Invasion*, *The Tempest*, and *Florizel and Perdita* and assisted with the Jubilee at Stratford in September 1769. Truculent in regard to his pay, Grimaldi once caused Garrick to remark that the dancer "was ye worst behav'd Man in ye Whole Company & Shd have had a horse Whip" (*Letters*, II, 741).

Hartry, John (d. 1774). First appearing at the Haymarket on 9 September 1760 in an evening of "Comic Lectures," Hartry offended part of the audience and published an elaborate apology. The following spring he appeared at Covent Garden; then he left the London bills until he was engaged at Drury Lane in 1766–67, opening as Tribulation in *The Alchemist* on 31 October and next playing Stockwell in *Neck or Nothing* on 18 November. He remained at Drury Lane for the next six seasons, playing modest roles, often old men. He was Lucianus in *Hamlet*, the Old Man in *King Lear*, a Shepherd in *A Peep Behind the Curtain*, a Justice in *Harlequin's Invasion.* He acted once in the 1774–75 season (Corin in *As You Like It*, 1 October) and died 4 October "impaired in health."

Havard, William (1710–78). First appearing in a booth at Bartholomew Fair on 20 August 1730, he soon moved to Goodman's Fields, where he played for several seasons before going to Covent Garden and on to Drury Lane in 1737–38. There he opened as the Duke in *Rule A Wife and Have a Wife* (3 September). He remained at Drury Lane for nine seasons, playing Edgar to young Garrick's King Lear on 3 May 1742. He wrote several plays, Garrick playing the title role in his *Regulus* on 21 February 1744. After a season at Covent Garden he reappeared at Drury Lane on the first night of Garrick's management (15 September 1747) as Bassanio in *The Merchant of Venice.* He played Lelio in the premier of *Albumazar* on 3 October of that year and thereafter played primary and secondary roles for Garrick during the next twenty years.

Hayward, Miss Clara (fl. 1770–76). The daughter of an oyster-monger, she first appeared at the Haymarket as Calista in *The Fair Penitent* on 9 July 1770, having been coached in acting "voluntarily" by Sheridan. Earlier that year a Mrs. Haywood, perhaps Clara, is mentioned in a Drury Lane bill. She played Emmeline in *King Arthur*, a Spirit in *The Institution of the Garter*, and Hero in *Much Ado About Nothing*, leaving the stage in 1776 as she had entered it, a kept woman.

Heath, Miss Ann. *See* Phillimore, Mrs. John.

Hippisley, Jane. *See* Green, Mrs. Henry.

Hippisley, John (1696–1748). Father of actresses Jane (Mrs. Henry Green) and Elizabeth, he was trained by John Rich as a harlequin and played Fondlewife in *The Old Bachelor* at Lincoln's Inn Fields on 7 November 1722. He went to Covent Garden in 1732 and to the provincial theatres and Bartholomew Fair in the summers, playing a phenomenal number of roles until his last recorded one, Trincalo in *Albumazar*, at Bristol on 3 November 1747.

Holland, Charles (1733–69). Making his debut at Drury Lane on 13 October 1755, he played Oroonoko to Mrs. Cibber's Imoinda and later that season was Florizel in Garrick's alteration of *The Winter's Tale*. A warm friend of Garrick, upon whose acting he modeled his own, he was at Drury Lane for the remaining fifteen years of his career. He acted in many of Garrick's important productions: Horatius in *The Roman Father*, Sir John Melvil in *The Clandestine Marriage*, Moody in *The Country Girl*, Ferdinand and Prospero in *The Tempest*, Thyreus in *Antony and Cleopatra*, Young Knowell in *Every Man in His Humour*, Osman in *Zara*, and Richard III in *The Jubilee*.

Hopkins, Miss Priscilla. *See* Kemble, Mrs. John Philip.

Hurst, Richard (d. 1805). Playing in London and the provincial theatres for more than forty-eight years, he first appeared in London at Covent Garden on 26 October 1754 as Tressel in *Richard III*. He may have been in the opening of *The Chinese Festival* at Drury Lane on 8 November 1755 and definitely was there in the 1765–66 seaon, playing Cornwall in *King Lear* on 22 October. He played Orasmin in *Zara*, Traverse and Sterling in *The Clandestine Marriage*, Macduff in *Macbeth*, Claudius in *Hamlet*, Antonio in *The Tempest*, and Posthumous in *The Jubilee*, remaining at Drury Lane through Garrick's management and into the fourth year of Sheridan's, through 1779–80.

Inchbald, Joseph (1755–79). Having played at York and Norwich, Inchbald first appeared in London at Drury Lane on 8 October 1770 as Osmyn in *The Mourning Bride*. He was Bowman in *Lethe*, Jaffier in *Venice Preserved*, and Linco in *Cymon* and developed a reputation for playing old comic characters and drunks.

Jefferson, Thomas (1728?–1807). Making his Drury Lane debut as Rossano in *The Fair Penitent* on 31 October 1753, he remained a utility actor there through most seasons of Garrick's management, later playing at York and Plymouth and for a time being manager at Richmond.

Johnston, Mr. *See* Bardin, Peter.

Johnston, Helen (fl. 1762–78). The wife of Roger Johnston, housekeeper at Drury Lane from 1762 until 1775 and a scenery painter and country theatre manager, she first appeared at Garrick's house in 1760–61 and became a regular member of the company in 1767. She remained through the 1780–81 season. Garrick thought Mr. and Mrs. Johnston to be "persons of great merit" (letter to A. R. Bowes, 23 April 1777).

Kear, James Thomas (d. 1796). A singer in Marlebonne Gardens about 1754, Kear first appeared on the stage under Theophilus Cibber at the Haymarket on 17 October 1757 singing "Dorus and Cleora" by Bryan and "Rule Britannia." In 1760–61 he was engaged at Drury Lane, first performing in the funeral procession in *Romeo and Juliet* (20 October). He played Hymen in the adaptation of *The Tempest* in 1765 and obscure characters in *Macbeth*, *A Peep Behind the Curtain*, *The Jubilee*, *Harlequin's Invasion*, and *Alfred*, appearing there into 1778.

Keen, William (1740–75). First listed on the Drury Lane bills on 16 May 1765, he was a supporting actor there until May 1775.

Kemble, Mrs. John Philip, née Priscilla Hopkins (1755–1845). The daughter of a Covent Garden prompter and of an actress, she was the widow of an Irish actor when she married John Philip Kemble in 1787. She was an actress and singer at Drury Lane from the 1771–72 season through that of 1776–77.

King, Thomas (1730–1805). First brought to Drury Lane by Garrick as the Herald in *King Lear* (unannounced, 8 October 1748), King was soon given a variety of roles, including Fribble in *Miss in Her Teens*, the Fine Gentleman in *Lethe*, and Valerius in *The Roman Father*. After two seasons in the provinces he returned to Drury Lane in 1762 and grew in popularity until he achieved eminence as a comic actor with his Lord Ogleby in *The Clandestine Marriage* on 20 February 1766. He became Garrick's close friend, and after that actor's death became manager of the theatre (1782).

King, Mrs. Thomas, née Mary Baker (1730–1813). A dancer and dependable supporting actress, she began her career at Goodman's Fields in a peasant dance on 27 October 1746, was at Covent Garden in 1748–49, and joined the Drury Lane company in 1749–50. Her debut in a speaking part was as Juliet in Dublin on 29 March 1751. There she met the comedian Thomas King and came to Drury Lane with him in 1759. She was a Fantastic Spirit and a pastoral character in the musical version of *The Tempest*, danced in *The Enchanter*, married Tom King in 1766, and continued to dance and play minor roles until she was "withdrawn" from the stage by King in 1772, Garrick playing for her final benefit on 1 May.

La Mash, Philip (d. 1800). Also listed as Lamash and Le March, he first appears on a Drury Lane bill on 29 September 1774 as Rovewell in *The Fair Quaker*. He remained at Drury Lane until October 1782, then going to Edinburgh and Leeds. He was said to be good in valet and coxcomb roles but poor at playing lords (Winston Ms.).

Largeau, Master (fl. 1756–57). Played Fripperel in *Lilliput* at Drury Lane from 3 December 1756 to 15 February 1757.

Lee, John (d. 1781). An actor and manager, he first appeared at Goodman's Fields in 1745, playing Sir Charles Freeman in Farquhar's *The Strategem* and the Ghost in *Hamlet*. His name appears on the Drury Lane bill of 14 November 1747 as the Bastard in *King Lear*. After a season at Covent Garden (1749–50) he returned to Garrick's house in 1750 to play George Barnwell in *The London Merchant*. He was also the Poet in *Lethe*. Later he went to Edinburgh as manager.

Leoni, Master Michael (d. 1797). Born Myer Lyon in Frankfort-on-Main, Germany, he came to Garrick's attention as a synagogue singer and had the part of Kaliel in Garrick's *The Enchanter* on 13 December 1760, the play apparently having been written to introduce the boy singer. After returning to the synagogue, he came back to the theatre, singing at Covent Garden and in Dublin.

Love, James (1721–74). Eldest son of George Dance, the architect, he became interested in the theatre and changed his name, presumably in order not to embarrass his socially prominent family. He played and managed in Edinburgh, built a theatre at Richmond, and in 1762 was invited to Drury Lane, where he remained for the rest of his life. He played Sergeant Flower in the first performance of *The Clandestine Marriage*.

Love, Mrs. James, née Hooper (d. 1807). First appearing at Drury Lane in May 1763, she was Mrs. Peacham in *The Beggar's Opera* on 17 September of that year. Hopkins remarks that she was "very bad."

Lowe, Thomas (d. 1783). A member of Handel's company (with Beard) in 1743, he became principal tenor in 1748 and remained until 1751. Later he sang at Vauxhall and managed and sang at Marylebonne Gardens. His first theatre appearance was as Macheath in *The Beggar's Opera* at Covent Garden on 26 September 1748. He played the same role at Drury Lane on 23 September 1760.

Lowe, Mrs. The wife of Thomas Lowe, virtually nothing is known about her career.

Macklin, Maria (c. 1732–81). The daughter of Charles Macklin, the well-known actor, she first appeared on the Drury Lane stage on 20 December 1742 at about the age of ten and made her official debut there on 20 October 1753. She retired from Covent Garden in the 1776–77 season.

Martin, Mrs. (fl. 1746–47). At Covent Garden through the 1746–47 season, she went to Drury Lane and remained there for her lifetime.

Matthews, Miss Catharine May (fl. 1772–87). A dancer, she had a long career at Covent Garden, ending her playing there in May 1785.

Messink, James (1721–89). Having come from Dublin with Barry, he first appears on a Drury Lane bill on 13 December 1750; he played Little John in the afterpiece *Robin Hood* by Moses Mendez. After an absence he returned to Garrick's house in 1767–68 and remained through the 1776–77 season, then played at Covent Garden through 1781–82. He assisted Garrick with the Jubilee and was known for his pantomime roles.

Millidge, Mrs. Josiah, née Elizabeth Matthews (d. 1800). Wife of the printer of the *Westminster Gazette*, she originally appeared in the late 1750s as a child actress and was first on a Drury Lane bill on 15 May 1767, playing, as Miss Matthews, the Chambermaid in *The Clandestine Marriage*.

Mills, Miss (fl. 1752–71). In the Drury Lane company from the 1752–53 through the 1766–67 seasons, she played Trusty in *The Clandestine Marriage* (20 February 1766) and next season went to Covent Garden with Colman, staying there through the 1770–71 season. She was also in the summer company at Richmond.

Minors, Sybilla (1723–1802). A well-known comic actress who specialized in playing awkward country girls, she was at Drury Lane beginning with the 1742–43 season, acting there and at Smock Alley, Dublin, through the 1757–58 season, at the conclusion of which she became Mrs. John Walker.

Moody, John (1727–1813). The principal tragedian at Norwich around 1750, his first appearance in London was as Thyreus in *Antony and Cleopatra* at Drury Lane on 12 January 1759, acting in the place of Holland, who was ill. He played Simon in *Harlequin's Invasion* and developed a specialty in Irish characters and old men.

Morland, Mrs., née Westray (fl. 1765–72). Coming to London from the Norwich theatre, she made her debut at Drury Lane as Juliet on 29 October 1770. Hopkins, the prompter, noted a speech impediment and "too long a waste." She played Fanny in *The Clandestine Marriage*, a Spirit in *The Institution of the Garter*, and Ophelia in *Hamlet*.

O'Brien, William (d. 1815). Making his debut as Captain Brazen in *The Recruiting Officer* at Drury Lane on 3 October 1758, he played the Fine Gentleman to Garrick's Lord Chalkstone the next month and ended his acting career as Lovet in *High Life Below Stairs* on 7 April 1764, when he undertook to enjoy high life above stairs by eloping to America with Lady Susan Strangeways, eldest daughter of Lord Ilchester. Several years later he returned to London as a playwright and produced two pieces, *The Duel* and *Cross Purposes*, on 8 December 1772, one at Drury Lane and the other at Covent Garden.

Packer, John Hayman (1730–1806). Making his Drury Lane debut on 19 September 1758 as Selim in *The Mourning Bride*, he remained at that theatre until 18 June 1800, last playing Brabantio in *Othello*. As "a Gentleman" he had appeared for one night at Covent Garden on 24 January 1758, playing Johnson in *The Rehearsal* and the Frenchman in *Lethe*.

Paget, William (fl. 1728–56). Having begun his stage career in Dublin as early as 1728, Paget came to the Haymarket in 1730, played the Bartholomew and Southwark fairs, and joined the Drury Lane company for the 1730–31 season, where one of his roles was Peachum in *The Beggar's Opera*. He played for John Rich at Lincoln's Inn Fields and later at Covent Garden, returning to Drury Lane for the 1733–34 season. After that he played at Covent Garden, the Haymarket, Lincoln's Inn Fields, Goodman's Fields, and at Richmond and Dublin.

Palmer, John (1742?–98). Called "The Younger," he was the son of "Gentleman" John Palmer and first played at Drury Lane on 9 November 1763 as Blunt in *I Henry IV*. He was the original Brush in *The Clandestine Marriage*, and died on the Liverpool stage during Act IV of *The Stranger*, 2 August 1798.

Palmer, Mrs. John. *See* Pritchard, Miss.

Palmer, William (d. 1798). Son of "Gentleman" John and brother to John the Younger and Robert, he played opera in Dublin and at Drury Lane (1768–69 through 1773–74) and at Covent Garden.

Parsons, William (1736–95). Coming to London from York and Edinburgh, he made his Drury Lane debut on 21 September 1762 as Filch in *The Beggar's Opera*, and appeared last there on 19 January 1795. Zoffany painted him as the Old Man in *Lethe*, with Bransby as Aesop and Watkins as the Servant. He died of asthma in the severe winter of 1795.

Peterson, Mr. (fl. 1730–31). Played Filch in *The Beggar's Opera* at Goodman's Fields on 12 October 1730, then went to the Haymarket and later acted at Southwark Fair.

Phillimore, Mrs. John, née Ann Heath (fl. 1755–67). A dancer, she was the wife of John Phillimore, a Drury Lane comedian. She danced there under the name of Miss Heath off and on from the 1755–56 season into 1767.

Platt, [Mrs. S. J.?] (1743?–1800). Perhaps the Miss Platt who spoke a prologue at Phillips Theatre, Bowling Green, Southwark on 26 September 1748 at the age of five, she was at Drury Lane as Miss Platt from 16 December 1769 to 6 June 1777, thereafter moving to Covent Garden, where she remained until 7 January 1800. After the 1787–88 season she was known as Mrs. Platt.

Plym, Miss (fl. 1763–67). First appearing at Drury Lane as Viola in *Twelfth Night* on 19 October 1763, she was described by Hopkins as "a pretty figure both in breeches and otherwise . . . thin weak voice." She played Melissa in *The Lying Valet* and the Chambermaid in *The Clandestine Marriage* and left the stage in June 1767.

Pope, Jane (1742–1818). A child actress at Drury Lane at the age of 14 (3 December 1756), she made her adult debut there on 27 September 1759 as Corinna in *The Confederacy*, succeeding Kitty Clive in chambermaid roles. She was the original Mrs. Candour in *The School for Scandal*, 1777.

Pope, Master (fl. 1753–65). A child actor and dancer, he played Jasper in *Miss in Her Teens* at Drury Lane on 5 April 1759 and appears on company lists for the 1753–54, 1758–59, and 1764–65 seasons.

Powell, William (1735–69). Having been introduced to the stage by Garrick, he became a well-known fixture at Drury Lane following his debut on 8 October 1763 in the title role in *Philaster*. It was said that only Garrick surpassed him in playing old men. He took some of Garrick's roles while the latter was on the Continent, and on his return Garrick paid him the compliment of discarding from his own repertoire those parts in which Powell had been particularly successful.

Pritchard, Hannah (1711–68). First known as Miss Vaughan, she began as a performer at Fielding and Hippisley's booths at Bartholomew and Southwark fairs, 1733–34, was engaged briefly at the Haymarket, and then joined Garrick's company as Mrs. Pritchard, wife of William Pritchard, the Drury Lane treasurer. Her final performance was as Lady Macbeth on 24 April 1768. She was the first and only player of Dr. Johnson's Irene.

Pritchard, Miss (d. 1781). The daughter of Hannah Pritchard, she made her debut as Juliet at Drury Lane on 9 October 1756. She married "Gentleman" John Palmer and retired from the stage in 1768, the year of the death of Palmer and of her mother. She later became Mrs. Maurice Lloyd.

Radley, Eleanor (d. 1772). A singer and actress, she made her debut at Richmond as Nysa in *Midas* on 24 June 1767 and first appeared at Drury Lane on 26 October 1768 as Leonora in *The Padlock*. She played Rhodope in *A Peep Behind the Curtain*, sang in *Romeo and Juliet*, played Sylvia in *Cymon* and Mademoiselle in *The Provok'd Wife*. Presumably she retired from the stage when she married William Fitzgerald.

Reddish, Samuel (1735–85). After a debut in Dublin on 12 October 1759 as Lord Townly in *The Provok'd Husband*, he eventually came to Drury

Lane on 18 September 1767. He became a lunatic in December 1785 and was placed in an asylum in York.

Reinhold, Thomas (1690?–1751). An esteemed singer with an "excellent bass voice," he sang in opera and at Vauxhall, Ranelagh, and Marylebonne Gardens. Born in Germany, he was reputed to be the natural son of the Archbishop of Dresden. He came to London to join Handel's company.

Reynolds, Miss [Lucy?] (fl. 1766–68). Making her debut at Drury Lane on 25 October 1766 as Miss Peggy in *The Country Girl*, she was in that company for the 1766–67 and 1767–68 seasons. Garrick dismissed her for careless acting. She became successively Mrs. Saunders and Mrs. Young and died an alcoholic.

Rogers, Miss (fl. 1766–67). Was an actress and dancer with the Drury Lane company through the 1766–67 season.

Scott, Mrs. John, née Isabella Younge (1741–91). A mezzo-soprano, she first appeared as Miss Younge at Drury Lane in 1747–48. She was with Handel's company from 1755 to 1759, continued at Drury Lane as Miss Younge through the 1767–68 season, and as Mrs. Scott sang there through the 1775–76 season.

Scrase, Henry (1717–1807). A bit player, he was at Drury Lane from 1750–51 to May 1762, apparently first playing Fenton in *The Merry Wives of Windsor* on 22 September 1750.

Simpson, Master (fl. 1756–57). A child actor, he played Bolgolam in *Lilliput* on 3 December 1756 at Drury Lane and was damned at the Haymarket on 31 October 1757.

Simpson, Miss (fl. 1756?). A child actress and dancer, she played Lord Flimnap in *Lilliput* at Drury Lane on 3 December 1756. She is listed among the Drury Lane company for 1755–56 and 1758–59. She may perhaps be sometimes listed as Miss Simson.

Simson, Mrs. Elizabeth (fl. 1752–74?). First appearing at Drury Lane in the 1752–53 season as the Gipsy in *The Stratagem*, she seems to have remained with the company through 1773–74.

Smith, Maria, née Harris (fl. 1772–96). Wife of the pianist and composer Theodore Smith, she made her Drury Lane debut on 20 October 1772 as Sylvia in *Cymon*. She remained at that house until May 1785 and retired from the stage in 1796. Hopkins notes that she sang Sylvia to "vast Applause."

Spencer, Miss (fl. 1759–70?). A singer, she was in *Harlequin's Invasion* at Drury Lane on 31 December 1759, and may be the Miss Spencer listed in the Covent Garden company of 1769–70.

Steele, Mrs. (fl. 1734–42?). A Mrs. Steele is mentioned in the bills as early as 1734, and an actress of that name played the Queen in Garrick's debut as Richard III on 19 October 1741 at Goodman's Fields. That Mrs. Steele is listed in the company for that and the following season.

Strange, Mr. (fl. 1762–68). Listed on a Birmingham bill of 14 July 1762, Strange first appeared at Drury Lane on 8 October 1763 as a Woodman in Beaumont and Fletcher's *Philaster* and was with that company until November 1769. He acted with Foote at the Haymarket in the summer of 1768.

Sutton, Mrs. (1756–97). Formerly dancing as Miss Fremont, Mrs. Sutton made her debut at Drury Lane on 23 October 1772. She also danced at the Haymarket and last appears on Drury Lane bills on 8 May 1779.

Taswell, James (d. 1759). A comedian, he appeared at Drury Lane on 16 January 1739 as Obadiah in Mrs. Centlivre's *A Bold Stroke for a Wife* and remained with the company until 9 November 1758, after which time he went to Dublin.

Usher, Howard (d. 1802). A bit player at Drury Lane beginning with the 1747–48 season, when he played Gildenstern in *Hamlet* on 22 September, he appeared at Covent Garden in 1753 and was again at Drury Lane through 1758–59.

Vallois, Mrs. (fl. 1746–57). Originally a dancer at Goodman's Fields, she was the wife of Jovan de Vallois, also a dancer. She appears on Covent Garden bills for four seasons, first in 1746–47 and last in 1756–57.

Vaughan, Henry (d. 1779). Mrs. Pritchard's brother, he first appeared at Drury Lane on 29 October 1751 as the Constable in *Eastward Hoe*. He retired from the stage in 1766.

Vernon, Joseph (d. 1782?). He first appeared at Drury Lane as a boy soprano in Mallet's revision of *Alfred* on 23 February 1751, and with Michael Arne he wrote the music for *Linco's Travels*.

Vernon, Mrs. Joseph, née Jane Poitier (fl. 1755–67). A dancer first appearing as Mrs. Vernon at Drury Lane on 27 September 1755, her marriage was annulled in 1764, and she appeared as Miss Poitier that year and as Mrs. Thompson about 1767.

Vidini, Signora Victoria (fl. 1769–82). A figure dancer, she came to England in 1769 and joined the Drury Lane company that year, remaining through the 1773–74 season. After retiring from Covent Garden in 1777–78, she was an occasional dancer at the Haymarket 1781–82.

Vincent, Mrs. Isabella, née Burchell (1735–1802). Said to have been originally a "milk girl," this soprano sang first at Vauxhall Gardens, 1751–60, under her maiden name. On 23 September 1760 she played Polly in *The Beggar's Opera* at Drury Lane. Later she sang at Marlebonne and played oboe in the Vauxhall band. She left performing upon marrying her second husband, Captain J. Mills.

Waldron, Francis Godolphin (1744–1818). Author, playwright, editor, bookseller, and actor, he came from Edinburgh to make his Drury Lane debut on 6 October 1769 as Scrub in *The Stratagem*, a "mean figure" with a slight speech impediment, according to Hopkins. He remained with the company until June 1796 and later was prompter at the Haymarket.

Walker, Mr. (fl. 1766–67). A utility actor at Drury Lane during this period, he is also listed in Beard's company at Covent Garden.

Watkins, Mr. (fl. 1760–67). An actor in the Drury Lane company during this period, he played the Servant in *Lethe*.

Weston, Thomas (1737–76?). The son of George II's head cook, he made his debut as Dick in *The Minor* at the Haymarket in 1760 and joined the Drury Lane company in 1761–62, remaining through 1766–67. He is said to have surpassed even Garrick in playing Abel Drugger.

Wheeler, John (d. 1789?). First acting at the Haymarket in 1768–69, he joined the Drury Lane company the next season and played through 1774–75, with an intervening period in Dublin.

Winstone, Richard (1699–1787). A friend of the actor Quin, his name appears on cast lists between 1734 and 1753 and as a member of Garrick's company beginning 1747–48. He also played at Goodman's Fields, the Haymarket, and Bristol.

Woodward, Henry (1714–77). A fine harlequin known for his nimble dancing and expressive gestures, he first appeared on the stage on 2 January 1729 in *The Beggar's Opera* with a children's company known as the Lilliputians. He went to Covent Garden as Lun Junior and to Drury Lane in 1737, playing there for the next twenty years. After a disastrous experience with management in Dublin, he returned to Covent Garden, where he remained until his death.

Wright, Mr. (fl. 1767–76). Played at Drury Lane from the 1767–68 season through 1775–76. A Mr. Wright, possibly the same actor, played at Richmond, Bromgrove, and Norwich in 1767.

Wrighten, James (1745–93). Trained as a copperplate printer, he early left his occupation to join the provincial theatre. He made his Drury Lane debut on 21 February 1770 as Burgundy to Garrick's Lear and remained with that theatre until January 1793, serving as prompter beginning 1786.

Wrighten, Mrs. James, née Mary Ann Matthews (1751–96). Wife of the actor James Wrighten, she played and sang at Drury Lane from her debut on 8 February 1770 as Diana in Isaac Bickerstaff's *Lionel and Clarissa* through the 1775–76 season. Later Mrs. A. M. Pownall, she also performed in America.

Yates, Richard (1706?–96). A rival of Henry Woodward as a harlequin, he was at Goodman's Fields when Garrick made his first appearance there, having joined Henry Giffard's company in 1737. He came to Drury Lane in 1747 and remained through the 1782–83 season. He was the original Sir Oliver Surface, and was acclaimed for playing Shakespeare's fools and low comic characters.

Yates, Mrs. Richard, Mary Ann (1728–87). Formerly Mrs. Graham and first wife of the comedian Richard Yates, she made her debut on 21 January 1753 as Anne Bullen in *Henry VIII*. She played at Drury Lane on 25 February 1754 (as Mrs. Graham), was dismissed in May 1755, married Yates in 1756, and returned to Drury Lane after having been tutored by her husband.

Younge, Isabella. *See* Mrs. John Scott.

Index to Commentary